The President spoke to the senator. His voice was hushed.

"They want me to go on television, to broadcast worldwide via satellite, and announce that the U.S. will unilaterally withdraw its forces from every allied nation on Earth. They want us to abandon every ally, every commitment. Total surrender."

"Tell them to go straight to hell!"

"At what cost, Senator? They have proved what they can do to New York, San Francisco, Los Angeles, Dallas, Washington. We surrender, or else millions of Americans die. That's what we face."

"But we spend billions on defense!" agonized the senator. "We cannot surrender without a fight!"

"So we will fight them," the President said. "And it will be merciless. We cannot honor the Geneva Convention. We cannot respect national borders. We will have ourselves a *dirty war!*"

MACK BOLAN
The Executioner

MACK BOLAN

STONY MAN DOCTRINE

A GOLD EAGLE BOOK FROM

WORLDWIDE

TORONTO • NEW YORK • LONDON

Second Printing June 1988

ISBN 0-373-61401-2

Special thanks and acknowledgment to Dick Stivers
for his contributions to this work.

"Who has to take a life
stands alone
on the edge of creation."
                              —*Adele Wiseman*

"I am Phoenix, from the Greek for crimson,
purple, all the colors of blood...
akin to *phonos*, which means murder,
and *theinein*, to keep away. A paradox,
yeah. Like the mind and the sword:
opposites that are in truth one.
Such an enigma is at the root of my creation."
                              —*Mack Bolan*
                    a.k.a. Col. John Phoenix

To the President of the United States
My Testament

NINE OF THE BEST MEN IN THE WORLD may die in this hour.

And I will have sent them to their deaths.

The enormity of that responsibility shakes me to the core of my being.

To you I am known as John Phoenix. Colonel John Phoenix, Retired—which only tells you I am a soldier.

The real story of who I am, and who my men are, is buried deeper—in my true identity, Mack Bolan.

When I am in combat, I see the same look flash across the face of each and every person I confront, one stricken glance that always asks the same question: what in hell is this?

The answer to that silent scream begins in war.

Ours would be a sad society indeed if the army was everyone's road—but it was mine. I became a soldier, a marksman, and an armorer. It was in Vietnam that

I became enlightened: I discovered I had certain qualities that were not shared by many others. I found a place for myself behind a sniper's scope.

I became a weapon for my nation's army.

Sniping is personal. You know your target close-up. I was one of the few who could do the job day in and day out.

Only because it had to be done could I bear the pain of doing it.

Then came the news about my family. Devoured by Mafia loan sharks, the sanctity of his life despoiled, my father turned a gun on his own family and then on himself.

After that, I could not return to a war ten thousand miles away. My guts were being chewed right here at home. I engaged the most immediate enemy. I took on the vermin responsible for my family's catastrophe. The Mafia.

Mack Bolan, Mack the Bastard, The Executioner—all faces of the same warrior, from whom the jackals scattered in fear.

I did *not* expect to win that war, nor even to withdraw with honor. In the minds of the vermin, I was already dead. In the minds of the police, too. And perhaps in my own mind as well. My intent was to take as many of them with me as I could. That simple.

Two thousand homicides later, I was done.

One of the first major battles in that war nearly proved my undoing. It was a trial by fire, a fire that cleansed all the deepest avenues of Hell, for it raged internally as well as externally. It raised the question again: what in hell is the apparition called The Executioner?

There were ten of us, the Death Squad, every man a veteran who could not ignore his country's enemy within. We crushed the enemy that time, but only I, Hermann Schwarz and Rosario Blancanales survived.

The death of seven others burned my soul. It was only then that I learned, in the crucible of mortal combat, to let my friends die.

Today I fight with nine warriors again. Able Team and Phoenix Force and G-Force. They live large. They live hard. They live!

So I have another squad now. And I have another weapon: Stony Man Farm, in the Blue Ridge Mountains. It is no ordinary farm. It is my command center for these nine very dangerous men. It is a stronghold of extreme complexity and formidable power, and it is run by the finest and bravest woman I will ever know, April Rose.

Yeah, I think of the farm all the time....

For the record, the Stony Man operation was set up for me by Hal Brognola. Only Hal was big enough to dream up such a drastic—and successful—strategy. A strategy that gave me a new name and brought me, through much war, to these deadly waters off Cuba.

Hal was top covert operations man back in the first days of my bloodletting against crime, and he secretly fed me logistical support. It was he who saw that I was self-destructing. It was he who needed me for this bigger war. It was Hal who connected me with the President of the United States. I owe Hal.

The base at Stony Man is kept humming night and day, every month, every year, by people who share a compulsion to execute their duty that is the equal of my own.

Aaron "The Bear" Kurtzman is one of the best. He stations himself at the computer console and cracks a whip that can shiver up the cybernetic spine of every organization that has joined my war: the National Security Council, the Justice Department, the CIA, the DIA.

From this matrix of superior mind and fire, polished to perfection by Andrzej Konzaki, my master weaponsmith, I launch my missions.

In some instances it is true that some of my warriors were once weapons without a target. But now they have all found their true aim in life: Justice by fire.

Let me tell you about these warriors.

"Gadgets" Schwarz is Able Team's wizard in the hellfire, a genius who came of age as a counterintelligence agent in Nam. Now he steers me straight as we zap across the crackling grid of real-world electronics.

"Politician" Blancanales is my wisdom man. He's Able Team's senior member whose Hispanic charm conceals an iron will.

Carl Lyons, Able Team's wildest hotshot, is an ex-LAPD cop who, for the sake of his country and the future of democracy, is one scary, scary guy.

Then there is Phoenix Force. Five more guys whom I may soon send to their deaths.

Phoenix Force joins me now at the peak of its legend. Its men strike with the violence of an exploding universe striking against infinity, for no glory other than the daily salvation of mankind.

Their senior member is Yakov Katzenelenbogen. Katz is the Stern Gang and the Mossad and the very wrath of God all rolled into one.

Gary Manning is a calm Canadian who can ignite the heavens when I tell him to. As in dynamite.

Rafael Encizo, the Cuban, is a survivor of the Bay of Pigs and had been looking to serve a wildcat force such as the Stony Man operation ever since. Now he does.

David McCarter is SAS. I need say no more, except that this Englishman has all the gall of Churchill and Field Marshal Montgomery beneath that fancy new London hairstyle.

Keio Ohara is my samurai, a Japanese kid six feet tall, unusual in every way. At the martial arts, he is like the name says: a knockout.

G-Force is Jack Grimaldi. He works on his own, for he has to operate his kind of machinery independently of the Farm. His kind of machinery is all kinds of planes. Jack and I go way back. Jack was a pilot for the Mob until The Executioner crossed his psychic flight path. I counseled him to change his ways. He did. He became king of the sky.

I love these men.

These men fight for justice. They would fight without me. And now, I believe I am sending them to their deaths.

I want it known, and always honored, that these

men have commanded themselves. Each man has lived and fought to the death as I have. Each of my warriors has stood alone on the edge of creation.

I act now under my own command, in these forbidden waters, in order to extend the limits of the possible. To hunt down and exterminate soulless monsters who, in their every imaginable horror and vileness, are the absolute obverse of my warriors.

My foes have lost any sense of soul. They killed their souls when they violated the sacredness of life.

The devouring has begun again. Death is everywhere. I am going to stop it, now, and I guess I'll have to seek your permission later.

Sir, I am a weapon that works in concert with other weapons: human weapons. Honor them for me always, please.

And I confess: I do what must be done.

I am content with that.

Now you know the history.

Pray for us.

Soon the battle begins.

Mack Bolan
off the coast of Cuba

1

Czechoslovakia

Monday
11:45 a.m.
(1045 Greenwich mean time)

EAST OF THE CZECHOSLOVAKIAN TOWN of Hanusovce, only one hundred twenty-five kilometers from the border of the Soviet Union, the man slowed his bicycle to a stop. He flipped down the kickstand.

His eyes swept the farming valley around him. A kilometer away, a worker guided a horse-drawn plow, turning over a green field touched with the yellows and reds of spring wild flowers to expose rich, dark earth. The worker completed one line, turned the horse and plow to cross the field again. In other fields, wind patterns moved across the virgin grass and the wild flowers like ocean waves. Trees swayed. Beyond the fields of the valley, a forest covered the hills. Smoke rose from a village hidden by trees.

Vyashesla Fedorenko pulled off his bright red sweater and draped it over the handlebars of his rented bike. Wandering into the roadside weeds, he waited, staring out at the fields. From time to time he looked to the east, where the road disappeared over a low hill. He saw no cars.

A man of average height and wiry muscles, wearing cheap slacks and a short-sleeved white shirt, Fedorenko might have been mistaken for a Czech on holiday from the factories except for the deep tan on his face and forearms. Squinting into the snow-glare of Afghan desolation and the furnace-brilliance of Yemeni deserts had cut deep lines into his narrow face.

Now, his eyes red-veined with the fatigue of three days' jet travel and waiting in international terminals, he watched the road for a car. He glanced at the cheap Hungarian watch he wore on his wrist. He tapped it. Taking a Texas Instruments digital chronometer from his pocket, he corrected the time of the Hungarian watch, then put the American wristwatch back in his pocket.

A Skoda sedan came over the hill. Fedorenko turned away, but looked back as the car approached. He recognized the driver, the driver recognized him. Striding to the edge of the road, he gave the driver a salute as the Skoda rattled to a halt.

The middle-aged driver, a pink-faced Russian with sagging jowls, wearing an overcoat over his huge gut, struggled from the small car.

"You have the tan of a movie star!" the fat driver addressed Fedorenko in Russian. "Travel agrees with you."

Fedorenko cut off the small talk with a bitter laugh. "Fifteen airports in seventy-one hours. Such travel is not a pleasure. Here." He gave the fat driver a cassette tape.

The Russian looked at the cassette, read the label in accented English. "The Beatles? Mag-ical Mys-ter-y—"

"I have encoded the changes since my last report. New gangs, their leaders, the numbers of fighters, their countries of origin. Liquidated informers. Changes in the shipment routes. Movements of weapons. The Directorate must have all that information."

"And the attack?"

Fedorenko closed his eyes, intoned like a saint describing a vision. "The Hydra moves.... A thousand fighters, the terror of a thousand nameless fighters...striking alone, striking in gangs, striking in armies...armies of silent death.... Death coming with the wind.... The cities of America are dead places, mausoleums to the Fall of Empire...."

"Colonel, you are a poet!"

"No." Fedorenko's black eyes turned to the other Russian. "A killer. Go. Take that tape. The Directorate must have the information. After Hydra, all of the Palestinians, all the Cubans, all the fighters must be destroyed."

"But there will be no failure. Without total victory—"

"Don't talk like a commissar! Total victory is impossible. You think the Americans have no security forces? But if we destroy one city, two cities, they will surrender. They will withdraw their international forces. All the people of the world will know. That will be our victory."

"Then why destroy the fighters? They will be heroes."

"They are only cheap weapons," Fedorenko sneered. "They are insects, lice on the face of my dream. After Hydra, they must die, or else they will betray me—us, our country. You hear my words? Liquidate all of them."

With a quick salute, the fat Russian pocketed the tape and returned to the car. Revving the old Skoda's engine, the Russian turned the car and drove away in the direction he had come, toward the border of the Soviet Union.

Alone again, Fedorenko stood at the roadside, his fists clenched at his sides, his back ramrod straight as if he stood on parade. He closed his eyes to the quiet farms and forested hills, focused on an image seething in the darkness of his mind, a vision of a plain of skulls, of an army of men and women rising from the skulls, howling, screaming, their necks and heads becoming tangled snakes that weaved and knotted, and whose scorpion-fang teeth glistened with poison....

2

Idaho

Tuesday
11:30 a.m.
(1930 Greenwich mean time)

THERE WAS A YELLOW SMEAR on the forest.

On the southeast slope of the mountains, the yellow glowed with the early-morning light, as if autumn had colored the trees. But Nat Blair, high over the Salmon River Mountains in a war-surplus Huey helicopter, knew that pines and Douglas firs and hemlocks did not change colors with the seasons. He looked for smoke or flame but saw only the splotch of unnatural yellow set amid the undulating green slopes of the mountains. He pointed it out to his copilot.

"Hey, Dean. Look at that."

"What?"

"That yellow patch. The whole mountainside."

Peter Dean peered at the unnatural splotch through binoculars. He passed the binoculars to Blair. "Looks like some kind of blight. A fungus maybe."

"Wasn't there last week. What's that look like, a quarter-mile across? If we have a disease that moves that fast, the company's got a big problem."

"Maybe they dumped some Silvex down there."

"Why would they do that? Besides, the Feds would have the company in court by now."

"I say it looks like a slop job of Silvex."

Blair watched the yellowed pines pass below him. He flicked on the switch of his radio. "Northwest International helicopter shuttle Charlie Three. Charlie Three to Center. Calling Center. . . ."

"Center. You got a problem, Nat?"

"Negative. No problem. We're at coordinates—" he read off a series of numbers indicating their position on the maps of the corporation's pulp and lumber forest "—and it looks like somebody did one hell of a Silvex job out here."

"That ain't possible. Don't even say it, friend. We'd have two thousand Forest Service investigators on our backs, them and those hippies—"

"Then we got a disease killing the trees. It's all died out down there. I'm circling it, taking a look. Over."

Watching the boughs of the pines, Blair eased the Huey down. The pines and ferns had a grayish-yellow color. Spots of black stained some branches. Blair saw nothing green.

Rotorwind whipped yellow forest debris. Dead needles and cones fell from the pines in sheets of yellow. Single needles and flecks of leaves stuck to the helicopter's Plexiglas. The skids touched the granite slab.

Dean snapped off his safety harness, then slammed open the copilot's door. Gripping the frame, he stepped down onto the skid.

Bits of dead vegetation swirled into the cockpit.

Blair waved the dust and leaves away from his visor, flicked bits off his face and neck. He watched his copilot run across the granite, and grab the gray yellow branch of a sapling.

Dean fell. Blair watched as his copilot struggled to his feet, clutched at his chest, fell again.

Easing back on the engine throttle, Blair let the helicopter rest on the skids. Even as he reached for the engine switch to stop the rotors, agony seized his throat and chest.

His hand groped at the radio switch. Lifting the microphone, he croaked, "Can't breathe...."

And he died, convulsions racking his body, his hands thrashing, his feet kicking the control pedals.

The helicopter jumped a few feet into the air and lurched sideways. A rotortip smashed into the granite mountainside. Inertia pitched the nose of the Huey into the granite as the blades shattered on the rock in a spray of metal and dusty soil. The tail finally fell, the Huey rolling over and over to crash against yellow pines two hundred feet downslope.

Silence returned to the dead mountain. Wind swayed the lifeless branches of the pines. Nothing moved in the next hours, no insects, no animals, no birds.

In the last light of day, another Huey helicopter approached from the south. The second helicopter bore the logo of the United States Army. The troopship touched down on the far side of the ridge.

Soldiers covered in plastic anticontamination suits and wearing helmets and oxygen tanks moved through the yellowed trees.

3

Kansas

Wednesday
4:30 p.m.
(1130 Greenwich mean time)

BEYOND THE MUDDY STOCK PENS and grain silos of the railroad yard, the Kansas wheat fields continued to the horizon.

Sheriff Milton parked his highway cruiser behind the town's one café and pool hall. The café's blue-and-gold neon Beer sign flashed despite the dawn light that paled the sky. The old, stoop-backed cook stood at the kitchen door, watching the town police and the county deputy sheriffs gather around the dead man. Sheriff Milton gave the cook a wave as he crossed the parking lot.

His new deputy, a boy who had quit the New York Police Department for the Rosemund County Sheriff's Department, took statements from two of the local people. Milton nodded, continued over to Police Chief Desmond and Deputy Sheriff Canfield. They stood over his friend Abe, the night watchman.

"You get the word on Senator Harper?" Deputy Sheriff Canfield asked.

Sheriff Milton nodded. He squatted. Abe was sprawled on the gravel in a clotted puddle of blood. His throat yawned with a neat, surgical slash circling his neck. But a knife had not killed him.

Crossing himself, Milton reached out and closed his friend's eyes. The dead man's face was cold, already stiff. Red beads clung to Abe's face like dew. The stuff came away on the sheriff's fingers. Milton pinched his fingers together, felt them stick. He took a clean piece of white paper from his jacket pocket, wiped the red mist from his fingers, carefully folded the paper and returned it to his pocket. Then he checked Abe's pockets. He found a wallet, warehouse keys, a .38 pistol still in its holster.

The sheriff finally spoke. "Canfield! Get a blanket to cover him. Chief Desmond, anybody know what happened to Abe?"

"Something weird went on out here. What, we don't know. See that?"

The police chief pointed to an aluminum tank standing against a boxcar. An electric pump unit sat on top of the tank. Wires led to a 12-volt battery on the gravel railbed. A long plastic nozzle extended straight up from the pump. A length of rope lashed to the boxcar secured the tank and pump upright.

"What is it?"

"It put out some kind of red syrup. The stuff's all over town. On cars, inside people's houses, on everything."

"Why would someone kill a man to do that?" the sheriff asked.

"Why would someone do that and then call Senator Harper?" the police chief responded.

A limousine roared off the highway to wheel in a wide turn through the parking lot, gravel rattling off its fenders. It slowed to a smooth stop. A young man in a gray business suit left the driver's seat, then opened the back door.

Wearing the denim pants, jacket and lace-front boots of a farmer, Senator Bradford Harper left the rosewood-and-leather interior of the limo. He strode across the parking lot, his paunch and jowls bouncing with each step. His aide-driver followed him. Police Chief Desmond saluted. Sheriff Milton did not.

The senator saw the corpse. He stopped and stared. Deputy Canfield returned with a blanket and spread it over the old watchman.

"So how'd you find out about this, Senator?" Sheriff Milton asked him.

"An anonymous call. Exactly what happened here?"

"What did this anonymous call tell you?"

"That there'd be a demonstration here. Why are you asking me? Am I a suspect, Sheriff Milton?"

"No, Senator. Someone called you. Just asking what they told you. What kind of demonstration did they tell you to expect?"

"That was it. They called on my private line. Only my senior aides and family have the number. I thought it'd be some kind of price protest, whatever."

"Is that why you wore the work clothes, to look like us common folk?"

"What happened here, Sheriff?"

"See that over there? That tank? Someone set that up and sprayed the town with red syrup. Right, Chief Desmond?"

"Covered the whole town. Everything's red and sticky. Don't know what the hell they were trying to prove."

"This some kind of joke?" the senator asked, incredulous.

"I wouldn't say that." The sheriff squatted again and raised the blanket from his dead friend's face and shoulders. "A good old guy. Worked here twenty years. Liked to play cards in the afternoon. His niece married my grandson's best friend. We got drunk together at the wedding, kissed some pretty young girls. And now someone's put a wire around Abe Miller's neck and nearly cut his head off."

The senator flinched at the sight of the open throat. The sheriff turned his friend's head to show the senator that only the spine joined the head to the shoulders.

"A knife didn't do that. It's called a garrote. That's a commando's way of killing. What kind of joke would that be? A political joke? Wish they'd done their joking in Washington, D.C. 'Cause I don't think this is funny."

4

San Francisco

RUSH-HOUR TRAFFIC streamed westward on the Bay Bridge linking the San Francisco peninsula to Oakland. The eastbound traffic on the bridge's lower deck traveled at sixty miles an hour. The upper deck, crowded with commuters driving from the East Bay cities and suburbs to their offices in the high rises of metropolitan San Francisco, maintained an even fifty miles an hour.

The cold wind that preceded a late spring Pacific storm whipped up whitecaps on the bay. As they drove, the commuters saw a panorama of the bay beneath a luminous blue sky, the wind sweeping away all mist and pollution. In downtown San Francisco, the TransAmerica pyramid and its neighboring towers of glass, steel and polished stone flashed gold with the light of the morning sun.

Then, at seven thirty-eight, at the center of the Bay Bridge, a car and a semi-truck and trailer suddenly stopped. Horns sounded in one vast cacophony. Drivers swerved from the right-hand lanes to pass the stalled car and truck. Traffic slowed as hundreds of cars braked, some attempting to change lanes.

The truck driver threw open his door and climbed down to the walkway. Later, witnesses could recall few details; he wore a ski mask pulled over his head, a high-collared jacket, and gloves. He hurried to the year-old Cadillac waiting in front of his truck. In seconds, the Cadillac disappeared into the flow of traffic.

Police found the stolen Cadillac burning in the Embarcadero district fifteen minutes later. Fire had gutted the expensive car, leaving only a scorched hulk.

Less than a minute after the driver abandoned the truck with the diesel engine racing, some machinery whining within the trailer, a high-pressure stream of fluid shot straight upward from the trailer roof. The fluid vaporized, becoming a mist as it continued a hundred feet in the air, feathering with the wind, drifting over the bay.

Mist rained down on the commuters. An odor like ammonia filled their cars. Thousands coughed. Their eyes stung as the irritant touched their faces.

A California highway patrolman stopped in front of the truck. He left his cruiser. He coughed as he walked through the raining droplets. He felt his eyes burning, his mouth filling with saliva. But he continued toward the truck. He tried the door handles, found them locked. The chemical soaked his uniform in the ninety seconds that he struggled with the doors.

Nausea heaved in his stomach. Hurrying back to

his cruiser, the officer reported the stalled truck and chemical spray, suggested that the police and highway patrol close the bridge.

Coughing, his eyes swimming with tears, his gut churning, the officer drove on to San Francisco. Paramedics hosed him clean with water, gave him medicated gargle, then oxygen until his symptoms disappeared.

In the bay, fishermen passing through the drifting mist coughed. Workers and residents along the Bayshore closed their windows to the ammonia stink. Police closed the Bay Bridge as the stream of chemical continued into the clear morning sky.

Before the highway patrol's hazardous-chemical unit could arrive with respirators and protective suits, the tanks inside the trailer went dry. In ten minutes, the truck's pump had shot thousands of gallons of the stinking, irritating chemical into the air of San Francisco.

5

Northern Lebanon

Thursday
5:45 a.m.
(0345 Greenwich mean time)

THE SUN ROSE LIKE FLAMES out of Syria. Mack Bolan squinted at the ragged shadow of the Qurnat as Sawda. The red disk of the sun appeared over the ridges and peaks of the mountains in the northeast of Lebanon. Bolan looked to the east. Lights marked farms around Sir ad Dinniyah, a small town ten miles away. He saw nothing on the rutted, weaving road. The graying hills and ridges obscured Tripoli, fifteen miles farther away. Despite the rising sun, night still held the wine-dark Mediterranean.

On a barren mountainside east of Tripoli, Bolan and a squad of Phalange commandos were waiting in cold shadows. They had para-dropped on the far side of the ridge and crossed over during the night. Now they waited for a plane to land on an airstrip gouged from the rocks and sand.

Only minutes to go, Bolan thought, *and a PLO gang dies.*

In the years since the Palestine Liberation Organization seized control of Southern Lebanon, holding the population hostage, the gang had earned billions of American dollars for their organization's campaigns of terror and atrocity by channeling heroin into the United States. With the complicity of the Soviet Union, Syria, Iraq and Iran, the gang gathered opium from thousands of poppy farmers as far away as Afghanistan and Pakistan. Transporting the raw opium paste to regional laboratories, the gang's Palestinian and ComBloc chemists refined the opium to pure crystalline heroin.

Then the White Death went to the cities of the United States. The drug became an attack-by-proxy on American society: every day of the year, armies of addicts robbed and murdered to pay for the heroin. The millions of crimes—the billions of dollars spent battling the crimes, the maimed victims, the shattered lives, the dead—all counted as victories for the Palestinian warlords who masterminded the drug flow and banked the American dollars. The Israeli invasion of Southern Lebanon had not stopped the gang's operation, only denied them the use of Beirut International Airport. Although the Palestinians in Southern Lebanon had been politically abandoned by their "brothers" in the Arab world, for fear of Israeli reprisals, the PLO in the north were entrenched and still active.

Glancing again at the graying countryside, Mack Bolan still saw no headlights on the road. Nabih, the Phalangist teenager assigned to be his spotter, swept the distant vista with his binoculars. A motorized Nikon with a telephoto lens hung by a strap around his neck. The photos would go into the files of Stony Man, the CIA, and the Mossad.

Bolan searched the shadows and darkness of the rocky mountainside around the PLO airfield below him. Nothing moved on the half-mile-long airstrip scraped from the rolling hillsides. He saw none of the soldiers who had accompanied him to this cold, windswept mountain.

The Phalange militiamen waited in the rocks, concealed beneath gray-and-black-patterned camouflage cloth. Bolan stroked the cocking lever of the 7.62mm x 54R Dragunov sniper rifle. Like Bolan, the Phalangists all had Soviet autorifles and rocket launchers. Without NATO weapons or cartridges to link this operation to the free world, the PLO would first suspect rivals within their own murderous regime. Even the American hand-radios they carried had been stripped of manufacturer's and country-of-origin identification.

Lights flashed from the shadowed valley. Bolan's hand-radio buzzed. "Colonel Phoenix!" a French-accented voice blared through Bolan's earphone. He recognized the voice of Jean Barakat, a French-educated architect who had returned home to lead a combat squad in the Phalange. "They come."

Nabih focused his binoculars on the yellow lights. He turned to Bolan. "Trucks...."

They watched the convoy approach. Headlights appeared, bobbed, disappeared as four Soviet transports drove through the folds and curves of the narrow valley. In the minutes that he watched and waited, Bolan calculated the numbers and considered what he saw.

Four troop trucks for a load of heroin? Why? And why did one of the transports tow a forklift?

Engine drone came from the east. A flurry of voices spoke Arabic and French in Bolan's earphone as Lieutenant Barakat checked his squad. Even as the lieutenant reported the men ready, Bolan's eyes spotted the distant speck. The speck became a four-engined turboprop aircraft; soon Bolan recognized an Ilyushin with the markings of Air Cuba.

The Air Cuba turboprop did not surprise him. The decline of the Russian economy had forced the Soviet overlords to limit their subsidies of the world's socialist slave states. The Cuban Communists now earned cash for the repression of internal dissent and external enemies by trafficking in drugs. Before leaving Stony Man for Lebanon, Bolan had dispatched Able Team to break an operation run by Cubans to transport marijuana and cocaine from South America to Florida.

As the Ilyushin banked in a wide circle, the convoy of trucks low-geared the final hundred yards, then screeched to a stop beneath Bolan's position.

Palestinians in *keffiyehs* and mismatched uniforms dropped from the trucks' tailgates to take sentry positions around the airfield, their AKM rifles still slung over their shoulders. Other Palestinians disconnected the forklift. One started the engine.

A fair-haired European-looking male left the cab of one truck.

"Get photos of that man," Bolan said to Nabih. He took the binoculars as Nabih steadied the long lens on a rock and snapped photos. Through the five-power lenses, Bolan watched the blonde direct the forklift operator. Then the man returned to the truck.

The Air Cuba Ilyushin made a flawless landing, bounced over the airstrip's gravel, the plane's props whipping up storms of dust. At the truck, the fair-haired man took off his shoes and pants and slipped into green plastic coveralls. He pulled on rubber boots and gloves. Slinging a pouch over his shoulder, the man returned to the forklift.

In the backs of the transports, Palestinians mus-cled fifty-gallon drums onto the forklift. The European pointed to the airliner. The operator bumped over the airstrip to the center door of the airplane.

Focusing on the door, Bolan saw into the interior. Despite the passenger ports lining the sides of the airliner, he saw no seats inside, only an empty cabin. The Cubans had evidently converted the Ilyushin to a cargo carrier, while maintaining its appearance as a passenger aircraft.

Lieutenant Barakat's voice came through the big American's earphone again. "When, Colonel?"

Snapping his hand-radio to his mouth, Bolan answered quickly, "Wait. Repeat, *wait*."

Bolan focused the binoculars on a fifty-gallon drum, read the stenciled numbers of a product code. Why the man in the anticontamination suit? Why the oil drums with the different product markings?

"Nabih, take a photo of those numbers on the oil drums." Bolan keyed his hand-radio. "Lieutenant Barakat. That European. Tell your men not to hit him. We need to take him alive."

"He appears to be a Russian, I think. I will instruct my fighters."

"Wait for my command to fire."

Bolan set the radio beside him and readied his Soviet rifle. Pulling off the soft plastic lens cap, he flipped the reticle switch to power the illumination of the cross hairs. He put his eye to the rubber eyeshield, found the airliner's side door with the scope's four-power optics. He set the cross hairs on the chest of a Palestinian struggling with an oil drum.

Estimating the distance to the trucks at two hundred fifty yards, Bolan adjusted the elevation knob and raised the cross hairs to the Ilyushin. A difference of fifty yards meant a point of impact approximately five inches lower. With a Leatherwood sniper scope, he could have made exact range corrections as he fired; but the inferior Soviet scope would force him to adjust by eye.

Keying his radio again, Bolan called his first shot. "I'm going to put a bullet through the European's leg. Open fire when he drops. Understand?"

Lieutenant Barakat instructed his men in Arabic. "They understand. And they are ready." Bolan looked to Nabih. The young man touched the Nikon and nodded. Bolan checked the row of ten-shot magazines ready at his left hand, then put his eye to the scope.

Sighting the cross hairs on the ankle of the European, Bolan flicked off the Dragunov's safety.

In the instant after Bolan squeezed off the shot and before the slug hit, the protective-clothed European moved. The bullet almost missed the man's leg. But the grazing hit spun him, slammed him into the gravel.

Autofire raked the trucks, shattering windshields, killing the drivers. Other riflemen put bursts into the scattered sentries. The PLO gunmen died before they could raise their weapons.

Bolan's next shot went into the chest of a Cuban. The dying flight attendant fell back into the airliner as the third shot tore into another Cuban's heart. Before the dead men fell, Bolan swept the cross hairs forward to the pilots' cabin. From his angle, he had no view of the pilots. He emptied the rifle's magazine through the fuselage and windshields, riddling the cockpit with high-velocity slugs.

A streak of fire hit the Ilyushin. The RPG tore into the side of the plane. Shards of aluminum and flaming plastic fluttered down. A hole two feet wide yawned in the plane. A second rocket hit a wing and the Ilyushin was engulfed in a ball of churning flame.

Other rockets hit the trucks. Bolan snapped a second magazine into the Dragunov and put the cross hairs on a PLO soldier cowering behind an overturned oil drum. Advancing the elevation knob one click, Bolan hit the soldier first in the back, then zeroed the rifle and hit him again in his *keffiyeh*.

Searching through the flaming trucks and diesel smoke, Bolan put single shots into terrorists. Rocket after rocket hit the trucks, killing concealed Palestinians, gutting the flaming hulks. Fluid from the burst oil drums flowed from the wrecks.

A Palestinian broke cover and sprinted for the rocks. Suddenly he fell. Bolan sighted on the terrorist's head but did not fire. Through the scope, Bolan watched the terrorist clutch at his throat, thrash, finally die with froth bubbling from his mouth.

A green cloud blurred Bolan's field of view. The Russian in the anticontamination suit ran, limping, for cover. Bolan followed him with the scope, noted that he now wore a gas mask and plastic hood.

Gas! Yeah, that's what they had in those drums. Not White Death this run, but the ultimate weapon of terror. Yellow rain in Laos and Cambodia, chemicals of mass murder in Afghanistan; why not poison gas in the Americas? No one in the United Nations had been willing to face the evidence coming out of Asia. Even in the United States, the bleeding-heart humanitarians had accused the Central Intelligence Agency of manufacturing the evidence to slander the "peace-loving" Soviet Socialists.

But now the Soviets' gas exterminated their Palestinian stooges.

"Watch the one in the plastic suit!" Bolan shouted to his spotter. Then he keyed his radio. "Lieutenant! Pull your men back! Now! That's gas down there. Poison gas. Get them back!"

Barakat did not waste time acknowledging. He commanded his men to retreat. Voices called back and forth among the rocks. Bolan covered the withdrawal with his Dragunov, sending slugs into wisps of black smoke, into fluttering canvas, into dead terrorists. Anything that moved or seemed to move took a slug.

"Where's that Russian?" Bolan asked Nabih.

The teenager pointed to a cleft in the rocks as he passed the binoculars to the black-suited American. Bolan focused the lenses and saw the Russian fleeing a Phalange soldier.

"Lieutenant Barakat, call your man back." Even as Bolan radioed, he saw the soldier tackle the protective-clothed Russian.

They fought, the soldier forcing the wounded man facedown on the rocks, looping a length of rope around his arms.

Then the soldier convulsed. He clawed at his throat, fell back. The Russian scrambled up and crabbed over the rocks. Then he, too, staggered and fell. His hands tore the mask from his face. He died thrashing.

"Don't go near that man's body!" Bolan shouted down the mountainside, hoping that his tone, if not his language, was understood. Bolting from concealment, he let gravity propel him down the rocks, jumping, hurdling, running a few steps, then jumping again. In seconds, Bolan stood on a ledge ten feet above the dead Phalangist.

Foam crusted the dead man's face, his eyes blindly staring into the sky. A few feet past him, the Russian sprawled on the rocks. Bolan saw several small rips in the protective covering he wore.

The gas had killed both men. Bolan wanted to take the dead Russian out for identification and laboratory examination.

And the brave Arab soldier deserved a decent burial. But Bolan knew that anyone who touched either man risked death. The squad did not even carry a body bag or plastic sheet. Bolan reached for the two white phosphorous grenades on his battle rig.

Footsteps. Bolan dropped into a crouch, his hand going for his .44 AutoMag. Lieutenant Barakat scrambled through the rocks and stopped beside him.

"Is Samir dead?"

Bolan nodded. "Does your faith allow cremation?"

"What?"

"Anyone who touches his body dies. It's either fire—" Bolan held up a phosphorous grenade "—or he rots there."

"Give him the grace of fire."

Bolan tossed the grenade. His accuracy and the grenade's phosphorous allowed only ashes and blackened bits of metal and bone to remain where the young soldier had died.

Marching toward their rendezvous with the helicopter that would take them to safety in the south, Bolan looked back. Smoke and flames rose from the wreckage of the Cuban Ilyushin, and from the gutted trucks. Nothing lived on the hellground of the airfield.

A victory.

But Bolan did not exult in the destruction of the gang and their horrible cargo. The victory cost too much. The death of the Phalange fighter—a college student, a volunteer in the struggle against the terrorists preying on his country and people—saddened the American warrior.

What had they stopped here? Who did the young man save with his death? A garrison of young draftees in El Salvador? A town in Guatemala? A Honduran army base?

Who had the Cubans intended to gas?

6

Jamaica

Thursday
2:00 p.m.
(1900 Greenwich mean time)

NEON COLORED HER SUN-BLEACHED HAIR. Carl Lyons watched the young blond woman lean into the taxi window to pay the driver. She was chic in her white linen slacks, white tube top and dark tan. Behind her, the neon of the private disco flashed in patterns that created dancers in motion.

She entered the club, but Lyons stayed in his rented car. There was no need to follow her. He knew who she would call. He knew where they would go. Rosario Blancanales and Gadgets Schwarz waited at a mountain airstrip. In an hour's time, when a plane carrying a million dollars' worth of cocaine landed at the airstrip, Able Team would spring an ambush on the blond drug dealer and her gang.

A cacophony of voices and disco rhythms blasted his ears. Lyons turned down the volume of the transceiver on the seat beside him. He grinned as he thought of the blonde's obsessive efforts to avoid surveillance—skipping from taxi to taxi, dodging through hotel lobbies, innumerable glances over her shoulder—while every step of the way she carried a combination mini-transmitter and directional finder in the plastic handle of her clutch bag.

"Hey, mon!" A Jamaican in a doorman's uniform leaned in the curbside window. "Park de car. You coom in here, you meet de girls. Dey cool you."

"No thanks," Lyons replied. "I'm waiting for my wife."

The elegant doorman grinned. "She coom in, too! Maybe she meet a boy she like."

Laughing, Lyons threw the car into gear and merged with the traffic. Tourists wandering across the avenue stopped the cars for a moment. In front of Lyons, four elderly visitors in an open jitney waved to friends, their white hair and pastel sport-shirts and sundresses lurid with neon light. A few car lengths past the door to the private disco, Lyons cut into a parking space and waited.

He thought of Mack Bolan, of Mack's Stony Man operation back in Virginia and the many Able Team missions already racked up in the name of America versus terrorism; he thought of America.

Despite the sultry evening, Lyons wore a sports coat. He had no choice. The sports coat covered his Colt Python. Sweat ran from his chest and armpits as he listened to snatches of conversation inside the disco.

The noise receded, the disco throb dropping to a distant beat in the background. He heard the voice of Carla, the blond gangster: "It's time. You ready?"

She was telephoning her partner. Touching his transceiver's channel switches, Lyons turned on the mini-transmitter hidden in the imitation ivory grips of the man's nickel-plated snub-nosed .38 revolver. The day before, Gadgets had crept into the couple's plush cabana, and as they made love in the Jacuzzi, he had exchanged one of the revolver's grips. Now, as the two smugglers talked, Lyons monitored both ends of the telephone conversation.

"Sure am, hon'. You see anything unusual?"

"Nothing. You?"

"No, babe. Had the eye in the back of my head open all day long. Be there in a minute."

Music and bar noise blasted Lyons's ears again. He heard the clink of glasses, laughter, then the sounds faded. He heard men's voices.

Glancing in the rearview mirror, Lyons saw the blonde in white waiting at the curb. A long-haired, bearded man in a cream polyester suit stopped in a white Chevrolet. Lyons keyed a transmitter and lifted the microphone to his lips. "Calling the mountains. The lovers are taking a drive."

Static hissed from the speaker. Lyons had to strain to hear Gadgets's words. "This is the Wizard. Repeat, please. Repeat message."

"They—are—on—their—way. They—are—coming."

"Message received. All systems go."

The Chevrolet sped past Lyons. "On my way. Over."

Staying a safe distance behind the car, Lyons followed the smugglers from the city, the steady beep-beep-beep of the DF unit leading him.

Once they had left Kingston behind, the couple's

car stopped on the shoulder of the highway. The mini-mike carried their words to Lyons, alerting him to the stop.

Switching off his lights, Lyons parked to watch them check the suitcases in the trunk of the car. Their conversation told him the suitcases contained $1,000,000 U.S. in fifties and hundreds.

Moving again, they resumed their nervous conversation. Lyons listened as they talked of condominiums in Utah and Malibu, hundred-thousand-dollar certificates of deposit, and investments in "front" businesses.

The road cut through sugarcane fields and banana groves, the lush growth sometimes walling in the highway. Fewer cars passed as the highway led into the hills. The scents of flowering citrus and spices perfumed the warm night.

Half an hour out of Kingston, the white Chevy turned east on a gravel road. Lyons drove on past the turnoff.

He keyed his transmitter. "Come in, reception party. This is a tourist from Virginia."

Gadgets's voice answered him. Only two miles separated them; the static was gone. "You don't have to talk in code," Gadgets said. "We're scrambled. Totally secure."

"Hey, that's not code. I talk like that all the time," Lyons said. "You ready? The ones with the money just left the highway."

"The doper soldiers are waiting at the airstrip. Pol's in position. I'll wait here for your signal."

"Maybe five minutes. I'm at the gate now. Over."

Swerving off the highway, Lyons stopped at a steel pipe barring a plantation's rutted private road. He jumped out of the car and went to open the old padlock with the crude key he had made earlier in the day. But he did not need the key.

The gate's rusty lock hung open, smashed. He turned the lock in his hand, examining it in the glare of the car's headlights. Someone had hit the old padlock several times with a steel tool. Lyons dropped to one knee, studied the mud and ruts of the plantation road. He saw the deep tracks of a heavy truck.

The truck had splashed scummy water from the ruts. Lyons watched tiny rivulets of water trickle from the ruts into the truck's tracks. The truck had passed through the gate only a few minutes before. What would Bolan have made of this?

Lyons considered the possibilities. Could it have been a freight truck, hauling bananas from the groves? No. Able Team had checked on the plantation; the harvest was weeks away, and plantation workers would not need to break the lock. Police? The gang had paid off the local constables. Soldiers? Impossible; Able Team's mission had the cooperation of the Jamaican government.

In fact, Able Team had more than total cooperation. To the government, Able Team did not exist. This was not the standard surveillance-and-seizure operation against drug traffickers. Able Team had no interest in the dopers. They might escape, they might die. Able Team wanted the pilot of the plane and his passenger.

Though the plane flew Bolivian cocaine from a Colombian airfield, Stony Man's South American informants had identified the pilot and passenger as Cubans. They were officers in the Cuban secret police, and they had a twofold assignment: first, to expedite the movement of vast quantities of marijuana, cocaine and heroin through the defenses of the United States, with the goal of poisoning American society; and two, to take the profits earned by the drug sales and distribute the millions of dollars to terrorist gangs throughout the hemisphere.

Able Team's mission: capture the Cubans.

The mission had gone like clockwork...until Lyons saw the smashed lock and tracks. But he had no more time for questions. That truck might be carrying police or soldiers or another drug gang. Lyons had to warn Gadgets and Blancanales. He switched off the car's headlights, then keyed the transmitter.

"Wizard, we got a problem."

"What's up?"

"I don't know." Lyons described what he had found.

"Maybe another crew of dopers," Gadgets said. "There are airstrips all over these hills. You want to abort?"

"Not yet. Maybe it's nothing. I'll check it out. Over."

Lyons could not risk continuing in the car. He reversed it and parked some distance from the gate. Stripping off his sweat-dampened leisure suit, the moist tropical air cool on his body, he slipped into a black cotton jump suit. Combat cosmetics on his face, hair and hands turned him into a shadow.

Then he strapped on his weapons.

First, his Colt Python in its shoulder holster. Then the Colt Government Model reengineered for silence by Bolan's Stony Man weaponsmith, Andrzej Konzaki. Finally, a CAR-15, a lighter commando version of the standard M-16.

He touched the pockets of the jump suit to check his speedloaders, magazines, knife and hand-radio.

Then he left the highway, jogging over the ruts and mud of the plantation road.

Moved by gentle evening winds, ink-black banana leaves swayed against the star-strewn night sky. Lyons moved as fast as he dared through the darkness, sometimes slowing to a walk and groping his way, sometimes sprinting a starlit stretch.

He carefully walked the curves in the road, listening, drawing long breaths through his nose, hoping to catch the sound or odor of the truck. Clouds of mosquitoes found him. He waved them away as he moved on.

A mile from the highway, he came to a plank bridge over a stagnant stream. Paralleling the stream, a path angled from the road, zigzagging up the hillside to cross and recross the water. Lyons left the road, walked a few steps up the path, then stopped.

Crouching in the darkness, he listened for a few seconds to the night sounds of the tropical mountainside. Wind rustled leaves against leaves. Insects flitted past. One moment the warm fetid odor of the stream drifted around him, then the soft wind swept the stink away with cool air that carried the scent of recent rain and flowers.

Lyons slipped a tiny penlight from his front pocket. He cupped his hand over it as he swept the faint glow over the trail's mud. Earlier in the day, he had flattened and smoothed a few feet of the trail. Now he examined the footprints. He saw only the tracks of an adult in sandals and two barefoot children.

A truck engine revved, then fell to a steady throb as the driver low-geared. Lyons snapped off the tiny light.

Avoiding the open area of the footpath, he hurried up the mountainside to a bend in the trail. The truck's headlights appeared on the road. A man in camouflage fatigues leaned out of the truck cab's passenger-side window, sweeping the mountainside with a spotlight. The light found the trail that led away from the road. The soldier slapped the roof of the cab, shouted.

Lyons recognized Arabic. As he lifted his hand-radio, he watched twenty camouflaged soldiers with Kalashnikov rifles jump from the back of the truck. No more thinking about Mack Bolan; now the decisions were up to him.

BLANCANALES WAITED. Cool mud oozed through his blacksuit's pants and shirt. The matting of mud and weeds beneath him sucked at his elbows when he shifted his weight. He stared through binoculars at several members of the drug gang.

Only a hundred feet from him, four of them stood

in a group, talking. They flicked the beams of their flashlights onto their maps or watches every few seconds. Another four of the gang's gunmen paced the perimeter of the airfield.

Focusing the binoculars on the far end of the field, Blancanales saw a gunman adjusting the gas flow of a camp lantern. A makeshift runway beacon, it hung on the end of a six-foot stick driven into the pasture. This beacon was the fourth. Blancanales had watched during the last hour as the gang installed lanterns at the other corners of the landing area, propping up the lanterns and testing them, then turning off the gas flow.

The light from the fourth lantern illuminated an expanse of the grassy pasture and first rows of banana trees bordering the flat field. Then the light died, returning the area to starlit darkness. Blancanales heard the gunman run across the pasture, shouting, "Ready!"

"Me too," Blancanales whispered. Invisible where he lay at the side of the landing strip, Blancanales waited for the Cubans to arrive in the plane. In front of him, an arm's reach away, was a three-switch radio detonator. To his side was an M-16/M-203 rifle/grenade launcher. He wore a silenced Beretta 93-R at his belt, a 9mm subsonic round in the chamber. The moment the Cubans stepped from the cabin of the plane, Blancanales would pop a surprise.

"Wizard! Politician!" Lyons's voice called through the earphone in Blancanales's left ear. He could not risk speaking. He clicked the "transmit" key on his hand-radio twice. He heard Gadgets answer, "Politician's too close to them. Can't talk. What's going on?"

"I'm on the other side of the hill from you," Lyons said, "where the trail meets the road to the banana farm. We got company."

"The truck?"

"It just pulled up. I counted twenty soldiers with AKs getting out. I don't know who they are, but they're talking Arabic and—"

"Could they be Jamaican military?"

"Negative. They're Arabs. They're standing around in the light arguing. I can see their faces. Some of them have those rag headdresses on, like in Egypt."

"See any Cubans with them?"

"No time to talk. Here they come. Lay low, pals. I'll try to get some information."

"Pol, you hear me?"

Blancanales clicked his hand-radio twice. Yes.

"What do you think? Can you talk?"

Three clicks. No.

"One thing I can say. If those guys from the truck are Arabs, something's gone weird. Over."

Two clicks. Yes.

Boots stomped through weeds. Blancanales heard the gunmen approaching. Like Lyons, Blancanales felt a long way from home, although travel had recently become a regular condition for Able Team; and as usual, the absence of an American environment made him think of Mack, and of their past together. Blancanales froze. The gunmen passed within ten feet of him. He heard their legs swishing through the low weeds. One man clicked a lighter, inhaled a long drag, coughed. He heard the other man take a drag. The smell of Jamaican marijuana drifted in the air.

"That bitch," one of the gunmen swore in a Texas accent. "Pays me a thousand dollars and thinks she's queen for a day. There is a limit."

"Call she a Yankee," the second voice joked in Jamaican patois, "and you sound like de local totes. Dey say, 'Yankee bitch dat, Yankee bitch dis.' All de time."

The Texan mimicked the Jamaican. "I grow my hair into de dreads. You tink I pass—"

"You pass for *hippie*!"

Both gunmen laughed. Blancanales eased his head up, chanced a glance at the two men. They stood a few steps away, silhouetted against the night-sky stars. Autorifles hung by slings from their shoulders. They passed a cigar-sized joint back and forth.

"A hippie like de chick with de curls. Like de cool blondie—"

"Hey!" the Texan protested in mock anger. "Don't you say I look like her, blond hair or not—"

"All you Yankees de same. Look de same, talk de same—"

The Texan flicked the huge cigarette at the Jamaican. Sparks exploded from his face, the cigarette falling somewhere in the weeds.

"You know, you even act like dat one! All you whites alike."

Laughing, the Texan searched through the grass

and weeds for the marijuana. He stepped toward Blancanales, crouching, sweeping his hands through the weeds.

A foot in front of Blancanales's face, the marijuana stogie glowed. He scooped up a handful of mud and matted grass and covered it, the ember hissing out.

"What you lookin' for, mon?"

"Can't find the smoke. It's here somewhere. Christ, it's muddy."

Blancanales eased the Beretta 93-R from its holster. Slowly, silently, he brought the pistol up. He kept his thumb on the hammer, but did not cock it. He could not risk the gunman hearing the hammer click back. If Blancanales had to shoot the gunmen, Able Team lost any chance of taking the Cubans.

"Don't worry 'bout it. In Jamaica, dere's ganja for all. De constitution, it say so." A lighter flared as the gunman lit another huge cigarette.

"Put that out!" a voice shouted across the pasture. "You're working tonight. Keeping moving. We paid you to watch this place."

"Yah, boss," the Jamaican replied. He walked away smoking, called back to the Texan, "Come on, mon."

"And that son of a bitch, too," the Texan muttered, following the other gunman. "Thinks his money makes him a Mafia man."

"Hey, mon. His money, it makes ma girl happy."

Their voices and laughter faded. Blancanales returned the Beretta to its holster. He took deep breaths to calm his nerves.

That was close, he thought. Two wandering dopers could have ruined the mission.

Gadgets's urgent voice blasted in his earphone. "Pol! They're coming. They're—" His voice cut off. To emphasize the proximity of the soldiers, Gadgets clicked his key code to Blancanales. Three clicks, then three clicks again.

"Oh, man," Blancanales muttered. Mack Bolan's Able Team was both the triumph of Pol's Chicano existence, and the bane of it. He decided to risk a whisper. "Wizard. Can you see them?"

Three clicks. No.

"Are they behind you?"

"They passed me," Gadgets whispered into his hand-radio. "They're down in between us. There! I see them. I count three of them. They're spreading out in the banana trees."

"But Ironman counted twenty."

"Bet they're spread out all around the strip."

"Bet someone's got the same idea we got," Blancanales countered. "Ambush."

"Ironman, answer," Gadgets called into the hand-radio to Lyons. "Dude of Iron. Thought you were going to get us some information?"

An answer came. Click, click. Yes.

LYONS DROPPED THE DEAD MAN. Pointing his silenced Colt into the darkness, he paused to click an answer to the voices calling through his earphone. Then he felt through the pockets of the soldier, searching for papers, cards, medallions—anything that would identify the soldier or the movement he represented.

Other than a folding knife and magazines for the soldier's AK rifle, Lyons found nothing. He rolled the dead man off the trail, continued uphill. Each kill was, Lyons knew, another shadow in the soul of Mack Bolan, a place where shadows defined a psyche and gave it its tragic but necessary shape.

Branches and vines overhanging the trail created a tunnel of darkness, sometimes total, sometimes dappled with pale blue starlight. Following the sounds of the soldiers' footsteps and clanking weapons, Lyons moved fast through moments of faint light, but stepped slowly through the black voids of shadows, lifting his boots high to avoid tripping on trailside growth that he could not see.

The muzzle of the silenced Colt preceded him into every nightshadow, his finger on the trigger and the fire-selector set on three-shot burst.

Voices stopped him at the crest of the hill. Lyons crouched and listened. He heard footsteps crushing the trail's matting of fronds, leaves and mud. Two soldiers appeared, their torsos and their Kalashnikov assault rifles silhouetted against the sky.

"Sayed!" one of the silhouettes called out. Then louder, "Sayed!"

The soldiers talked in Arabic. One of them continued down the trail, calling out, "Sayed! Sayed!"

The other soldier paced the trail, his AK at port arms. He peered into the impenetrable black of the mountainside's jungle, turning to stare in the direction of every small sound.

Groping through the mud and rotting debris, Lyons found a pebble. With a flick of his left thumb, he shot the stone into the foliage directly across the trail from him.

The soldier pointed his rifle at the sound and hissed, "Sayed?" When no one answered, he searched for the source of the noise, pointing his AK, stopping every few feet to stare into the dark.

Lyons stood up behind him, clamping his left arm around the man's throat. He jammed the Colt's suppressor into the side of the soldier's head. The man thrashed and kicked.

"You speak English? Drop the rifle. *¿Habla español?*"

The soldier continued struggling, slamming the AK's buttplate back, trying for Lyons's groin but only hitting the Colt's empty holster. Lyons shot him, the point-blank slug smashing his skull.

He let the corpse fall. Wiping blood from his face, he grabbed the man's AK and kicked the corpse off the trail. Lyons returned to the shadows to wait.

Running feet thudded up the path. Making no effort at silence, the other soldier was double-timing through the darkness. As he approached the spot where he had left the other man, he spoke quickly in Arabic. The silence halted him.

"Assad?" He stood in the center of the trail, turning in circles.

Taking one step from the shadows, Lyons threw his arm around the soldier's throat and dragged him backward. He forced him to sit down. Again, with the Colt's muzzle against his captive's head, Lyons demanded: "You speak English? *¿Habla español?*"

"I speak, I speak. What you want?"

"You want to live? Drop the rifle."

"Yes. I want live."

"Who are you?"

"Saroush Rajavi."

"No, I mean, what's your organization? Group. Name of your force."

"We are fighters for the Anti-Satanic Army."

"Palestinian? PLO?"

"Believers. Muslims who fight the imperial forces of the Great Satan, in—"

"Where are the others? Are they waiting for you?"

"They go on to fight. We guards. We look to find Sayed."

"You want to live?"

"Yes. No death."

"Okay, Saroush, you're a prisoner. Do as I say, keep quiet, and you live. You understand? You live."

"Yes, I your prisoner. I no make—"

Lyons pressed the pistol against the young man's back as he released his grip on the throat of the "believer." He picked up the AK from the trail and tossed it into the darkness.

"Now stand up," he said. "Strip off that gear. The knife, the ammunition. Throw it. Now open your shirt. All the buttons. Turn around."

Grabbing the back of his collar, Lyons jerked the shirt down the soldier's back, then lashed his arms together.

"How old are you, Saroush?"

"Eighteen years."

"You have a wife? Brothers and sisters? A family?"

"No wife. Mother and brothers in Iran."

"You cooperate, and you live. You see your family again. I promise. No death, no—"

The drone of a twin-engined plane interrupted Lyons.

THE PLANE CIRCLED THE FIELD ONCE, the engines' roar overwhelming the earphone of the hand-radio. Blancanales cupped his hand over that ear to listen to Lyons brief Gadgets. At the corners of the pasture, the brilliant points of the lanterns seared away the night, creating patterns of tropical green that faded to gray and black.

"They're backups for the Cubans," Lyons was saying. "No business tonight. Straight rip-off and bang-bang."

Gadgets laughed. "Leave it to Ironman to grab an Iranian terrorist in Jamaica who speaks English. What luck. Wish Mack was here to help figure out this shit."

"Wasn't luck at all. He's the third one I took," said Lyons. "And there will come a time, man, when Mack will most certainly be with us in our kind of night—that much I know, I can feel it. Hey, is the plane landing?"

Blancanales broke in on the conversation. "I'm looking up at it. It's finishing a go-round. Its lights are on. It's coming in."

"There's no bad guys around you?" Lyons asked. "What can you see?"

Xenon spotlights at the wings' tips lit the pasture like a sudden sunrise. The plane dropped down, cutting treetops, then skipping across the weeds and wet grass. The xenons went black as the plane slowed. Lantern light gleamed from the twin-engined Cessna's midnight-blue enamel. Blancanales watched the plane pivot.

"I'm in the clear. What's the plan?"

"We have to let the Anti-Satan boys make their hit. If there's a firefight, it'll cut the odds. If the dopers surrender, that's just more confusion when we make the grab. Hope those pre-sets can knock down that crowd."

"We'll find out," Blancanales muttered, touching the radio-trigger of the charges positioned in a pattern around the improvised airstrip. "Now the plane's coming this way."

Propeller wind rippled the grass and weeds as the Cessna taxied over the pasture, bumping and pitching, rapidly approaching Blancanales. Had the pilots spotted him as they landed?

Swerving in a wide arc, the plane cut behind Blancanales. A wing passed over him.

The Cessna completed its turn and stopped its engines only thirty feet from Blancanales. The plane's tail almost touched the brush and banana trees at the end of the field.

The drug-gang leaders—he in his cream-colored sport suit and the blonde in scorching white—hurried across the field toward the plane. The man carried a heavy suitcase. Two gunmen with Uzis followed steps behind, togged in Western-style hats and shirts. Long hair hung down over their shoulders.

An instant of light in the plane's cockpit revealed the faces of two swarthy men. Blancanales keyed his hand-radio and whispered, "The dopers have Uzis. The Cubans are climbing out. Looks like the exchange."

The four dopers waited for the Cubans. The gunmen stood two steps behind the man and woman. They held their Uzi machine pistols in their right fists. Except for the modern weapons, the two young men looked like players from an old Western movie.

The Cubans looked dapper in slacks and gold-braided pilot jackets. They approached the gang leaders with smiles and handshakes. As the Cubans shook hands with the bosses, one put his arm around the man's shoulders. The embrace became a choke-hold.

Pulling an autopistol, a Cuban fired into the chest of one cowboy, then the other, knocking down both men before they could raise their Uzis. The second Cuban held the blonde in white, and struggled to fire a pistol as the woman screamed and struggled and clawed at his eyes.

A cowboy took several chest hits. On his back, he fired a one-handed Uzi burst through the legs and back of his boss, the 9mm high-velocity slugs punching through the American gangster to send the Cuban who held him staggering backward.

As he watched the wild slaughter, Blancanales recalled the jive he had overheard between the ganja smokers: nobody liked anybody in this gang....

Muzzle-fire flashed from the trees. High-velocity autorifle slugs found the gang's sentries. A gunman's sawed-off shotgun blasted once. Slugs from five rifles ripped him.

Despite the pistol shots to his chest, the cowboy continued firing his Uzi. A burst caught the wounded Cuban, the wild spray of bullets hitting him in the legs, body and face. The cowboy aimed at the second Cuban.

The Cuban shoved the woman into the cowboy's autoburst. She jerked twice, fell. The Cuban fired as the cowboy jerked the trigger of an empty weapon. The slug snapped the wounded man's head back. Then the surviving Cuban stepped forward to fire into the heads of the dying cowboys.

Screaming and bleeding, her white clothing now red-splashed, the woman scrambled to her feet and ran, her hair streaming behind her. The Cuban aimed at the back of her head, but did not fire.

Camouflage-uniformed soldiers ran from the darkness. Soldiers laughed as they captured the wounded woman. They called out for the others to join them as she struggled and screamed.

Two soldiers held the woman down. A third soldier extended his AK's spike bayonet, then raised the rifle like a spear. A scream tore through the night. The men laughed.

Blancanales looked away, whispered into his handradio. "It's over. All the dopers are dead. One of the Cubans got hit. The second one's trying to help him, but I think he'll be dead of wounds. Anytime you want, I'm ready to go."

"What's going on with the Anti-Satanist Army?" Gadgets asked. "Is that woman dead or what?"

"They executed her," Blancanales answered. He looked over to where they had thrown the woman. He'd assumed the bayonet killed her. But now he heard crying and pleading under the laughter of the gathering soldiers.

"Looks like a gang bang to me," Lyons broke in.

"Ironman! Where are you?" Gadgets demanded. "Time to make our move."

"Second the motion. Heads up. I'm coming in with a prisoner."

Blancanales watched the group of men rape the wounded woman. "Even if she's the doper queen, we can't let this crap happen."

"What do you want to do?" Gadgets asked him.

Lyons's voice cut in. "Let's exploit the opportunity. How many can you count around the woman? You see any others?"

"One man's pulling up his pants, walking toward the Cuban," said Blancanales. "I don't see any others wandering around. They all came to the party."

"I'm moving to the edge of the pasture," said Lyons's voice in Blancanales's earphone. "Soon as I get there, we'll drop them with the pistols. Won't know what's hitting them—"

"And when they do, I'll trigger the charges!"

Gadgets's voice spoke from their earphones. "I tied the prisoner to a tree. I'm moving into position to cover you."

"Here's the plan," Lyons told his partners. "Politician, you and me hit the gang. Wizard, wait until it gets noisy, then hit whoever we miss. Ready? Now!''

Sighting his silenced Beretta on the center of the approaching man's body, Blancanales squeezed off a three-shot burst. The grinning rapist fell on his face. Blancanales flicked the pistol's fire-selector up to single shot and aimed at the back of an Arab's head.

Silent slugs punched into the soldiers. The 9mm slugs that Blancanales fired lacked the velocity for through-and-through wounds, the bullets only slapping heads forward. The soldiers lurched against the backs of their comrades, then slid to the ground.

Lyons fired .45 ACP hollowpoints, the impact of the slugs throwing soldiers to the grass. The others, still oblivious, leaned over the woman, cheering and whistling as their comrades violated her.

One soldier turned, saw a friend jolt and stagger as a .45 slug tore into his chest. Alarmed, the soldier rushed to his friend. He saw the blood gushing from a chest wound. Instinctively, the soldier glanced at the trees, searching the darkness for the unseen sniper. A 9mm steel-cored slug punched into his eye. He fell backward, jerked and thrashed as he died.

Blancanales paused to key his hand-radio. ''Full auto, then I pop the charges—''

Arab soldiers raised their AKs, looking for targets in the tree line. At their feet, the woman—her tight jeans and tube top slashed open—sprawled on the trampled grass, her arms out wide. She struggled. She could not lift her arms from the grass.

Lyons snatched a magazine from his belt, gripped the fold-down handle of his modified Colt and aimed single shots into the soldiers as fast as he could sight.

Over the iron sights of his M-16/M-203 rifle/ grenade launcher, Gadgets watched the scene. The Arabs crouched in a tight circle around the spread-eagled woman. The pale light from the lanterns at the corners of the field threw multiple shadows, leaving the faces of the men gray, their eye sockets black.

Deadly slugs from two directions slammed down the soldiers. Gadgets sighted on three still-standing soldiers, sprayed twenty rounds from his rifle in one sustained burst.

He guessed at a target for his grenade launcher and fired. The 40mm concussion/flash grenade missed a man shouldering an AK, but tore into the body of a dead Arab. The explosion sprayed flesh as it ripped into the fallen man.

Blancanales flipped switches #1 and #2 on the radio-trigger. He pulled himself into a ball, eyes closed, hands over his ears.

Lyons and Gadgets saw the puffs of smoke in the field. They covered their ears, put their faces in the dirt.

Eight concussion/flash charges popped into the air, then exploded with a mind-shocking flash and roar.

The Cuban near the Cessna and the wounded Arabs, all fell semiconscious.

The Cessna's windows shattered. At the other side of the pasture, car windows fell in sheets of sparkling cubes.

As one, the three warriors of Able Team rushed

the Cuban. Running across the field, Lyons dropped
the spent magazine from his modified Colt and
snapped in another mag. A moment behind him,
Gadgets came from the banana trees. Blancanales
reached the plane first.

Crawling, temporarily blind and deaf, the Cuban
groped in the grass for his pistol. Blancanales place-
kicked the man in the solar plexus, the kick throwing
the guy onto his back, gasping and choking.

Gadgets went to the open door of the Cessna and
glanced inside. Then he went to one knee and
watched the field while Blancanales slipped plastic
handcuffs on the Cuban.

Lyons stopped short of the plane. Gadgets pointed
to the woman. Lyons nodded, approached the tangled crowd of dead and wounded in the center of the
field.

A wounded teenager reached for an AK. Lyons
kicked the rifle away and pointed his pistol at the
teenager. The boy raised his hands, begging Lyons
for his life. Lyons did not fire, continued on instead.
He kicked rifles from dead hands.

He heard the woman moaning. A soldier sprawled
on her, as if covering her nakedness. As Lyons approached, he finally saw why the woman could not
move her arms.

Bayonets crucified her, the spike blades of several
AK rifles pinning her arms to the earth, one spike
through her right forearm, two through her left palm
and upper arm. Lyons dragged the dying soldier off
her to observe her wounds.

They had cut her clothes away. Slashes streamed

blood over her chest and abdomen. Even as he knelt to check her pulse, he saw her dead, staring eyes.

Methodically going from man to man, he shot each in the head. The wounded teenager whom he had spared raised his hands. Lyons shot him in the forehead.

Gadgets and Blancanales watched Lyons kill all the wounded, then shoot all the dead again. Finally Lyons jogged over to the plane, changing magazines as he ran.

"We got one of them," Blancanales called out. "But the other Cuban's dead."

"I'm going back for the boy I brought in." Lyons started for the banana rows.

"Hey, bad man!" Gadgets shouted. "Let him slide. He didn't have anything to do with that. Besides, we need him."

"Nothing's going to happen to him. I promised him he'd live. I keep my word."

"Where are the other two?" called Gadgets. "The ones you captured on the other side of the hill."

"Gone." Lyons jogged into the trees.

Blancanales and Gadgets knew what Lyons meant. They exchanged a look. Gadgets chuckled ironically. "Glad Lyons likes me."

The Iranian teenager walked from the banana rows, Lyons one step behind him.

He questioned the boy as they walked. "Who's back at the truck?"

"My friend, Abbas."

"Is he your officer?"

"No. Soldier."

"Who's your officer?"

The teenager turned toward the center of the field. For the first time, he saw the sprawled corpses of his comrades. He stopped in midstride, a wail of fear and grief starting low in his throat.

Lyons grabbed his collar to lead him to Blancanales and Gadgets.

The boy cried, pleaded in English, sometimes lapsing into Persian. "No, I only soldier. They take me from village. They shoot me, they shoot mother, family if I no come—"

"Saroush, quit it. You'll live. I keep my word." Lyons forced the boy to sit down. "Stay there. You're going to America—"

"America? Prison in America?"

Blancanales laughed. "Probably a taxi. All the Iranians I know started off driving taxis."

"I tell truth. I only soldier."

Gadgets motioned his partners to the side. They stepped away from their prisoners where they could not be overheard. "Dig this, we're operating in mysteryland here. The Cubans spent years building up their dope trade. There's ten- and twenty-million-dollar dope deals happening in Miami and La Paz. But this one's a surprise—the Cubans have ripped the dopers for only a million. Why not wait till they got five, ten, twenty million? And why do they import a kill-squad of PLO and Iranian teenagers as back-up?"

"World's full of surprises," Lyons offered. "But what we have to do is airfreight these prisoners back to Stony Man. And quick."

"Let Kurtzmań think about it," Blancanales agreed. "He gets paid for it—"

Lyons cut off the conference. "We gotta move. Otherwise the next surprise could happen to us."

Without another word, they jerked their prisoners from the marshy pasture and marched them into the darkness.

7

Santa Barbara, California

Thursday
11:00 p.m.
(0700 Greenwich mean time)

A CIRCLE OF BRILLIANCE crowned the hill in the night-shrouded wilderness of the Santa Ynez Mountains.

His hand gripping the door latch, Senator Bradford Harper waited for the helicopter to touch down on the estate's mountaintop landing pad. In the distance, grids of sparkling blue marked the cities of Goleta, Montecito, Santa Barbara. Beyond the cities, the scattered lights of oil platforms jeweled the Pacific.

The pilot eased the executive helicopter from the sky. It floated to rest on the concrete helipad. Senator Harper threw open the door as the rotors derevved. A young man in a three-piece suit ran across the pad to help the senator down.

Senator Harper had flown from Kansas at the invitation of his old friend and political ally, the President.

The Man waited in the nightshadow of a wide-branched oak. "Brad, I'm glad you could make it. How's Bette? The kids?"

"Never better. They wanted to come, too. But I told them it wasn't that sort of get-together."

"It isn't. I asked you to come West because we can talk here without all the news services speculating on what's going on. You had an . . . incident in Rosemund yesterday morning."

They walked through the darkness, a quarter moon lighting the hillside path. The senator noted that his friend wore faded denims and hiking boots. The President pushed aside fragrant branches of flowering sage. The young man followed several steps behind.

"You were right not to believe what the FBI told you," the President continued.

"They said it was an environmentalist protest gone wrong," the senator snorted. "Who are they kidding? We don't have any of those kooks in my district. We sent them all out here—"

The two friends laughed.

"But what did happen?"

"I need to make a decision," the President said. "Even with your security clearance, I would not tell you any of this if we didn't go way back. Does the Armed Forces Committee keep up with developments in international terrorism?"

"When it concerns the military."

"This concerns the military. But it's nothing we can stop with the Army or the Navy." The President stopped and turned to the aide. "Bill, show him the note."

The young man stepped forward. He flipped open a folder, snapped on a flashlight. The beam illuminated the first page.

Centered on the page, the senator saw a column of eight numbered notations and names. Numbers 1 through 3 listed latitudes and longitudes. Numbers 4 through 8 listed cities: New York, Los Angeles, San Francisco, Dallas, Washington, D.C.

Another word appeared at the bottom of the page, like a signature: HYDRA.

"What does it mean?" asked the senator.

"Number one is a latitude and longitude in the Salmon River Mountains," replied the President. "Two helicopter pilots working for a lumber company saw a stand of dead trees. They landed, apparently, to check it out. They died almost instantly. It was a combination of Agent Orange and something called Agent VX. Do I have it right, Bill?"

The aide nodded. "Yes, sir. The senator has of course heard of Agent Orange, the defoliant. Perhaps, however, the term 'VX' requires explanation. Agent VX, known to organic chemists as one/two/two/trimethylpropylmethylphosphorofluoridate," the aide quoted, "is a binary chemical weapon in our military arsenal and is exceedingly lethal. One milligram kills."

"A nerve gas?" the senator interrupted. "Terrorists have that? But why out in the forest?"

"A demonstration," the President sighed bitterly. "To show us what they had. The nerve gas to threaten us, the defoliant to mark the spot."

"But they didn't mean to kill the two men," suggested Senator Harper. "They only meant it to be a threat. They can't be completely insane."

"The second latitude and longitude was Rosemund," the President continued. "That was another demonstration. And another murder."

"He was a night watchman," Harper pointed out. The three men were walking again. "He caught them and got killed. Maybe he panicked them. Maybe one of them is a hothead or a psycho."

"Brad, you're hoping they're not capable of doing what they say they will. Listen to me, they hit Rosemund because they know you're the chairman of the Armed Forces Committee. And they know we're friends. First they demonstrated they could hit anywhere in the country, now they've demonstrated they can wipe out whole cities. They parked a semitruck on the Bay Bridge. A high-pressure sprayer shot a chemical hundreds of feet into the air. You have the details, Bill."

"Yes, sir. The truck contained approximately one thousand gallons of water mixed with a chemical called OPA, which is a combination of isopropyl alcohol and isopropylamine, in a five-percent solution, that is, approximately fifty gallons of OPA diluted with one thousand gallons of water. The wind spread the spray's mist over an area five miles in diameter. Isopropylamine is one element in the binary agent, GB. If the terrorists had combined undiluted OPA with the other element, methylphosphonic difluoride, everyone in that area would have died. It would be unwise to believe this group does not also have methylphosphonic difluoride in its possession. If they were to strike a city with GB or VX, we could expect millions of casualties."

"Oh, dear God," Senator Harper groaned.

They stopped in silence on the moonlit trail. A gentle wind swayed the oaks and sage, carrying the scents of dust and pines.

An electronic tone buzzed somewhere in the darkness. A low voice answered. Two men in midnight black appeared.

Senator Harper spun his head in surprise. The President gave the two Secret Service men a nod.

"Good evening, sir," they responded simultaneously. Then they passed on, only the faint, almost unheard sound of their foam-soled boots on the pathway's sand betraying the patrolling agents.

The senator waited until the men disappeared before he spoke again. "What do the terrorists want?" he asked.

After hesitating a moment before answering, the President spoke so quietly the senator had to lean forward to hear every word. "They want me to go on television, to broadcast worldwide via satellite, to announce that we will unilaterally withdraw our military forces from every allied nation on Earth. Every soldier, military technician, advisor. They want us to abandon every ally, every commitment. Total surrender."

"Tell them to go straight to hell."

"At what cost, Senator? They've proved what they can do. You read the list. New York, Los Angeles, San Francisco, Dallas, Washington. We surrender, or else millions of Americans die. That's what we face."

"We can do something," spluttered Harper. "*Something*. We have the best soldiers in the world!

We spend billions on the Rapid Deployment Force, the CIA, the FBI, the NSA—all of them. We can't surrender without a fight!''

The President put his arm around his friend's shoulders and led him away from the young aide, who did not follow the two senior statesmen.

When the President knew he would not be overheard, he asked: "You know the phrase, 'Dirty War'? If we fight them, it will be merciless. We cannot honor the Geneva Convention. We cannot respect national borders. Maybe we can keep it a secret, maybe we can't. But I cannot do anything without the support of every responsible congressman and senator. I won't even be able to tell most of them why, but I will need their unconditional support. Because I'll tell you this. I won't go on television and surrender. I won't do it. So, you with me?''

"Come hell or high water, one hundred and ten percent."

"Good," beamed the President. "There's an Air Force jet waiting at LAX. It'll take us back to Washington tonight. Tomorrow we start a war. And I pray to God no one will ever know.''

8

Eastern Mediterranean

Friday
8:30 a.m.
(0630 Greenwich mean time)

In a business suit, carrying a briefcase, Mack Bolan strode through the mechanics and technicians in the hangar, then marched across the service apron to the executive jet.

He ran up the aluminum stairs and stepped smartly into the United States Air Force plane marked with a corporate logo. A Lebanese worker slammed the cabin door shut.

Bolan smelled the cigar before he saw his friend.

Hal Brognola, the President's liaison to Stony Man Farm, waited at a forward conference table. Bolan seated himself in a leather swivel chair across from the head Fed. The fuselage trembled as the pilot powered the engines to taxi for takeoff.

"I monitored your report," Brognola told Bolan, an unlit stogie clamped between his teeth. "Show me the photos."

Snapping open the attaché case, Bolan found the envelope containing the thirty color exposures, enlarged to eight-by-ten by a Mossad photo lab.

Brognola flipped through the prints.

As the jet accelerated over the asphalt of Beirut International Airport to soar into the clear morning sky, Bolan looked down at traffic-jammed boulevards and artillery-shattered camps. The plane banked away from the city, and its shadow raced over beaches to the open waters of the Mediterranean.

The horizon returned to the window as the pilot eased out of the wide turn and started to gain altitude.

"I wanted to take that European, Russian, whatever he was," Bolan told Brognola. "But it didn't happen. He got clear of the gas, then the boy who tackled him tore his anticontamination suit. The gas killed them both."

Nodding, Brognola divided the stack of photos by subjects: all the prints of the Russian in one group, the photos of an Air Cuba flight attendant in another, the photos of the Palestinians in the last group. He flicked his lighter's flame at the cigar stub.

"Able Team got one of the Cubans in Jamaica. He's on his way to Stony Man now. Would've got both but things went wrong—"

"Casualties?"

"Not on our side."

"What went wrong?"

"Twenty PLO 'front-line fighters' showed up. Lyons took one of them alive."

"Palestinians in Jamaica?"

"Hard to believe. But we have an explanation now."

"What's the explanation?"

Brognola did not answer. He picked up an eight-by-ten showing the Russian in profile and compared it to a frontal angle of him. "You had a good photographer. Kurtzman will love this—"

"What's the story on the Palestinians?" Bolan insisted.

"How much gas do you think they had in the trucks?"

Bolan shrugged impatiently. "Four trucks. Hardmen in one, the others carried the oil drums. Work it out on your calculator, Hal. They had a forklift to move the stuff to the plane. Now give me an answer on those Palestinians."

"Not until I have clearance—"

"What! C'mon, Hal...."

"Where do you think that gas was bound for?"

"Ask Fidel. What's this about clearance? You know I have highest authorization."

"Look at this one here—" Brognola held up a photo of one of the Air Cuba crewmen. "Doesn't look like a Cuban. Chinese? What do you guess?"

"Could be any nationality—sign up with the Kremlin, see the world. I want to know exactly what's going on, my friend. Since when do you fly to the Middle East to debrief me, Hal?"

"This isn't a debriefing. Like I said, I monitored your report."

A buzz sounded from the door to the cockpit. Brognola unlocked the door. The copilot stepped into the cabin and placed a slip of paper on the conference table.

"The message you expected, sir."

"Thanks." Brognola relocked the door before taking a code pad from his coat pocket. The pilot had penciled two short columns of numbers on the paper. Brognola decoded the numbers into two words that he wrote on the paper. Then he tore up the code pad. He pushed the paper across the table.

"Here it is, Mack," grunted Hal. The two words on the paper stood out in their capitalized isolation. "This is my authorization. This commands me to brief you on your immediate next mission. It is also your go-ahead to initiate the mission."

Hal Brognola pointed a chubby finger at the two words on the paper. DIRTY WAR.

9

Offshore New Jersey

Friday
4:45 a.m.
(0945 Greenwich mean time)

TEN MILES SOUTHEAST of the Port of New York, the
Atlantic stank of oil and sewage.

Their collars turned up against the chill predawn
wind, Rafael Encizo and Gary Manning gripped the
guardrail of the bucking tug as the old workboat
chugged through the rolling swells.

A mile to the west, a line of lights defined the black
form of a freighter, the *Tarala*.

Voices came from the tug's pilothouse as the Stony
Men's commander, Colonel Yakov Katzenelenbogen, argued with the Coast Guard captain. They
heard only snatches of words over the wind and
engine noise.

"...two hours...extreme difficulty...endan-
ger...."

"...not your concern!"

Encizo glanced at the luminous numbers of his
watch. "We could have had it done in the time
they've talked."

Since sunset of the previous day, the old tug had

drifted in the Atlantic as the three men of Phoenix Force waited for the arrival of the Panamanian-registered freighter from the open sea. The *Tarala* was due early in the night. But the rusting freighter arrived eight hours late.

An informer in South Yemen had reported a coastal schooner transferring cargo to the *Tarala* as the freighter coursed through the Gulf of Aden, bound for the Red Sea and the Suez Canal. Under surveillance by the Mossad, the *Tarala* did not turn north as expected for the port of Tripoli and the armories of the Syrians occupying northern Lebanon, but instead continued due west through the Mediterranean. British counterterrorist units had taken over the surveillance, expecting the freighter to attempt to deliver its cargo to the Provisional Irish Republican Army.

But the *Tarala* continued west, cutting a course for the United States.

International law allowed for customs inspection when the *Tarala* neared the coastal waters of the United States. However, customs and Coast Guard commanders knew that the crew would offload the cargo for pickup by speedboats before customs inspection.

Even if the *Tarala* did not evade interception, seizure of any weapons aboard would not lead to the identification or capture of the terrorists expecting the delivery. Restraints on both the FBI and the CIA prevented direct action by antiterrorist officers. Therefore the CIA called in Stony Man.

A straightforward mission. Except that the men of

Phoenix Force knew they could not search all the ship's holds and cargo containers. Hundreds of weapons, tons of explosives could be hidden anywhere on the freighter. Only a meticulous, lengthy examination of every compartment and crate could reveal expertly hidden contraband. And no search would discover the identity of the terrorists who intended to use the weapons.

Gary Manning, the Phoenix Force member with the most training and experience in counterespionage and electronic surveillance, decided to place microtransmitters throughout the ship. The microphones would allow Stony Man to monitor any attempt to transfer the cargo. The Coast Guard would wait at a distance, ready to strike when terrorists attempted to take the shipment.

To accomplish the boarding, Rafael Encizo had requisitioned scuba gear and a Sea Horse II. Encizo and Manning had used the Sea Horse Swimmer Delivery Vehicle (SDV) once before, when they intercepted and boarded a Soviet SSG submarine in the course of a mission against a "Jeddah" dragonnade.

Yakov had originally thought that this latest mission—boarding an anchored freighter under cover of ink-black darkness—would involve a few hours of leisurely infiltration. Then the freighter had been eight hours late. If they went in now, at four in the morning, they would be racing dawn.

Yakov slammed the pilothouse door shut. Limping down the steel stairs, he shouted at Encizo and Manning. "Why aren't you ready? Into your suits!"

"*Inmediamente,* Colonel!" Encizo answered as he and Manning rushed into the deck cabin.

As the two younger men stripped to their Speedo trunks and pulled on their wet suits, Yakov explained the change in plans. "No time for a quiet approach. We will tow the Sea Horse to within a few hundred yards of that scum bucket. You'll cut loose while we continue ·past. That'll save thirty minutes."

"And what about the exit?" Manning asked. "If it's daylight when we duck out—"

"You sound like him up there." Yakov pointed his artificial hand up toward the pilot's deck. "You worry too much."

"I will worry, and I'll worry now, thank you, sir!" said Manning, belligerently but without disrespect. "If they put a burst in our backs, I won't ever be worrying again."

"Then I should advise you that you may need two hours on board. At light, if you have not left the ship, we will create a diversion. Speedboats, shooting, sirens. Like television, but no pretty girls. This diversion will occur to the west of the *Tarala*. You will proceed east, into the rising sun. Do you understand?"

"No matter," said Encizo as he checked the Velcro closures on his knife sheath and the holster of his silenced Beretta 93-R. "We will not need the excitement. This will be a very simple thing. A swim in the moonlight."

Minutes later, Encizo and Manning slid the Sea Horse into the water, then followed it themselves.

The foul, freezing seawater splashed over them as they strapped themselves into the SDV's open cockpit. Manning spit out a mouthful of scum. He felt cold water wash over his face with a slap of pain. Then the water penetrated his neoprene suit at the ankles, the wrists, the neck. His muscles spasmed against the chill. He began subtle isometrics to warm his muscles. He felt the conflicting sensation of cold water intermingling with the sweat that coated his tightly suited body.

"Moonlight swim, my ass!" he cursed. "Like swimming in frozen crap."

He heard Encizo laugh. They buddy-checked each other's air tanks and valves. The battery-powered electric motor started up and churned the surface water for a moment. Then the SDV's buoyancy chamber blew out air and the miniature fiberglass submarine settled horizontally in the water. They jammed in their mouthpieces and signaled to Yakov.

The tug eased forward. Soon, at the end of a nylon line, they were trailing a hundred yards behind the churning screws. Planing through the choppy wake, they watched the lights of *Tarala*. The two men touch-checked their regulator hoses for kinks, then soaked their face masks to prevent fogging.

Designed for a maximum speed of three knots, the Sea Horse bucked and throbbed as the tug reached a speed of ten knots.

Suddenly a swell hit from the side and flipped it. The SDV spun like a lure on a dragline in the turbulent black water, and only the cockpit straps kept Encizo and Manning from falling free. Finally, another swell slapped the Sea Horse and stopped the spin.

Manning peered through his mask, hugging the curved fiberglass deck as his senses reeled. His stomach was heaving. He did not pretend to be an underwater expert.

He felt an elbow nudge him, then the Sea Horse suddenly slowed. Encizo was emptying the buoyancy chamber, and the SDV began to slip below the surface as he pushed the control stick forward.

In the calm, undersea darkness, they heard the tug's screws fade into the distance. Encizo watched the luminous needle of the compass that was set into the SDV's deck and maintained a course toward the *Tarala*.

At the count of three hundred, he eased the control stick back to slowly fill the buoyancy tank. He kept the SDV below the ocean's choppy surface and arched his back to raise his head above water.

A steel wall loomed above him. Pushing the control stick hard to the right, Encizo brought the SDV parallel to the *Tarala*'s hull. Manning finally looked up. Encizo pointed to the prow. Manning nodded.

The SDV's electric motor pushed them silently through the water. Encizo kept the miniature submarine a foot below the water. The surface chop slapped and buffeted their heads as they watched for the anchor chain.

The hull curved over them and protected them from observation. Any crewman at the *Tarala*'s deck would need to lean far over the rail and look straight down to notice them. From time to time, patterns of pale illumination from the ship's lights touched the two black-clad fighters. They ducked beneath the chop, surfaced only when darkness returned.

When the craft reached the freighter's anchor chain, Encizo stopped the SDV and blew air from the buoyancy chamber. As the SDV sank, he unsnapped his safety strap and slipped a line through a chain link. In seconds he had secured the SDV. It drifted six feet below the surface, tethered by the line.

Manning freed himself from his safety strap. They helped each other shrug out of their tanks, then swam the few feet to the chain.

Choppy waves slapped at them as they watched the deck. An amber bowlight lit the *Tarala*'s prow. They would be climbing into the full glare of the light. Anyone on the deck or bridge would spot them.

"What do you think?" Manning asked Encizo.

"Maybe I don't get paid to think," the Cuban expatriate answered as he started up the chain, climbing hand over hand on the slick iron, using the chain links like he would rungs on a ladder.

From the water, Manning watched Encizo near the rail, the amber light on him like a spotlight.

THROUGH HIS BINOCULARS, Yakov Katzenelenbogen saw nothing moving on the decks of the *Tarala*.

He saw vignettes of shadow and drab color around lights, the jagged silhouettes of superstructure and antennas black against the stars. Water sprayed from a midship scupper, but Yakov saw no crewmen, no sentries, no Phoenix Force commandos.

The pilothouse door slammed open behind him. "Sir!" one of the Coast Guard men called out to him. "Message on your radio."

Yakov strode into the warmth of the cabin. The monitor of his portable long-distance radio buzzed again and again. He unlocked the console, keyed his identification code.

A voice, denatured and made monotonic by the radio's electronic encrypting, came from the monitor. Yakov recognized the voice as that of April Rose, Mack Bolan's woman and Stony Man's resident electronics and communications specialist. "Phoenix One. I am relaying a message from Stony Man One. Repeat, Stony Man One."

Yakov switched off the monitor and plugged in the headphones. "Continue."

"Suspend operation. Return to Stony Man. Stony Man One has issued call for all members of your team to assemble at Stony Man Farm. Stony Man One inflight from Middle East, ETA eight hours. Repeat, suspend operation. Return to Stony Man. All members of your team."

"Impossible. Repeat, impossible. Insertion of personnel achieved. Operation in progress."

"When can personnel withdraw?"

"Unknown. No contact since insertion. No visual contact, no radio communication. This member very concerned."

"Withdraw personnel first opportunity. Stony Man One has canceled all operations. On command of America One. Repeat, America One."

Yakov did not speak for a moment. All operations

canceled at the command of the President of the United States.... What had happened?

He could think of only one reason to assemble all the Stony Man soldiers. War.

Yakov's religion and patriotism conflicted with his professional commitment to Mack Bolan, a man and a warrior he respected with all his heart. If the United States came under attack by the Soviets, the Arab hordes encircling Israel would launch a unified assault on his country. That would be the war his people had always feared—the Jihad.

As a citizen of the one democracy in the Middle East, a Jew, and an ex-officer in the Israeli Defense Forces—though maimed and middle-aged—he knew his duty. He calculated the flight time between New York City and Tel Aviv. How long until the war? Hours? Days? His nation of three million men, women, and children would face the combined armies of all the Arab and Muslim nations on Earth as those armies stormed Israel in waves of infantry and armor and aircraft, driven on by lies and hatred as the Muslim fanatics attempted to annihilate the Jewish state, to devastate the cities, to scorch away the achievements of generations, to leave only bones and sand and broken stones where the desert had flowered with orchards and farms, to destroy all things that represented the twentieth century, to return the Middle East to the Dark Ages, when Arab kings and their prophets ruled empires of slaves and impoverished, obedient subjects. It would be Armageddon.

"Phoenix One, are you there?" said the disembodied voice of April Rose.

He started to speak. The words caught in his dry throat. He coughed, turned to see if any of the Coast Guard men could overhear him. He whispered into the microphone, "Is it War Number Three?"

April's voice hesitated. "Maybe."

God grant my people mercy, he thought.

LIKE SHADOWS WITHIN SHADOWS, they crept along the deck, Encizo first, Manning ten steps behind him, their feet silent in their thin neoprene socks.

Encizo wore only his wet suit and weapons. Manning carried the pouch of micro-transmitters.

The *Tarala* stank of human filth and rot. Moving through the containers stacked on the freighter's foredeck, another smell assaulted the men: an acrid, vaguely nauseating stink from the cargo inside the eight-by-eight-by-ten-foot-long steel boxes.

Encizo paused beside a cargo derrick. He pointed at the control box and stood watch as Manning placed a micro-transmitter near the operator's phone. If and when the crew used the derrick to offload cargo, the microphone would catch the operator's voice and the voices of the men around the controls.

Gary Manning paused to examine the controls. Unlike the other rusting, salt-encrusted equipment on deck, the control panel gleamed, factory-new. The phone line and power cables flexed in his fingers, the plastic showing no cracking from ultraviolet exposure. He examined the deck where the panel was bolted to the steel. Even in the faint light from the bridge and crew's quarters at the other end of the deck, he saw the scratches and burr marks of recent installation.

Rafael Encizo nudged him. The Cuban motioned him on. But Manning shook his head. Continuing his examination, he saw cables leading to a heavy pumping unit.

When he had worked in civil engineering, Manning had used high-pressure pumps. Later, as the head of his own security company in eastern Canada, his accounts had included maritime and freight-handling firms. The pump in front of him exceeded the requirements of an old ship like the *Tarala*. More suitable for a fire boat or an oil tanker, the pump could suck fluid through six-inch-diameter pipes at a volume of thousands of gallons a minute.

Properly valved and plumbed, the pump could quickly fill or empty a tanker's holds, or shoot water hundreds of feet. This unit had been installed for a use that Manning did not understand.

The six-inch-steel output line went to the derrick mast. There, an assembly of steel fittings and a cast-iron valve reduced the output's diameter to only one inch. The one-inch line went straight up the mast. At the top of the mast—though he could not be certain because of the poor light—he thought he saw the pipe bend at a forty-five-degree angle. The pump would shoot an ultrahigh-pressure stream of fluid far from the freighter.

Without the proper nozzles and swivel joints, such a pump would be useless to fight an on-board fire.

And it had no utility whatsoever for unloading a liquid cargo. As installed, the pump could only spray the cargo into the sky.

Manning hissed to Encizo, "Here! Come here!"

The Cuban slipped back silently. "What?"

"What is this?" Manning pointed at the pump, at its six-inch output, at the thin line running up the derrick mast.

Looking at the pump, then the lines, then the huge pump again, Encizo shook his head. He went to the base of the unit. Two six-inch pipes emerged from belowdecks to enter the pump. Each line had an electric solenoid valve. Encizo only shrugged, motioning Manning to move on.

They continued to the superstructure. Voices stopped them.

Frozen in the shadows, they listened as men argued in Arabic. Encizo crept across the deck to the yellow circle of a porthole. The Cuban sneaked a glance inside, then motioned Manning to join him.

Through the filth-streaked glass, they saw several men crowded around a television. Two appeared to be Arab, three others Hispanic. Beer bottles and video cassettes littered a table. The two Arabs were struggling to insert a cassette into a video player. The others were glancing at one another, smiling. Finally, one Hispanic turned the cassette over. The video deck operated. A pornographic scene flashed onto a color television. The men clapped, whistled. One Arab shoved the other away.

The shoved Arab sulked. He wrapped a *keffiyeh*

around his head then took something from the wall beneath the porthole and left the crew room.

Kalashnikov rifle in his hands, the Arab walked past Encizo and Manning. They waited until the sentry disappeared into the deck's shadows before moving to the deep darkness beneath a flight of steel stairs.

Encizo keyed his hand-radio and whispered, "Phoenix Two and Three. On board."

"Acknowledged." Yakov's voice came through their earphones. "Transmission received from Stony Man. This mission canceled. Evacuate objective immediately."

"Negative," Encizo spit. "Arab *putos* spotted."

Manning hissed into his own hand-radio. "Something's going on here. Not just weapons smuggling."

"Mission canceled on orders of Stony Man One. Return immediately. Pick up point one mile due west of objective. Repeat, one mile due west. We will show lights."

No one argued with Mack Bolan. Encizo sighed. "We come back. *Inmediamente, mi coronel.*"

"Damn!" Manning cursed. "Back in that filthy ice water."

"There is no hurry," Encizo told him. "First, we finish our job. Then we play in the ocean."

"No objection here."

They listened for a minute, heard only the wind and creaking steel as the old freighter swayed with the swells.

Slipping from concealment, Encizo took the lead, creeping silently up the stairs.

On the next deck, they froze as footsteps passed on the walkway above them. A steel door squeaked shut. Encizo pointed to the right and left, to the rows of doors and dark portholes on that deck. Manning shook his head, no. He pointed up, to the bridge. Encizo continued up the stairs.

Following his Cuban friend, Manning glanced down to the main deck to see the sulking Palestinian hunched against the wind, staring out at the Atlantic, his Kalashnikov slung over his back. Among the stacked cargo containers, another sentry's cigarette lighter flared. Manning went low on the stairs and began to climb with his hands and feet, his back lower than the handrail.

A hiss stopped him. Flat on the walkway, Encizo pointed to the bright circle of a porthole. As they watched, a silhouette crossed the window.

To their side, a door handle clicked. Encizo moved fast. He disappeared. Manning crept off the steps and pressed himself against the bulkhead.

Their neoprene-black bodies were jammed into the right angle where the superstructure's wall and walkway met when Encizo and Manning heard the door open. The interior's brilliant light bathed the walkway and handrails. A figure in green fatigues that were tucked into black leather combat boots stepped from the doorway, hand groping for the railing.

The walkway went dark again. The boots went past their faces, then down the steps. They caught a glimpse of a *keffiyeh*-wrapped head and an AKM muzzle before the Palestinian descended to the lower deck.

Manning slowly rose to his feet. He went to the porthole and peered inside. He saw radios, electronic consoles, shipboard telephones, a door in the opposite wall. He scanned the room. He saw no one, only an empty chair in front of the radio.

Motioning to Encizo, he whispered, "The wireless room! Stand watch, I'll put one in there."

Encizo nodded. Manning went to the door, turned the knob infinitely slowly, and pushed the door open. He looked inside, froze.

The radio operator slept on a floor mat. Manning started back, then looked. Empty beer bottles stood at the side of the mat. Reaching into his pouch of micro-transmitters, Manning took out one of the coin-sized devices and peeled off the plastic that covered the self-adhesive back.

He pushed the door open, took two steps to the radio console and slapped the transmitter under the table. Beyond the inside door, he heard voices. Two steps brought him back to the wind-whipped Atlantic night.

"Now the bridge," he whispered to Encizo.

Molding themselves against the steel wall, the two warriors moved slowly to the superstructure's corner. Their legs were fluid, their feet never left the walkway; no footfall, no creak of old steel betrayed them.

Encizo went flat, his cheek against the walkway, and he peered around the corner.

As his partner watched and listened, Manning waited, his eyes sweeping the decks. He noted the one Palestinian still hunched against the rail, another pacing the deck and smoking a cigarette that lit his face with each drag.

Encizo rounded the corner like a snake. Manning dropped to a crouch and watched Encizo crawl under the wheelroom window. The long rectangle of plate glass glowed with the phosphor green of a radar screen. Encizo motioned Manning to follow.

Their backs flat against the superstructure's steel, they inched up toward the long window, keeping their heads to the side of each end. When they gained the height, they turned slowly to peer through the glass into the interior of the room.

Brilliant light filled the wheelroom. A silhouette moved against the radar glow. Manning snapped his head back. He looked across to Encizo. Encizo looked at Manning. He touched one eye, pointed inside. He licked his thumb, mimed sticking something to the window. Manning nodded.

While Encizo watched the interior, Manning prepared another mini-mike. Accumulated filth and corrosion along the bottom of the window forced him to wipe the glass clean before pressing the adhesive-coated transmitter to the extreme corner of the window. He scraped up some flaking paint and gull guano from the window's ledge to conceal the device. The window would now serve as an extension of the microphone, gathering the voices of the crew and captain for transmission.

Motioning Manning to follow, Encizo continued

to the opposite side of the superstructure. Around the corner, they saw another steel stairway leading down. While his partner listened for movement below them, Manning pressed a mini-mike to the porthole of the cabin immediately behind the bridge. Then they crept down to the second deck.

An aluminum outboard-powered boat hung in the lifeboat racks. In contrast to the rust and salt-encrusted paint of the freighter, the boat's aluminum gleamed. The factory's plastic cover protected the outboard motor. Manning put a transmitter on the underside of a wooden seat, then followed Encizo to the main deck.

Across the deck, the sentries talked. A lighter flared for a cigarette. Encizo crawled across the open area between the superstructure and the stacked cargo containers. He rose to a crouch and watched the upper decks for other sentries. He signaled to Manning.

Staying against the lip of the hold hatches, Manning crawled to the shadows of the containers. The two men darted from row to row, glancing down the length of the rows, listening for unseen sentries, then crossing.

Manning saw a container door swinging with the ship's sway. He hissed Encizo to a stop.

Peering inside the door, he saw oil drums. The interior stank of some nauseating chemical. He looked at a tangle of plastic tarp under a container. He tore a patch free. Gulping a breath of air, he leaned into the fumes and wiped the floor of the container with the patch. The stinking chemical coated the plastic.

Manning folded the plastic into a tight wad and jammed it deep into the ankle of his boot where the neoprene would hold it tight.

A minute later, first Encizo, then Manning dropped into the Atlantic. The slap of their bodies hitting the water was lost in the wind and waves.

10

Virginia

Friday
3:00 p.m.
(2000 Greenwich mean time)

SQUINTING AGAINST THE GLARE of the afternoon sun, the assembled personnel of Stony Man watched the Army helicopter descend.

The Huey's side door slid back. Mack Bolan jumped the last six feet, then ran for the perimeter of the helipad. Hal Brognola waited until the skids touched concrete.

Throwing her arms around her man, April Rose welcomed Bolan with a kiss, the rotor-storm whipping her auburn hair around their heads. The noise obliterated her words.

Aaron Kurtzman, data director of the Stony Man HQ, allowed them only a moment's embrace before shouting, "There's a shipload of nerve gas anchored ten miles east of New York City! We got a lab report just five minutes ago—"

Bolan gently separated April's arms and pulled her along with him as he strode for the Stony Man command center, the War Room. The others knotted around him—Kurtzman, Yakov Katzenelenbogen,

Gary Manning, Rafael Encizo, Brognola—all shouting to their commander and at one another to make themselves heard over the rotorthrob of the helicopter as it soared away. Bolan glanced to his friends, his brother warriors—would they all survive the coming week of desperate war?

Bolan and Brognola had flown by Air Force jet from Lebanon to Paris. At Charles deGaulle airport, they had jogged across the tarmac to a Concorde supersonic transport.

Bolan had welcomed the civilian flight. With businessmen and movie actors in the seats around them, Brognola had not been able to continue the briefing. They could not discuss strike options. Bolan had slipped headphones over his ears and slept deeply as stereo orchestral music drowned out the vibrations of the SST's engines.

On arrival at Kennedy International, Bolan had run to a waiting limousine for a ten-minute meeting with a government official. Meanwhile Brognola had met with a CIA courier to exchange the negatives of the Lebanon photos for a folder of Agency background information. Then they had run again, to the Huey waiting to take them to Stony Man.

Bolan had told his friend nothing of the limousine conference at Kennedy: neither to whom he had spoken, nor what they had discussed. Brognola did not press Bolan for the information. He knew Bolan would tell them all at the briefing.

Keio Ohara, the shy young Japanese martial artist of Phoenix Force, waited at the entry to the War Room. Awkward with the still unfamiliar ethnoeccentricities of his American and European compatriots, Keio bowed to his commander. He handed over yet another folder thick with papers and photos, then bowed to everyone in the group as he also gave them folders.

The drill instructor's voice of Andrzej Konzaki, the Stony Man weaponsmith, boomed. "Take your seats, please. Keio, pull the blinds for me and turn on the screen's power. Mack, everyone's got info for everyone else. Let's get this briefing in gear."

Setting down his aluminum canes, Konzaki took a seat in the front row of chairs. His artificial legs were stretched out in front of him. In his conservative gray suit, with his information folders and his open briefcase placed on the seats around him, Konzaki looked like a Washington bureaucrat, not an ex-Marine master of weapon technology. Bolan gave Konzaki a friendly mock salute as he took the lectern. "Where's Grimaldi?" the big guy asked.

"Checking aircraft," Konzaki answered. "Reported in, then went to work."

"Good. And McCarter?"

"His flight was delayed," Yakov reported.

"IRA popped one at Heathrow," Manning added. "Bloody bastards. Killed three kids and their grandfather. Wish we could clean out those morons."

"They're on the target list," said Bolan, "but not this week. You've all had briefings. You know what we're up against. You probably know more than I do. Hal and I flew over on the Concorde. What's developed in the last few hours? What did you say about nerve gas in New York, Bear?"

Aaron "The Bear" Kurtzman held up a torn teletype sheet. "Just came off the machine. Manning's sample turned out to be methylphosphonic difluoride. It's half of the nerve gas GB."

"There's a whole shipful of it," Manning reported. "Cargo containers stacked twenty-five feet high. High-pressure pumps. Couldn't see what they were for, the pipes going straight up in the air. Thought the machines were a miracle of Arab engineering—totally bungled!"

Yakov interrupted. "Colonel, I took the liberty of assembling the equipment and weapons necessary for the assault."

"On what?" Bolan asked. "It's on a ship? On the docks, what?"

"The *Tarala*. The freighter my comrades in the Mossad tracked from Yemen."

"So what's your plan?"

"Hijack it," Encizo announced. "Take it out to deep water, and—" The Cuban grinned, pointed down.

"We want prisoners, remember," Mack Bolan said, his blue eyes cold as ice. "We're up against unknown enemies. Hal, the photos from Lebanon— please pass them around. We have already dropped the negatives with Langley. They'll be searching their files for those faces. These are the facts as I have them. A Russian appeared to be the officer in charge of the chemicals. He wore a protective suit and a gas mask. The Cubans came in on the Ilyushin. Keio, there's an Oriental in a Cuban uniform. Maybe you can tell us his nationality, or his ethnic group.

Yakov, I don't know if I can recognize whatever gang those Palestinians came from—"

"Kalinin!" Kurtzman shouted out. He waved the photo of the Russian killed in Lebanon. "Alex Kalinin. You're a rich man, Mack. The Afghans have a reward for this one. One kilo of gold."

"They can keep it. What do you know about him?"

"Off the top of my head... won the Lenin prize in the Communist Youth Corps, degree in biochemistry from the University of Moscow, taught at Patrice Lumumba University, fluent in Spanish and English. Chemical Warfare officer in the KGB—" Kurtzman turned to the others "—you know the Soviets have two separate armies, the KGB army and the Red Army. Went to Afghanistan to test experimental poisons. Gassed a mosque full of women and children. Was careless enough to walk in front of a Red Army photographer. The Afghans captured the photographer, took his film and notebook. That's how we identified the unit and the location. United Nations wouldn't accept the evidence, by the way, when they had the Afghan hearings. The Rule of the Three Monkeys—See No Evil, Hear No Evil, Speak No Evil, *unless* it's the United States."

"He have any links to the Cubans?" Bolan asked.

"Who knows? The KGB's got links to every crazy in the world. We do know that he's been connected with a character called Fedorenko, who was one of Andropov's artsy-fartsy friends, used to go with Andropov to beatnik Russian art galleries back in the seventies. But Fedorenko's disappeared, could be dead for all we can find out. We may never hear about him again."

"What about the others?" asked Bolan. "Anybody got anything on them?"

Heads shook, no.

"Too much to hope for," April sighed.

Konzaki spoke up. "We got names from the Cuban that Able Team took in Jamaica. We'll cross-check for names, places, organizations—"

"How's the interrogation of that Cuban pilot from Jamaica going?"

Bolan rubbed the unshaven stubble of his broad chin.

"Just came from Langley," Konzaki replied. "Got few hours of cassettes for you to hear. Señor Bru is a very pragmatic young Communist. He wants to live. We're cross-checking what he's told us with what the Iranian soldiers told us—"

"Able Team captured Iranians? In Jamaica?"

"Affirmative. A soldier and a truck driver. They're no one important. Teenagers. Mullahs came to their villages and grabbed all the young men. Some went to the Iraqi front, others got sent to 'freedom-fighting' units. But they had names and details. Able Team will use the information in Nicaragua."

"What?" Brognola asked, incredulous.

"We have every kind of creep and they're all in on this Hydra operation," said Konzaki. "With the information they've given us, we have identified bases in Nicaragua and Florida."

"Hope this doesn't end up on the six-o'clock news

as American crimes in Central America,'' commented April Rose.

"Where are the camps in Florida?" asked Bolan. "Who are the leaders, Andrzej?"

"The Iranians don't know. They had contact only with their unit leaders. But the Cuban pilot heard two Orientals speaking at the Florida base. They spoke Spanish to his commander, spoke Chinese or whatever to each other."

"What did they look like?"

"The pilot didn't see them. He was outside the office, never saw who his commander talked with."

"We're moving!" Bolan said. He pointed to Yakov. "Colonel, when David McCarter gets here, you go back to New York. We'll review your plans while we wait for him. Bear, we want *anything* you've got on those bases in Nicaragua and Florida—"

"Already done, Mack," Konzaki interrupted. "Give your okay, Able Team's on the way."

"Good. Konzaki, Yakov. Set up briefings for me. Kurtzman, the War Room's yours. You're responsible for managing the information flow from all sources, and to all agencies. Briefings will be continuous. We'll have personnel from other agencies coming here. You'll need to transmit updates to me, to Able, to Phoenix wherever they are in the world. You and Konzaki and April will be coordinating the movement of teams and equipment. Understand this, all of you. This is the big one. I talked with the President. He said no surrender. *No surrender.*''

Mack Bolan scanned their faces for a long, silent

moment. "Now go to it. You all have your work. Konzaki, Yakov, Kurtzman, come up front, please. Hal and I have some points to check out with you."

The confusion of voices returned as the warriors gathered their intel folders and left their seats. Yakov spoke quickly with the members of his team before going to Bolan. Encizo and Manning argued with each other. Keio attempted to mediate. April made a phone call, then dashed out.

Gathering in a tight group around the lectern, the senior members of the Stony Man forces held their questions while Bolan leafed through interrogation transcripts, glanced at maps and satellite photos. Bolan waited until all of the others had left the War Room.

"The President said more than 'No surrender,'" Bolan told them quietly. "I met with him only a few minutes ago. Hal, that's who was in that limo. The Man himself.

"He told me that all the evidence we have indicates this is more than an attack on the United States by fanatics and political criminals. We have the involvement of radical anti-U.S. terrorists, the Cuban DGI, the Nicaraguans. We've faced these groups before, but never all at once, never in a coordinated worldwide assault.

"One organization links all these groups. One organization funds them, trains their recruits, plans their atrocities, provides sanctuary for the killers, pleads their insane causes to the world. We know who they are, but we cannot stop them. It would mean war to attack their command center.

"The President told me 'No surrender.' Even if we fail, there will be no surrender. We will not abandon the people of the world to the slave-masters.

"Even if they hit our cities.

"That is what the President told me. If we can stop them, good. The story will never make the newspapers or history books. There will be no confrontation.

"But if we fail, the President will go straight to the center of this terrorism. He will inform the Soviet Union that any attack on the cities of the United States by the KGB or its proxy forces is an act of war.

"Problem is, the Soviet Union has spent the last twenty years preparing for this. We have not. Our allies have not. You know the Europeans. Our country cannot expect help quickly. Only talk and debate, while millions die.

"There it is. America alone. Against the most powerful military regime in history. War. And only we can stop it."

Mack Bolan's steely eyes glared at each man in turn. Behind the hard gaze was a soul torn by primal forces.

But the steel of those eyes expressed a will, a determination to seek the balance within the tempest, a balance within himself and within his men, that by virtue of its intrinsic power and faith would ensure final victory in a struggle that even now pitched the world precariously toward a full fall to Hell.

Yeah, it would be a dirty war, but it would be illuminated by a doctrine that could light the very heavens.

When the mind is right, the sword is right.

11

Straits of Florida

Friday
3:30 p.m.
(2030 Greenwich mean time)

CRUSTED SALT STIFFENED HIS FACE to a mask.

As his power cruiser closed the last mile to the yacht, Kinosuke Yoshida stood on the flying bridge. The spray from the prow misted his white shirt and white deck pants. He saw Cuban crewmen on the yacht furl its sails.

Yoshida's eyes continued scanning the wind-whipped Straits of Florida for the patrolling cutters of the United States Coast Guard.

The rented power cruiser was manned by his bodyguards. Kizu piloted the craft, Kampei monitored the multi-band radio scanner and searched the frequencies for signals from the Coast Guard.

To the moment that they tied up beside the yacht sailing north from Cuba, Yoshida and his men did not fear an encounter with the Coast Guard. They had the correct immigration stamps in their passports. They carried receipts proving they had rented the cruiser. In their deck suits, purchased from an expensive shop in Miami, they appeared to be only

Japanese tourists lavishing American dollars on a visit to Florida.

But he had no confidence in the documents and disguises of his comrades aboard the yacht. Yoshida knew the United States maintained continuous surveillance of the Straits of Florida—from ships, high-flying radar planes, satellites. If the Americans had detected the departure of the yacht from the secret marina in the islands of the Cuban Archipiélago de Sabana, their security services would maintain their surveillance until the yacht reached its destination. Yoshida knew a satellite could even now be replaying their coordinates to a Coast Guard ship.

Any encounter with the Coast Guard involved questions. If the false identities of the Cubans and Palestinians failed to pass the inspection of a Coast Guard officer, the Americans could link Yoshida to Hydra.

And he would lose his victory.

Kinosuke Yoshida, leader of Japan's United Red Army, known and feared internationally as a demon of assassination and random terror, had invested a year in the planning of Hydra. Though the Russian, Fedorenko, had conceived the attack on America, and the Cuban, Munoz, had managed the shipments of chemicals and weapons, it was Yoshida who had assembled the army of terrorists.

Crisscrossing the Middle East, he recruited young men and women from the Soviet camps in South Yemen, the Palestinian bases in northern Lebanon, the radical Muslim fortresses of Iran and Libya. He traveled through Europe to find the exiled survivors of the Uruguayan *Tupamaros* and the Argentine People's Revolutionary Army. He recruited members of the Italian Red Brigades and the German anarchist gangs.

No other terrorist leader in the world could have recruited soldiers from such a spectrum of psychotics. Secrecy did not allow Yoshida to detail the attack, nor the weapons, nor the sponsors. He promised only an attack on America. The fanatics of the world knew Yoshida as a master terrorist utterly beyond politics. No treaty, no shuttling negotiator, no change in government leaders anywhere in the world would prompt the cancellation of his unnamed and mysterious project. The fanatics accepted his promise, joined Hydra without questions.

For they knew Yoshida plotted and executed terror for the pleasure of murder, for the pleasure of seeing mass death.

Before the terrorists reported to the isolated training camps, Yoshida purged his recruits. Soviet KGB officers reviewed the backgrounds of the men and women, cross-checking every detail and name in their past. Informers died. A Mossad agent disappeared. Assassins contracted from the Muslim Brotherhood murdered a CIA operative.

Purified, his terrorists received coded instructions. Zigzagging from one country to another while Yoshida and his personal assistants watched for surveillance, the terrorists finally assembled in isolated camps.

To begin with, the terrorists were trained in languages and conventional assault weapons. Yoshida's men and Cuban DGI agents continued the purging of informers and agents. Only after months did the terrorist army receive its first training in chemical weapons.

In the camps of the Soviet Union's worldwide military empire, where most post-cold-war terrorists received the know-how for their careers of murder and mayhem, KGB instructors would introduce their pupils to grenades and small bombs; advanced students, such as the IRA Provisionals, went on to study the fabrication of 100-kilogram bombs.

But now, in the camps of Yoshida's army, the terrorists learned of chemical weapons, agents of death that required transportation by freighters and fleets of trucks. The scale of their mission dawned on the fanatics. They were not going to attack a government office. They were not going to hit a school bus filled with children. Not an airliner, nor a hundred airliners.

Yoshida plotted the murder of cities. American cities. Millions of Americans.

The army of terrorists came to share his lust. They became his disciples.

Though he had not conceived of Hydra, the conspiracy of mass murder crowned the career of Kinosuke Yoshida. His lifelong rage at all living things would climax with the devastation of American cities.

As a child playing in the gutters and ditches of post-war Tokyo, he tortured and killed small animals. In the fire-bombed ruins behind his mother's brothel, he knocked birds from the air with stones, opened their bodies and watched as ants ate the internal organs of the still-living birds. He trapped rats, then soaked them with gasoline; a touch of a match sent the rats fleeing from an agony they could not escape.

Once, when his mother's bouncer threw a drunken pimp into the street, Yoshida stalked the man until he passed out in an alley. With a sharp piece of glass, he slashed the pimp's eyes. He ran away laughing as the blinded, screaming man thrashed in agony.

Yoshida grew to be six feet tall, a giant in Japan. The taunts of other children, the stares of adults reinforced his psychopathic behavior. He never abandoned his childhood fixation with torture and killing. As a teenager, his appearance and mental illness condemning him to the fringes of society, he joined the criminal gangs ruling a devastated Tokyo: the Yakuza.

Traditionally, the Yakuza controlled the Japanese underworld. In the sixteenth century, Iyeyasu Tokugawa unified Japan through military conquest. Chaos swept the cities and countryside as thousands of samurai of defeated lords wandered in search of new masters. Most of the samurai never found positions in other armies. Destitute, disillusioned, the warriors starved or accepted work as laborers.

They took jobs in the labor gangs building the capital of Tokugawa Japan, Yedo—now known as Tokyo. The shōgun's architects, as men of culture and art, had no experience in managing men who earned their rice with their muscles. It was gangsters from the gambling underworld who bossed the labor gangs that dug the ditches, cut the lumber and stone to fashion the stately temples and palaces of the overlords.

Work camps had no law but the sword. The samurai-turned-laborers lived short, brutal lives, sweating for their money during the workdays, then drinking and gambling and whoring away their money during the nights.

The gangster princes promoted the samurai to maintain discipline in the labor gangs. They introduced the warriors to the Seven Endurances of the Code of the Gambler: cold, heat, hunger, pain, imprisonment, generosity and willingness to sacrifice life. The Yakuza evolved from this chaos.

In time, the Yakuza gangs became the spies and bodyguards of minor lords. Often, when lords from the remote regions traveled to the capital, they could not afford to bring their own samurai. Instead, they hired a retinue of Yakuza warriors for the procession into Yedo.

The Yakuza also came to control any venture the nobility would not touch: prostitution, blackmail, assassination. For three hundred years, the Yakuza ruled the underworld without challenge.

At the end of the nineteenth century, civil war again tore Japan. Following Commander Perry's forced introduction of foreign ideas and technology, the leaders of Japan debated the future of their nation. Conservative lords wanted their people to continue in their traditional isolation, to live without technology, without the contamination of barbarian concepts such as liberty, equality, or the rule of law.

Other Japanese wanted the end of the shōgun's absolute rule, the end of the rigid womb-to-grave caste system, and the entry of their nation into the modern world.

Military forces loyal to the emperor destroyed the shōgunate. With the restoration of the Meji Emperor, thousands of defeated samurai swelled the ranks of the Yakuza. Ironically, the criminal class of the Yakuza became the most conservative faction of Japanese society. They preserved the traditions of the samurai and the feudal past.

When the American Armed Forces destroyed the Tojo military regime, the Yakuza ruled the devastated cities. The underworld lords commanded the police. Businessmen took Yakuza as partners, for only the Yakuza had money to invest. And the Yakuza, through their banks and their ruthless soldiers, controlled the central industries vital to the reconstruction of the cities: lumber, stone, concrete, steel, labor.

The Yakuza banked billions of yen and American dollars. Acting as fronts for the underworld, the banks then loaned the billions to the Yakuza's partners in the emerging corporations of Japan. The ancient society of pimps, gamblers, extortionists, and assassins thus extended their domain to the quiet boardrooms of Japan, Inc.

But Kinosuke Yoshida did not join the Yakuza to participate in the economic miracle of post-war Japan. He did not lust after money.

Yoshida desired only blood and horror.

The street hoods who employed him recognized his

natural talents. Subsidizing his karate and kendo studies, training him in the use of pistols and rifles, they used him to exact revenge on other petty hoods. He accepted assignments revolting even to rapists and murderers.

Once, to halt a rival gang's grab at the prostitution profits of a slum district, Yoshida's boss ordered him to kidnap one of the gang's leaders and somehow terrorize the gang. He left the technique to the imagination of Yoshida. The kidnap occurred, and a series of notes told the rival gang where they could find their leader. They rushed from place to place. They found an arm, a leg, the other arm, the other leg, finally stumbling onto the screaming, dying hulk of their commander. As a joke, Yoshida left it to the leader's own men to grant him the mercy of death.

When he did this, he had not yet celebrated his sixteenth birthday.

As he became a young man, proficient in the martial arts and possessing the unnatural strength of a fanatic, yet also a cold, calculating intelligence uncommon in the underworld, he gained the notice of Yakuza lords who had transcended their criminal origins to attain executive positions in Japanese financial corporations.

In the early 1960s, Communist and anarchist riots disrupted Japanese society. These riots disgusted the Yakuza lords. The radicals' politics offended the traditions sacred to conservative Japanese. The influence of the Soviet Union and Maoist China frightened all Japanese.

In response to the affront of the riots and to protect their vast wealth from any possible Communist victory, the Yakuza executives sent Yoshida to intimidate the radicals.

A propagandist who denounced the emperor from Communist podiums died with a microphone jammed down her throat.

A Red shock-trooper, known for his violent assaults on police, received a tiny wound in his neck vertebrae from a rusty needle. The resulting infection left the radical leader a quadriplegic.

·A leader whose face appeared almost daily on the front pages of radical newspapers disappeared. The next day, a thick envelope arrived at a newspaper office. The envelope contained the leader's face.

But the mutilations and murders accomplished nothing. The Left continued disrupting Japanese universities. Students and radicals protesting one cause or another generated newspaper and television news throughout the decade. If right-wing thugs broke a loudmouthed student's legs or assassinated a Communist Party leader, another radical took his place. The Yakuza lords abandoned their campaign of terror against the radicals. Yoshida returned to assassinating upstart hoods.

Yet he continued attending the rallies, watching the riots of the Communists. The radicals fascinated Yoshida. He admired their seething rage. Though the ·young Communists offered many reasons why they despised the Japanese culture and people, Yoshida saw through their polemics. Like himself, they only wanted to destroy. They used politics as he used the Yakuza: as a means to fulfill their desires. They had no interest in the political process, they only wanted to destroy.

Yoshida had no interest in criminal profits, he wanted only to murder.

Then came international terrorism. Yoshida abandoned the Yakuza without a thought, to join the ultraradical United Red Army of Japan.

The Communist governments of North Korea and South Yemen welcomed Yoshida to their "freedom fighter" training camps. He accepted basic instruction in weapons and explosives, but told his instructors nothing of his past. Later, in the classes of unarmed combat and interrogation, his natural abilities and experience betrayed him as a professional.

Assuming their pupil to be a common criminal from the slums of Japan, the Cuban and Palestinian and Soviet teachers—themselves masters in torture and murder—selected Yoshida for intensive training.

He surprised them. He advanced so rapidly in his studies, and demonstrated such skill in assassination and combat and torture, that the camp administrators seriously doubted his teachers' reports.

Yoshida's first assignment proved his teachers correct beyond question.

He had traveled to Beirut to spend three weeks watching a Kuwaiti prince. Posing as a Japanese businessman, he persuaded the Kuwaiti to invite him to his fortified office complex. With only his hands, Yoshida killed the prince's personal bodyguards, seized the prince and fought his way out of the fortress. Kuwait secretly paid a ten-million-dollar ransom to Al Fatah. The United Red Army received a five-million-dollar share.

Now a hero of the Revolution, Yoshida became a leader. Under the leadership of two other alumni of the Soviet terror schools, Ilich Sanchez—or "Carlos the Jackal"—and Zeko Tanaga, Yoshida planned the United Red Army's attack on Israel's Lod International Airport in Tel Aviv. In solidarity with the Palestinian Revolution, three Japanese gunmen murdered twenty-seven people, wounded seventy-eight others. Most of the dead and wounded were Puerto Rican Catholics on a pilgrimage to the birthplace of Jesus.

The Arab world ComBloc nations hailed the outrage as a great victory of the Japanese Communist "freedom fighters" over the Zionists.

Yoshida remained a shadowy figure in the maelstrom of international terror. Though he crafted victory after victory, he had no interest in following his soldiers on their suicidal missions. He studied the world, found his targets, formed the kill squads. He watched his dramas in lurid video as his Japanese and Palestinian and European soldiers achieved glorious martyrdom on international prime-time television.

Then Fedorenko brought Yoshida the concept of Hydra.

MIDWAY BETWEEN THE FLORIDA KEYS and the Archipiélago de Sabana-Camagüey, Yoshida approached the yacht to meet with his coconspirator, Jorge Munoz y Villamor, an officer in the *Dirección General de Inteligencia* (DGI) of the People's Republic of Cuba.

At the helm of the power cruiser, Kuzi backed off on the throttle and cranked the wheel hard to the right. The cruiser bobbed to a perfect stop, the port rail bumping against the yacht's hull as the two pleasure craft rose and fell with the light wind-chop.

Cubans stepped down from the yacht to lash the craft together. Kampei continued monitoring the Coast Guard frequencies as Yoshida and Kizu, the bodyguard carrying an Uzi, climbed up to the yacht.

"Comrade!"

Munoz attempted to greet Yoshida with an *abrazo*, the macho embrace of friendship between Hispanic men. Yoshida avoided the Cuban's embrace, gave him only a perfunctory nod. He nodded also to the Palestinian beside Munoz, Saeb Shyein, an Al Fatah liaison officer. Shyein knew Yoshida well; he made no attempt to even shake hands.

The Japanese terror-master never allowed any man or woman to touch him. He considered it a violation of his personal security.

Yoshida opened the meeting without wasting words. "Anything from the Americans?"

"Let us have our conversation in the comfort of the cabin."

"One moment." Yoshida glanced at Kizu. They watched as Kizu went ahead into the yacht's cabin. After a minute, the bodyguard returned; he nodded to Yoshida. Only then did Yoshida follow Munoz and Shyein down the narrow stairs. Kizu remained on the deck, watching the crewmen.

"Señor Yoshida," Munoz commented, "the distrust of one's comrades in revolution only strengthens the forces of empire and fascism—"

"Any word from the Americans?" Yoshida repeated, sitting on a leather benchseat in the walnut-and-brass cabin. He looked at the tray of American and European liqueurs on the table, took nothing.

Shyein, the Palestinian, disregarded his Islamic prohibitions and poured himself a half glass of bourbon, with ice.

"Not yet," Munoz answered.

"Any movement in their armies?" the Japanese asked.

"It is too soon. But the surrender will come. Even they will see the futility of resistance to our—"

"How much money have your Cubans taken?" Yoshida interrupted.

"From the dope gangs? Millions. My men struck everywhere in the Western Hemisphere. They have taken over twenty million dollars in the past week. Already, I have transferred much of the money to our allies in the United States."

"Mercenaries!" Shyein cursed. "Americans sell themselves like Jew whores."

"Amigo," said Munoz, "our comrades the Black Liberation Army, the FALN, the Chicano-Mexicanos—they all need funds to operate. In the Russian struggle, remember, Lenin operated on funds seized from the czarist banks. But the FBI storm troopers of repression in the United States are far more efficient, far more dangerous. Our friends suffer many casualties with every attempted expropriation—"

"But will dollars buy bravery and sacrifice?" Shyein demanded.

"It will." Munoz smiled. "I gave them only down payments. If they do not fight, they will not be paid."

Shyein gulped bourbon, splashed more into his glass. "If they fail us, they die."

Munoz laughed. "That is understood."

Yoshida stopped the argument. "And the Russian. When does he return? When do we meet again?"

"Security does not allow another meeting," Munoz told him.

"We agreed to meet again before the deadline."

The Cuban shrugged. "Things change."

Yoshida stared at Munoz for a long moment. He knew the Cuban lied. The talk of security did not mean they feared the Americans. Munoz and Fedorenko feared him, Yoshida the warrior. As they should, for he despised them.

Munoz, the bureaucrat, the accountant, the pretender to Revolution who mouthed slogans and posed for photos with his gray-beard leaders; Fedorenko, the Russian who played chess for relaxation, who read French novels, who enjoyed the ballet. . . . They thought they could save themselves from the flashing blade of his hatred. But Yoshida the warrior despised them.

Yoshida felt the sea salt crusted on his face crack as he smiled. "Yes. Things change."

"Tell me, how goes it with the many fighting groups?" Munoz asked him.

"As we planned. In the movements of the fighters,

there has been no change." Yoshida stood. He looked to the Palestinian. "Come. I return to Miami now."

Gulping down the last of his bourbon, Shyein staggered to the deck. A Cuban crewman handed him a suitcase and a vinyl case the shape of a Kalashnikov. Kizu helped the Palestinian down to the deck of the power cruiser. Munoz waved goodbye. "*Adios*, my Japanese comrade. And Shyein! Give my regards to my Cuban brothers, wish them luck for me."

"Victory to the People!" the Palestinian called out as the cruiser's engine roared. Like a tourist departing on a world voyage, he stood on the flying bridge waving until they left the yacht far behind. Then his drunken grin dropped. Turning to Yoshida, his face twisted into a sneer. "That Cuban dog. That coward. He is like an old woman with his books and computers. He knows nothing of war. He should be a Jew shopkeeper."

"Did he talk of the attacks in Lebanon and Jamaica?"

"What? Our forces were attacked? By who, the Mossad?"

"In Lebanon, yes, perhaps. It is not known who struck in Jamaica. Two Cubans and a group of your fighters disappeared. I think the Americans."

"But the Russian said they would surrender. He said the Americans would not fight! How can we fight them? So many against so few of us?"

"Did Munoz not tell you of the city killing, that the Russian would kill cities?"

'He said it would not be necessary. He said—"

"Munoz said?"

"Yes, Munoz. He said the Americans would surrender. The Americans are soft. He said we would have an easy victory."

Yoshida scanned the horizon with binoculars for the United States Coast Guard. "They will surrender. But only after we have killed a city."

"Good! Death to America. Victory to our people—"

"Then we kill all the cities."

"Why do you say that? If they surrender, why continue the killing?"

Lowering the binoculars, Yoshida turned to face him with his wide face. For the second time he smiled.

"Why not?"

12

Miami

Friday
7:00 p.m.
(2400 Greenwich mean time)

WHEELS SCREECHING, a Gulfstream jet decelerated on the runway of the Fort Lauderdale Executive Airport. It was painted flat-black, and marked with multicolored corporate logos.

In the cockpit, Grimaldi throttled down, letting the aircraft's momentum carry them to the last turn-off at the far end of the field. The former Mafia pilot swept the jet around, then hit a switch to unlock the boarding stairs. He hurried from the cockpit to join his passengers as they opened the cabin door.

"Miami was my old stomping grounds, Sarge," Grimaldi reminded his leader. "You sure you can't use me here?"

Bolan shook his head, glanced at Encizo. "You're on your way to Nicaragua. Brief Able Team, put them in motion."

"*Adios, hermano,*" muttered Encizo.

"Watch out, you two," said Grimaldi. "Everything you hear about Miami is true."

"You're telling me?" Encizo laughed. He gave

Grimaldi a brotherly punch in the chest as they stepped into the torrid Florida evening.

A Cadillac El Dorado convertible, its polished red finish alive with .the lights of the airfield, squealed to a stop only a few feet from the jet's folding stairs.

Bolan and Encizo carried heavy suitcases down the stairs. They stared when they saw the Cadillac's driver.

Her lustrous black hair flowed over a blouse of white satin. Light glistened on the deep red lipstick of the lovely Hispanic woman who waited behind the wheel. Without comment, she returned their stares as they approached.

Bolan and Encizo set their heavy cases on the white leather of the back seat. Encizo swung over the convertible's side and sprawled on the back seat, leaning against the cases.

"Who are you?" Bolan asked as he took the front passenger side bucket seat.

"My name is Flor Trujillo. DEA."

"And like a flower you are." Encizo leaned forward to smell the scent of her hair and neck. "What a delicate flower, a beautiful flower...."

Flor jerked her head to shake away his hand. "Back off, you Cuban bozo!"

Encizo laughed.

"Thank you for delivering the car. Where can we drop you, Ms. Trujillo?" Bolan asked her.

"I'm your contact, gentlemen. It's my operation you're interrupting. I take you where you want to go, I make the introductions."

"We have Highest Authorization," Bolan reminded her. "You will follow your orders."

"And my orders are to take you there, make the introductions. I am this operation. If I don't go with you, no one will talk to you."

Bolan turned in the seat and looked at Encizo. The Cuban grinned, nodded. Bolan accepted her.

Spinning the steering wheel, Flor accelerated the huge convertible into a power drift across the asphalt. She straightened the car and hurtled for the gate at sixty miles an hour. Her raven-black hair glistened with lights as it flagged in the slipwind.

"This vehicle have the equipment we requested?" Bolan asked her.

"Agency seized this car from a Colombian gang. Turbocharger. Steel armor. Bulletproof glass. Then we spent some money. Multi-band radio in the dash. False compartment in the trunk. Weapons inside. Uzis, magazines of 9mm in two bandoleers. An M-16/203 with tear gas and stun grenades."

Encizo chortled at the Drug Enforcement Agency arsenal. "We brought our own weapons, *chiquita*."

"I know who you are!" Bolan shouted to her over the roar of the slipwind. "You helped some friends of mine in the Caribbean. You remember Carl Morgan?"

Flor gave him a half-smile. "I remember him."

"He told me you are one hard-core professional. You caught a round from an M-60, still had it in you to join in a firefight."

"Not really," she laughed. "Slug went through a

brass railing and the yacht's wall. My Kevlar stopped it. It hurt, and my arm didn't work right for days. But you don't need both hands to fire a Colt AR. What else did Carl tell you?''

"Just that story."

A few short blocks brought them to Tarmarac and the ramp of Florida's turnpike. Swinging onto the broad highway, Flor stomped on the gas again. The acceleration of the turbocharged Cadillac snapped their necks back.

Bolan told the story of Able Team's Caribbean battle to Encizo. ''...helicopter's doorgunner was ripping up the boat with an M-60, point-blank fire. Flor gets hit. But she keeps putting out rounds with her commando rifle. Carl goes up on top of the yacht to punch out the helicopter with one of those XM-17 revolver grenade launchers, a wheel gun. He goes back to the pilot room, Flor's putting a cold can of beer against where she got hit. Then she pops the top and drinks the beer!''

Laughing, they sat back as Flor gunned the car down the turnpike as it swung west and then south, bypassing all traffic on the narrower roads. Out of Broward County into Dade County, they roared southward. At Pennsuco, near 125th Street, they exited the turnpike and picked up U.S. 27, Okeechobee Road. They continued southeast past Hialeah and into the northwestern part of Miami.

Just past Miami International Airport, they swung onto Route 122 through the city itself, exiting onto U.S. 195 and across the Julia Tuttle Causeway to Collins Avenue.

When they left the causeway, Bolan said, "Flor, pull over. Now I drive."

Without a word, she parked at the curb. She opened the door, swung her legs out, then stopped. She reached back and pulled the keys from the ignition, then she left the car.

Flor walked around the front of the Cadillac. Her blouse billowed around the waist of her tight designer jeans. Bolan moved to the driver's seat and took the keys as Flor got in.

Easing away from the curb, Bolan drove slowly through the Miami streets and boulevards. He scanned the sights like a tourist. But he was no tourist.

Collins Avenue. An address from another time and another battle. He had been here before—more than once—in the days when his war had been against the Mafia. Now he fought here again.

His ice-blue eyes scanned the lights and neon of the tall hotel fronts. Lined up on the avenue, the hotels' windows overlooked the sand beaches of the man-made island. Flor pointed to the newest high rise, the Imperial Colonnade.

"We booked reservations there," she said.

"The Colonnade! Just like old times, Mack!" Encizo reminded him.

"Yeah, that's where the action was," Bolan commented. "And is."

Inside one of his suitcases, Bolan carried an attaché case containing stacks of hundred-dollar bills with nonconsecutive serial numbers. One hundred thousand dollars. A down payment in the universal currency of drug deals.

They swept into the curved, landscaped driveway of the luxury hotel. A uniformed doorman met them as the car came to a stop.

Bolan assumed his role. Casually tossing the doorman the keys, he commanded, "I want my luggage in my suite, pronto!" His voice was loud, arrogant.

"Yes, sir!" The doorman snapped his fingers at a bellhop. As Bolan passed the doorman, he slipped a bill into the man's hand. The doorman glanced at the corner. One hundred dollars!

Playing her part, Flor took Bolan's arm and clung to him as they entered. She laughed softly at Bolan's act. "Who are you supposed to be? Some hotshot dealer from up North?"

"You got it."

Five minutes later, they entered the penthouse suite. Bolan snapped open one of his cases and switched on a counterelectronic surveillance unit.

"I swept the rooms for transmitters," Flor told him.

Bolan extended the unit's "wand" and walked through the suite. It detected no electronic surveillance. Finally he sat down. But he left the unit's power on. Some designs of micro-transmitters avoided detection by remaining off until the operator activated the power by radio pulse. Bolan took no chances.

"We need information," he told Flor. "You work in the Cuban expatriate community. Your contacts include the paramilitary groups. We captured a pilot named Bru. You've received the names of the men we want."

"Why do you want them?"

"For questioning."

"But they work for you."

"What?"

"All the paras are Agency or ex-Agency. They dream of invading Cuba. Some of them finance their armies with the drug money. They operate in a gray area, moving back and forth between politics and crime. We always clear a target with Langley before busting them."

"We want that gang for questioning. You can use this as an opportunity to close them down without going through the, ah, process—"

"Without going due process of warrants, arrests, trials?" Flor completed the presentation.

Bolan nodded.

"But you want them alive? That will be difficult."

"Not all of them. Only the main man."

"Well, we can't get him. He'd be out at the camp."

"The Esperanza Camp?"

"The Cape Esperanza Youth Rehabilitation Center."

"What do you know about it?"

"Nothing at all. We thought it was an Agency operation. Didn't want to know about it."

"Can you set up a meeting at the camp?"

Flor shook her head. "No. It has to be a bar in town. Maybe we can take his lieutenant, but he'll have his men with him. There'll be shooting."

Encizo laughed, a quick, cynical hack. "Have no

fear, *niña*. I will hold you in my arms, protect you from the bad men."

Flor stared at the Cuban, demanded, "The Agency wants them terminated? Is that the word for killing men who want to free their country but won't go along with Washington's political fads?"

"They're not Agency," said Bolan.

"Mister, I've read their files. All of the groups out there in the swamp are Agency. Fascists who fought for Batista. Socialists who fought with Fidel himself. Veterans of the invasion. Sons of men who didn't make it back from the torture chambers. They fight for the Agency, but all they get is betrayal after betrayal. And now liquidation, right?"

"What did you read in their files?" Bolan asked her.

"Well, not theirs. The Cape Esperanza gang has buried their past. I've never met the leader. And his officers have all the marks of first-class plastic surgery. We have nothing on them. But the Agency won't let them escape, right?"

"Wrong initials, Ms. Trujillo," said Encizo. "Not CIA. DGI. The DGI of the People's Republic of Cuba."

Flor blinked, realizing the error of her interdepartmental suspicion. "I did not understand."

"Now you do," said Encizo. "Now you know why this hotshot dealer from up North wants your cooperation. We all work for the same government. With that clarified, can we get this operation moving?"

"I'll make the calls," Flor answered, her voice quiet.

Encizo laughed again.

A NEON JUKE BOX blasted out the rhythm of an old rhumba. Bolan followed Flor through the dim club. He noted the few patrons at the tables and bar. Two middle-aged Hispanic men at a table saw Bolan, slapped money on the table and left. A man at the bar spoke quickly with the bartender before following the other men out the door. Flor continued to a doorway marked Private and pushed through the bead curtain. Bolan followed two steps behind her.

Two swarthy men in crisply pressed white suits and tropical print shirts looked up from their drinks and conversation.

"Why are you here, *señorita*?" the first Cuban asked.

"Business," Flor told them.

Swinging the briefcase onto the table, Bolan snapped it open. The Cubans looked at the money, their expressions unchanging.

"What business?"

"As we discussed on the telephone."

"We discussed nothing. We don't know you."

Flor laughed, throwing her head back, watching the Cubans. "It is your loss. Come, my friend. We go."

They pushed through the beads again. Flor caught Bolan's arm, pulled him to the bar. She leaned close to him, whispered, "The one that talked is Mujica."

"Who's the other one?"

"A soldier."

"When the time comes," Bolan told her, "I'll take care of the soldier. They'll need a few minutes for their other soldiers to move into position. You watch Mujica. I'll watch the door."

She signaled the bartender and ordered orange juice in rapid Spanish. "Why are you so sure they will shoot?"

Bolan scanned the interior. The last patron put money on the bar and left. Alone in the club with her, Bolan leaned up against Flor as if they were lovers, whispered, "They're hot for money. The smuggling operation has been fronting for the Cuban DGI, earning money for Communist crazies in Colombia, El Salvador, Guatemala. Recently, they shifted their base from Cuba to Miami. Last night in Jamaica, they murdered a drug gang to rip off a million in cash. Colombian and Bolivian authorities report a number of wipeouts like that. Apparently, the DGI operation intends to cash out all its accounts. We believe the money's flowing into a KGB operation. We want to follow that flow if we can. If it's not too late."

A beep sounded in the earphone Bolan wore. He listened as Encizo's voice whispered to him. "Two cars out front, two gunmen each car."

"Are we ready to go?" Bolan asked Flor.

"Anytime."

Bolan spoke to the mini-mike in his lapel. "We'll take our man. Don't let any of them make it in here."

"No problema, hermano."

His lips touching Flor's fragrant throat, he whispered, "Four gunmen out front. Stay low as we go out. Let's take him."

She moved her body against him. He felt a breast brush his arm. "They're DGI or KGB, right? No doubt about that?"

"Most definite."

"Let me go first."

"What are you intending to—"

Before Bolan finished his whispered question, Flor kissed him, spun away. Her heels clicked quickly on the barroom floor as she went to the private room. At the bead curtain, she turned as if to glance back to her lover. Her right hand went under her blouse, to her waistband.

A .45 ACP slug smashed through the face of the soldier, the impact bouncing him off the wall behind him, blood spraying from his shattered skull. The small-frame Detonics autoloader dropped on line as Flor rushed forward two steps and fired a second slug point-blank into the gunman's chest. Even as her arm arced upward with the heavy recoil, she turned to Mujica and slammed the small pistol down on the bridge of his nose. He froze with his hand under his coat. Blood trickled down his face.

"Puto de Stalin!" Flor spat into Mujica's face as Bolan rushed up behind her. Her hands and arms shivering with adrenaline rush, she held the Detonics on the Cuban's forehead. Bolan snatched the Colt Python out of Mujica's shoulder holster.

Whirling, Bolan double-actioned three rapid shots, the slugs destroying the glass beads in the doorway.

The bartender flew backward, a double-barreled shotgun falling from his hands. It hit the floor in front of him, both barrels exploding, the simultaneous blasts of 12-gauge birdshot destroying his groin and abdomen, shattering bottles and mirrors behind him. Tissue sprayed the broken glass. Blood misted the air.

Flor still pointed the Detonics at their prisoner, her hands shaking. Bolan gave her a grin as he cinched the Cuban's hands behind him with plastic handcuffs.

"Let's get him out of here."

As Bolan jerked Mujica out of the chair, Flor reached down to the dead gunman and found a Browning High-Power in his shoulder holster. She touched the ejector to confirm a round in the chamber.

Bolan strong-armed their prisoner through the bar. Flor stayed two steps ahead, her eyes flicking from side to side, the Detonics and Browning in her hands.

Shots popped outside. A gunman staggered through the door. Blood spurted from a chest wound and a gash across his forehead. He pointed an Uzi back at the street to spray 9mm slugs into the night.

Flor raised the pistols she held, but Bolan's .44 AutoMag thundered first. The impact of 240 grains of high-velocity hollowpoint slammed the gunman against the wall. The corpse collapsed in a tangle of dead arms and legs, tripping Mujica. Bolan and Flor struggled to drag their prisoner through the narrow entry.

On the street, Encizo sprinted across the asphalt, a

Heckler & Koch MP5A2 9mm silenced submachine gun with a passive infrared nightsight in his hands. He executed a wounded man crawling behind a car, the slug hitting the gunman's skull with only the sound of a slap.

In his peripheral vision, Encizo saw another gunman raise a pistol-grip 14-inch Remington 870.

The first blast of double-ought balls tore past his face. Even as he spun, desperately spraying low-velocity 9mm slugs to hammer car steel and smash tempered glass, Encizo waited for the shotgun's second blast to kill him.

Flor burst from the bar's entrance. With a pistol in each hand, she advanced on the shotgunner, fire flashing as she hit him again and again, the gunman's body slamming against the car, .45 blasts and the pops of 9mm shots echoing in the neighborhood.

One step behind the deadly beauty, Bolan dragged out the man in the blood-splattered white suit. Running three steps, Bolan jerked Mujica off his feet and pitched him into the back seat of the El Dorado.

In seconds, Bolan had the Cadillac fishtailing through the side streets. Flor sat in the front seat, still clutching a pistol in each hand. She swept her arm across her face to wipe away clots of blood. Blood patterned her white satin blouse like tropical flowers.

Encizo leaned from the back seat and put his hand on her shoulder. He felt her shaking. He spoke loud to be heard over the windrush and roaring engine.

"*Hermana*, forgive me for my indiscretions tonight. I will never again show you disrespect."

Bolan looked back at Encizo. His glance showed total agreement.

Encizo laughed, then said sincerely, "And, if you forgive my earlier indiscretions, perhaps you would consent to accompany us to another investigation tonight?"

13

Jamaica

Friday
10:30 p.m.
(0330 Greenwich mean time)

BLACK-AND-WHITE PHOTOS, contour maps and building diagrams spilled across the limousine's back seat. Grimaldi looked anxiously at the glass partition that separated him and Able Team from the uniformed driver. Rosario Blancanales and Carl Lyons glanced through their folders. Gadgets Schwarz reassembled his collection of photos and maps.

"I rented this limo from the hotel," Grimaldi told them, quietly but urgently. "It isn't Team equipment, so we can't talk much. We'll be flying south in about five minutes. The company talked with your friends and got some interesting leads. So here's your next account." He glanced at the partition again. "All I can tell you for now is get ready to take a big step."

They gazed at maps of Nicaragua, photos of mountains and pine forests. Lyons grinned. "Interesting."

Gadgets laughed. "The places we go. Wow."

Leaving the tourist and commercial center of Kingston, the limousine followed the highway around the eastern end of the harbor, then turned onto the broad modern boulevard along the natural break-water of the Pallisadoes Peninsula. The lights of the wharves and Kingston high rises shimmered on the black waters of the harbor and broke the early-evening horizon. The festive lights of yachts and pleasure cruisers swayed on the gentle swells of the bay.

Able Team ignored the scenery. They leafed through the pages in their folders. The top of every page, the corners of the photos and maps bore the stamp CLASSIFIED.

"They put all this together since last night?" Gadgets asked. He checked his watch. "In only sixteen hours?"

"You haven't been back to the Farm," Grimaldi told him. "You don't know what's going on. You'll get a complete briefing on the plane. Let's just say that business is hot."

Speeding past the entrances to the international terminals, the limo continued to the hangars serving the freight flights. The driver braked at a private terminal that catered to corporation executives. The driver jumped out to open the doors for the four "salesmen." Grimaldi checked the seats for forgotten papers, then tipped the driver twenty dollars. In another moment, the limo pulled away.

Grimaldi stood at the curb while Gadgets, Lyons and Blancanales started into the executive terminal. Grimaldi watched the limo leave the terminal grounds. Then he called out to the others, pointing to a gate in the chain link fencing. "Forget the VIP treatment. Through the fence. Like the rest of the hired help."

Hurrying through the employee entrance, they darted through parked trucks and vans. Inside the hangar, technicians serviced Lear jets bearing the logos of multinational companies. Reflexively, the four men stayed in the shadows. They turned their faces when they passed workers or executives. On the runway, they broke into a jog.

Grimaldi led them to a flat-black executive jet. As the rear door opened, Grimaldi peeled a self-adhesive company insignia from the fuselage.

"Snappy plane, *ese*," Lyons joked in Los Angeles gang-jargon. "But can't you pay for some paint? Cruisin' in the primer don't make it."

"Primer?" Grimaldi asked. "Ah, the night black. Talk to the Air Force. Too late for this trip, but maybe the next time we drop you into Indian country, we can fly you there in cherry-red metalflake. Get in the plane, joker."

Blancanales and Gadgets saw the parachute gear immediately. Lyons followed them, still laughing at the teasing of the ace pilot. Three steps into the cabin, Lyons spotted a weapon. "All right! Konzaki sent us the good stuff."

He picked up an M-249 Squad Automatic Weapon. Made lighter than the standard military model by the use of titanium, it fired belt-fed SS109 5.56 slugs at a cyclic rate of 750 to 950 rounds per minute. Konzaki, the Stony Man weaponsmith, had modified the M-249 for long-distance killing by reengineering the sear mechanism to fire semi-auto and three-shot bursts in addition to full-auto, then mounting a twenty-five-inch precision barrel, and finally adding a Leatherwood ART II variable 3x-9x sniper scope. A lock-on titanium suppressor served to muffle the report and conceal the muzzle-flash.

Lyons marveled at the weapon, at its Fabrique Nationale design, the custom titanium work, the monster scope. At a thousand yards, its 62-grain, hardened steel-cored slugs would punch holes through lightweight body armor and steel helmets. On days of perfect weather at the firing range, Lyons had scored deadly hits on silhouette targets placed at six hundred yards.

Opening a wardrobe closet, Grimaldi stripped off his sports coat, tie and shirt, and neatly arranged the clothes on a hanger. He pulled on a T-shirt sporting Playboy Club insignia. As he tucked the T-shirt into his slacks, he watched the three men of Able Team.

They were preparing a high-altitude, low-opening paradrop into the central mountains of Nicaragua. There could be no failure, no surrender. Serious wounds or capture meant death. Yet they had not shown a doubt or hesitation. They were checking through their HALO rigs and weapons with cool professionalism, their hands steady and unhurried.

Grimaldi thought of the report on the double-ambush the night before on the banana farm. Able Team took one day off to lounge in the sun and rest, now it's off to Stalinist Nicaragua on a do-or-die mission. Where did Bolan get such men?

"You got an hour, tourists," Grimaldi told Able Team. He went to the pilot's cabin. "Then it's out that door."

14

Nicaragua

Friday
12:01 a.m.
(0601 Greenwich mean time)

MOONLIGHT STREAKED ACROSS the blades of month-high corn. Gadgets lay in the damp field, his head pillowed on his wadded parachute. Rows of corn screened him on both sides. He leaned up and saw the moon low on a horizon of forested ridge crests. He found north by the twinkling of the Big Dipper.

His hand-radio clicked. Lyons. Another code came through. Blancanales. Gadgets plugged in his earphone and keyed his code: three clicks to identify himself, then two more to indicate he was down and ready.

Silence. A breath of wind moved the corn. Gadgets scanned the farmland around him. He lay on a slope overlooking a small valley. The valley's checkerboard pattern of fields continued uphill almost to the ridge lines; above them, the steep mountainsides became pine forest.

Perhaps a mile away, he saw a tiny light. A house. What seemed a mile farther were several lights clustered along the pale stripe of a gravel road. Gadgets decided to risk voice radio.

"The Wiz speaks. I'm in the middle of a cornfield. I came down to the east of the flare. There's a rise to the west of me. I think the flare was on the other side of the rise. Talk to me."

"Lay cool," Blancanales cautioned. "I'm on the rise. After I came down, I got a good fix on the flare before it went out. I'm moving slow, looking and listening. Ironman, talk. Where are you?"

"Just missed the trees. I'm way, way up the hill from you."

"Problems?" Blancanales asked. "You need any help getting downhill?"

"I like it up here," Lyons answered. "It's beautiful and it's peaceful."

"Up and moving, tourist," Gadgets told him. "You didn't come here to meditate."

"Yeah, yeah. I'm on my way. Over."

"What about you, Wizard?" Blancanales asked.

"Thirty seconds."

Gadgets opened the case protecting their long-distance radio. The radio incorporated a scrambler and tape unit to produce a "screech" transmission of incomprehensible electronic noise. Without an automatic tape to record and slow the burst of transmission, then a unit to decode the message, the message remained only electronic noise. The first message went to Grimaldi, now on his way back to Miami, confirming Able Team's touchdown and safety. Later messages would travel via NSA retransmission to Stony Man Farm in Virginia.

Gadgets received a coded response from Grimaldi. Closing up the transmitter, he gathered his wadded parachute, his pack of radio and electronics, and his weapons. He keyed his hand-radio. "Okay, Pol. Let's go meet our friends."

LYONS LAUGHED. "Teenyboppers!"

"Easy, man," Blancanales advised him. "They're qualified."

Lyons looked incredulously at his fellow warrior. "We're going up against the PLO, radical Muslims, Cubans, and the cadre of the Red Army Faction. And those two—" he pointed at the teenaged boy and girl with autorifles "—they are the backup squad? Get serious!"

A tiny fire of corncobs and sticks sputtered, throwing intermittent light on their faces and swirling smoke into the sooty ax-hewn rafters of the hut. The five of them crowded within its earthen walls, Able Team's packs and weapons competing with dried corn, chilies and farm tools for space.

Maria and David talked back and forth with Blancanales, their voices low but angry, Blancanales's voice soothing. Maria threw back her knife-cut black hair and glared at Lyons. A hateful sneer twisted the angelic beauty of the teenaged girl's face. Then she turned again to Blancanales and hissed in quiet, rapid Spanish.

Gadgets grinned to Lyons. "Shouldn't have said that. She knows English."

"So what?" Dropping down the bipod legs of the M-249, Lyons pointed the weapon at the hut's plank door. He checked the fiberglass-and-foam case protecting the scope. He pulled out his silenced Colt Government Model, wiped mountainside mud from it, and returned it to his web-belt's holster. Then he adjusted the straps of the shoulder holster carrying his Python.

"No dig in, mister," David told Lyons in broken English. "We go, *inmediamente*. One minute."

"Not with you, kid," Lyons answered. "I don't take teenagers to the cemetery."

Blancanales spoke. "There's no one else. If they—"

Holstering his Magnum, Lyons leaned past Blancanales. He put his hand on the girl's shoulder. "Maria, how old are you? Thirteen? Maybe fourteen? And your brother, how old—"

She twisted away from Lyons's touch. "My brother dead. My father dead. My mother dead. This my country, my war. You come here, tell me no. Who are you? Here, you foreigner. Here, you work for me."

"Their unit got ambushed a day ago," Blancanales explained. "Her father and brother and the older men did not come back."

"How'd you two get rifles?" Lyons asked the teenagers.

"This my rifle!" Maria snapped back. She shook her M-1 carbine. "I carry it one year."

"I kill Cubano," David declared, holding an AK-47. The scuffed stock still bore a stenciled spray paint armory number.

"They're qualified to lead us there," Blancanales

told his partners. "They're qualified because there's no one else to guide us."

"We have maps," Lyons countered.

"Is our war," Maria stated simply.

"Four to one," Gadgets concluded the argument. "Looks like you're outvoted, Carl."

Once the moon had set, Maria and David led them from the valley.

They followed a rutted dirt lane past farms and family compounds. Dogs barked from dark houses.

As they passed one house, a voice called out in Spanish. Maria answered. A man came out carrying a long-barreled shotgun. David ran through corn to talk with the man for a moment. The man slung his shotgun over his shoulder, then scrambled across the cornfield to join them.

Lyons's right hand went for his silenced Colt. María spoke quickly in her schoolchild English. "No, mister. He brother of my father. *No problema.*"

Her uncle looked at the three combat-clad men of Able Team. He pointed to the sky and mimed a parachutist pulling on his shroud lines as he descended.

"I don't like this," Lyons told Blancanales and Gadgets. "Everyone in town's going to know—"

"The brother of my father saw you come," Maria interrupted. "David tell him we go kill *comunistas*. He say he help us."

"Why did we have to come here?" Lyons groaned. "Everybody wants to kill the Sandinistas."

"Mister!" Maria hissed. "We are Sandinistas.

True Sandinistas. The others are *comunistas*. They steal our revolution."

"Can we get moving?" Lyons asked, impatient, staring around at the dark fields. "Let's talk politics when the crazies are cold."

Blancanales laughed softly. "You would've loved Vietnam, Ironman. Politics in five languages, all night long."

Maria spoke with Blancanales quickly in Spanish. Blancanales turned to Gadgets and Lyons. "Give the uncle some of your weight to carry. He'll go with us to the top of the mountains. It'll be downhill past there."

The newcomer shouldered 800-rounds ammunition for the M-249, a pack of six Viper rockets and two pouches containing claymores. He trudged behind them as they climbed the hillsides. They left the fields and the occasional houses behind, and hiked on through pine forest. Beyond the pale smear of the starlit path, the forested mountainsides became depthless voids of pitch-black.

Every sound—the cry of a night bird, a dislodged rock bouncing down the hillside—made the three men of Able Team freeze for an instant. Maria and David ranged far ahead of them, always returning to point out the correct fork in a path, but usually stayed in the darkness.

"How do we know these people aren't leading us into a trap?" Lyons whispered to Blancanales.

"We don't."

After another hour of steep, switchbacking trails, the pines thinned out as the mountainsides became sheets of black volcanic rock.

They went over the crest. As a wind whipped at their sweat-soaked clothing, Able Team paused for Maria's uncle to return to them the ordnance he carried. He shook hands with Lyons, Blancanales, and Gadgets Schwarz, then slipped away.

"Adios, yanquis y niños."

They paralleled the ridge line for miles. Above them, the vast dome of the night swirled with stars.

They rounded a fold in the mountain and saw the distant lights of the terrorist training camp. Blancanales glanced at his watch. He called the teenagers back. They spoke in Spanish.

"It's eleven now," said Blancanales. "By our maps, we're six miles from the camp. How fast can we cover that distance?"

"For first part, very quickly," Maria told him. Her voice was mature beyond her years. "But near camp, becomes dangerous. They have patrols. Land mines."

Gadgets and Lyons waited as the teenagers briefed Blancanales in rapid Spanish. Then Blancanales turned to his partners.

"The terrorists train up here. They set booby traps, ambush each other with noisemakers and blanks. If we contact one of those squads and can slip away, great. But if they identify us, they can get their helicopters up here in ten minutes."

"How many helicopters do they have?" Gadgets asked. "What kind and how many soldiers do they carry?"

"The kids say they're Alouettes. Six men in each. Seems the socialist governments of Nicaragua and

France exchanged gifts, and the terrorists got troop-ships."

Lyons interrupted. "What about the patrols?"

"We shouldn't encounter any serious patrols until we're almost at the perimeter. They've got cleared fields of fire and mine fields out for a hundred meters. Maria and David can take us to the wire. Their job with the local militia is to steal the mines. They go in there twice or three times a month."

Lyons stared at the two teenagers. "Someone sends these kids to steal land mines? That's sickening. And you guys call me cold."

"Mister," Maria told him, "we volunteer."

Blancanales looked at Lyons. "Don't let it bother you. This is the last night. Let's go."

Hiking again through the darkness, they followed networks of tiny trails downhill. Gravity accelerated every step, helping them move quickly despite their heavy packs and weapons. At a switchback, Gadgets stood side by side with Lyons for an instant. A little breathless, Gadgets spoke quietly to his ex-cop partner. "Sometimes I forget you weren't in Nam. There, you would have learned the meaning of the word 'sickening.'"

Then Gadgets hurried on, trying to keep up with the quick-footed girl and boy.

CANS AND BOTTLES AND CARTRIDGE CASINGS littered the hilltop. On this side of the mountain, the winds carried moisture from the distant Pacific and the jungles of Honduras.

Lyons crawled through ferns and vines.

Trash scraped at his nightsuit. Beneath a pine, piled trash smoldered, a gray wisp of smoke drifting up from time to time. Lyons stood up beside the tree and looked downslope four hundred yards to the training base.

Gadgets and Blancanales came up. Blancanales lifted a can to the starlight. He strained to read the label, but could not. It was printed in Arabic.

He squinted at the label on a beer bottle. People's Republic of Cuba.

"I got a good line on the parade ground," Lyons told them. He scanned the compound with a telescope. "I got all the guard towers. A few of the streets in between the barracks. All of one road going into the base. Most of the other road. Yup. I'm going to make them hurt."

"If we don't get them," said Blancanales, "you will."

"Don't talk that way," Lyons told him. "When they get a fix on where I am up here, everything in the camp—recoilless rifles, RPGs, pistols—everything's coming this way. It's up to you guys to keep the heat off me."

Blancanales laughed quietly. "Come on, Wizard. We got another half mile to go. *Adios*, dead-eye. I'll send one of the kids back to stand sentry for you."

Gadgets gave Lyons a quick salute as they went.

A COIN FLIP DECIDED which of the teenagers stayed with Lyons. In the darkness, Blancanales ran his fingers over the peseta. He offered it to Maria to touch. She felt a profile.

David would go to the wire with the *norteameri-cano* commandos. She stayed with the bad one.

"Maria, aquí. David, con nosotros," Blancanales said simply.

She spit in the dark. "No like that man. Damn *yanqui.*"

Blancanales and Gadgets shouldered their gear. Gadgets leaned to her. "He has a child your age. He is very concerned. So he talks like a father."

"U.S.A. long way away," she answered. "Here he father to nothing."

She quickly kissed David, then watched him lead the two *norteamericanos* into the blackness. Ten meters away, she heard the other commando, digging in. Clutching her M-1, she dodged through the trees and branches. She found Lyons gouging the stony soil with a folding shovel.

"I stay," she told him. "Watch for Cubanos."

"If you see them, if they see you," said Lyons, "lead them away. Run as fast as you can—"

"No! I fight."

The man stared at her. Finally, he asked, "You have ammunition?"

"Twenty-three bullets."

He laughed. "Won't last long in a firefight, *chica.*"

"I fifteen, mister. I Sandinista all life. I fight for my country, for my people. I soldier."

"Well, happy birthday and merry revolution." Still laughing, Carl Lyons gave her a hand grenade. "That'll even up the odds a little. Maybe you'll live to be sweet sixteen."

THEY CRAWLED THROUGH an abandoned village. Only weed-grown fields, the furrows flattened by trucks, and the bullet-pocked earth walls remained of the community. The boy had described to Blancanales and Gadgets the continuous training and target practice that had occurred here, indeed everywhere around the base. Brass casings rolled under their feet. Spent cartridges scattered on the bare concrete slab of a burned house, glinted with the lights of the perimeter fences. A hundred yards from the camp, they stopped.

Beyond a tangle of barbed wire, they saw scraped bare dirt extending to the camp fence. David showed the men a crawl hole through the wire. He gave Blancanales information in whispered Spanish.

Blancanales summarized to Gadgets. "If we want, he can take us halfway across the no-man's-land. After that, we chance the lights. Or we can set up here. He says patrols pass here, but not often. Sometimes there aren't patrols for one or two nights."

"We don't need to risk it," Gadgets whispered. "Unnecessary with appropriate technology."

Retreating on their bellies to the ruins of a farm hut, they crouched against a stone-and-mud wall and opened the pack of modified Viper rockets.

The Viper Light Anti-Armor Weapons, solid fuel rockets in plastic disposable one-man launchers, differed from U.S. Army specifications. Originally designed to attack armored vehicles, Stony Man's weaponsmith Andrzej Konzaki had instructed the factory to manufacture some with concentric wraps of notched steel wire and white phosphorous. Though the warheads presented no threats to tanks, the redesigned weapons would shred and scorch any soldiers within a hundred-foot kill zone.

There was a second modification that radically altered the use of the rockets. Able Team would not rest the launchers on their shoulders, aim, then press the trigger bars to fire the rockets. Gadgets and Konzaki had modified the launchers to fire by radio impulses.

Gadgets slid three launchers from their packing case. He checked the radio-triggers, then picked up one of the Vipers. He crawled a few feet to a fruit tree sawn short by bullets. Studying the stump for a moment, he went on to the next living stump.

Sighting along one side of the tree stump at the camp a hundred yards away, he saw two Alouette helicopters under floodlights. Orange and white, they still bore the stenciled markings of the Department of Agriculture. Gadgets put the Viper's fiberglass launch tube to the bullet-hacked tree and lined it up on one of the helicopters. He lashed the tube securely with heavy tape.

Careful not to break the new green shoots growing from the splintered stump, he snapped down the shoulder stop and slid out the extension tube. He heard the firing-pin mechanism cock. Squinting through the launcher's sights, Gadgets adjusted the aim with a final length of tape. He checked his aim again. Perfect.

Blancanales and David stood watch as Gadgets

ranged in a semicircle around the base, placing and arming the six Vipers. After two hours, he was done.

"No problems?" Blancanales whispered.

"Perfecto," Gadgets answered.

15

Offshore New Jersey

Saturday
1:00 a.m.
(0600 Greenwich mean time)

WITH ONLY HIS GREASE-BLACKENED FACE above the dark foul water of the North Atlantic, Gary Manning stared up at the prow of the *Tarala*. An arm's length away, their heads bobbing with the swell, Keio Ohara and David McCarter secured the mooring line of their Sea Horse II Swimmer Delivery Vehicle.

Like the night before, when Rafael Encizo led Manning to the old freighter, the amber glare of the prow beacon glistened on the huge links of the anchor chain. Again, only luck would conceal him as he climbed the chain. But this time, Manning would take the risk of climbing first, not that *mas macho* Encizo.

Why he watched the deck, he did not know. From his extreme angle—almost straight down from the prow—he was unable to see if a sentry stood at the rail. And every second he watched, he endured another splash of the cold sewage-tainted tide surging out from the rivers and harbors of New York City.

Finally, he shrugged off his dread. If he could not

see them, they could not see him. Those terror merchants abhorred deck watch. The night before, he and Encizo had no problems with the sentries; the Hispanics and Palestinians had stayed out of the wind and salt spray. And the Coast Guard technicians, monitoring the mini-transmitters placed in the radio room and bridge, reported no talk of intruders.

Manning checked the Velcro securing his knife and Beretta 93-R. Then he put his neoprene boot into a chain link and grabbed another with his hands.

"Hope they're staying warm with their skin flicks," he whispered to McCarter and Ohara.

"Get up that chain!" McCarter hissed. "Cold as all hell in this place."

"Think I like it?" Manning asked. He climbed slowly, hanging from the chain as it swayed with the swells and motion of the freighter. He struggled to secure a positive foothold in the links before reaching up for the next handhold. Not trusting the grip of his textured neoprene gloves, he put his hand and wrist through each slick, oily link of the chain.

Above him, nothing moved. He saw no forms at the rails, no glowing points of cigarettes.

Halfway up, he paused to listen, arching his neck back to watch the rail. He heard the creaking of the ship, a steel door banging as the ship rolled with the sea. Nothing moved on the prow.

He continued cautiously, careful not to click his Beretta, knife, or radio against the chain. Every few seconds, he looked up at the railing, the angle of the chain forcing him to arch his back and strain his neck.

Only a few more links separated him from the hawsehole. The anchor chain ran through the hull in a steel housing that was too small for a man's body to pass through. The night before, Encizo and Manning had crawled through the hawsehole and over the coiled ropes on the deck. Now Manning secured an arm through a link, reached for the stamped steel of the safety grid under the railing.

Metal clinked against metal. He listened. Boot soles squeaked. He heard boots scuff.

The wind shifted for an instant. He smelled a sickly sweet tobacco. No, tobacco and cheap hashish.

Manning waited, resigned to hanging on the chain for a few minutes. He counted to sixty, then sixty again. The wind chilled his face. Sweat ran under the tight neoprene of his suit. Above him, the boots scuffed the deck. His legs cramping from his awkward stance, his arms aching, Manning counted to sixty again. He looked up. He saw a lighter flare again.

A transistor radio blared. A New York rock-and-roll station blasted the Atlantic silence.

Bloody damn! Manning realized the sentry had found a hiding place where he could smoke and listen to American music without an officer finding him.

The electronic rhythms covered the sound of Manning's Velcro holster flap ripping open. Forcing his cramped hand to clamp tight on the Beretta's grip, he pushed his gloved index finger through the trigger guard and pulled out the pistol. He flipped up the safety.

He tapped the safety grid with the silencer tube. He repeated the taps, click-click-click.

The radio went off. Manning tapped again, click-click-click. He saw the sentry's hands on the railing. Pointing the pistol straight up, Manning made a low wailing sound, like a sound effect from a childhood ghost story. "Woooooooooooow...awooooooo-ooooow...awooowhoo...."

A *keffiyeh*-framed faced peered down, searching for the source of the strange noise. Manning double-actioned a 9mm slug into the Arab's forehead.

As the dead man fell back, Manning set the safety and jammed the pistol into the holster. In a second, he had climbed through the hawsehole and onto the deck.

The dead Palestinian lay sprawled against coiled ropes, his mouth agape, his eyes staring up at the swirling stars. Manning crouched low to watch for other sentries along the railing. He could see no farther than the containers stacked on the forward deck, where the curve of the bow straightened. He slipped through the ropes and cables and checked the other side. He saw no one.

He returned to the railing. Cupping his hand around a blue-lensed penlight, he signaled Ohara and McCarter. A shadow rose from the gray water. Manning crouched in the coils of rope and stripped off the waterproof casing on his hand-radio. He put the earphone in his ear and watched the deck as he buzzed Yakov on the Coast Guard tug.

"Phoenix One. Phoenix One. This is Fish One. On the boat. Fish Two coming up. Any noise?"

"No alarm," came Yakov's voice. "No extraordinary talk. Have you observed any change in cargo or personnel from last night?"

"Nothing here on the bow. Can't see amidships."

"I will alert you if there is an alarm. Over."

Glancing over the rail, Manning saw Ohara's wet-suited form ascending the chain. Manning watched the deck and listened for boots as he waited. When he heard the safety grating creak with Ohara's weight, he pulled the tall Japanese through the hawsehole. Manning checked the seals of the heavy waterproof satchel that Ohara carried on his back.

"What happened? Why did you wait?" Ohara whispered.

"Him." Manning pointed at the dead Arab.

Ohara leaned back through the hawsehole and flashed his blue light to McCarter.

In a minute, the brawny SAS veteran joined them. McCarter carried a second waterproof satchel. They tore the plastic seals and opened the satchel of weapons. Each man took a silenced MAC-10, a bandoleer of magazines, and a web belt carrying two pouches of the new Italian MU-50G controlled-effect grenades. Designed for urban and antiterrorist warfare, the hand-thrown grenades—so small a man could hold two in one hand—had a 100 percent lethal blast radius of five meters, yet presented no danger to personnel beyond twenty meters.

Manning led Ohara back along the starboard rail. McCarter crossed the bow deck to check the port rail. They slipped along the opposite sides of the stacked cargo containers.

As he came to the corner of the stack, Manning pressed his back against a container door, then crept forward. When he reached the corner, he eased his head out. He saw no one around the foremast, no sentries near the huge pump or the controls. He raced silently across to the containers stacked amidships. From there he directed Ohara to the pump.

Manning watched the deck as Ohara finished with the pump cables. Finally Ohara joined McCarter at the other rail.

They continued toward the holds. Manning had a clear view of the rail to the superstructure. He moved slowly along the deck, his shoulder brushing the wall of stacked containers. At every opening between the containers where a sentry might find shelter from the wind and Atlantic chill, he paused for an instant, the MAC-10 at chest height, to snap a look into the shadows. But he found no terrorists on the foredeck.

At the superstructure, Manning signaled the other two Phoenix Force soldiers to follow him. He retraced his route of the previous night. As before, he saw light in the porthole of the crew quarters. Tonight, two Hispanics watched a New York program on their television.

The Phoenix Force soldiers circled the superstructure. Manning and McCarter watched the doors and walkways as Ohara moved along the railings. Every ten paces, Ohara lashed a fist-sized packet to the rail with tape.

When they completed their circle of the first level, they crept up the steel steps to the next. They glanced into lighted portholes, saw one empty cabin, another cabin where a Palestinian read the Arabic script of a torn newspaper. They circled that deck, continued up the stairs to the command level. Below them, on the main deck, sentries paced.

The Phoenix men did not attempt a complete circle of the third level. Avoiding the pilot's long plate-glass window, Ohara taped packets along three rails of the superstructure.

He took the last packet from his satchel and taped it with its convex front facing down the steps.

Manning pointed to the radio room. Ohara nodded, crept to the door. He crouched against the steel of the superstructure to wait. Manning and McCarter eased around the corner.

McCarter crouched at one end of the pilot's window. Repeating Encizo's maneuver of the night before, Manning snaked under the wide window. They inched up and peered into the wheelroom.

Manning saw a Hispanic leaning back in a swivel chair, his feet on the radar console. He looked at the screen from time to time as he talked with a Palestinian. Beyond the two men, the door into the radio room stood open.

Viewing the interior from a different angle, McCarter saw the two men, and on the wall behind them a map of New York City. As he watched, the Palestinian suddenly glanced to one side, breaking off his conversation with his companion at the radar console. McCarter ducked down. He waited for a signal from Manning.

The Palestinian went into the radio room. Manning crawled under the window to McCarter. "I saw two. How many you see?"

"Two."

"Let's get it over with."

They returned to the side of the bridge. Manning held up two fingers to Ohara. The Japanese nodded. The three men touched the safeties of their MAC-10s.

Ohara glanced through the radio room's porthole. He saw a Palestinian seated in front of the radio, transcribing a message. He turned to his compatriots, held up a hand. Wait.

Faint buzzes came from their hand-radios. Manning keyed an answer on his set and heard Yakov's voice whisper through his earphone.

"Fish One. Transmission in progress. Wait until message received. Repeat, wait. Acknowledge."

Manning did not risk a whisper. He clicked his transmit key, twice, then twice again.

"Are you ready to assault?" said Yakov's muffled voice.

Two clicks.

"Wait in position until I signal...."

Boots sounded on the steel steps. Simultaneously, the three Phoenix men shrank to the walkway, their neoprene-black forms going flat.

Voices speaking Arabic preceded two *keffiyeh*-wrapped heads. The Palestinians carried AKMs—one with his autorifle slung over his shoulder, the other swinging his folding stock Kalashnikov by the pistol-grip. They talked as they came up the stairs. They started across the walkway toward the door to the bridge. One reached for the door.

He stopped, stared down at Ohara as if his eyes could not be sure what they saw.

A .45 slug from Manning's MAC-10 sprayed brains from the Palestinian's forehead. A three-round burst slammed into the other terrorist's gut and chest as he swung up his Kalashnikov. The impacts of the slugs threw the Palestinian backward down the stairs, his body crashing to the walkway below, the rifle's steel clanging on the steel steps.

"Move it!" Manning hissed. Surprise had been lost.

Throwing open the doors, they rushed in, Ohara into the radio room, Manning and McCarter onto the bridge.

Keio Ohara saw the Palestinian radio operator rising from the chair, his hand going for a shoulder-holstered pistol. Driving a front-kick into the terrorist's side, the hundreds of foot-pounds of force ripped the cartilage of several ribs and sent the Palestinian's right kidney into shock. Ohara had neutralized him without killing him. The terrorist fell to the floor, vomiting. Ohara stooped to grab the automatic from his shoulder holster, and continued on.

Manning and McCarter held their fire as they entered the bridge. The Hispanic at the radar console did not have time to sit up before McCarter slammed the butt end of his MAC-10's receiver down on his head. The man fell to the floor, stunned, his hands over his bleeding head.

No cries, no shots, no alarm. No alarm yet. The Phoenix men swept the bridge room with their eyes, the muzzles of their MAC-10s on line. They saw no one. As Ohara and McCarter looped plastic handcuffs around the hands and feet of their prisoners, then jammed check-patterned *keffiyeh* cloth into the men's mouths, Manning held his submachine gun on the other doors.

One door opened to the outside. The other, to another small room behind the bridge. When Ohara finished with his prisoner, Manning motioned him to the side of the second door.

Throwing the door open, Manning rushed in, surprising a terrorist in bed with a lurid girlie magazine in one hand, his other hand pumping up and down under the blanket. The man screamed. Manning jammed the MAC-10's muzzle against his face. The scream cut off. But Manning's laughter continued.

"I caught a commie jerking off!" he called out to the others.

A door squeaking stopped his joking. Hurrying out of the cold Atlantic night, a Palestinian startled Ohara and McCarter. Slugs slammed into the Arab's chest, the impacts throwing him against the door. His body sprawled in the doorway. McCarter grabbed it by an arm to pull it inside. He locked the door.

Manning dragged his prisoner out of the bed and put a knee on his back as he jerked plastic handcuffs tight around his wrists and ankles. He jammed a wad of bedsheet into the man's mouth.

The seizing of the bridge had taken less than sixty seconds.

Manning keyed his hand-radio. "Phoenix One. Objective Number One secured. Phase Two ready."

"Your action interrupted reception of command message. Secure all writing, note frequency on radio before proceeding. Imperative. Repeat, secure writing, note—"

"I got you, Katz. Over." Manning hissed to Ohara. "Grab whatever that guy wrote down, and write down the exact wireless band."

Returning to the radio room, the Japanese Phoenix fighter saw a notepad of meticulously penciled Russian. A voice was speaking repeatedly from the radio monitor in Russian, then in Arabic. Ohara gathered all the papers and booklets in the room, then copied down the numbers on the receiver's digital display.

In the bridge room, Manning and McCarter examined the many controls and switches. They found the switch for the general alarm. Manning called out to Ohara.

"Keio! You set?"

The bundle of papers in his hand, Ohara nodded. He took a radio-pulse transmitter the size of a walkie-talkie from one of his belt pouches. He folded the notebook and papers and sealed them inside the waterproof pouch. Examining the pulse-transmitter for water or other damage, he switched on the power. He waited as the circuits went through an automatic diagnostic mode. The power light blinked green.

"I am ready."

Manning flipped up the red safety cap, hit the switch marked GENERAL ALARM.

Sirens wailed. Throughout the *Tarala*, Palestinians and Cubans and Europeans rolled from their bunks, grabbed their Kalashnikov rifles. Sentries ground out their cigarettes and rushed to join their comrades.

The terrorist "freedom fighters" had rehearsed the defense of the freighter many times. Trained for combat in the Soviet camps in South Yemen and Syria and Lebanon, trained for their attack on New York City during the months of their voyage from the Middle East, they knew they might face attack from the Coast Guard or the United States Navy.

But looking out at the wind-whipped Atlantic, they saw no ships in sight. They heard no helicopters. Officers grabbed intercom phones to call the *Tarala*'s bridge. They received no answer.

Men found two dead Palestinians, shot at point-blank range with large-caliber weapons. Gathering on the decks, the terrorists saw their officers running up the flights of steel stairs to the command deck.

Calling out in Arabic and Spanish and Russian, the officers beat on the steel doors of the bridge.

Inside, Manning looked to Ohara. "Now, Keio."

Ohara pushed the pulse transmitter's power button.

In one wave of shock, hundreds of thousands of steel fragments swept the decks and walkways.

The storm of steel from the carefully placed radio-triggered mini-claymores sprayed death in all directions.

Every terrorist on the *Tarala*'s superstructure died at the same instant, their torn bodies falling as one.

After the blast, the Phoenix men heard only the Atlantic wind, and the creaking of the old freighter as it swayed with the swells. Manning nodded to

Ohara, who keyed a distress signal on the ship's radio.

"Calling the Coast Guard. *Tarala* requests assistance...."

When the Coast Guard cutter *Cape Horn* finally approached, the captain hailed the crew of the old freighter with a bullhorn. No one answered. The boarding party found only the dead.

16

Florida Everglades

Saturday
2:00 a.m.
(0700 Greenwich mean time)

TURBOCHARGER WHINING, the El Dorado raced through the humid Florida night. Bolan drove, Flor beside him, Encizo in the back seat.

The shoot-out at the Club Cabana had changed their relationship. Despite the chance of combat, Bolan had not hesitated to bring Flor as backup. Encizo had invited her. More than a compatriot, Encizo and Bolan accepted the lovely though deadly young woman as a friend.

They followed Highway 41 west from Miami and through the savannas and cypress swamps north of Everglades National Park. Rafael Encizo told Flor a story.

"Under the dictator Batista, Cuba was a country of the very rich and the very poor. My family was among the very poor. I made money for my family by diving for coins in the harbor, like many boys my age. The tourists threw coins for the boys to catch. Even then I was as much fish as boy, and I made much money.

"But one time, one *hijo de perro*, *un perro rico* in his own yacht, held up a gold five-peso piece and tossed it into the water. But at the bottom, what I found on the sand was a brass washer. I came up and I heard him and his friends laughing.

"I knew what *el Europerro* had done—"

Flor laughed at the word. Encizo had deliberately mispronounced the Spanish word for European to say "European dog."

"—but he didn't just laugh. He shouted down that I was a bad diver, to dive until I found a coin. That was an insult, of course."

Behind Encizo's words, the night seethed with life. Insects chirped in the darkness.

"Understand. I spent much time in the water. I was still a boy, but my shoulders were wide. My mother worked so hard providing for us, so that our poverty would not stunt us. I was strong. When I fought, I fought with men and I won.

"The European had wounded my pride, yet I could do nothing. But later, his watchman, a Cuban, comes to me. He gives me a peso. He felt very badly about what the rich man had done. He told me he hated the rich man and that this would be the last night. The Cuban would sneak away to his village.

"I did not take his money, but I remembered what he said. That night, after the watchman went away, I slipped onto the yacht.

"I put the brass washer on the European's pillow, as he slept. When he woke up, he had his washer back, but no watchman.

"He thought I killed the watchman. He thought I

killed the watchman, then crept up to his own pillow as he slept. . . . He and his yacht were gone from the harbor in minutes.''

Laughing, the three friends sped through the night. Swarms of flying bugs splattered on the windshield.

After thirty minutes at ninety miles an hour, Bolan slowed as they approached the town of Paolito.

They cruised through streets vaulted by arching cypresses. Moths orbited streetlights and flickering neon. Passing a roadside bar with only one pickup truck in the gravel parking lot, Bolan flicked on the high beams and accelerated. He watched the odometer and slowed two miles later. Exactly as Mujica, the Cuban DGI captured in the nightclub attack, had told them during their interrogation of him, an unmarked and ungated road appeared on the left.

Bolan wheeled in a slow turn and killed the headlights. He let the Cadillac idle in neutral until his eyes adjusted to the starlit darkness, then he eased the car forward, the big convertible lurching and swaying in the rutted, muddy track. A few hundred yards from the highway, Bolan steered the car under the overhanging branches of a tree.

Taking a flashlight from the glove compartment, Flor got out. She slowly pushed the door to shut it without a slam. A quick sweep of the flashlight— Flor cupped her hand over the lens to allow only an indistinct glow of light—revealed a path for the convertible.

Crouching beneath low branches, mosquitoes swarming around them, they dressed for the infiltration. Bolan and Encizo pulled on night-black fatigues, and smeared blacking on their faces and hands. Flor put on a black Kevlar windbreaker over a black denim jump suit. She, too, smeared her face black, then knotted a black scarf over her forehead and hair. From the Cadillac's arsenal, she took an Uzi submachine gun and a hand-held infrared monocular.

The Stony Man warriors carried more sophisticated equipment. Over their shoulders they slung Heckler & Koch MP5A2 silenced submachine guns with mounted infrared scopes. Encizo carried a silenced Beretta 93-R with luminous sight. Bolan buckled on his .44 AutoMag and loaned a silenced Beretta to Flor. They both slipped secure-frequency hand-radios into their thigh pockets. A spare radio went to Flor.

"Frequency's scrambled," Bolan whispered to her. "Unless someone has one of the radios, anyone monitoring the band will only hear bursts of static."

But they took no assault weapons. The fragmentation and phosphorous grenades, the Armburst antipersonnel rockets, the M-16/M-203 autorifle/grenade launchers remained in the trunk.

Tonight's infiltration would be for information only. They needed to find the leaders of the group threatening the United States. For electronic eavesdropping, a pouch on Bolan's web belt contained four mini-transmitters and a multi-band monitor with a miniature cassette recorder.

Bolan signaled Encizo. Invisible in their nightblack clothing, their boots silent on the soft earth and mud, they moved forward.

As they had agreed hours before when they discussed the operation, the two men—more qualified than Flor with their years of infiltration training and jungle fighting—alternated on point. One man went ahead, while the other and Flor crouched in the shadows, listening for sentries or patrols, sweeping the darkness with their infrared optics. When the pointman advanced fifty yards, he stopped to cover their advance.

They moved fast, sometimes running, for the first mile.

An amber flash lit a wall of branches and marsh grass. Bolan and Flor saw Encizo run from the shadows to the complete darkness of the cypresses. They crabbed from the road and went low in the tangled grasses. Using only one eye, Bolan peered out.

Headlights appeared around a curve in the road. They heard gravel rattling against the sheet metal of fender wells.

Bouncing on its heavy-duty suspension, a pickup truck rattled past them. A buzz sounded in Bolan's earphone. Encizo reported.

"Stony One, I counted two men in the front. Heard tools in back. What did you see?"

"The same. Let's get going."

They trotted along the road until they saw the camp lights. Slipping into the high grasses, they circled to the west, crouch-walking, then finally crawling to a bulldozed perimeter. Tangled mounds of rotting grass, branches and roots concealed the three nightfighters. They sprawled a few steps from one another, scanning the abandoned installation.

Originally built in the last few days of World War II as a fourth-phase training base for B-24 bomber crews, the airfield and barracks were abandoned by the U.S. government until May 1959. President Eisenhower, irritated by Fidel Castro's Marxist posturing, accepted Vice-president Richard Nixon's suggestion to arm and train Cuban exiles for an overthrow of the revolutionary regime. A covert CIA operation repainted the barracks and cleared the overgrown runways and parade grounds.

After John F. Kennedy assured air cover for Brigade 2506's assault on the beaches, but abandoning the fighters, their landing craft and the supply ships to merciless strafing and bomb runs from the Cuban air force, the U.S. government closed the secret camp.

Years later, freed from Principe prison for a ransom of tractors and medicines, the survivors of Brigade 2506 returned to the camp—but without their CIA officers. The embittered Cuban exiles, hardened by betrayal and the horrors of Castro's People's Justice, accepted no leadership from Washington. They waged endless war-by-attrition against the Communists, fighting into the 1970s, the aging first generation initiating their sons in the techniques of guerilla combat as the war continued into the 1980s. Various groups used the camp and training fields, sometimes staging maneuvers one weekend, then evacuating the camp during the week—hauling out generators, radios, and weapons—when "old friends" from the CIA appeared.

The latest group of Cubans to use the camp appeared no different from the others, except that the membership included women. In the glare of light bulbs strung over a parade ground of rutted mud and gravel, they gathered around cars and trucks. Bolan saw men loading boxes—some the length of rifles— into pickup campers, others into the trunks of the passenger cars. Some of the Cubans wore fatigues, most wore street clothes. The women wore Levi's or casual fashions.

Across the camp, Bolan saw the lighted windows of an office. He watched forms cross the bright rectangle. Slipping a pair of Zeiss folding binoculars from a belt pouch, he focused the 9-power optics on the window.

A check-patterned *keffiyeh* passed through the light. Inside, a wide-faced Cuban sat on a desk. No, not a Cuban! An Oriental. Bolan keyed his hand-radio.

"Phoenix Two, can you see into the office?"

"*Sí*, I see. Is that an Arab?"

"Do you recognize the head cloth?" Bolan held his tiny binoculars steady on the window. The form wearing the *keffiyeh* paused in his view.

"I recognize the AK," Encizo told him.

"Do you see the other one?"

"No. A Cuban?"

"I see an Oriental. Looks Japanese. Maybe Chinese. Flor—"

"Here. Ready," she said.

"Phoenix Two, give her your H&K," said Bolan. "Flor, watch the camp, keep us informed as we go in. We'll place the microphones and take a look around. If there's shooting, snipe at those soldiers—''

"My friend," Encizo interrupted, "that little German gun did not kill when I fired from across the street tonight. At one hundred yards, even if she hits them, they might not fall down."

"Even at this distance, a steel-cored slug moving at—'' Bolan calculated the approximate loss in velocity "—750 or 800 feet per second will do it. She can keep their heads down if we get into trouble."

"And what if she gets into trouble? She'll be alone against—''

"That's their problem!" Flor answered.

Encizo and Bolan laughed quietly. Encizo crawled to Flor and passed his silenced, infrared-scoped weapon to the black-clad woman. He left her his bandoleer of 30-round H&K magazines and wished her luck.

"Buena suerte, guerrera." The word meant woman warrior.

"Y tu, hermano," Flor whispered in return.

Creeping silently through the tall grass and brush, Bolan and Encizo continued two hundred yards to the west. Buildings with long-collapsed roofs and leaning walls blocked the view of the Cubans on the parade ground. Bolan and Encizo lay shoulder-to-shoulder for minutes, watching the camp streets and shadows with the binoculars and infrared scope. They saw no sentries.

"Straight across," Bolan told his friend.

They crawled over the scraped marshland. A bulldozer had leveled all the trees and brush months before. Since then, the grass had grown more than two feet tall. At the edge of the camp, they came to a collapsed, weed-overgrown chain link fence. They slipped through the weeds and ran to the shadows of a dilapidated barracks.

For cooling and to discourage tropical insects, a two-foot airspace separated the barracks from the soil. Bolan crouched where steps met a doorway. Hidden from view on two sides, he leaned under the building. The damp, always-dark airspace smelled of rot. Despite sections of collapsed floorboards, he had a view of the opposite side of the building. Nothing moved.

Bolan pointed toward the office. Encizo nodded, then led the way. They stayed against the rotted barracks, stepping over fallen boards and piles of trash.

As they neared the center of the camp, Encizo froze. His hand stopped Bolan.

The sweet stink of mentholated tobacco smoke cut through the odors of mildewed wood and mud rot. They heard voices, a laugh. Boots crunched on sheets of wind-torn asphalt roofing.

Bolan and Encizo could not take cover in time. They squatted where they stood, going low to the ground, rolling onto their sides, letting their shoulders come to rest in the mud beneath them, as if their bodies had flowed onto the earth.

Two men in camou-patterned fatigues wandered around the corner. They stood in the open, talking in Spanish. One spoke quickly, the other deliberately, sometimes pausing to think of a word. One flicked his cigarette away.

Sparks showered Bolan and Encizo. The glowing cigarette butt bounced off the barracks wall above them. Bolan heard a gunman tap a cigarette pack. A butane flame spotlighted a Northern European face, a moon face with fat cheeks and thick lips. The face returned to darkness as the gunman sucked the cigarette.

Bolan smelled burning cotton-polyester. He saw the still-glowing butt on Encizo's back, between his shoulder blades. Moving his arm infinitely slowly, Bolan strained to reach the butt burning into Encizo's flesh, but could not reach it. As the two gunmen continued their loud conversation, Bolan leaned farther, finally flicked the butt into the mud.

They lay without moving for minutes. At last the sentries continued on their rounds. When the sounds of their pacing faded, Encizo rose to his feet, cursing under his breath.

"Hijos de la puta grande! They did it to me again! When I was in Principe, they put out a hundred cigarettes on me. Those two die, I swear to God. It is a promise to God!"

"Maybe tomorrow night. What did they say?"

"Their commander has received conflicting orders. There is much argument and confusion with their leaders."

"What were the orders?"

"They did not know. They hear only the argument. They talk also of the Revolution. Of the honor of fighting in this battle. Of world victory. You know the crap.''

"Let's hear the rest. . . . '' Bolan touched the pouch of micro-transmitters he carried and motioned for Encizo to move.

Peering down the street between the rows of barracks, they saw no one. Encizo stood tall, strode across the open area, then dropped into shadows. Bolan followed him, swaggering like the Cubans, but with his shoulders slumped to minimize his height.

Ahead, they saw lighted windows. Unshaded bulbs projected long rectangles over the mud and gravel of the camp's street. Voices went loud as someone raved in Spanish and others tried to shout him down. Staying in the shadows, Encizo strode forward, swinging his arms, trusting to darkness and daring. He also thumbed back the hammer of his silenced Beretta and held it against his leg. Bolan followed him.

A sentry stepped out of a dark doorway calling out, *"¿Roberto?"*

Encizo answered without breaking stride. *"No, Juan. Roberto está allá. . . . "* He swept his left arm toward the center of the camp.

The silhouette held up his hand. *"¿Tiene un fósforo?"*

Slapping at his pockets, Encizo stopped a step away from the sentry. *"No, pero. . . tengo una bala!"*

He jammed the silenced Beretta under the sentry's chin and pulled the trigger twice. The bullets smashed into the man's soft throat with sounds like two fist strikes. Encizo caught the dead man with his left arm as he pointed the Beretta into the doorway. But no second sentry stood there.

They dragged the corpse up the steps into the doorway and stripped him of his Kalashnikov. Encizo buckled on a canvas vest of long "banana" magazines for the AKM and slung the autorifle over his shoulder.

Footsteps passed the doorway. They saw two Cubans patrolling with AKMs in their hands. Encizo whispered to Bolan, "I place the bugs."

Nodding, Bolan unhooked the belt pouch. He took out the multi-band receiver and miniature tape recorder, and put the four coin-sized microtransmitters in Encizo's hand. Encizo glanced from the doorway, then slipped away without a sound.

Checking the receiver's volume control, Bolan flicked on the power and heard the faint scratching and clicking of the transmitters in one of Encizo's pockets. Crouched in the doorway of the rotting barracks, his H&K silenced submachine loaded and locked, Bolan waited.

Encizo forced himself to walk in a natural swagger. Despite his familiarity with the language and mannerisms of his enemies, despite his easy killing of the sentry, he knew the danger he faced. In the lighted parade ground beyond the rows of barracks, he saw men and women waiting. From time to time, he heard voices inside the barracks to either side. Footsteps creaked on the old floorboards.

He dropped to one knee for an instant, still a distance from the office building, and looked through the airspace beneath it. The camou-fatigued legs of sentries paced on the opposite side of the barracks. If they continued around the building, he would meet them face-to-face. In his silhouette and voice, he seemed like one of them, but if they checked him with a flashlight....

Moving quickly, he closed the distance to the lighted window of the office. Shouting continued within. He heard a fist pound a desk. Snapping looks in all directions, Encizo ducked into the airspace and crawled into the stinking darkness. Strips of light glowed here and there above him. Feet crossed the floor. The slashes of light disappeared as the boards bowed, flexed closed.

Snatches of multilingual conversation came to him. Then the argument continued in accented English. He heard several accents, could only recognize Spanish. What other languages did he hear? Arabic? Russian?

He searched the floorboards above him. Light came through a hole where a knot had fallen from a board long ago. Looking up, he saw the crumbling edge of the linoleum and a peeling ceiling. Stripping the plastic from the self-adhesive mini-transmitter, he jammed it into the knothole. A handful of mud sealed the hole.

Clicking his hand-radio, he alerted Bolan, then whispered, "First one in place."

Bolan switched on the receiver and recorder. He plugged his earphone into the receiver and listened to what was happening in the office.

"...I will repeat for the tenth time. The interception of the shipment from Syria has betrayed the duplicity of the fascists. Even as they attempt to negotiate, to bribe us with promises, they attack our allies. There is nothing to debate. We must stand fast in our resolve. They will not capitulate to history without the death-blows of our—"

"There is no question of resolve," another voice interrupted. "We will do as agreed, when we receive the order. Not until—"

"The order will come! But how will the front-line units receive it? We must issue instructions now, not later! Now! Tell them to strike on the day as planned. If we do not order the destruction of the city now, the fascists could jam all frequencies, cut all lines, spread confusion and lies to deceive our fighters."

"Tonight they travel. Then they prepare their weapons, and then they wait for the order. Perhaps the Americans will surrender. I will not go beyond my instructions—"

"These are new instructions!"

"You did not bring the code. I do not know if you are authorized to command me. . . ."

Bolan's hand-radio clicked again. Transferring the earphone, he heard the shouting continue through the hand-radio as Encizo whispered, "I put the second one on the window. Did you hear what they said?"

"Affirmative. We hit them."

"How? All we got is these little guns and knives."

"We go back for the heavy weapons."

"We can't. The Cubanos, the ones talking in Spanish, they say they are late, they talk of leaving immediately. They will escape."

"Forget the other microphones. Soft probe canceled."

"How can we attack?"

"There is no alternative."

In the minute that he waited for Encizo to return, Bolan calculated the numbers against them. He had counted twenty-plus terrorists at the cars and trucks. More soldiers waited in the barracks, or patrolled the camp. And he knew nothing about the airfield beyond the camp. Could there be more terrorists there?

Two men—and a woman—with only light weapons against a multinational terrorist force of unknown numbers. Bolan did not like it. He had more weapons in the Cadillac, but to return to the hidden car risked losing the chance to hit the terrorist teams before they disappeared into the crowded millions of a distant city.

How could they even up the odds?

Like a shadow with eyes, Encizo returned. His commander's whispered instructions did not surprise him.

"We'll capture what weapons we can," said Bolan, "and reduce the numbers with the silenced guns until it starts."

"Two of us, against all of them? In this junkyard? It will be a miracle if—"

"There is no alternative. We'll never find those terrorists once they're in Boston or Detroit or Washington. Monitor those goons. I'll buzz Flor and brief her."

Bolan passed the receiver and recorder to Encizo, then clicked his hand-radio.

"No change," she answered. "They stand at the cars. Waiting. They do nothing."

"Situation has changed. We've come too late for information. Hold your position. When the firefight starts, you're on your own. Hit everything that moves. We will not, repeat, will not go into your field of fire. Retreat to the car if we don't return."

"You're attacking them? But you left the rockets and grenades in the car!"

"We can't risk going back to the car," said Bolan's voice. "The terrorists are in motion. We stop them here or they're gone."

"Then I will stop them!" said Flor. "I will block the road while you come out."

"You alone? Not smart."

"Yes, it is stupid. One woman against many cars of Communists. Almost as stupid as two brave men against an army. But there is only one road out. I can block it. I can give you time."

"If they have a plane, the leaders will escape—"

"We have the car's transmitter," said Flor. "We can alert the Coast Guard, say they are dopers. You are wasting time. Hurry and we can make it. It is only two miles back to the car. We can run it in a few minutes."

Encizo grabbed his arm. "They are radioing their leader for confirmation of the new orders. The captain of these Cubans will not change his instructions unless he gets the orders from 'the Russian' himself. He said that, 'the Russian.' "

Pausing for an instant, Encizo listened, then relayed new information. "And they must translate it into code! Luck just came to us. We have time.''

Keying his hand-radio, Bolan informed Flor. ''We just got a reprieve. A few minutes. Move to the road and wait for our signal.''

''Thank God! Dead heroes do no one any good.''

They retraced their route quickly. When they came upon two sentries, Encizo ordered the sentries to put out their cigarettes, then he and Bolan continued on in the darkness without breaking stride. They jogged across the cleared ground, thrashed through the grass and brush beyond the perimeter. They did not need to signal Flor. She hissed them to a halt.

''Why not ring bells? I heard you a hundred yards away! Here, take all this—''

She passed them her Uzi and the silenced H&K, and pulled off her heavy Kevlar windbreaker. ''I will run to the car. I run miles every morning. If you guard the road, I can run without looking back—''

''Good idea,'' Bolan agreed.

She sprinted away without another word.

''Is there a word in Spanish for female macho?'' Bolan asked his Cuban compatriot.

''They are fighting!'' Encizo monitored the mini-mike receiver, a hand cupped over the earphone he wore. He strained to interpret the chaos of sounds and voices. Finally, he turned to Bolan.

''They killed the Cuban captain and his lieutenant,'' he said.

''What?''

''Knifed them, beat them. The Arab and the Oriental are laughing. I cannot understand what they say. I think they talk in Arabic. Someone else—''

Encizo listened again. "Now they're speaking Spanish. They say the captain they just killed had lost his nerve. That he could not follow his orders. It is one of the other Cubans they talk to. The Cuban asks if they must abandon the war against the Americans. No! The war will go on. Without mercy. Without quarter. The Oriental says he will talk to the freedom fighters. This Oriental is the worst yet—he says they will gas the cities. He goes to give them the orders to do so."

What was it he had read once, Bolan thought, what was the phrase? "The children of the Revolution devour one another." These revolutionaries, these "front-line fighters," murdered one another in their lust to murder Americans. They had abandoned the goal of their conspiracy—the bloodless evacuation of all American forces stationed in allied countries, leaving the few free nations of the world naked against Soviet power—in order to satiate their psychotic fantasies of mass murder.

When the President had summarized the evidence linking the conspiracy to the KGB, Bolan understood the motive: a quick Soviet victory over NATO and the other American alliances. The end of the cold war, the end of the propaganda war, the end of the wars of national liberation. Victory without casualties to the Red Army, victory without the destruction of Soviet military bases, victory without the threat of incineration of Russian cities.

But now? What had they overheard? Did the Soviets think they could murder entire American cities without risking the most horrible revenge in history? The knowledge of this madness stunned him.

"Amigo!" Encizo said. "Listen...."

A voice blared from a loudspeaker. The Spanish drifted through the torrid night. Feedback shrieked. The volume of the loudspeaker fell. Encizo translated.

"His Spanish is not good. He says...the facist Imperialists have betrayed the negotiations. They must wage war without quarter. The front-line fighters are to go to their secret places...no thought of mercy. Think of the martyred cities of my country, Hiroshima, Nagasaki. The martyr cities of Hanoi, Beirut. Total merciless war. Death to the monster."

Cheers rose.

"Yeah," Encizo agreed. "Death to the monster. But he's it."

"No," Bolan corrected. "He's a leader. We have to take him. Alive. He said 'the cities of my country'? He's Japanese."

Amber parking lights bobbed and wove toward them. They rushed to the Cadillac as Flor braked, simultaneously hitting the remote-control trunk switch. Bolan jerked heavy cases from the trunk's interior. Stripping off their bandoleers of 9mm magazines, they threw the ammunition and silenced Heckler & Koch submachine guns into the trunk.

Bolan and Encizo armed themselves for the assault. Black Kevlar battle armor, fitted with steel trauma plates, protected their torsos, groins and throats. One of the Stony Man teams had battle-proved the armor; in Egypt, only weeks before, Carl

Lyons took a point-blank AKM burst to the chest, but suffered not even a bruise.

They buckled on bandoleers of thirty-round 5.56mm magazines, loaded with alternating rounds of SS 109 steel-cored · NATO and hollowpoints. Pouches of 40mm steel-wire fragmentation and white phosphorous grenades hung on their web belts. Bolan tore open a case of the new Italian MU-50G controlled-effect grenades, and filled his thigh pockets and the pockets of his battle armor. He passed the case to Encizo and Flor.

Both men loaded their M-16/M-203 hybrid assault rifle/grenade launchers over their shoulders. Flor took all the bandoleers of ammunition for the DEA Uzis, then buckled a web belt with a Colt Government Model .45 and ten magazines around her waist, and jammed her Detonics in a back pocket of her jump suit.

"We ready?" Flor asked them, her voice quiet.

Shaking his head, Bolan pulled a last suitcase from the trunk. It contained six Armburst rockets. Remanufactured for antipersonnel effect, the armor-piercing warheads had been replaced by RDX—an explosive with a rate of expansion of twenty-five thousand feet per second—laminated with four layers of notched steel wire.

"Now we're ready. Flor, you drive. Phoenix Two, up front with the rockets. You pull the safeties, pass them back to me as we charge the camp. I want to hit them with all the rockets before we go through the gate. And we watch for the Japanese one. We want him alive. Questions? Flor?"

"I'm ready. Ready to go."

Hearing her voice quaver, Bolan took a moment to check her weapons and bandoleers, then slapped her on the back to move her toward the driver's seat. "Just drive. You're one cool soldier. When the firefight gets heavy, you'll do great. Like at the bar."

Flor laughed. She revved the engine as they jumped in. "I never shot anybody before tonight," she insisted. "I mean, face-to-face. That I know of."

Now Bolan and Encizo laughed. Encizo turned to her. "Had me fooled."

"Move it!" Bolan shouted over the roar of the engine and the clattering of gravel and stones against the undercarriage. "Just keep your head down, Flor—you'll learn fast. Remember, we need the Japanese one alive. Alive."

As the car raced from the trees, Bolan stood up in the back seat of the bouncing Cadillac and shouldered the first rocket. He leaned forward to steady the launch tube on the windshield, but he did not fire.

"Flor! Stop!"

She hit the brakes and skidded to a stop on the rutted gravel track. Ahead of them, one of the pickup trucks was leaving the parade ground. Terrorists sat in the other cars and trucks while Cubans in fatigues directed traffic, or loaded the last truck with boxes. They paused in their work to look at the Cadillac.

The launcher popped. Dead on target, the first low-velocity rocket punched through the windshield of the moving pickup truck. The blast shredded the sheet metal of the body and camper shell. Glass and bits of razor-sharp steel flew into the night in a glittering cloud of fragments.

Encizo passed back a ready launcher, then tore open the seals on the next as Bolan sighted on the Cubans who had AKMs, and fired. Ten thousand steel blades scythed the soldiers, killing them before their blast-thrown bodies fell, killing the terrorists in the nearest cars and trucks.

The third rocket hit a truck on the other side of the parade ground as the driver threw open the door and dived out. He never touched the ground, the Armburst hitting the truck's rear fender only an arm's length away. The blast and thousands of steel razors reduced the driver's body to a splash of tissue and scattered bone fragments.

"Hard right!" Bolan commanded. Flor cranked the steering wheel and fishtailed across the bulldozed perimeter. Waiting until he had a different angle of fire, Bolan sent the fourth rocket into the bumper-to-bumper cars and trucks.

The white flash of death caught a dozen terrorists as they scrambled from the vehicles. It slammed them aside. A woman lifting a Kalashnikov died on her feet, a hundred steel needles ripping through her.

A sheet of fire roared up across the parade ground as spilled gasoline ignited. Flaming figures ran blindly into the night. Trapped terrorists beat at windows, clawed at doors. Screams rose and faded as throats gulped fire, then were sealed closed with clots of seared lung tissue. A paralyzed Cuban dragged himself by his hands from a flaming hulk even as the gasoline incinerated his dead legs.

They who would have committed mass murder died in a mass pyre.

"Wait on the last rocket!" Bolan shouted to Encizo. Holding an Armburst ready, Bolan searched for a target. He saw a lone Cuban soldier with an AKM, but did not fire.

He shouted to Flor, "Hard left! Into the camp!"

Encizo's M-16/M-203 popped. A 40mm grenade arced into the flame-lit camp and hit the ground a few steps from the running Cuban. White phosphorous peppered him, though it did not knock him down. But an instant later, he dropped his rifle to claw at the metallic fire burning through his flesh. Screaming, he thrashed and fell. The phosphorous would continue through to the bone or internal organs, and would burn until exhausted.

Cranking a hard right, Flor stood on the accelerator and the Cadillac's rear tires spun on the wet marsh grass, throwing mud. She steered for a gap in the tangle of brush and old fence. Too late, she saw a mound of dirt and debris that had been piled by a bulldozer. Hitting it straight on, the Cadillac left the ground.

Bolan looped his left arm around the passenger seat's headrest. For a long instant, the Cadillac hurtled through the air, then slammed down, the frame scraping the gravel.

Flor did not take her foot off the accelerator. Fighting a drift to the left, she steered between two barracks, the left rear fender and bumper hitting the corner of one building, smashing the termite-eaten four-by-fours that supported it.

Decades-old dirt and rotten slats crashed down. Bolan saw a group of Cubans silhouetted by flaming gasoline as they ran between the barracks. One-handed, he pointed the fifth Armburst and fired. The Cadillac skidded past the scene before Bolan saw the rocket hit. Flor fishtailed through a right turn.

"Next rocket!" Bolan shouted to Encizo.

A Cuban in fatigues ran from the shadows, his AKM flashing. Slugs hammered the Cadillac. Flor swerved to hit the gunman. He jumped to one side.

Bolan swung the empty Armburst launcher like a baseball bat, shattering the plastic tube against the Cuban's face. Drawing his .44 AutoMag, Bolan put a 240-grain jacketed hollowpoint slug into the stunned gunman. Slamming into the man's ribs at 1,400 feet per second, the expanding hollowpoint liberated a thousand foot-pounds of shockforce, which exploded from an exit wound four inches across. Bolan turned away from his somersaulting kill and searched the darkness for other targets.

Flor braked and turned, skidding to avoid hitting the burning hulks on the parade ground head-on. She hurtled the Cadillac through walls of flame and the stench of burning flesh.

Completing a circle around a row of barracks, Flor accelerated. Bolan glanced ahead and saw a tangle of corpses, the Cubans he had killed with the fifth Armburst. Flor held the wheel steady as the heavy Cadillac lurched over the corpses. Something clanged on the hood.

"Grenade!" Encizo shouted.

They all ducked down. The grenade bounced over

the Cadillac. Her head below the dashboard, Flor heard the explosion. She straightened up, saw only a crystal network of shattered windshield. She drove blind, then heard a smash.

A bloody face flopped against the shattered glass. Hands clawing at the windshield, the Cuban screamed. Encizo fired a point-blank burst from his hybrid assault rifle. He next used the butt to smash out glass until he had cleared a hole for Flor to see through.

She peered through the hole, had to swerve to avoid the corner of a barracks, skidded sideways, overcorrected, smashed through a wall. As the Cadillac rocked on its springs, boards and plaster and filth falling on them, Flor shifted into reverse. The Cadillac did not move. Eyes wild, Flor jammed the transmission into drive, snapped the car forward, shifted to reverse again. Frantic, she stood on the accelerator, the turbocharger whining, the tires spinning. Burning rubber smoke choked them. But the Cadillac did not move from the cave of broken walls and flooring.

Encizo grabbed her arm, shook her. "Joyride's over! Out!"

AKM slugs punched through the wood walls around them and hammered the trunk of the Cadillac. Bolan slung the last Armburst over his shoulder and gripped the M-16/M-203. He kicked open the door and saw the camp street outside. Slugs ripped through the doorway. Encizo shoved aside the boards that covered him in the back of the Cadillac and stepped out over the hood.

"Where's Flor?"

A burst of Uzi fire came from behind the Cadillac. A Cuban staggered back. Flór emerged from the confrontation, pushing aside a ceiling panel. She walked across the El Dorado's hood to join them. They saw the muzzle-flashes of three AKMs facing them.

"Out the back." Bolan rushed to a door, kicked it open, and sprayed a burst of 5.56mm slugs into the night. Encizo leaned past him and fired a 40mm grenade.

In the gray, flickering light of flaming white phosphorous, they ran toward the offices, two rows of barracks away. The fire from the parade grounds had spread. Flames and black smoke rose into the night.

They came to a camp street lit by orange glow. Bolan crouched in a shadow and motioned for Flor to take cover as Encizo checked a doorway. Then Bolan sprinted forward. He went flat in the airspace beneath the barracks. He motioned the others forward.

A form moved against the wall of flames. Bolan sighted on its legs, sprayed a burst. An AKM flew from the gunner's hands. Waiting until Encizo gained cover, Bolan ran for the wounded Cuban. A pretty young woman writhed on the gravel, her shattered legs twisted under her.

The Cubana saw Bolan approaching, screamed, not with fear but with hatred and fanatical rage, and pulled a revolver from her belt. Bolan fired a three-round burst into the snarling face, then took cover beside a flight of steps.

Boots stomped across the floorboards. Glass shattered above him as hands jammed a Kalashnikov through a window. Another pair of boots ran across the gravel behind Bolan. Spinning, his autorifle on line, Bolan held his fire as Encizo tossed an Italian controlled-effect grenade through the window.

For a second, the boots inside the barracks scrambled, the rifle clattering to the floorboards. The sharp crack of the RDX stopped all movement inside.

An engine roared, gears clashed. Careering through the flames and corpses, a pickup truck raced at them. Simultaneously, Bolan and Encizo snapped their assault rifles to their shoulders, but flinched as they looked directly into the flashing muzzle of an AKM, and at the demon grin of a Japanese face behind the Kalashnikov.

Slugs ripped over them. Bolan felt a shock to his shoulder, rolled aside, lifted his M-16/M-203 to spray high-velocity 5.56mm slugs at the taillights of the swerving truck. Twenty yards down the camp street, an Uzi fired wild, Flor holding down the trigger until the magazine went empty.

"That was him!" Bolan shouted. "The Japanese leader!"

Encizo snapped a 40mm grenade at the pickup truck as it skidded around a corner. He fired the last burst of his M-16's magazine as the barracks corner exploded. But the barracks's wood caught the steel wire shrapnel of the fragmentation round, and the 5.56mm steel-cored, hollowpointed slugs scored only the tailgate and bumper.

Breaking cover, Bolan sprinted after the pickup, the weight of his battle armor and weapons slowing him. A last AKM sent a slug past his ear. Bolan did not break stride as a cross fire from Flor and Encizo eliminated the terrorist gunner behind him.

At the corner of the barracks, Bolan raised his rifle as he saw the taillights disappear around another corner.

"Flor!" he shouted back. "Grab an AK. Watch the road out. Encizo, I think he's going to the airfield."

Already in motion, the Cuban exile ran through the street of death, spraying quick bursts of high-velocity 5.56mm hollowpoints into his dead and dying enemies.

A crawling terrorist pointed a pistol. Encizo fired the last round of his rifle's magazine and saw flesh spray from the wounded Cuban terrorist's shoulder. Changing mags, Encizo kicked an automatic from the terrorist's grip. The young man raised a bloody hand for mercy. Encizo put the M-16's muzzle to the Cuban's forehead.

"Leave him alive!" Bolan shouted, "We need prisoners."

Encizo fired a single shot through the terrorist's unwounded arm. He kicked him over on his back. He grabbed the three-time wounded boy's collar, tore his shirt back and down over his shattered arms, and left him screaming in the mud.

Running after Bolan, Encizo saw the black form of the Stony Man commander running toward the airfield, and he followed him.

Straining against the weight of his armor and weapons, Bolan kept his stride. At the barracks where the truck had turned, he stopped short and ran up a parallel street. He slowed to a silent walk as he came to the end of the barracks. Behind him, at the far side of the camp, flames leaped high into the sky, but all firing had ended.

Bolan crept around the corner, staying in the shadows. He snapped a glance into the next street. No truck. He had thought they might have waited in ambush for him. But they had gone. Encizo's footsteps approached. Bolan signaled him. Together, they ran toward the airstrip.

Rotorthrob beat the night's silence. Bolan stopped to scan the night. His mind raging, he saw the silhouette of a helicopter rise against the stars.

Sighting his grenade launcher, Encizo fired, but missed as the form banked. Light flashed on the underside of the helicopter as the grenade exploded in the air. Encizo fired aimed bursts.

Bolan tore the last Armburst launcher from his shoulder, aimed ahead of the silhouette and fired. But the rocket arced over the helicopter as the pilot dropped down to treetop height. A half mile away, the blast tore cypress branches.

The rotorthrob faded into the distance.

17

Virginia

Saturday
3:30 a.m.
(0830 Greenwich mean time)

WHEELING A CART OF MAPS and satellite photos from a Stony Man Center storage room, April heard Mack Bolan's voice. She whirled her head around, her eyes searching for her man. But the words—stripped of warmth and personality by electronic encoding—came from Kurtzman's radio monitor. She ran the length of the corridor to the com-room.

"Is Mack all right?"

Kurtzman nodded, scribbled on a pad. He read back a description. "...Japanese, looked older than thirty, between five eleven and six feet tall.... Wide-shouldered, moon face.... What else?"

"We heard him speak Spanish to the Cubans," said Bolan's voice. "Encizo said it was basic Spanish punctuated with revolutionary clichés. We think we heard him speaking Arabic with one of them who looked like a Palestinian...."

"What about mannerisms? His clothes? Did he have an unusual weapon?"

"Negative. Standard AK. Wore a light-blue summer suit, sportshirt."

"That's a good detail right there. Maybe he's traveling in the United States under a legitimate cover."

"Follow it up. We passed two prisoners on to the Agency. We're hoping to get a name out of them. But they're both low-ranking terrorists. One of them isn't expected to live."

Kurtzman looked at his notes. "Anything else on the Palestinian? Anything that might link him to a group or country? If we can spot an association—"

"Nothing that we saw or heard. The Feds said they'll sift through what's left of the camp at dawn. Langley get anything out of that Mujica?"

"Not yet. He's a tough nut, they said. They're putting him through drug interrogation, but we won't have any details on that until midday. They said it could be weeks before he broke down and—"

"We don't have weeks. The crazies in this conspiracy are out of control. What's the word from Phoenix and Able?"

"Good news. Phoenix is batting one thousand. Three prisoners plus taped communications and captured documents. One prisoner started talking before they could get him on the shuttle jet to Langley. He said they had just received instructions to move into the East River and wait for the right wind conditions—"

"—to spray New York. . . ." Bolan completed the statement.

"Not the ones on the ship. They were to pick up a

squad trained to use the chemicals. The squad would work the machines.''

"Bear, Phoenix monitored all their communications, right?''

"For the past twenty-four hours—''

"Get a dupe of that tape, have Ohara listen to it. I want to know if any of the messages—''

"Right, if any of the radio messages came from a Japanese. Will do.''

"Apparently the Japanese one is launching the attack,'' Bolan continued. "The Cuban leader wouldn't issue the order to his soldiers until he got confirmation from 'the Russian.' That's when the Japanese and the Palestinian killed him. I want to know if the order to the freighter came from the Russian or the Japanese. What about Able?''

"They're down. Grimaldi's waiting for their signal in Honduras. He's got a plane ready.''

April could not wait any longer. She took the microphone from Kurtzman. "Mack, are you okay?''

"Tired, that's all. How're things at the Center?''

"Busy. But we'll be ready tomorrow to brief the other law-enforcement agencies.''

"Don't bother to analyze or summarize the information. This is happening too fast. Just have the information ready.''

Another radio buzzed. Kurtzman flipped a switch. An electronically neutralized voice spoke. "Air Force Liaison calling.''

"Stony Man Center. Proceed.''

"We have a report from the Texas coast. We are

tracking a low-flying aircraft. We believe the flight originated from the northern shore of Cuba...."

"April, start the tape recorder!" Kurtzman grabbed the microphone from her. "Sorry to interrupt, Mack. They think there's a low flyer from Cuba heading for Texas."

"Brief me when you have the details. Over." And the frequency to Miami went silent.

"... the aircraft has not responded to requests for identification."

"You have planes in the air?"

"Affirmative. The aircraft has employed electronic countermeasures but we continue tracking—"

"Do you have *armed interceptors* in the air?" Kurtzman stressed.

"We have alerted our interceptors, but—"

"But nothing! Stop that plane!" Kurtzman clicked off the microphone. He turned to April. "Buzz Phoenix Force. Tell them to stand by."

"For Texas?" she asked.

Kurtzman nodded..

18

Nicaragua

Saturday
5:00 a.m.
(1100 Greenwich mean time)

THE RED LIGHT OF DAWN colored the far mountains, the peaks eight miles to the west catching the first rays of daylight, the mountainsides and valleys still in darkness. Electric light spilled from the windows of the camp buildings. White fluorescent smears illuminated the fences.

Carl Lyons watched the line of daylight descend the mountain. He looked back at the ridge crest and saw a blue sky above the shadowed pines and oaks. Dew beaded the ferns and wild grasses around him.

He lay in a shallow trench behind his M-249. The Parkerized gray weapon stood on its bipod, its black titanium suppressor aimed down at the camp. During the night, Lyons had filled several plastic bags with soil. Bags braced the bipod to steady the weapon. Other bags stacked around the trench gave Lyons more protection.

Looking down at the terrorist camp, he considered the simplicity of the attack strategy. Genius. *Bolan's plan, but our execution,* Lyons thought. *We all made our contributions. Grimaldi, the nightblack jet; Konzaki, the customized M-249; Gadgets the radio-triggered Vipers; and I'll pull the trigger.*

The girl padded silently through the trees. Red-eyed and squinting with fatigue, she crouched at the side of Lyons's ditch.

"You ready, mister?"

Lyons keyed his hand-radio. "Wizard. Politician. You guys awake?"

"The Wiz here. Thanks for the wake-up call."

Blancanales's deep voice came on. "We'll hear a bugle before they assemble. But you're the one who gives the word."

"When I've got my targets, I'll give you a buzz. Over." Lyons turned to the teenager. "We're ready."

"And David? How is David? We *novios.*"

"Engaged?" He handed her the radio. "Buzz them. Press here, talk."

After a delay, Blancanales gave his hand-radio to David. The teenagers chatted in rapid Spanish. Maria concluded the conversation with a smack of her lips into the mouthpiece. She saw Lyons laughing again, and she glared at him.

"You ready now, *señorita?*"

"Yes, I ready all the time. I wait for—"

The loudspeakers of the camp blared reveille. The morning light touched the parade grounds. Uniformed terrorists formed ranks in front of a reviewing stage.

"Waiting's over," Lyons told her. "Watch my back."

He put his right eye to the scope.

PETER KRANTZ STOOD IN FRONT of his full-length mirror, turning from side to side to admire his commandant's uniform. As the last notes of the recorded bugle died away, Krantz's aide-lover, Miguel, brushed the last tiny flecks of lint from the tailored uniform. Krantz peered outside. In the gray morning light, his soldiers assembled in ranks on the parade ground.

Today, another platoon of front-line fighters left for the United States. Yesterday, Krantz had embraced each member of the group that would take terror to Los Angeles, California. They would be there soon, perhaps tonight.

Posing in front of the mirror, he closed his eyes, saw the horror of their operation there: the mass death, the announcement, the panic sweeping the United States.

That one strike against the Empire of the United States would crown his career. But there would be more. *Today, a platoon left for New York. Tomorrow, Detroit. The next day, Chicago.*

He felt dizzy with excitement. His fighters would make the cities of the United States mausoleums to the Decline of Empire, peopled with millions of corpses frozen where the gas killed them. These achievements would make Krantz one of the new masters of the world.

The son of a prosperous German couple—his

father a technician and designer with a manufacturer
of luxury German autos, his mother a professor of
English in a university—he had learned the philo-
sophy of terror from his National Socialist parents.
His father and mother and their neo-Nazi friends lec-
tured the boy endlessly on the duty of the next
generation to destroy America.

As a teenager, he joined the embryonic terrorist
movement in Berlin. The gangs bombed nightclubs
serving American soldiers. Once, in a daring attack
that filled his comrades with admiration for Krantz,
he kidnapped a young American soldier too drunk to
defend himself, then tortured the soldier to death.
That act admitted him to the ranks of the Terrorist
International.

In the ten years since then, he rose from recruit to
leader. He received basic training from the PLO in
Lebanon and Syria. He went on to advanced training
by Soviet and Cuban instructors in South Yemen.
After proving himself on missions of atrocity in
Israel, England and Ireland, he gained the attention
of Fedorenko.

Under the leadership of the troika, Krantz hoped
to fulfill the dreams of his Nazi parents.

The voices of the instructors outside halted his
daydreaming. He gave his lover a kiss, but pushed
away the teenager's groping hand.

Striding from his office door, Krantz heard the instructors call the ranks to attention. Krantz thought
of his idols, the martyred leaders and commanders
who he worshiped and served. He adored them as if
they still lived. He felt sometimes as if he knew them,

he had heard so many stories and records, seen so many films. He modeled his life after them. To please the spirits of Hitler, Hess, Goebbels, Goering, he would murder millions of Americans.

A hundred twenty-three faces turned to him. Young men and women of many nations, of all races, born to injustice and suffering, hardened by years of training: fanatics. Foremost stood the ten members of the New York attack force.

Krantz ascended the three steps of the parade stand. At the back of the concrete platform, the two senior instructors, a Pole and a Cuban, stood at attention. The political officer, a Palestinian, adjusted the microphone and then went to the back of the platform, where he snapped to attention.

Krantz went to the lectern.

"Comrades! Front-line fighters in the war against the American Imperialists! Today—"

Blood exploded from his mouth and eyes. His forehead burst open as slugs slammed into the back of his head. Even as the impacts threw him face forward, more slugs punched him. His arm flailed wildly, his chest and gut spewed gore. A second burst cut down the officers behind him.

For a long moment, the lines of terrorists stared. In the milliseconds before they reacted, they watched their leaders twitch like spastic marionettes, first in the air, then on the slab of the stand, as high-velocity slugs shrieking from the rising sun raked the dead men, their arms, legs and torsos jerking in a supine death-dance.

Even as the ranks of terrorists threw themselves

into motion—some diving, others crouching, many running—the slugs found the first row. The front-line fighters died.

CORDITE STINK SEARED LYONS'S THROAT. Raking across the parade grounds four times, he fired the first hundred rounds. He stopped, touched the receiver. The hot metal seared his fingertips, then his thumb as he clicked the fire-selector up to semi-auto. He could not risk burning out the weapon.

The M-249's recoil and vibration had numbed his face and arms. Despite the suppressor and the earplugs he wore, his head rang. He took a few deep breaths as he watched the panic far below him.

He felt more than saw someone move behind him. Thumbing back his Python's hammer, he spun, only to see the girl crouching behind him. She had left her position to watch the slaughter.

"Go! Watch for *comunistas*!" he shouted at her. He pointed to the plugs in his ears. "I can hear nothing. Stand guard."

Lyons put his eye to the scope and scanned the parade grounds. Inside barracks, flashes blew out windows. A half second later, he heard the pops of 40mm grenades. Blancanales and Gadgets were hitting the camp with their M-16/M-203 grenade launchers, firing and reloading and firing, sending fragmentation and white phosphorous into barracks and offices.

Through the Leatherwood's optics, he saw the terrorists finally raise their Kalashnikovs. They fired wild at the mountainside where Lyons hid. He sight-ed the cooled M-249.

He fine-tuned the trajectory cam ring, adjusting the framing bars for the slight difference in range from the parade grounds to the barracks. He sighted on the chest of an OD green-uniformed terrorist and squeezed off a round. The terrorist staggered back. Lyons fired again and again, killing a terrorist with each shot. He tried a head shot, missed.

He took his eye from the scope and looked down at the camp. He watched the black smoke pouring from a barracks. The smoke drifted to the southwest. He glanced downslope to the treetops and saw the branches sway with a gentle breeze. Putting his eye back to the ocular, he corrected slightly upwind and sent a slug into the face of a terrorist. He tried another head shot, missed.

Don't be a show-off, Lyons told himself.

With rapid fire he punched 5.56mm holes in ter-rorists' chests and backs. He saw the white flash of a phosphorous grenade scatter several soldiers from cover. Lyons shot three. He saw two others jerking and thrashing as metallic phosphorous burned into their chests and skulls, but he did not waste car-tridges on them.

On the far side of the camp, a pilot ran for a helicopter. A group of soldiers dashed from cover to cover, Kalashnikovs in their hands. They gathered their comrades, some with rifles and RPG-7 launch-ers, others with no weapons. Through the scope, Lyons saw a black man with an AK shove a pan-icked, bleeding soldier away from the helipad. Lyons killed the black, then two other soldiers in the side door of a French Alouette III helicopter.

But the copters' prefab steel hangar screened the other Alouette from his fire. He dug the protective plug out of his ear, then keyed his hand-radio. "Wizard! Wizard!"

In the seconds that he repeated his call again and again, he heard AK slugs ripping through the trees. He ignored them. None came close.

A blast threw flame and debris. An RPG rocket left a flaming hole three feet wide and twenty feet long in the mountainside's brush and small trees. Six inches of wood from a large pine had been splintered away. He could not ignore that. Anywhere an RPG hit was too close.

"Wizard! Fire those Vipers. Hit that scum! They're getting organized."

Another RPG screamed into the mountainside a hundred feet wide of him. He shouted into the hand-radio again. "Wizard. Hit them."

"Just a second," Gadgets answered calmly. "They're loading up the helicopter. I'm waiting for a full bus. All right!"

Simultaneous blasts wiped away the French helicopters, the hangar and the fuel depot. Aviation fuel and munitions exploded in a vast churning ball of flame.

"Hey, man!" Gadgets raved. "Think that shook them? Here come four more...."

A wave of flame and debris flashed across the camp. Striking waist-high, the four carefully targeted rockets hit two barracks, an office and the blazing ruins of the hangar. The blasts scattered sheet steel shrapnel.

Blancanales's voice came on. "The kid and I are pulling out. Don't let anyone follow us."

Lyons watched the black smoke billowing from the fires. The southwesterly breeze had faded. Then he returned his eye to the optics. He braced the weapon with his left hand around the stock's titanium tubing, exhaled as he held the forehead of a terrorist in the cross hairs. The terrorist officer scanned the mountainsides with binoculars. Lyons squeezed off the shot.

Shattered lens glass sparkled in the air. The dead man fell back.

Firing the last three cartridges of the first belt, Lyons tore open another plastic magazine. He pulled out his ear protection and listened for the girl. He did not hear her.

Lyons plugged his ear again and threaded in the next cartridge belt. He searched the wrecked and burning camp for targets. He killed crawling wounded, shot exposed legs and shoulders, played peekaboo with an RPG gunner. He missed twice, then the gunner fired a rocket and missed Lyons.

The gunner lunged out once again, his launcher on his shoulder, but ducked back as Lyons fired a single shot. The bullet missed, the gunner lunged out to fire, and Lyons triggered a five-round burst. The gunner flew back, dead, the rocket flying wild, self-destructing at 3,000 feet above the earth.

Rifle slugs continued ripping through the trees. Lyons sought out the AKs. The scope's aspect slid over the faces of the terrorist army—Europeans, blacks who would certainly be Africans, black and white Americans, Hispanics, Asians. Most of them sprawled in the dust and gravel of the camp, dead or dying. Others searched for Lyons over the sights of Kalashnikov rifles. Lyons found them first.

He put the cross hairs on a face displaying tribal scars. He saw a pretty European woman with her hair in stylish pincurls. He also saw a Hispanic wearing a Castro-style beard. Then a girl with American Indian features. None would return home.

A blur of motion made Lyons look up from the scope. He saw a truck careering through the camp's streets. A man with Slavic features jumped from the cab's passenger side to roll aside the chain link gate. Lyons put a burst through his chest and head. He shifted his aim to the truck and punched holes through its windshield, engine and radiator. He sighted on the fuel tanks on the side. His bullets tore open the metal. Pools of diesel fuel spread around the truck.

A line of orange tracers jackhammered the mountainside. Lyons heard the fire of a 12.7mm heavy machine gun. Branches and leaves fell around him as if an invisible chainsaw slashed the trees.

Scanning the compound and guard towers, he found the weapon's muzzle-flash. Before he could pull the trigger on the target, a 40mm frag arced into the side of the guard position. A blinded terrorist thrashed in the open guard-tower window. He fell over into the crossbars of the tower and hung there. The other guard sprayed more slugs at Lyons.

"Ironman!" Blancanales called through the radio. "You up there? You all right?"

Putting a burst through the sentry in the tower, Lyons keyed his radio. "What do you need?"

"I thought you'd been hit."

"No."

Another RPG blasted the mountainside. Lyons squinted against the dust. He threw open the weapon's feed cover. He wiped the action. The hot metal scorched the cloth. When he squirted oil into the receiver, it smoked.

He watched the camp. No terrorists left cover. No other trucks tried to race the gate. Slugs continued snapping through the trees, but few now. No more rocket fire came.

An M-1 popped behind him. Grabbing his silenced Colt, Lyons peered into the brush and listened. The M-1 popped again. Autofire replied. Crawling from his sandbagged trench, Lyons wormed silently through the mountainside's growth.

He saw green-uniformed soldiers thrashing through the brush. One dragged a wounded comrade to the safety of rocks. A .30-caliber slug slapped into the man's back as he crouched. The two other terrorists, a sunburned Northern European with crew-cut white-blond hair and a thick-necked Hispanic woman, shouted to each other in Russian. The blond man fired a long burst from his Uzi as the woman pitched a grenade.

Lyons killed them both with .45 hollowpoints to their heads. The grenade sent slivers of steel zipping through the trees.

"Maria!"

"*Aquí....*"

Crawling again, Lyons went to the wounded terrorists and finished them. He crouch-walked through the tangled brush, pausing behind pines, watching for a movement. Finally he found Maria.

Sitting against a tree, she held her intestines with her left hand, pointed her carbine with her right. A second wound through her leg poured blood into the soil.

He forced his face to show nothing. Easing the girl back to reduce shock, Lyons talked quietly and slowly, saying nothing, talking only to calm.

Maria did not respond to his English. She stared into the forest around them, her eyes darting from place to place. Her breathing remained strong.

Taking her hand away, Lyons examined her gut wound. A fragment had slashed her side, laying open a flap of flesh and exposing her abdominal membranes. Though he saw intestines under the membrane, the gash did not continue into her abdominal organs.

He covered the wound with a field dressing and put her hand over the bandage to hold it in place. He examined her leg wound. A 9mm slug had passed through her left calf. When he felt the bones, she screamed, thrashed. His fingers found the mismatched ends of a bone.

"Come on, Maria." Lyons lifted her in his arms. "You're going to be all right, but you can't stay here."

She did not drop her carbine. Lyons shouldered

her through the brush, running and lurching across the mountainside. Crying out, Maria opened her eyes wide, stared, as if watching for other attackers. Lyons avoided a ten-yard-wide slab of bare, open rock. Keeping to the shadowy pines, he thrashed through the last few branches and put her down beside his emplacement.

"Pol, Wizard," he called into his hand-radio. "Maria's hurt. Doctor time, right now. Move it."

Looking downhill, he saw terrorists sprinting across the camp to drag comrades to safety, to grab weapons. Others sprinted for the gate. Lyons touched the M-249. The barrel and receiver had cooled.

"We're two hundred yards below you," Blancanales said. "We heard a firefight up there."

"Yeah. They're dead, she's hit. Nine millimeter, lower leg. Simple fracture of a bone. Gut wound, left side. She'll live but she needs a hospital."

"We'll take her out with us. How about you? What's the problem? I see them moving."

Lyons jammed his weapon closed, gave Blancanales a quick jive line. "Hey, *compañera* . . . like, you know, it's cool now."

He saw the girl push herself upright against one of his improvised sandbags. Her face white with shock, she braced her M-1 over her good leg and sat there watching the approach behind them. Lyons reached over to her to grip her hand. He felt her fragile, long-fingered hand shaking.

"You're hard-core, Maria. Don't worry. We'll get you out. I promise."

When he took his hand away, he saw her blood on his palm. He did not stop to wipe it away. Snapping back the action to feed a round, Lyons put his eye to the scope of his automatic weapon. What he saw, he killed.

19

Texas

Saturday
6:00 a.m.
(1300 Greenwich mean time)

IN A CAVERNOUS HANGAR at Houston International
Airport, the men of Phoenix Force waited. Outside,
jetliners roared away as commercial flights carried
early-rising Texans to the cities of the United States
and Central America. But the Phoenix Force crew
went nowhere. They waited.

Manning and McCarter paced, McCarter kicking a
cola can across the hangar's oil-stained concrete.
Ohara sat on a folding chair, his back straight, his
hands folded in his lap, his face serene. He seemed to
sleep.

On the far side, Yakov rushed into an office.
"This is inexcusable! Where are the helicopters?
Where is the officer responsible for this...."

Yakov's voice faded as the office door swung shut.
David McCarter laughed.

"Those bastards will moan this day. Feel like giving them a what-for myself."

"Let the colonel handle it," Gary Manning told
him. "Bet those choppers are shuttling some

bloody general and his staff to his golf game."

"You're on!" McCarter told him.

"What?"

"How much?"

"No, you don't! No more bets with me. Never again."

"In for a hundred bucks."

"Not against me—"

"I say the general's still out whoring. Instead of watching for those low-flying Cuban buggers, he's out buggering—"

"I said no!"

Ohara opened his eyes, blinked as the English rowdy shouted into Manning's face, "Then you're in default. Pay up!"

"I didn't bet—"

"You said you bet."

"A figure of speech—"

"Figure of speech, bull. You're trying to worm out of it now. What you were doing was trying to cheat Keio. Figured you suck him into it, then take his pay."

"Forgive me," Ohara apologized. "But what do you speak of? I don't understand to what you refer."

"That Englishman's got salt water on the brain," Manning answered.

"Listen to that," groaned McCarter. "You're the wily one. Look, just pay up. You can afford to be honorable with your debts, I made you enough money the other weekend—"

"What money?"

"Don't you 'what money' me. From the race."

McCarter gave Manning a brotherly slap on the shoulder that would have knocked down most men. "The race! In Kent!"

Manning grinned. "Somehow managed to keep it, too."

"A competition?" Ohara asked.

"If you could call it that," Manning answered. "It was his idea. I'm in Kent, England, trying to get a proper rest and he tells me about the local marathon. With the low quality of the Kent runners, McCarter thinks I can win it. He didn't realize there were others who could play that game too."

McCarter broke in. "Manning could've beaten the local boy without working up a sweat. But the pub owner had this 'nephew,' he said—"

"Some 'nephew'. Six-foot-six with legs by Ferrari."

"Those legs helped the odds. I got ten to one on our Canuck of the North—"

"Get rich fast. Invest in Canada. I put three hundred pounds on myself."

"Then Manning asked me where to ambush a runner," McCarter said. "Truly turned my head, the thought of a proper Canadian bloke resorting to head bashing."

"I just thought the local boys would bash my head for what Trudeau did to the queen."

"Who is Trudeau?" Ohara asked. "What did he do to the queen?"

"Said Canada might not print her face on its money anymore," laughed McCarter. "So Manning's telling me to wait until the pack goes by, because he'll be last, then he gives me another three hundred to bet. Tells me he's running last and then he bets more.... I thought he'd been soaking his head in maple syrup—"

"I ran last because of the weather. Awful, cold, stormy," explained Manning to the Japanese. "The pack of runners takes off from the start like they're all sprinters. I let gravity carry me. I keep my legs cool. Then come the last few miles, when the course goes uphill, and they can't keep their pace. They slow down, their muscles cramp up with the cold. Two or three drop out. I'm gaining on the others. Then comes the ambush."

"Someone attempted to attack you?" Ohara asked in complete innocence. "During a sporting event? Did you call the police?"

"I called McCarter." Manning laughed.

"These two bloody bastards jumped out of the woods at Manning," McCarter said. "So I jumped out of the woods too. One of the bushwhackers goes down holding his jewels, the other one goes down holding his head. Manning sprints for the prize."

"What was your time for the distance?" Ohara asked.

"Who cared? Nobody cared," Manning said. "We wanted the money. I come in first. While I trot off for a hot soak to keep my muscles from knotting up, McCarter collects the money."

"But they didn't want to pay! Those Kentish sods thought we'd cheated them."

"I walked into the pub, and the pub lord's raving

about us 'interfering' with his nephew. We had no idea what had happened to the nephew.''

"And the two buggers from the woods are standing right there, calling us cheating foreigners. Me, an Englishman!'' McCarter snorted.

"I pointed the two men out,'' Manning said. "Told the people to question them if they wanted to know what happened to the nephew. Wrong thing to say. After a moment, I realized Mr. McCarter and I would need to conduct the debate back-to-back, that is, by the 'Alley Rules of Discourse.' ''

"They rushed us like a pack of devils. We took some bruising, it was nip and tuck there for a while, us two against about fifty of those sods.''

"Yeah,'' said Manning, "but sportsmanship prevailed.''

"In other words, they all stood in line to get a swing at us—''

"When the scene calmed down,'' Manning continued, "we searched for the two ambushers through all the unconscious and bleeding citizens, and then we dragged them out—''

"And we knocked their heads together, we did. Interrogated them on the spot. Seems *they* tripped the poor little nephew and removed him from the race. Had no problem collecting our money after that—''

"Yeah, the debate ended,'' said Manning. "God save the queen.''

All heads turned at once. The whup of rotors throbbed through the metal walls of the hangar. Yakov left the office and limped toward the hangar doors.

"If the general's got his golf shoes on," McCarter shouted to Yakov, "Manning wins a hundred bucks."

"What are you jabbering about?" the Israeli demanded, venting his impatience and frustration.

"The Canuck knows where our helicopters have been."

"Oh, yes? Perhaps he also knows where the Cuban aircraft landed? He should inform me, so that I can inform the United States Air Force."

Yakov slammed open a corrugated steel door and stepped out into brilliant sunlight. McCarter followed him out. Shielding his eyes against the light, McCarter saw the silhouettes of helicopters descending from the sky.

Air Force markings identified the Huey. McCarter shouted to the others.

"Off your duffs, mates!"

Five minutes later, the men of Phoenix Force left Houston behind, flying west on a search for a DC-5 somewhere in the flatlands of Texas.

20

Miami

Saturday
9:00 a.m.
(1400 Greenwich mean time)

SKIDDING TO A STOP on the airfield, the DEA unmarked Plymouth rocked on its springs. Flor threw open the door. She ran back and unlocked the truck. Bolan and Encizo lifted out their heavy suitcases. They shook hands with the exotic young woman agent who had guided them through Miami and the Everglades.

"Flor, if you ever get bored chasing dopers," Bolan shouted over the screaming engines of two waiting Lear jets, "send a résumé to Stony Man Farm. You can give Colonel John Phoenix as a reference."

"Thank you, sir."

"Mack to my friends—"

"Señorita," Encizo urged. "Please consider the offer. We need fighters like you."

"With your charm and intelligence," Bolan continued, "I'm sure we could send you anywhere in the world. You could be very valuable to us."

"And very dangerous to *las comunistas*!" Encizo laughed.

"I will think about it," Flor said, turning away from the engine noise. "But I don't know if I would be effective in countersubversion. My politics, my ideas—you would consider them very socialist. My father, his brothers, my mother's family, all were very well-known in the Socialist parties of Bolivia, before the fascists and the Communists drove us out, murdered—no, that is history. This is my country now. Now, I'm fighting a war here. A war against dope."

Bolan looked at her long and hard. "Many battles. One war. Give us a call sometime. Stony Man pays better than your Agency. *Adios*."

"*Hasta la vista, guerrera,*" Encizo told her.

The Stony Man warriors strode to the two waiting jets. Encizo passed his suitcase to Bolan and jogged to the plane that would take him to Texas to join Phoenix Force's search for a DC-5 carrying binary chemicals. A case of weapons in each hand, Bolan marched up the aluminum steps to his jet's cabin.

Bolan turned, waved even as he saw the Plymouth speeding away, the brave woman already returning to a war no less dangerous than his own.

As a joke, he had offered her more pay than the Drug Enforcement Agency. But what value could he put on an American like Flor Trujillo?

Did a civil-service salary pay her to face death every minute of her career? Perhaps a hideous, drawn-out death at the hands of sadistic drug traffickers? He had seen her fight with fear shaking her body. For a government paycheck, did she risk the terrible wounds and disfigurement of modern weapons?

In an era when popular philosophies preached self-enrichment and the pleasures of wealth, she gave her intelligence and spirit to her adopted country for a few hundred dollars a week.

Even as he posed the questions, he knew the answers. Flor Trujillo loved America, loved the idea of America. She felt her responsibility to freedom, and her character, her spirit, her soul—whatever word described the mysterious element that made a person different from all the other people of the world—gave her no choice but to serve that country, that idea, with everything such selfless service entailed.

Bolan had met a kindred spirit. Another warrior like himself.

21

Nicaragua

Saturday
11:00 a.m.
(1700 Greenwich mean time)

HEADING STRAIGHT NORTH, toward the Honduran border, they littered their trail with bloody bandages and ration packets. The three men of Able Team took shifts carrying Maria's stretcher.

After the attack on the camp, they had delayed only to hack down two saplings and fashion a stretcher. Now, Gadgets and Lyons raced along woodcutters' paths, plodding uphill under the weight of the semiconscious Maria and their own packs, trotting when the trails went downhill.

Ranging far ahead of them, David surveyed the trails for ambushes or signs of Nicaraguan army re-act squads. He knew the mountains and the people.

As Gadgets and Lyons rounded one bend, they saw a peasant woman waiting with the teenaged boy.

"Water," David told them, pointing to the plastic jug the woman offered them.

The woman leaned over Maria, kissing her cheeks, making the sign of the cross over her. She washed

Maria's face as Gadgets and Lyons gulped the cold spring water.

"*No bueno*, kiddo," Lyons told David, nodding toward the woman. "Maybe she tell *comunistas*."

"She no talk. She sister of friend of mother of Maria."

"When the Communists come," Lyons explained to the boy, "they will see our tracks. They will know she saw us. If she does not tell the Communists about us, she dies."

"*No problema*," David replied. "She help us, she help the *comunistas*. She already send boy to *comunistas*, tell them of many, many *Somocistas* in mountains—"

"What? She's informed on us? What the—"

"Boy walk to army camp. Walk six hours. Army comes tonight. We gone. *Comunistas* give her money. *Todo es bueno*, yes?"

Gadgets tore open a foil packet of hikers' trail mix. He ate the mixed nuts and fruits in a few swallows, and tossed the wadded packet on the trail. If their pursuers missed Able Team's bootprints, they could follow the trash.

"I do not like this," Lyons told his partner, looking down at the woman who comforted the wounded girl. Lyons squatted, grabbed the handles of the stretcher. "Time to move. Make distance."

They continued north. The cool mountain air warmed to tropical temperature as the morning became midday. Sometimes they came to stretches of over-logged and eroded mountainside. Leaving the shadows of the pines and oaks, they immediately felt the heat of the direct sun. Red orange dust swirled from the denuded, gullied slopes; walls of gritty, desert-hot wind enveloped them.

In other places, the trail took them through deep folds in the mountain. Lush tangles of ferns and mosses enclosed the footpath. Bromeliad—orchid-like parasitic flowers in red and pink and soft purple—hung in pine boughs.

Where the trail crossed a ridge crest, they stopped. Blancanales jogged up to where the others waited with the stretcher. In addition to his pack, Blancanales carried the M-249 machine gun and two hundred rounds of ammunition. Though they had used all the Viper rockets and most of the ammunition during the attack, the weight of his pack and the M-249 made every step an effort. His camouflage fatigues were sopped with sweat under his straps and back.

"This is it," Blancanales told them. He took a plastic-protected map from his chest pocket. Sweat from his face dropped on the map and beaded away as he scanned the topography. "Now we cut west. Give the kid whatever trash you got left."

David bent over Maria and talked quietly with her. Gadgets and Lyons dug through their packs. They found a few foil envelopes of presto-food. Lyons gnawed at a granola bar. Blancanales took a syrette and another dressing from his medical kit.

Making quiet conversation in Spanish with Maria, Blancanales changed the blood-soaked bandage on her leg and gave her an injection of painkiller. The boy took the bloody dressing and empty syrette, and gathered the empty food packets and.wrappers. He ran ahead on the path to create a false trail for their pursuers.

"I think we should bury this monster," Blancanales told Lyons, patting the M-249. "We don't need it. And we could move faster without it."

Lyons bugged his eyes. "No! Never! I'll carry it. That thing is a precision instrument—"

"Twenty-five miles."

"I'll carry it. We get jammed by a re-act unit, that monster's our ticket out and away."

"Here you go. Twenty-five miles." Blancanales and Lyons exchanged weapons, Blancanales reclaiming his M-16/M-203 rifle/grenade launcher, Lyons the M-249 Squad Automatic Weapon.

Blancanales slung the hybrid autorifle over his back, then gripped the stretcher.

As Blancanales and Gadgets marched west with the girl, Lyons cut a long leafy branch, then followed them. Behind him he carefully whisked away the bootprints that betrayed their new direction.

22

Texas

Saturday
12:00 p.m.
(0700 Greenwich mean time)

CUT BY THE BLACK LINES of the highways and the red tracks of dirt roads, the Texas range extended to the horizon. Water holes flashed like coins.

In the distance, a few miles from the helicopter, a swirl of wind created by the heat of the morning's sun swept across the land, gathering strength, becoming a column of whirling dust and debris. Yakov followed the dust devil with his binoculars. His mind drifted from the search for the DC-5 cargoliner, and he thought of the *suffat chol* created by the heat and winds of the Sinai and Negev deserts.

The ancient Hebrews had seen God in those columns of wind: the unseen form of God, walking the Land of Israel clothed in wind and swirling desert sand.

Yakov blinked hard against the fatigue stinging his eyes. He turned his thoughts away from his home and his God.

Scanning the range with the binoculars, he saw clusters of isolated ranch buildings, sometimes a town, sometimes light reflecting in flashes off a speeding car's windshield. But no DC-5.

Actually, he did not expect to see the aircraft itself. In his years with the Israel Defense Forces, Yakov had often patrolled the Sinai. He remembered incidents of Israeli planes lost or terrorist planes intercepted, the many other incidents when radar had indicated the incursion of a low-flying aircraft. In those searches, he and the other patrolling soldiers had looked for the tracks of the landing gear. An aircraft may be a hundred feet long, yet still be cleverly hidden. A crash could scatter metal over a large area, yet the debris might go unnoticed in a rocky, sand-blown area.

But the tires always left scars. Sometimes even windstorms could not erase the marks. Yakov had seen truck tracks remaining from Turkish pursuits of Lawrence and his Bedouins during World War I. The face of the desert healed very slowly.

A DC-5 required a long landing strip. Yakov looked for parallel lines a kilometer in length.

Yet in the vast heartland of Texas, a kilometer diminished to insignificance, merely a fleck on a horizon-to-horizon plain of green brush and dusty earth.

Yakov pressed the helicopter's intercom buzzer and shouted over the roar of the rotors.

"Billions of dollars for your high technology and we do this with binoculars?"

The copilot answered. "We'll get a report from the eyes in the sky soon. We grab these grass smugglers all the time—"

"We'd better get this one!" Yakov did not correct the copilot's misinformation about grass smugglers; in their briefings, the Air Force personnel had received no information on the binary gases. Their officers spoke only of the intruding aircraft, not of the crew or cargo.

Keying his electronically encoded hand-radio, Yakov heard a static, blurred voice answer. He looked to the south and saw the speck of another Huey. Even with direct line-of-sight transmission, the distance taxed the small radio's power. He spoke slowly, distinctly.

"Phoenix One. Calling all Phoenix soldiers. Have you sighted anything? Anything?"

Bursts of static answered.

A faint voice he could not recognize said, "No."

McCarter's voice came through clear. "Bloody zilch."

Yakov turned. Behind him, McCarter faced out the helicopter's opposite side door. With the safety strap looped around his waist, he held binoculars to his eyes with one hand and the radio to mouth with his other.

Yakov tapped the Englishman on the shoulder, shouted, "You need not use the radio, young man!"

McCarter shouted back, "Bloody zilch! This is a waste of time!"

The copilot's voice spoke through the intercom headsets. "Message from the airport. Changing channels. . . ."

A click brought the voice of Rafael Encizo. "This is Phoenix Two. I wait at the airport. They have no helicopter for me."

"Phoenix One speaking. Do not, repeat, do not join us. This search is not productive. Contact the local law-enforcement liaison, coordinate our search with the police in the countryside and the highway police—"

"The highway patrol."

"Correct. We will continue in helicopters until they return to refuel. What news from the Farm?"

"Stony Man One on his way back. There was fire in Miami. I cannot say more."

"A success there?"

"Two. But a big fish got away. I go now to speak with the police. Over."

Yakov returned his binoculars to the heartland of Texas.

23

Over Virginia

Saturday
1:00 p.m.
(1800 Greenwich mean time)

BOLAN FOUND A CHESS SET in one of the Lear's compartments. He spread a map of the Western Hemisphere over the conference table and used the white pawns to plot the positions of his men. Three pawns marked Able Team's mission in Nicaragua. He placed four pawns in Texas to represent the search by Yakov, Ohara, Manning and McCarter for the DC-5 cargoliner. The last pawn marked Encizo's arrival at Houston.

A rook represented Stony Man Farm. He took a knight for himself, glanced out of the port to confirm the Virginia countryside below, and placed the knight south of Washington, D.C. The other knight went to Honduras, where Grimaldi waited for Able Team's extraction signal.

Nine men and himself. Against how many? He did not even know who he was fighting.

Grabbing a handful of black pieces, he placed a rook and a pawn in Nicaragua. The black king in Florida represented the Japanese terrorist leader who escaped. He put two more black pawns in Texas.

The cargoliner had popped onto the Air Force radar screens somewhere west of Cuba. Had it taken off from a Communist airfield? The Ilyushin in Lebanon bore the company logo of Air Cuba. He placed a rook on Havana.

Where did the other terrorist-forces hide? The deathlist to the President had named five cities: New York, Washington, D.C., Dallas, San Francisco and Los Angeles. Had the terrorists pre-positioned murder squads in all the cities? Were millions and millions of people held hostage in a waiting game that would soon explode into bloodletting? He placed a pawn on each city.

But how many other squads waited in the United States to do mass murder?

There could be no answer. Not until they revealed themselves. And now, with the breakdown in the discipline of the terrorist leadership, he could not expect the assaults to come in any order or logic.

How could he tactically respond to chaos?

A buzz came from the intercom.

"Are we over Dulles?" Bolan asked the pilot.

"No, sir. You have a communication on your secure line. Three more minutes to landing."

Bolan flicked on his monitor. April spoke urgently.

"Mack, there's a tanker off the Carolina coast. A Coast Guard cutter attempted to stop it for a search. It opened fire on the cutter with machine guns and automatic weapons."

"I'm on my way. Call ahead and arrange for a

helicopter to take me out to the Coast Guard ship."

"I will. We just got a call from the chemical-warfare squad decontaminating the *Tarala*."

"They confirm the nerve gas?"

"Confirmed. But it wasn't just nerve gas. The freighter had that superpump and tanks of chemicals, but in the containers on deck they had rockets. Short-range rockets loaded with binary agent. Mack, that tanker's only a hundred miles from the White House."

"Warn the Coast Guard. Tell them to hold the attack until I get there. Over."

He took a last look at the map of the Western Hemisphere, at the positions of the chess pieces. Now he knew where another Hydra pawn moved. But what of the others? The hidden terrorist squads, the DC-5 somewhere in Texas, the hidden Cuban base?

His fist opened over the map, scattering black pieces everywhere.

If the terrorists hid, the Stony Men would wait. If they appeared, the Stony Men would attack. He and his nine warriors would hack away the many heads of Hydra.

Mack Bolan stripped off his sports coat and prepared for the next battle.

24

Texas

"I DON'T KNOW WHY THOSE GENTLEMEN in the Air Force didn't call us hours ago," Sergeant Bragonier of the Texas Highway Patrol told Rafael Encizo.

Passing the dispatchers' room, the sergeant waved. The young woman at the consoles returned the wave. Though balding and scarred by a career in law enforcement in the extremes of Texas weather, Sergeant Bragonier presented a formidable image in his motorcycle officer's uniform: high boots, jodhpurs, black leather jacket, Ruger .44 Magnum. Commendation and marksman medals marked a shirt stretched tightly across his chest by powerful muscles.

"Maybe they think we're still men who ride around on wheels," the Texan continued. "Can't make it in the space age. I mean, what's so top secret about dope? Got those marijuana smugglers coming out of sky most every night. Maybe we could get a Federal Aviation ordinance enacted. All aircraft flying below one hundred feet are highway patrol responsibility...."

Encizo laughed. Where was that DC-5 and its cargo of nerve gas?

They pushed through double fire doors. The clatter and whir of computers filled the corridor. Sergeant Bragonier motioned the Cuban through a doorway.

A lanky young man in faded jeans and a red rayon cowboy shirt, his lizard-skin boots propped on a printer, watched phosphorescent green numbers flash across video screens. Perforated paper spilled out of a high-speed chain printer, thousands of names and files descending into a chromed paper stacker. The cowboy-operator wore his hair in the short crew-cut brush of an English reggae-rock pop star.

"Well, say, Sting," the sergeant joked. "This is a Mr. Torres from some federal agency. That's what he told me. What do we have in the way of aircraft reports?"

"De-bop-bop..." "Sting" replied, scooting his rolling chair across to a keyboard terminal. He typed in codes. Columns of one-line crime-report summaries—each line identifying the town, county, time, date, then numbers indicating the crime or accident—rolled through the video screen. A flashing line appeared.

"Zip."

He typed in more codes. Another line flashed.

"No UFOs."

He typed in a third code into the computer.

"No unexplained phenomena," "Sting" told them.

"Too bad, Mr. Federal," said Sergeant Bragonier. "Looks like it's back to the Air Force—"

The young cowboy stopped them. "Wait. I'll key in Miscellaneous. Some people not experienced with these machines think computers are smart. Sorry, it ain't that way. They don't think, period. Only record. Put in a mistake, they record the mistake, forever. Therefore, I think...."

Typing the numbers of individual reports, "Sting" flashed through screens of green letters and numbers. One made him laugh. He pointed it out to the other men.

"We got a wacko tourist from Washington, D.C. Bit off some chicken heads."

Sergeant Bragonier laughed. "Probably one of our esteemed congressmen. In a cocaine seizure. Only way to explain what happens in Congress."

"Here's an interesting one." "Sting" pointed to a report displayed on the screen.

The sergeant interpreted the codes and abbreviations for Encizo. "A hit-and-run driver...drunk... speaks only Spanish. Hmmm...reason it's crossfiled in Miscellaneous is because they can't imagine what he hit. He's got a dent and skid marks on the roof of his van. But the van hadn't rolled over, they know that for sure."

Encizo reached for a phone.

25

Carolina Coast

Saturday
3:30 p.m.
(2030 Greenwich mean time)

PARALLELING THE COURSE of the tanker *Al Karem*, the Coast Guard cutter maintained a separation of two miles. Beyond the range of the *Al Karem*'s rifles and machine guns, the crew of the USS *Jefferson* waited for the unnamed "specialist from Washington." The crew monitored the maritime frequencies, meanwhile kept their vessel's single 4-inch cannon aimed at the terrorists.

In the clear cold weather, the American crewmen stood on the deck watching the distant ship. Through binoculars, they saw the Palestinians and Hispanics running on the decks, throwing back hatches.

Gunners on the superstructure started to aim bursts or single shots at the Coast Guard cutter.

From time to time, slugs clanged into the *Jefferson*. Pelicans and sea gulls following the cutter dived into the water where bullets splashed, thinking the crew had thrown garbage. The Coast Guard men, most of them teenagers, crouched behind steel and laughed at the danger.

Flying in fast from the west, Bolan leaned against his safety strap and watched the crewmen on the *Jefferson* wave to him. The helicopter's pilot took the Huey troopship in a circle around the cutter.

The voice of the *Jefferson*'s captain spoke through the Huey's intercom.

"Colonel Phoenix? Is that Army, Air Force, or Marines?"

The Huey's doorgunner, listening in on his headset, looked over at the black-clad colonel. Bolan wore his battlesuit, the nylon combat armor still crusted with dried slicks of blood and mud from the assault on the Esperanza Youth Rehabilitation Camp. He carried the M-16/M-203 over-and-under hybrid assault rifle/grenade launcher. A bandoleer of 5.56mm magazines crossed his chest. He had a bandoleer of 40mm grenades belted around his waist.

Trusting that Bolan would not hear him, the doorgunner covered his microphone and shouted across the Huey to the other gunner, "Colonel Phoenix of the Spook Patrol!"

The Stony Man warrior ignored the captain's question and asked one himself. "Any communication with the tanker, Captain?"

"Nothing. The only response we get is bullets. I got a coded message from Washington preempting my authority in this deal. So you give the word, Colonel, and we'll put some four-inchers past that scum bucket's bow. They'll understand that communication."

"What I want you to do is load smoke rounds," Bolan commanded. "Stand ready to put the first round into the bridge, then walk the rounds forward. I want that ship smoked solid while I board it.''

"What are you talking about, Colonel? Board that tanker? Did you bring a platoon of Marines with you?"

"No, sir. But those terrorists won't surrender—"

"*You* are going to assault that ship? Alone? Isn't that a mite overconfident?"

"I need prisoners, and I intend to take some. Get that smoke loaded, Captain. I'm hitting it in—"

As Bolan spoke, he saw a tongue of flame flash from the *Al Karem*. A rocket shot toward the *Jefferson*.

"Get your crew off the decks!" Bolan roared. "Seal up! Sound a chemical warfare alert!"

The captain did not answer. The rocket soared high and wide, exploding in the ocean several hundred yards behind the helicopter and cutter. A flock of pelicans rose from the ocean in a thrashing of white wings.

"I don't think I'll bother, Colonel," the captain told Bolan though the ship-to-chopper intercom. "Their targeting ability is not exactly threatening my ship."

A cloud of greenish mist drifted over the explosion-churned water. Bolan watched pelicans fly through the mist, then fall out of the sky.

"Captain, I suggest you reconsider—"

Sirens sounded below him. Bolan saw the crewmen clear the *Jefferson*'s decks. The cutter veered to the west as a second rocket flashed from the *Al Karem*.

"Loading smoke, Colonel Phoenix!"

Bolan spoke through the intercom to the Huey's pilot. "Start a wide circle aft of that tanker, as if you're giving it a look-over from a safe distance. When the first smoke round hits it, go straight for the superstructure. Look for a deck or platform where I can exit. When I'm on the ship, clear out. Gunners, hit anything that moves."

The second rocket screamed past the Huey to explode a thousand yards away. Another green cloud spread over the ocean's surface.

"Yes, sir. One wide, wide circle coming up."

The Huey banked as the pilot's voice continued. "Tell me, sir. What is that they're shooting at us?"

"You see the birds dying?" Bolan asked. "What do you think?"

"Jesus...."

Bolan slipped off his headset and shouted across to the gunners. "You got some rope back here?"

They nodded. One gunner reached into a gear compartment. He pulled out a hundred-foot coil of 5000-pound-test nylon line.

Bolan took the line and secured one end of it, then double-checked his knots. He planned to slide down to the *Al Karem* if masts or wires barred any other approach.

Slapping the end of his M-16/M-203's box magazine to check the seating, Bolan snapped back the actuator to strip the first cartridge; then he set the safety. He unlocked the M-203 and shoved in a 40mm buckshot round; he flipped down the grenade launcher's safety. By touch, he counted the Italian MU-50G grenades in his thigh pockets.

He looked at the *Al Karèm* and saw the muzzles of autoweapons sparking as the Palestinians directed their fire at the Huey. Bolan continued his equipment check, securing the Velcro flap on his AutoMag, putting the long nylon loops of plastic handcuffs in the front pockets of his battle armor.

The teenaged doorgunners stared at him. He gave them a quick command through the intercom. "Check your weapons. Load and lock."

Their hands fumbled at the cocking handles of the M-60D machine guns. One gunner, in his nervousness, snapped the cocking handle back twice. The cartridge bounced off the helicopter flooring, rolled out the side door.

On the Coast Guard cutter, the 4-inch cannon boomed. The shell shrieked into the *Al Karem*. Phosphorescent yellow smoke clouded from a lower deck. A second shell slammed into the superstructure as the Huey banked.

The pilot weaved and bobbed at a hundred miles an hour, taking the Huey up to a hundred feet, then dropping down to skim the water. He banked the troopship from side to side.

Shells from the cutter screamed into the *Al Karem*. A yellow cloud obscured the bridge. It poured out of shattered ports. A crewman threw open a door and staggered from a cabin, smoke billowing out the open door. Two Palestinians, one carrying a heavy machine gun, the other two boxes of cartridge belts, ran for the aft railing. A shell slammed into the deck and enveloped them in yellow smoke. Another shell hit amidships.

"Colonel, I can't risk the bridge!" the pilot shouted through the intercom. "Looks like they got VHF and long-wire antennas all over—"

"Swing around the far side," Bolan ordered. "We'll try the prow. Tell the captain to keep putting in smoke."

"But we'll be in his line of fire!"

"Put me down there and you can lift out."

Slugs hammered the Huey's aluminum. A ricochet whined past Bolan. The doorgunner behind the black-suited Stony Man looked down at a gash in his boot. Blood poured from the AK wound in his foot.

Soaring up, then dropping to within feet of the water, the pilot banked the Huey around the stern of the *Al Karem*. A Palestinian at the railing lifted an AKM.

The doorgunner beside Bolan sprayed .308 NATO. The Palestinian fell back as the helicopter flashed past.

Rotorstorm whipped yellow smoke. Bolan watched the ship pivot beneath him, the Huey holding a tight circle. Then he looked directly down at the main deck.

Instead of the pipes and valves needed to move liquid cargo, he saw an open hold. Canvas painted the same gray as the decking had been rolled away to expose rocket launchers. Hundreds of long tubes lay in racks made of welded angle-iron. He could not identify the type of rockets or country-of-origin. Nor did he see any radar dishes or antennas indicating a rocket-guidance system.

A single rocket shot away as he looked, streaking toward the *Jefferson*.

There was no guidance system. The rockets and launchers had not been designed for the pinpoint accuracy needed to destroy warships and combat aircraft. The technicians who had modified the *Al Karem* and fabricated the rocket launchers had no intention of waging war, only committing mass murder.

The crude rocket launchers and their binary gas warheads had only one target: the capital of the United States of America.

Palestinians in *keffiyehs*, Hispanics in denim work clothes jerked Kalashnikov rifles to their shoulders. Bolan hit the side door's edge as the pilot banked the Huey into a wild S-turn, the ocean dropping away, blue sky appearing.

Bolan looked through the opposite side door and saw ocean. The pilot whipped through the S, the *Al Karem* suddenly ahead of the Huey again.

"More smoke!" Bolan shouted into the intercom.

"Going past again, Colonel. You tell me when you think you can offload. I don't think you'll make it."

The doorgunner next to Bolan, entrusting his life to his safety strapping, leaned from the side door and poured continuous fire at the decks and railings of the old ship. Hot brass showered Bolan. A gunman appeared at a railing; he died. Another one staggered sideways, blood pumping from a shattered arm.

But other terrorists put their Kalashnikov sights on the Huey hurtling toward them. Slugs punched steel, some screeching across the helicopter's sheet metal to shatter Plexiglas.

Beside Bolan, the teenaged doorgunner suddenly lurched, his left leg kicking backward. Wounds to his calf and thigh spurted blood into the slipwind. The teenager fell back, clutching at his bleeding leg, the gyrations of the helicopter throwing him against the rear bulkhead. Only his safety webbing saved him from falling to the ocean.

As blood poured through his hands, the young soldier's panicked eyes looked to Mack Bolan.

Bolan had seen those eyes a thousand times—as teenaged Americans died in I Corps rice fields, as fourteen-year-old VC conscripts died entangled in the wire of fire bases, when his brother Johnny looked up from a hospital bed....

The other doorgunner continued firing, blood puddling around his wounded foot. The Huey hurtled onward. The pilot was determined to follow Bolan's orders.

The wounded gunner struggled to sit up. His hands reached for the twin grips of his weapon.

Bolan knew these young men would die before they failed him. But he could not throw their lives away. If it was Grimaldi who piloted the Huey, or if he fought with the hard-core warriors of Able and Phoenix, men who had already had some years of life, Bolan would chance it. But not with these kids. He shouted into the intercom.

"Pull up! Get out of range. You got two wounded back here."

"And one up front...."

The Huey went straight up. The G-force pressed Bolan against the flooring as he slid through blood to the wounded doorgunner. Linking two of the plastic handcuffs end-to-end, he looped them around the gunner's thigh and pulled the plastic bands tight to slow the flow of blood.

He put the boy's hands over the more serious of the two thigh wounds. "Press hard, we'll have you in hospital in fifteen minutes."

He spoke into the intercom. "Pilot, put me though to the captain of the *Jefferson*."

"Yes, sir."

"Well, Colonel, how's it going?"

"It's going down. High explosive. Sink it."

"You do have the authority to order that, right?"

"Your commander briefed you?"

"That he did. And it will be my pleasure...."

"Pilot, take us to a thousand feet. Circle that ship."

"We're there now."

Bolan took the M-60D. Resetting the machine gun's rear sight, he aimed for the racks of rockets far below him. He squeezed off long bursts.

Figures on the deck of the *Al Karem* ran for cover. Sweeping the lines of .308 NATO over the deck, Bolan shot out the first belt. As he threw open the feed cover to insert another length of cartridges, the first high-explosive shell tore through the tanker's bridge.

Another punched into the crew quarters. Bolan continued firing at the rocket launchers as the pilot held the slow circle. A shell hit the main deck.

The captain's voice returned to the intercom. "Say, Colonel, how about a missile?"

"Put it amidships, at the waterline."

Bolan heard the captain issuing orders to his crew. "Stand by...."

Bolan put a last burst into the terrorists, then held his fire. He reached to the wounded doorgunner and helped him sit up.

"This is it."

A streak of fire left the *Jefferson*. Skimming along the sea surface, the high-tech, computer-guided missile took only seconds to cross the miles separating the two ships.

Flame blossomed from the holds of the *Al Karem*. An instant later, the sound of the blast reached the helicopter.

Smoke and flame rose from the holds. As they watched, secondary explosions popped like strings of firecrackers. At the stern, a group of terrorists dropped a lifeboat into the water.

A greenish haze spread around the *Al Karem*. The terrorists in the lifeboat went strangely still. A man struggling in the water sank beneath the surface. On the burning ship, nothing moved.

"What do you think, Colonel?" the captain asked. "You think that was worth three hundred fifty-eight thousand dollars of the taxpayers' money?"

The *Al Karem* rolled onto its side. Explosions continued inside the hull.

"You realize, Captain," Bolan cautioned him, "that this didn't happen."

"Yeah, guess not."

Bolan took a last look at the Hydra death ship. "Pilot, let's get these men to a hospital."

As the helicopter turned for the Carolina coast, the *Al Karem*, gutted and lifeless, slipped into the depths.

26

Nicaragua

Saturday
5:30 p.m.
(2330 Greenwich mean time)

ROTORTHROB BLASTED the late-afternoon quiet.
Lyons threw himself down under a pine's shadow.
He scrambled through the dust and pine needles to
the trunk. He searched the network of branches and
sky above him for the helicopter. A buzz sounded
from his hand-radio.

"It's passed," Blancanales told him. "It came
over the top and followed the ridge line. You see it?"

"No, just heard it, all of a sudden," Lyons
answered. "Noise fading now."

"It went straight north. Another of those French
helicopters."

When the helicopter's throb diminished into the
distance, Lyons got to his feet. His black cotton
jump suit was muddy where the dust mixed with his
sweat. Hot afternoon sunlight slanted through the
pines, a slash of light across the black cotton of his
shoulder. Even with the altitude and winds, sweat
poured from his body. He stepped into the shadow
and keyed his hand-radio again.

"How far to the river?"

"Coming up real soon," said the voice of Blancanales.

"Hope so."

"That monster heavy?"

Lyons laughed. "You talking about my Black Beauty? She is my true love. Over and out."

Adjusting the wide padded sling of the M-249, Lyons strode through the woods, scanning the hillsides and gullies, listening for the sound of pursuers. He glanced at the trail behind him every few seconds. Sometimes he stopped to watch and listen from concealment. Then he jogged ahead.

Blancanales and Gadgets made excellent time despite the stretcher. Maria slept, or stared around them at the terrain. She still clutched her M-1 across her chest.

At one point she pointed to the charred stumps of pines in the woods around them. "Here, my father and brothers and everyone work. In the revolution, the *Guardia Nacional* kill schoolteacher, burn school. My father cut wood for new school here."

Laying back in the stretcher, she closed her eyes against the heat and pain. "We make school. Government sends Cubano, who teach only Marx. *¿Somoza o Fidel? ¿Qué es la diferencia?* It is not revolution when you change kings."

"Tell it to Jane Fonda," Gadgets joked.

"We know all about 'people's democracies,' " said Blancanales. "Hey, smell it?"

"What? A people's democracy?"

"The river. Maria, you know the area—"

"Yes," she replied. "Soon is a road. Then the lake. There is fish. And boats."

Blancanales signaled to Gadgets to stop. He keyed his hand-radio. "Ironman, we're here. Time to plan our boat ride."

ROCK AND ROLL BLARED from the lieutenant's tape player. He pulled off the highway. He looked in the rearview mirror that was edged in white plastic fuzz and saw the prison truck following him.

Lurching over the rutted side road, the lieutenant swerved from pothole to pothole, guiding the 1957 Chevy's undercarriage safely around rocks. The road cut over an utterly denuded hillside, every pine and oak gone.

The Chevy and the truck continued over the hillcrest. On a ridge, an army work crew had cut the trees. The lieutenant's chain gang would not cut the wood for sale as firewood. The work of the counterrevolutionaries made money for the people. And more money for the lieutenant.

The revolution had been kind to the lieutenant. Rising from a start as a teenaged pimp serving national guard officers, to informer, to assassin and streetfighter, he finished the war in the army of liberation. He bribed a colonel in the new government for a commission in the Sandinista army. Posted to a remote garrison, he proceeded to build his financial future. He took the responsibilities of employing prison labor, of the sales of "surplus" military rations, and of supervising the use of the nationalized estates of wealthy exiles. Soon, when the economy collapsed and a coup threw out the Communists, the lieutenant would retire from the army and devote his full attention to his enterprises. But now he bossed chain gangs.

Parking at the edge of the road where he overlooked the long narrow lake, the lieutenant switched off the tape player and left the Chevy. He glanced at his watch, then at the sun, low over the mountains. There was perhaps an hour's work before dark.

He took a Marlboro from his silver cigarette case as he watched the guards unload the prisoners. Chains linked the prisoners' ankles. The prisoners— ex-national guard soldiers, the sons of Somoza officials, and minor businessmen—climbed from the truck, whereupon soldiers with Kalashnikov rifles herded them into line distributing tools.

A prisoner stumbled, dropped a saw. When the middle-aged, paunchy man bent to pick it up, a soldier kicked him onto his face. All the soldiers laughed. The lieutenant did not. He snapped his fingers at the soldier and motioned him back. The prisoner scrambled to his feet. The lieutenant gave the businessman one of his American cigarettes, then pointed him toward the tangle of downed pines. The businessman gave the lieutenant a nod of thanks.

The lieutenant could not allow maltreatment of the convicts. He hoped someday to do business with these now-imprisoned bankers and merchants. How else could he advance in life? The study of Marx and Engels earned no profits. A million revolutionary slogans bought nothing.

All heads looked up at the sound of the plane. Its

pontoons almost touching the pines, a blue-and-white seaplane roared over the mountain's crest. The lieutenant saw the pilot in the cockpit. Seconds later, the plane cut chevrons into the bright mirror of the lake.

"*Somocistas!*" a soldier shouted.

"*Yanqui imperialistas!*"

The lieutenant called out to the truck and had the driver bring him the field radio. The driver lugged the heavy radio and batteries to the Chevy. The lieutenant sat on the Chevy's bumper and turned on the set. Several hundred meters below the road, he watched the seaplane taxi in a half-circle. A small boat left the shore.

Flicking the power switch repeatedly, the driver tried to turn on the radio. The lieutenant held the handset to his ear, waiting for a frequency.

A soldier fired his Kalashnikov at the tiny plane and boat. Then all the other soldiers fired. The lieutenant laughed. Trying to hit something 500 meters away with one of those sheet-tin and plywood Russian rifles? A joke. Maybe if they had American M-14s or German G-3s....

Blood and flesh exploded from the back of a soldier. High-velocity slugs kicked dust on the hillsides below and above them. Slugs buzzed past. Soldiers staggered back with blood gushing from small-caliber wounds. Throwing himself into the dirt, the lieutenant felt the weight of the driver and radio fall on him. He shoved the man away. His hand came back gory. The driver choked to death as blood filled his lungs.

The lieutenant took cover behind the Chevy. Slugs punched through the body of the car. Slugs shattered its windows. One of his dashboard ornaments, a plastic figurine of Fidel Castro, flew from the vehicle. The lieutenant looked at the splintered figurine at his feet, with its ridiculous pink face and brown beard, and kicked it away.

How could he get another Chevy? As the unseen machine gunner hammered the young officer's car to junk, the lieutenant considered the thousands of Nicaraguan cordobas and American dollars he would need for another car.

It was not fair. Why couldn't the machine gunner restrict his fire to the Russian truck? The government had hundreds of those ugly wrecks. Why his Chevy? Couldn't the counterrevolutionary firing from the lake see that he destroyed a classic American auto?

The lieutenant wept at the injustice of war.

BRASS AND BELT LINKS flying in the slipwind, the cartridge casings collecting on the seats and rolling onto the cabin floor, Lyons finished the belt and pulled the M-249 into the plane. It had been a long and arduous journey to get both himself and the weapon to the river, and thence to meet up with Grimaldi and the plane. But it was worth it. A thousand feet below them, the Nicaraguan army truck burned.

"All right!" Lyons exclaimed, laughing. "Black Beauty does it again. My true love. Makes the world safe for democracy. We're going to go down in history."

Grimaldi turned to the ex-LAPD cop-gone-commando. "Before you get out the party hats, crazy man," he said, "I got your next assignment for you. An attack platoon left the camp yesterday. You didn't get them all. The terrorists made it to Los Angeles."

Lyons's laughter died.

Blancanales and David tended to Maria. She sprawled back in a seat, watching the mountains and valleys below her color with the light of sunset. The plane bucked through updrafts. The lurches caused her face to contort with pain. Blancanales wiped her face with a sponge.

"You'll be okay," he told her. "We'll take you to a hospital in the States. You and David. Everything's arranged. The war's over for you. You'll be safe in the States."

"No!" she shouted at him. "The war over when my country free! War never over. I come back." Sadly she looked down to the mountains of her home.

"I come back."

27

Texas

Saturday
6:00 p.m.
(0100 Greenwich mean time)

PLASTIC DOMES, SUN-FLASHING SPIRES, the rusting steel skeleton of an unfinished high-rise hotel rose from horizon to horizon in the central range of Texas. No ranches, no farms, no homes broke the desolation of the dust and scrub brush around The City of Big Top.

The sprawling network of theme parks and amusement centers, interconnected by the plastic tubes of elevated monorail lines, and surrounded by seas of black asphalt parking lots, appeared to be a lost city, the gaudy abandoned capital of an unknown people.

A wide expressway linked Big Top to the small town of Junction, twenty-five miles away. Now, as the sun began to set on the straight line of the horizon, only one pickup truck traveled the eight-lane expressway. Encizo saw no other cars or trucks as Sergeant Bragonier—a faded denim jacket concealing borrowed battle armor—drove on to Big Top.

The other men of Phoenix Force, reinforced by the

Special Weapons and Tactics squad from Goodfellow Air Force Base, waited in Junction, only minutes away by helicopter.

Sergeant Bragonier of the Texas Highway Patrol had offered to act as unofficial liaison with the state's law-enforcement agencies. Encizo and the sergeant, dressed as ranchers, with fence wire and truck tires and stock feed in the back of their pickup, reconned Big Top for Phoenix Force.

"Arab oil money built it," the sergeant told Encizo. "Out here in the middle of nowhere. Some sheikh wanted to outdo Disney World. Never you mind that no one wanted to come to the middle of Texas to go to the biggest circus in the world. After all, who says no to easy money?

"The Arabs pulled the state into it. Said they needed a highway linking Big Top to the interstate, for all the millions of tourists in cars. They built most of the parks and attractions, started the Holiday Inn, surveyed the site for an international airport—they expected tourists from all over the world. . . .

"Then the price of oil went down. The Arab money stopped. The state said they'd finish the project, then tried to sell it. Finally, they laid off the construction workers. Trailer parks disappeared as thousands of men and their families moved on out of here.

"So this is what we're stuck with now. They used to have a guard company patrolling the place, keeping kids and vandals out. I had to come out here one time when the guards caught someone dismantling one of the domes—those things are big, the biggest can fit a football field.

"Later on, the sheikh got himself another guard company. Foreigners. Arabs and Hispanics. And Africans. The rent-a-cops griped about the foreigners taking their jobs, but I never thought anything about it. Figured if the sheikh wanted his own men guarding his property, good enough.

"Haven't been out here since. Nobody has. Except maybe people sightseeing. That drunk Mexican probably took a wrong turn to end up out here—"

Encizo broke the sergeant's monologue. "The plane could have landed on this freeway. One of the wheels hit the roof of his van. Perhaps."

An Air Force high-altitude photo-recon plane had transmitted video images of parallel lines marking the windblown parking lots around Big Top. But Phoenix Force could not risk confirming the information in helicopters.

Encizo and Sergeant Bragonier confirmed it from a pickup truck. "Look at these skid marks...."

Long black smears streaked the expressway's smooth asphalt. The pickup passed over the marks. As they neared Big Top, the steel frame of the unfinished high-rise hotel loomed before them. Encizo scanned the horizontals and verticals for movement.

The red light of the setting sun painted the rusted steel crimson. Something flashed. Encizo flinched, thinking he had seen the muzzle-flash of a weapon pointed at him. But no bullets struck the truck.

A sun-flare off binoculars? Encizo studied the skeletal hotel, but could identify nothing in the gridwork of steel and shadow.

"Look over there...." With a nod, the sergeant indicated a parking lot.

Eight feet of chain link fence encircled Big Top and the parking lots. At one section, footprints and the tire tracks of cars marked both sides of the fence, Lines in the dust and sparse shrub—three bands of parallel lines—curved from the expressway, across the roadside, to that section of the fence. Then the lines continued through the windblown dust and debris of the parking lot.

The bands continued straight across the parking lot's hundreds of acres of asphalt to a geodesic dome of steel and day-glo orange plastic.

"The plane is there," Encizo stated matter-of-factly.

Fatigued by days of continuous action and travel and anxiety, the Cuban veteran of a hundred battles made a mistake.

Lifting the microphone of the long-range Texas Highway Patrol radio, Encizo uttered seven words. "Phoenix Two reporting. It is there. Over."

Only after he spoke did he remember the highway patrol radio, unlike the Stony Man radios, had no electronic encoding. As the only source of transmission in this area, his message could have shouted out their identity. He cursed his exhaustion, warned the sergeant.

"Maybe I have made a problem for us. I forgot this radio, your radio is not like—"

Flame flashed from the top floor of the skeletal hotel. A rocket-propelled grenade shrieked into the expressway only a few feet to the side of the pickup.

Asphalt shrapnel shattered Encizo's window, spraying tempered glass into the interior of the pickup.

Reacting instantly, Sergeant Bragonier whipped the steering wheel from side to side. Encizo grabbed the radio mike again.

"RPG! They're shooting."

Yakov answered. "We come immediately. Over."

The pickup swerved over all four lanes as automatic fire from the hotel pocked the expressway. A slug hit the truck's cargo bed like a hammer smash.

Another RPG hit the expressway. The RPG-7 warheads, designed for penetrating armor and concrete, punched deep into the asphalt and roadbed as their cone-shaped charges exploded.

Fortunately for the two men in the pickup, most of the explosion went downward and straight up. Hunks of asphalt clanged into the truck's hood and side panels, but no real shrapnel.

Accelerating, braking, swerving, the Texas Highway Patrol officer exploited his long experience of chasing suspects on the highways and roads of Texas. As RPGs exploded around them and high-velocity autofire pocked the asphalt and ricocheted, Sergeant Bragonier left the hotel behind.

A blast rocked the truck. Out of control for an instant, the pickup skidded sideways at eighty miles an hour. The sergeant expertly steered into the skid, then fought the wheel as the truck fishtailed violently.

"Faster! A mile, two miles!" Encizo shouted.

He knew what had hit them. If a Soviet RPG-7 misses a target, the warhead continues to its maximum range, 900 yards, and self-destructs. The fire-ball and concussion of a self-destructing warhead had almost done the work of a direct hit.

The sergeant looked in his rearview mirror. "We're burning! The load's on fire."

Encizo looked through the shattered rear window and saw the tires in their load belching black smoke into the evening sky.

A flame flashed behind them, the blast shock of another self-destructing RPG hitting Encizo in the face like a fist. He clung to the edge of the open window, the tempered glass remnants crunching in his grip as the truck whipped from side to side.

Cars pursued them! Encizo saw the muzzles of autoweapons flashing. An AK slug punched through the pickup's cab and starred the windshield.

Grabbing his M-16/M-203 assault rifle/grenade launcher from the floor of the cab, Encizo loaded a 40mm high-explosive grenade into the launcher. He snapped back the actuator to chamber a 5.56mm round in the M-16.

"When I say," Encizo shouted, "drive straight for the count of two, then—"

"Go to it, federal! Just tell me when you want to make your shots."

As the truck lurched and swerved, Encizo stuck the M-16/M-203 out the back window, sighted through the flame and smoke.

"Now!"

The wild swerving stopped, the sergeant holding the wheel steady while Encizo fired.

Squeezing the M-203's trigger, Encizo sent high-explosive into one car's windshield. He whipped the rifle to the side, sprayed out thirty rounds of 5.56mm slugs at the second car. Windows shattered, glass sparkling in the air.

The 40mm had hit the gunmen of the first car. Speeding out of control as the dead driver's foot jammed the accelerator, the car drifted across one barrel of the expressway and hit the gravel separating the northbound from the southbound lanes. The car flipped sideways and tumbled. Doors opened, bodies flew out—one man still holding an AKM, another already dead.

But the second car still pursued them.

Reloading his weapon as the sergeant swerved to evade the fire of the AKs, Encizo saw arms extend an RPG launcher from the car.

"Hit the brakes!"

Deceleration threw him against the dash. White smoke from the skidding tires and the foul soot from the burning tires filled the pickup's cab. The terrorist car skidded past them, gunmen leaning from the side windows trying to bring their AKMs in line. On the other side of their car, the RPG launcher shot a rocket uselessly into the air.

Flooring the accelerator, the balding, middle-aged highway-patrol motorcycle officer gave a rebel yell. He held the pickup steady and ahead as Encizo braced his hybrid assault rifle on the passenger door, sighting on the terrorists.

Over the rifle sights, Encizo saw the man with the RPG loading another rocket in the launcher. He waited as the rocket man inside the car pulled off the warhead's safety cap and cocked the launcher's hammer.

Encizo laughed as he shot the 40mm frag into the car. Thousands of tiny razors ripped the gunmen, a second explosion coming an instant later as the RPG's warhead blasted a gaping hole through the roof of the car.

Twice dead, the terrorists died a third time as their car whipped sideways, overturned and rolled. Metal slammed and tore, and doors and weapons and bodies were scattered over the expressway. Before the terrorists' car came to rest, gasoline whooshed aflame.

Sergeant Bragonier gave another rebel yell. He slowed the pickup to a stop.

"Damn fine shooting, even if you are a *federal*. Now you take the wheel, 'cause I want to shoot too."

"The fire, man! We're on fire, too!"

"Oh, yeah...."

Scrambling from the pickup, Encizo saw he could do nothing. The tires burned in balls of sooty, choking flame. The sergeant ran to the tailgate and jerked it down.

"Let's go!"

Back in the pickup again, the Texan screeched the tires as he accelerated in reverse. Speeding backward for a hundred yards, he jammed on the brakes.

The bed's load flew from the tailgate. The burning tires rolled along the expressway to bounce into the scrub brush.

The sergeant gave Encizo the driver's seat, and he took up the M-16/M-203. With the speed and assurance of long familiarity, he loaded a 40mm high-explosive round.

"I'm also a sergeant in the National Guard," Sergeant Bragonier explained to Encizo. Scanning the road for cars, he saw none.

"Damn," he muttered.

Encizo laughed. "Be patient. This may be a long night...."

Helicopters approached from the south.

FROM THREE THOUSAND FEET, Yakov scanned the huge amusement park with binoculars. He saw the tire tracks from the expressway cross the parking lot to the orange dome. Searching for the terrorists, he swept the binoculars over other areas.

The setting sun flashed from glass and chrome spires, but left the streets and squares in deep shadow. He saw a single form dash from one building to another, but no one else. He knew there could be a thousand enemies hiding in Big Top.

To the north, past the towering unfinished hotel, a car burned on the highway. Yakov let the binoculars hang by the strap around his neck as he took the hand-radio from his combat-uniform's web belt.

"Phoenix Two. Report."

"We have you in sight. We are waiting one mile north of the hotel."

"Where is the enemy?"

"They fired rifles and rockets from the hotel. Two cars came out. But they are dead."

"What nationality are they?"

"I saw one Palestinian. The others...I don't know."

"Wait for instructions. Over."

Yakov returned the radio to his belt. He stood in the Huey troopship's side door, considering the problem. He tapped the stainless-steel hook of his prosthetic right hand against the helicopter's sheet metal, then turned to the young men waiting for his command.

Manning, McCarter and Ohara, blacksuited in their combat armor, their weapons ready, studied the circus city beneath them.

The six men from the Air Force SWAT team checked and rechecked their gear, from time to time looking to the older man in the beret who would command them.

One of the Air Force men could not help staring at Yakov's long-ago lost right hand and forearm, and the prosthetic device that served in place of his limb.

The young man thinks I am a cripple, Yakov guessed. *But I don't need two hands to lead him and these other soldiers to victory.*

But what would constitute victory in the garish monument to ignorance and greed below?

The destruction of the binary gas? Killing all the terrorists? Or as Yakov's commander, Mack Bolan, stressed in every communication: *Prisoners, information, anything that can lead the Stony Man warriors to the psychotic leaders of Hydra.*

To defeat Hydra, it would not be enough to neutralize the binary gas threats to the cities of the United States. Not only must every gram of chemical agent be seized or destroyed, but the Stony Man warriors must confirm the destruction of all the vehicles, equipment and weapons assembled for the attack.

And the destruction of every terrorist soldier. If the terrorists trained to commit mass murder with binary chemicals escaped, then their psychotic leaders or the Soviets would simply resupply the terrorists with more binary agents. While they remained alive, they threatened all the decent people of the world.

Finally, and most crucially, the madmen who conceived and coordinated the Hydra must be eliminated. They must die or be confined within the deepest isolation cells of a high-security prison.

Yakov smiled at the absurdity. He and the other Stony Men raced from one country to another, from one battle to another, fighting terrorists, fighting mind-numbing fatigue, when they knew perfectly well who sponsored, armed and paid the terrorists.

But they could not attack the nexus of terror. An attack on the Kremlin meant war.

Instead, he and Bolan and the others must hack off the thousands of devouring heads of the KGB's monstrous Department of Terror.

The Israeli ex-army officer knew he must do the obvious. The Hydra monster must die. Yakov spoke into the intercom.

"Pilot, go down. Draw fire from the enemy."

Find, then kill.

MCCARTER SAW THE FLASH of the rocket launcher. The warhead streaked down from the uppermost floor of the hotel's steel frame. It exploded in the parking lot below the helicopter.

The pilot took the troopship up and away. McCarter sprayed a magazine of 5.56mm slugs from his M-16 at the rocket launcher's position, then the helicopter returned to three thousand feet.

Even over the rotor-roar, McCarter heard Yakov screaming into the intercom, ordering the pilot to resume the low-altitude search.

Bloody fly-boy. Someone shoots at him, he forgets what we're here for. And those Yank SWATers. Waiting for us to do something. They haven't even pulled the wrapper off that door gun.

Slinging his M-16, McCarter grabbed handholds and crossed the Huey to the one machine gun. He ripped off the plastic sheeting protecting the M-60. He examined it.

At least somebody had some wits about him, McCarter admitted.

Rather than sending an M-60D doorgun with the troopship, the armorer had sent a standard M-60 with a swivel-mount adapter. The weapon still had its bipod legs and shoulder stock. A quick pull would free the M-60 from the swivel-mount to be used away from the helicopter.

He broke open a can of linked cartridges and loaded the weapon. Looking over to Yakov, McCarter pointed down to the hotel. The Israeli finally persuaded the pilot to return to the search.

As the helicopter descended, McCarter opened fire almost straight down on the hotel's top floor. Watching for movement, he raked the shadows hiding the terrorist with the rocket launcher. Three-ought-eight tracers ricocheted from the steel-and-concrete structure.

No one returned the fire.

McCarter continued putting bursts into the hotel as the helicopter dropped. Finally he swept the top floor with a level burst. Tracers skipped off the concrete floor to spark against steel verticals.

Still no answering fire.

At a hundred miles an hour, the Huey circled Big Top, dived through its plastic avenues, soared over the domes, dropped to within a few feet of virgin pavement.

The pilot completed a circle of the parking lots and returned to the vast parking lot between the hotel and the dome hiding the DC-5.

Watching the hotel's upper floors, McCarter saw the rocket flash. But before he could lift the M-60, the rocket hit the tail rotor.

Metal screamed. The frame shuddered as the tail blades disintegrated. The Huey dropped ten feet to the asphalt. The skids crumpled, the helicopter bounced up. The fuselage spun once in counter-revolution to the main rotors, then the pilot shut down the engine and the aircraft crashed to the ground.

Shouting, falling over one another, Phoenix Force and the Air Force SWAT team evacuated the wreck. McCarter grabbed an extra can of linked cartridges for the M-60, then he jerked the weapon free of its door mount.

Autofire came from the domes. Another rocket streaked down from the hotel. Its miss peppered them with bits of asphalt. The helicopter pilot fired at the hotel with his .45 pistol.

Another rocket hit the helicopter, this time punching through the engine and banged-up fuselage. Avgas exploded in a sheet of flame.

Backlit by the fire, the men of Phoenix Force snapped into action, spreading out on the parking lot's asphalt, functioning like a microarmy as they fired and maneuvered, then advanced for the cover of Big Top. The SWAT unit added their firepower to the rush.

Forty-millimeter grenades, continuous M-16 bursts, deadly accurate fire from McCarter's M-60 preceded the SWAT team.

Gaining the shelter of a walkway's low wall, Yakov buzzed Encizo.

"The helicopter's down. We are now in the park."

"We saw the rockets. Want us to clean out that hotel?"

"No. Join us. First we attack the aircraft and the chemical weapons. Over."

Yakov shouted to the men around him. "The aircraft!"

Pushing back the cocking knob of his Uzi with his stainless-steel hook he used as a hand, Yakov led the way, McCarter one step behind.

Lights came on as dusk faded to night. Crouching behind Yakov, McCarter saw a shadow move ahead of them. A three-shot burst from the M-60 spun an Arab in a security-guard uniform out of the bushes. An AKM clattered to the walkway.

A muzzle flashed. Concrete chipped near Mc-

Carter's leg. Ohara's and Manning's M-16s ripped the area. An Air Force man threw a grenade far ahead of Yakov.

After the grenade's pop, McCarter rushed ahead of Yakov, firing the M-60 from his hip, chopping ornamental bushes, shattering windows, punching holes in walls. A shadow broke cover.

Nine-millimeter slugs from Yakov's Uzi sent the terrorist sprawling.

Ohara ran to the wounded man and tore the AKM out of his hands. The helicopter pilot took the captured weapons, plus the stripped bandoleers and grenades from the Palestinian's uniform.

Firing came from the far parking lot, one weapon an M-16, the other a booming .44 Magnum. A 40mm grenade exploded against the front of the day-glo orange dome.

Swerving wildly across the open asphalt, the bullet-pocked, fire-scorched pickup truck with the shattered windows and windshield dodged AK fire from the hotel and the dome. The .44 from the pickup boomed again and again, the revolver's heavy slugs crashing through the dome, continuing through the interior.

Yakov motioned the group forward in a rush. He led them to the base of the dome, spraying fire. Behind the cover of an eight-foot-tall clown's head, he gripped his Uzi in the pincers of his steel claw and worked the magazine release with his left hand, then jammed in the new magazine.

Every shadow, every place of concealment took bursts of autofire from Phoenix Force. The pickup screeched to a stop. Encizo popped a high-explosive

40mm grenade at the terrorist gunmen before sprinting to rejoin his *compañeros*. The highway patrolman, squatting behind the pickup to reload his Ruger, spotted a gunman perched in the dome's steel frame and dropped him.

Crouched with Yakov against the clown-head, David McCarter saw how the terrorists had converted the dome into a hangar. A wide flat lawn fronted the dome, with only a low curb separating it from the parking lot. To allow the entry of the DC-5 cargoliner, the dome's steel struts had been cut away for approximately twenty-five percent of the circumference. Through the large space, the terrorists had towed or pushed the plane inside. Tire and bootprints marked the lawn in front of the dome.

But on three sides of the dome, the steel strutwork rose undamaged from its foundation wall. On those sides, a sunken garden framed the dome. McCarter, the SAS veteran, knew where he would attack.

"What are we waiting for, the bloody Marines?" McCarter shouted out.

Yakov answered him. "You first, young man."

"And so I am...."

Sprinting ahead, holding the M-60 ready, McCarter heard a roar of automatic fire as his compatriots sprayed the dome. AK slugs zipped past him. He jumped from the walkway and thrashed through the garden's decorative shrubs.

McCarter threw himself against the foundation wall of the dome. He set the machine gun on its bipod. Then he aimed three long bursts at the muzzle-flashes in the landscaping.

The line of men reloaded, the firefight dying out for a moment. McCarter lay in the shrubbery. He heard the clatter of magazines against receivers.

Inside, voices shouted in Arabic, Spanish and Russian. McCarter heard metal scrape on concrete. He looked up.

An AKM barrel slid through a hole in the dome's plastic skin. With weapon braced, one of the terrorists was waiting for the attackers to rush.

McCarter took a grenade from a thigh pocket. He pulled the pin. He eased up. The terrorist's AKM barrel wavered only inches from his face.

Phoenix Force and the Air Force SWAT team suddenly broke cover in a surging line of men and fire.

In one motion, McCarter wrenched away the Kalashnikov and shoved the grenade through the hole in the plastic. Someone screamed. An AKM sprayed a point-blank burst above McCarter as he threw himself flat again.

The advancing SWAT team sprayed the area. Only an arm's reach above him, slugs pocked the concrete. McCarter drew himself into a ball as chips of concrete rained on him. Ricocheting slugs thumped into the ground. One punched into a box magazine on his bandoleer.

"Watch it, mates!" McCarter shouted.

His grenade had popped. Bits of plastic were fluttering in the air like confetti. Jerking the cotter pin from another grenade, McCarter let the lever flip free, counted to three, and exposed only his hand as he threw it inside the dome. He waited for the pop, then lifted his M-60 over the low wall.

Through shredded plastic fabric, he saw a death-black DC-5 cargoliner. Worklights bathed the interior in a glare brighter than day. He saw fighters and technicians everywhere.

Trucks clustered around the cargoliner. Pickups carried tools and pipes. Three heavy trucks, stakes sticking up from their flatbeds, carried drums of aviation fuel. A pumpline ran from the drums to the plane's wing tanks.

Palestinians in checkered *keffiyehs* and desert khaki uniforms ran from place to place inside the dome, peering out at the attack, firing bursts, running to new positions.

Hispanics in street clothes and security-guard uniforms argued with a Palestinian officer in a beret.

A young African with tribal scars patterning his face ran directly at McCarter, not seeing the Englishman as he stooped to check two bloody comrades. The African left the dead men and took his RPG launcher to the dome's perimeter wall. Not more than two steps from McCarter, he set down a vest of rockets and loaded a warhead.

As the African peered into the night for a target, McCarter shot him point-blank with the M-60.

McCarter reached through the geodesic struts to grab the RPG launcher and the vest of rockets. He keyed his hand-radio.

"Yakov! What's the delay?"

Figures thrashed through the shrubbery. McCarter raised the M-60, saw the Israeli and Encizo side by side. He motioned them over and pointed inside.

"Looks like they're refueling that bugger," Mc-

Carter told them. "I took an RPG from one of them. What do you say we do a quickie on them? With all that petrol there—"

His Israeli leader did not answer. Letting his Uzi hang by its sling, Yakov keyed his coded hand-radio.

"Manning, Ohara. Do you have your positions?"

"Here with two of the SWATs," Manning answered.

"I am in position, sir. An American waits with me."

"Keio, cease firing. Move yourself and the American with you to the other side. Manning, we wait now. Do not fire unless you must. Encizo—" Yakov turned to the Cuban "—circle the dome. Fire only if you must. Check the positions of our men. We cannot allow any of the enemy to escape. One of them may be a leader."

Encizo nodded. Crouching below the level of the foundation wall, he moved away. Yakov keyed his radio again.

"All of you, listen. When you have your positions, I will demand the surrender of the terrorists. Do not resume firing unless I order you to do so."

"What's with you now, Father Time?" McCarter demanded. "You're going to let those bloody murdering lunatics live? That helicopter hit you in the head?"

Without taking his eyes from the scene inside the dome, the veteran of two desert wars and a hundred covert operations answered the rude young brawler.

"One does not win by killing. That only litters the world with corpses. If I must kill to take the victory,

I will. But my first and only intention is victory."

"When we kill them all and we can go home," Mc-Carter said, "we've won. Why get philosophical in a firefight?"

Yakov indicated the terrorist fighters and technicians with his steel pincers. "If we kill them all, do we know who sent them?"

"Everybody knows...."

"Who? The people of the world? Corpses give no confessions. And if we kill them all, do we learn where the others hide? Do we learn who are their leaders? If we kill them all, other groups still threaten American cities. The other groups threaten the world. It would have been best if these vermin were never born, but killing them is not the victory. Victory is to eliminate the threat. Therefore I will offer them surrender. If they cooperate, they live."

"You of all people, going soft on crazies. Old man, that's the PLO in there. Libyans. Cubans."

"You want only to fight, David. If you must fight, first win. Win, then fight."

"If you say so."

"My young friend," Yakov added, "load that rocket launcher immediately."

Gunmen continued firing into the night. Phoenix Force and the Air Force SWAT team held their fire, silently moving into their positions. One by one, Ohara, then Manning, then Encizo reported from their positions.

In the dome, the Palestinian officer in the beret gathered a squad of front-line fighters and directed them toward the parking lot. The squad ran across the cavernous interior. They crouched near the improvised entry for the DC-5, then waited as their leader continued arguing with two Hispanics.

"We are ready," Yakov muttered. Taking a deep breath, he shouted into the dome, first in Arabic.

Palestinians fired at his voice. AK slugs clanged off the steel struts to buzz into the night. Yakov ducked. He stood up again to shout in English.

"Surrender and you live! Fight and you die!"

A Palestinian boy with a Kalashnikov ran toward Yakov. As the teenager brought up the assault rifle, a .44 Magnum revolver boomed, the young terrorist's life ending as a slug smashed through his chest, spraying blood and flesh into the air behind him. The corpse fell back, still gripping the AKM.

The other terrorists took cover among the trucks and landing gear and stacked crates. Voices shouted to one another in several languages, some raving, others imploring, one barking sharp commands.

Another voice called out in Spanish. Other voices answered in Spanish. Shouted arguments broke out.

One terrorist threw down his AKM and ran for an exit, his hands high. An autoburst from a Palestinian killed him.

Hispanics sprayed slugs at Palestinians and Africans. Two young Hispanics in khaki fatigues broke cover and fired their Kalashnikovs wildly at the other men. They ran for a hole in the dome's fabric.

One of the running men pointed his AKM behind him and fired a one-handed burst to empty the weapon. He dropped the magazine, kicked it away as he ran, pulled another from his web gear. The man reloaded as he ran into the muzzle of a Palestinian's rifle. A burst through his gut, then a three-shot burst into his head ended his escape.

The second man dived at the plastic fabric of the dome. The material did not rip. Stunned, one arm hanging limp, he crawled along the perimeter, looking for a hole or rip, a way out of the killing ground. Palestinians fired at him, hit a leg, wounded him a second time in an arm. Other Hispanics, concealed throughout the area, returned the fire.

A knife slashed through the fabric. An arm grabbed the wounded Hispanic and dragged him out. Another one sprinted for the hole in the dome, died as three AKMs fired.

Yakov's hand-radio buzzed. Encizo reported.

"I have him. They are Cubanos *comunistas*. He says the Arabs have gone insane."

"Who is the Palestinian officer? Ask him."

Inside the dome, the Palestinians exterminated the Cubans. Darting from cover to cover, the Arab gunmen searched out every one of the Cubans, shot them or battered them to death with AKM butts.

Encizo answered. "He is a big man. A leader. This *comunista* says the Arab brings orders to kill the city of Dallas. But that was not the plan, he says. I tell you, Katz, this is exactly what happened in Florida. The crazies want only to kill. They kill each other."

"What are his wounds?" Yakov asked.

"He will live. Until maybe I kill him."

"No. To break the conspiracy, we must have information. Hold your position."

Yakov shouted out in Arabic. The Palestinian officer answered him with a grenade. It hit the dome's fabric, bounced back to the floor. Yakov and McCarter ducked as steel-wire shrapnel cut a thousand tiny holes in the plastic.

The officer shouted out a command. Obeying instantly, the squad of PLO fighters ran into the night, screaming as they jumped from the entry level down to the gardens surrounding the dome. Their Kalashnikovs sprayed slugs in all directions.

"Well, now, Mister Right Honorable Katzenelenbogen," McCarter demanded sarcastically. "May I have your leave to shoot those creeps?"

Katz's Uzi answered. Aimed bursts of 9mm slugs killed the first two terrorist soldiers. McCarter leveled his M-60 and fired, sweeping the weapon's muzzle from right to left, then left to right. The heavy slugs scythed down the purveyors of terror.

A moaning Palestinian flailed his arms above him, beseeching Allah for mercy. But surcease came from the M-60.

Again, Yakov demanded the surrender of the Palestinians. No one answered.

"Too quiet..." McCarter hissed.

An RPG blasted through the dome. It sprayed fire over the gardens. Yakov motioned McCarter to shift positions as the Palestinians fired another rocket at the voice tormenting them with the fact of their defeat.

Dragging the weapons a few steps to the side, McCarter found a rip in the plastic. He surveyed the interior.

Palestinians crouched among the trucks. Carrying several OD green satchels, one of the Arabs dashed from group to group. Another gunman tossed the green satchels to his comrades. McCarter saw arms thrashing in green plastic sleeves. One Palestinian stood for an instant as he pulled on plastic pants, then dropped behind the crates protecting him.

"Look at that." McCarter had slashed a hole in the dome's plastic for Yakov.

"Hmm," the Israeli commented. He keyed his hand-radio. "Encizo, what do you observe?"

"They put on gas suits."

"Manning. Report."

The Canadian answered quickly. "Looks like they're suiting up for a counterattack. A chemical counterattack."

"Ohara. What do you see?"

"The leader. . .he moves near the airplane. . .he is in the airplane. What are your orders?"

"Yeah, General," McCarter demanded. "You want them to pull a gasser on us?"

Yakov issued quick commands. "Manning, Ohara. You and the Air Force men withdraw to the south end of the town. Encizo, you care for the prisoner. Carry him to the assembly point. Is that police officer with us?"

"Yes, he is here."

"All of you go. McCarter and I stay—"

"I'm not going to stay for the bedbug treatment!" the brawler protested. "I wanted to blast them from the first."

"And now you will. The rocket."

Twisting free the warhead's metal safety cap, Mc-Carter shoved the RPG-7 through the torn plastic dome cover. Palestinians in plastic suits scurried from cover to cover. One climbed into the plane. Another dragged a tow chain from the bumper of a truck and looped the chain around the landing gear.

"They're trying to get the plane out," McCarter said. "They're crazy. They think we're just going to let them fly away?"

Shouting in Arabic one last time, Yakov offered the terrorists their lives. None of them responded.

Starters whining, the DC-5's props turned, the engines spewing smoke as they warmed. The props created a wild artificial wind within the dome. Yakov and McCarter felt air blow from rips and holes.

"Tell me when, already!"

Yakov nodded.

Sighting on the drums of aviation fuel, McCarter squeezed the launcher's trigger.

A spray of flame lit the interior of the dome, the rocket's warhead ripping through the steel drums, simultaneously vaporizing and igniting the high-octane fuel.

A vast, churning maelstrom of flame, fanned by the cargoliner's propellers, consumed the cars and trucks and men. Fire blossomed around the cargo-liner. Its engines continued to whip the fire-storm, even as the plane's sheet metal buckled and melted.

Yakov and McCarter retreated from the furnace. Behind them, the highly volatile plastic of the dome burst into flame. Sheets of sizzling plastic fell into the inferno, while the updraft lifted more burning plastic high into the night sky.

Flaming pieces fell on other domes. The fires spread. Plastic melted, flowing in noxious-smelling rivers of fire. Big Top burned.

Waiting at the south entrance to the circus city, the men of Phoenix Force joked with one another and the Air Force personnel. Encizo pressed field dressings against the wounds of their one prisoner.

Sergeant Bragonier of the Texas Highway Patrol watched the flames rising from the abandoned fun metropolis.

"Those terrorists.... Why wouldn't they surrender?"

Yakov answered. "To live the rest of their lives in prison? I only promised them life. And to them, that means nothing."

28

Twenty-Nine Palms, California
Sunday
5:00 a.m.
(1300 Greenwich mean time)

POINTS OF LIGHT marked the darkness of the predawn desert. Through the executive jet's portholes, Able Team saw the purple band of the horizon tilt as the jet banked. The lines of the airfield's lights rotated to parallel.

"Twenty-Nine Palms Marine Corps Base," Grimaldi announced from the cockpit. "Estimated time of arrival, right now."

Deceleration pushed them forward against their seat belts. Landing lights blurred past. Leaving Nicaragua fourteen hours earlier, Able Team had changed planes in Honduras. After putting Maria and David in an ambulance, they had showered away the dust, sweat and blood of their attack on the terrorist training camp, then had flown north in the nightblack Air Force jet. They slept en route to the California desert.

The jet taxied to a Huey troopship. Grimaldi shut down the engines. He hurried to the door and threw it open. Cold desert air swept into the warm interior.

"Off, you three," he told Able Team. "You got people waiting for you."

"Thanks for the ride," Lyons said as he passed. "But next time, bring a stewardess along."

"Hey, joker. You got to get rank before you get privileges."

"I second the motion," Blancanales told Grimaldi. "Next time, we want some comforts."

"You want all that, run for office. Only real politicians get the comforts on Air Force planes."

"Don't insult us," Gadgets snapped cockily. "We may be with the government, but we work for a living."

"Then go earn your money!" Grimaldi shouted boisterously to them as they ran laughingly down the stairs. He watched Lyons, Blancanales and Schwarz run across the asphalt to the Huey. "*Adios*, gentlemen," he said quietly. "Go with God."

Lyons pulled his sports-coat collar closed against the chill blast of the Huey's rotors. Marines in desert-yellow camouflage fatigues and combat gear reached from the side door to help him in. He turned and pulled in his partners.

Marines jerked the doors closed as the helicopter lifted away.

A gray-haired man in a dark blue business suit motioned for them to join him on the folding bench. Under his conservative coat, he wore a Kevlar vest.

"I'm Torres," he said over the vibrating rotor-throb of the helicopter. "DEA. Last night we thought we had a standard drug plane coming in. Mexicans spotted it skimming the ocean in the Gulf of Cortez. They notified us, we got ready to intercept it. It was big—airliner size. We knew we had a multi-ton load coming in. When it crossed the border, our planes tracked it on radar. It dipped off the screens for a minute, then reappeared. But it wasn't the same plane.''

Around them, the teenaged Marines and their officer watched the four huddled men. One Marine nodded toward the strangers as he touched helmets with another Marine. "Spooks. CIA.''

"Nah, man. Just narcs.''

"Then what are they doing with us? And what's with the gear?'' He pointed to a box containing rifles, bandoleers of ammunition, other equipment. The second Marine shrugged.

"When the helicopter got back to where the DC-6 had landed,'' continued Torres, "he saw a group unloading cargo into trucks. He reported that he saw a semi and trailer and several pickup trucks. The last thing he said was 'rocket.' Then we lost contact.

"Our people reached the scene fifteen minutes later. They found the plane burning, and the wreckage of the helicopter. Blown out of the sky. That's when we called in the Marines. That was almost twenty hours ago.''

The Drug Enforcement Agency officer unfolded a map of the southern California desert. "We closed all the highways leading out of the area. We have the highway patrol, the sheriffs, the FBI, and all the local police departments helping us maintain the checkpoints and search the desert. We don't think they could have gotten the semi past us. It's only a matter of time."

Gadgets pointed to the city of El Centro, on the U.S.-Mexican border. "That's an agricultural area, right? How many trucks a day from the farms use these highways?"

"Today, none," Torres told him. "We're rerouting all through traffic."

"You get any description on the smugglers?" Lyons asked.

"The fire destroyed most everything. What our people did get, we'll get results on today sometime."

Blancanales leaned close to speak over the noise. "They had two planes. What about a third? Could they have transferred the load to another plane?"

"We have people at the El Centro airport and all the smaller airfields," Torres said. "Nothing got out."

"But the truck could be in the desert," Lyons commented.

"We have thousands of officers and soldiers looking for it. We even got a call from Washington. They're putting a spy satellite on the problem. It's only a matter of time. Let me introduce you to the captain."

Torres motioned for the Marine officer to join the huddle. A tall, angular young man, the captain had a face of sharp cheekbones and a resort-quality tan. His desert-camouflage fatigues and flack vest made his face and neck appear thin. But the muscles of his neck and forearms flexed wire-taut as he moved. He squatted on his heels and looked at the three strangers. He swayed slightly, riding the bucking and lurching of the helicopter. Blancanales got off the bench seat to squat next to the officer so that the group could talk.

"I guess you fellows are the specialists," the captain said, speaking with an East Texas accent smoothed by years of university attendance and officer training. He studied them for a moment, staring each of them straight in the face, appraising Blancanales, then Gadgets, then Lyons.

"Captain Powell," Torres told them. "He will be your Marine liaison. Equipment or transportation. Anything you need, you get it through him."

Powell glanced at the men's hands. His eyes noted the clothes they wore, what kind of shoes they wore, how they tied them. Gadgets and Blancanales extended their hands.

"Pleased to meet you," Gadgets told him, shaking his hand.

"Likewise."

"Wish you'd been with us yesterday," Blancanales joked.

"Yeah? Where was that?"

"Chasing these crazies—" Blancanales began.

"Can't say," Lyons interrupted.

There was a long pause as the captain waited for Blancanales to continue. When he did not, Captain Powell turned to Lyons.

"So why didn't you get your crazies yesterday, specialist?"

Lyons shrugged. "Maybe today."

"Well, we shall see," the captain commented.

"We'll be at the scene of the crime real quick." He grabbed the box and dragged it over. "Washington telexed your specifications. We've got boots and fatigues in your size, plus vests and weapons. Instructions are for you secret agents to look like soldiers."

"Great." Lyons took a plastic-wrapped bundle marked with his name. Able Team changed into the uniforms. Lyons put his shoulder holster over his camouflage shirt, then pulled on his flack jacket. Blancanales and Gadgets put their shoulder holsters in the box with their street clothes. They slipped their Beretta 93-R autopistols into the web-belt holsters furnished with the uniforms. They transferred magazines from their sports-coat pockets to the ammo pouches on the web belts.

"Never seen pistols like those," Captain Powell shouted to Blancanales. "Can you give me a look-see?"

Blancanales dropped the magazine from his Beretta and snapped back the slide. With the slide locked back, he glanced into the chamber to check it, then passed the weapon to the officer.

"Fancy...." The captain examined the fold-down left-hand grip, the suppressor, the fire-selector. He pointed to the triangle of three enamel dots.

"It fires three-shot bursts of semiautomatic," Blancanales said. "Effective rate of fire is about a hundred rounds a minute. But with the silencer, it gets hot fast. With subsonic loads, it's silent death."

"Secret agents and silent death, huh?" The captain laughed. He returned the autopistol.

Folding down the left-hand grip, Blancanales

demonstrated two-handed aiming. He pointed the pistol toward the door's Plexiglas port, sighting on the distant spinning disk of a helicopter's rotors. Against the violet of the western horizon, the far helicopter was banking over the landscape, dawn light flashing gold and red from the blades.

"I'll keep my point-four-five." The captain slapped the holster of the auto-Colt he carried.

Lyons tapped Blancanales's shoulder and motioned to him. Lyons leaned over, closing off the Marines and DEA man from his words. "We have to talk this over, we only got a minute—"

"Not here," Blancanales told him. "Got to wait until—"

Even as he spoke, the rotors flared. The Huey dropped like an elevator, to touch the sand without a lurch. Marines threw open the side doors.

Able Team ran through the helicopter's dust storm. The gutted hulk of the DC-6 lay on a pre-World War II airstrip. A bulldozer blade had recently scraped the sand and weeds from the cracked, buckled concrete. Several hundred yards away, only a decrepit and vandalized building remained of the old Army Air Corps base.

Unmarked cars and black-and-white patrol cars were parked near the wreckage. Marine Corps helicopters waited in a wide circle on the airstrip. Groups of soldiers waited.

Lyons looked over at the blackened hulk. "Think there's anything the lab teams could have skipped?"

"Don't know where else to start," Gadgets commented.

"Let's have a talk with the captain." Blancanales signaled Captain Powell. The Marine moved through the desert brush. Soot, like a black frost, tainted the weeds.

"Want me to take you on tour?" the captain asked. "The DEA helicopter went down a few hundred yards thataway."

"No thanks," Lyons told him. "One thing I'd like to know. What exactly was the story issued on what happened here? What do all these highway patrol, police and Marines think they're looking for?"

"Two stories. For the civilians, police, newspapers, television, all those people—a gang of smugglers shot down a Drug Enforcement Agency helicopter. Now what they've told us is that a gang of terrorists brought in a load of weapons. They used an RPG or SAM missile to bring down the DEA. So what's the *real* story?"

"That's it," Lyons answered. "Weapons."

Blancanales looked from Lyons to Captain Powell. He saw that the Marine officer did not much like serving the outside "specialists." A telex from Washington D.C. had instructed the officer to risk his life and the lives of all his troopers for three civilians who would not tell him the truth. Blancanales turned to Lyons.

"Tell the captain what the crazies have got," he said.

Lyons shook his head. "Classified."

Captain Powell looked at the ashes of the four-engined airliner. "They brought in a nuke for L.A.?"

Able Team did not answer him.

"Well, gentlemen," the captain began. "This trooper speaks English, Spanish, Arabic, and lately I been learning French. They sent me to atomic-warfare school. They sent me to chemical-and-biological-warfare classes. So what did I think when they assigned me to chase these terrorists? I thought, 'This is it. This is the Big One.' So you see? You got no classified secrets from me."

The walkie-talkie at the captain's belt buzzed. He keyed a reply, listened for a moment, voiced a confirmation. He grinned at the three men of Able Team.

"A semi-truck and trailer and two pickup trucks shot their way through a roadblock. Want to mosey on that way for a look-see?"

"Moving."

ACCELERATING to a hundred miles an hour on the straightaways, only slowing to sixty for the highway's few curves, the trucks hurtled across the desert. Early light glinted from the windshields. The two pickup trucks cruised ahead of the semi.

The Huey stayed parallel to the trucks, flying at chapparal height four hundred yards to the east. Lyons and Blancanales stood in the side door, watching the terrorist convoy. Behind them, Captain Powell and Gadgets huddled at the radio.

A streak of fire came from one of the pickups. The helicopter veered as the pilot reacted, reflexively gaining altitude and banking. Holding safety straps near the side door, Lyons and Blancanales watched the RPG flash beneath them.

A second rocket passed wide.

"What's going on?" Gadgets shouted. He handed Lyons and Blancanales headsets with microphones for the intercom.

Lyons slipped his on. "They're taking potshots at us with rockets."

"Okay, dig this." Gadgets briefed them. He pointed to the speck of another helicopter above them. "The colonel's directing this from up there. He's already filled me in. There's a road-blocking force two miles ahead. They will stop the trucks. The Marines in the other troopships will close the trap behind the terrorists. But the colonel's keeping the Marines back at combat distance. If anyone wants prisoners, or wants to take that truck intact, it's up to us. The colonel has instructions to destroy all of it, if we don't succeed."

"End of the road coming up," the captain interrupted.

"If the binary canisters get hit..." Blancanales cautioned.

Lyons broke in. "Wizard, radio him. Tell him to keep the firing away from the trailer. That'll give us a chance. We need information from those—"

"He already issued instructions," Gadgets interrupted. "He knows what's inside. No one will shoot up that load."

Able Team watched the action. Closing on a barricade of earth movers and semi-trucks with flatbed trailers loaded with telephone poles, the terrorist trucks hit their brakes, the semi fishtailing slightly, the pickups leaving the highway. As one of the pickups bounced along the shoulder, a terrorist stood up in the back and braced an RPG launcher on the cab roof.

The rocket flashed away. The warhead splintered poles.

But the barricade held, even when other rockets blasted a semi's cab and a highway-patrol car.

Swerving across the sand, the pickups cut across the desert, looking for a route around the trailers, tractors, and flaming car and truck. They met machine-gun fire from the doorgunners of the other troopships, forcing the pickups to wheel circles in the rocky chapparal.

Squads of Marines unloaded from the troopships to take positions on ridges overlooking the highway. Slugs from the Marine fire-teams kicked up dust around the weaving, bouncing trucks.

A lurch bucked a terrorist from the back of a truck. He rolled across the sand and rocks, came up still holding his Kalashnikov. Rifles and M-60s found him simultaneously, a barrage of high-velocity slugs ripping him to rags.

Surrounded, the trucks raced back to the semi. Unable to maneuver like the pickups, the driver of the semi slowed to a stop on the highway. Several gunmen jumped from the cab and the trailer, and took cover in a network of shallow gullies fanning out from a culvert. The semi and the highway's raised roadbed protected them on one side. They sprayed wild autofire at the Marines taking positions two hundred yards away.

The squads held their fire as they closed in on the terrorists.

"From the other side!" Lyons pointed at the semi as he shouted to the captain. "Put us down on the far side of the truck."

Nodding, the captain spoke into the com-line. The helicopter banked in a half-circle. One of the pickups protected the other side of the semi and trailer.

A terrorist rose to one knee with an RPG launcher on his shoulder. He aimed at the onrushing troopship.

Lyons leaned against his nylon safety strap and lined up the sights of his M-16 from the side door. He aimed for the terrorist's chest and sprayed him.

An instant before the terrorist jerked the launcher's trigger, twenty 5.56mm slugs punched into his chest, arms and gut, throwing him back. The launcher fell forward, the rocket exploding at the dead man's feet.

Flame and sand churned up and the low-flying helicopter lurched as it shot through the blast cloud. Lyons looked back. Nothing remained of the terrorist.

"Ready to get, you two?" Captain Powell shouted.

Blancanales snapped back his rifle's actuator and unhooked his safety strap. Lyons dropped the empty magazine from his rifle, then slammed in another.

"Cocked and locked!" Lyons shouted.

"Go!"

The helicopter hovered in the air. Lyons and Blancanales stood in the side doors, waiting for the skids to touch sand. Terrorist autofire hammered the

Huey's sheet metal. A round zipped through one door and out the other.

Lyons jumped the eight feet to the sand. He rolled on impact. Squinting against the dust and debris of the rotorstorm, he saw Blancanales drop from the other side door, landing in a crouch. Lyons signaled Blancanales to cover him.

Running wide of the terrorists around the pickup, Lyons sprinted for the highway. Bullets zinged past him. He threw himself down in sand and rocks. A hundred yards away, terrorists left cover to cut him off. Lyons sighted on a head, saw it spray bone and brains as a slug from Blancanales's rifle killed the man. The other terrorists dropped flat. Lyons sprayed a burst over them.

Now Blancanales ran. Staying low, pointing his rifle like a pistol, he fired two- and three-round bursts to keep the terrorists down. A Hispanic teenager in a windbreaker rose above the chaparral, putting his rifle to his shoulder. Lyons put a three-round burst through the boy's chest. Then the ground exploded around the terrorists.

A machine-gun team from Able's helicopter put down M-60 fire on the two terrorists lying prone in the open. Firing from a slight rise, the Marine gunner chopped the bodies apart with 7.62mm NATO slugs.

Blancanales advanced on the semi and took cover. He popped single shots at the few terrorists left firing from the pickup truck. One of the helicopter machine gunners turned his M-60 on the truck, slugs jackhammering the sheet metal and shattering the windows. Lyons sprinted to the highway.

As Lyons started up the banked shoulder of the road, a terrorist leaned from behind the semi cab, pointing an AK. Lyons dived. He heard slugs rip over him. He brought up his M-16, but did not aim at the terrorist's head or chest. He needed a prisoner.

Lyons sighted on the feet of the young gunman and fired a burst. The terrorist slammed to the asphalt, his Kalashnikov clattering away. The young guy screamed for what seemed like a minute, his cry of pain and shock rising and falling, becoming a choking wail.

Under the cab's chassis, Lyons saw another set of feet run up to the wounded man. The second terrorist went to one knee as he tried to help his wounded comrade. Lyons sighted on the knee and feet, fired again, then sprinted the last thirty feet to the truck.

The wounded kid had one foot gone. The other foot and ankle twisted at a right angle to his leg. The second man had a mass of flesh and splintered bone for a knee. His other leg—hit three times—flopped as he screamed and writhed. Lyons kicked away their rifles, jerked a pistol from one terrorist's holster and threw it aside. He leaned down to tear the shirt from the first terrorist. He knotted the shirt around the spurting stump of the young guy's ankle to slow the flow of blood. As he went to the second man—

"Down!" Blancanales yelled.

Lyons dropped flat.

A line of slugs punched into the truck's cab.

Blancanales fired. The terrorist autobursts stopped.

Marine sniper fire killed terrorist after terrorist.

Lyons and Blancanales lay flat on the asphalt, watching the battle around them end.

"It's all over," Blancanales said into his handradio.

Lyons gave his partner a punch in the shoulder. "We got the truck. And we got some prisoners. Mission accomplished."

A last terrorist popped up, a rocket launcher on his shoulder. He aimed at the trailer. Even as Lyons and Blancanales sighted their rifles on him, he fired. An instant later, the terrorist died, slugs from their rifles and unseen Marine snipers ripping him.

But the rocket roared through the sheet-metal siding of the trailer. Blancanales grabbed Lyons, half lifting him, half dragging him away from the truck. Lyons stumbled into a run. They dived for cover as the semi's tanks poured diesel fuel over the highway.

Blancanales saw flames rise from the truck. A gaping hole yawned in the side of the trailer. Blancanales grabbed his hand-radio.

"Marines! Pull back, get out of here! There's binary gas in there. That was a suicide shot."

Captain Powell's voice answered. "What about you, mister?"

"Save your men, we're gone—"

Lyons interrupted him. "Nothing's happening."

"What?"

"No gas, nothing."

"Maybe they missed the canisters."

All the weapon fire had stopped. Lyons broke cover and ran for the flaming trailer. Engulfed in flames, the two leg-shot terrorists screamed and thrashed. Lyons raced toward them. He reached into the flames. He grabbed one man.

Fire burned Lyons's hand. He lost his grip on the dying terrorist's uniform. He staggered back. Hearing no more screams, he abandoned the two terrorists to the flaming fuel. He ran to the trailer's doors.

Blancanales helped Lyons throw the doors open. Inside, daylight shone through the rocket holes. Lyons climbed into the trailer.

Near the doors, jackets and fast-food garbage littered the floor. The terrorists had left an empty ammunition crate and fiberboard RPG rocket packing tubes. At the far end of the trailer, fifty-five-gallon barrels lined the trailer walls. The rocket blast had torn open several barrels, spraying fluid over the interior of the trailer.

Lyons read the stenciling on the sides of the barrels. Some said lubricating oil, others said detergent. Lyons scooped some of the fluid from a ripped-open barrel and smelled it.

Oil? He looked at the fluid, saw a faint shimmering. He smelled the handful of fluid again, then tasted it.

Oil-fouled water.

"They faked us."

WHITE EXTINGUISHING FOAM glistened on the semi. FBI and DEA pathologists snapped photos of the charred terrorists on the highway. Other agents transferred the contents of the trailer to a government truck. Marines policed the area, collecting weapons and ammunition. One Marine found a terrorist's foot, still in its shoe. He tossed it over to the pathologists.

Gadgets prepared a taped report for Stony Man. Blancanales and Lyons went through the pockets of the terrorists, finding only loose cartridges and folding knives. The terrorists did not wear uniforms, only street clothes: black slacks, khaki pants, T-shirts, windbreakers.

"They're all Hispanics," Lyons commented to Blancanales.

"The team we hit down south was multiracial," Blancanales added. "For L.A., I would've thought they'd have blacks and whites and Asians."

Captain Powell strode up to them. "What's the body count on your terrorists? You get them all?"

"This was a decoy operation," Lyons told him. "I don't think any of these losers are the creeps we're chasing."

With his boot, Lyons turned the bullet-shattered head of a young man. His face showed fistfight scars. Lyons crouched, looked closer.

"Hey, specialist," Captain Powell joked. "Interrogating that one is a waste of time."

Two tiny tattooed teardrops marked the left cheek of the corpse. Lyons picked up the dead man's hand and studied it. On the back of the hand, in the space between the thumb and the first finger, he saw another tattoo: a tiny Christian cross. Both tattoos had been done in blue.

Searching the body more closely, Lyons found a third tattoo. On the dead punk's neck, in the stylized script of a street-gang's graffiti, he saw the inscription: 23rd.

"Wrong, Captain. I recommend you take a street-warfare class. Because this *vato* just told me where we're going next."

THE FBI HELICOPTER LIFTED AWAY as Able Team jogged to the waiting unmarked car.

Across the street, a group of Chicano teenagers in undershirts and khaki pants, some of them wearing stocking caps despite the midday sun, watched the helicopter soar from the vacant lot. They drank beer, shared cigarettes. The teenagers watched the three men with attaché cases get into the waiting car.

Spray-painted gang symbols marked every building and street sign on the block.

"The chief sends his regards," Detective Bill Towers of the LAPD told Lyons as they left the side street to merge with the traffic of Whittier Boulevard. "Of course, he doesn't know anything about you. Never saw you. Never heard of you. Never wants to hear of you. But he wishes you luck."

"How're things going for you?" Lyons asked the middle-aged officer. "Notice you're not wearing your uniform. Is that just for today? Or did you make the grade?"

"Detective Towers now."

"You with us today?"

"Yup."

"Who else?"

"I don't know the FBI. They're not my kind of people."

"We got no federal backup? I thought—"

"Chief won't do it. As it is, he's risking his head sending two of us."

"Two of you? We ask for backup and we get two men?"

"Hey, we're both gang detail," said Detective Towers of the same police force that had trained Carl Lyons. "We know the boys. The Bureau's giving you your backup. We're giving you the names and addresses. It's the most we can do. Christ, do you know what's going on in this city? You're asking us to help you wipe out some lower life forms, when we can't even make arrests."

Detective Towers drove through side streets. "We come up to a jerk who's gone berserk, we can't even administer tear gas without a class action suit. 'PCP Psychos of the Slums Versus the People of California.' A billion dollars punitive damages for restricting a doper ax-murderer's right to self-expression."

Lyons laughed. Blancanales leaned forward, asked Towers, "How long you guys known each other?"

"We were partners for a while," Lyons answered.

"Still get the nightmares," Towers taunted.

"You both sound exactly alike," grunted Blancanales. "Same humor. Or is it that all cops sound alike?"

"What do you mean, humor? Who's joking?" Towers continued. "I'm telling the truth. Just the facts, ma'am."

Another turn brought them to an industrial area. Parked cars and pickups lined the street. A group of workers clustered around a catering truck. Detective Towers right-turned into a parking lot. He honked his horn. A rolling door cranked up, its steel squealing on wheels. Towers continued into the windowless plant, then pulled the parking brake and turned off the engine.

Men and cars waited. Agents dressed as cabdrivers sat in taxis. Others wore delivery-company uniforms to match their panel vans. Two others were dressed as nondescript citizens with economy cars. Three others sat on the hoods of two customized cruiser cars. Those agents, Hispanics, looked young; they wore the khaki pants and T-shirt uniform of the local gangs. The windows of their cars had been tinted almost black.

"See? You got backup, Carl." Towers pointed to the agents around them.

"Great. Fantastic. Starting right now, Towers, don't use my name, all right?" Lyons turned to Gadgets and Blancanales. "Standard nicknames? Politician, Wizard?"

"And what's your name?" Towers asked.

"He's Hardman One," Blancanales told him.

Towers laughed. "You work Vice, now? Sounds like a porno movie."

"How about Ironman, then?" Blancanales suggested.

"Ironman's okay," Lyons told them. "Time to work."

Disguised agents gathered around them. Using their code names, Able Team introduced themselves to the agents. They looked over the cars and special equipment. All the agents had questions. Lyons finally interrupted the confusion.

"Gentlemen!" He pointed to Detective Towers, used only his first name. "Bill there has the basic information for you. Neighborhood maps, names, addresses. Criminal records, gang charts. Three of you will chauffeur me and my associates around. Others will be tail units and observers. If we don't put you in motion, wait. Just wait for a call. Maybe we won't even need all of you. And one last thing. This is life and death. We can't brief you on all the details, it's classified. But remember, it's life and death multiplied by between ten and twenty million times. If we can't kill the problem, it goes public."

Lyons and Towers ducked into a heavily customized low-rider car. They sat in the back, screened from view by the tinted windows. Blancanales took a taxi, Gadgets a panel van. Gadgets stowed his radio and electronic gear in the van, then threw in an M-16/M-203 rifle/grenade launcher.

The agent masquerading as a gang punk turned to Lyons. "All right, Señor Ironman. *¿Dónde vamos?*"

"This address—"

CARS AND TRUCKS CROWDED THE CURBS. Lyons saw LAPD black-and-whites, a fire-department car, a van from the coroner's office, and mobile news units of several television stations. Neighbors stood on their lawns and porches, watching the officials and sightseers gawk at the house.

A stripped car rusted on the house's lawn. The RPG had hit near the corner of the house, to the side and below the window of the front bedroom. A police officer and a fire-department investigator looked through the three-foot-wide hole. They continued through the house to the backyard.

The low-rider agent cruised slowly past. Even with the smoked windows, Lyons stayed low in the seat, only his eyes and the top of his head above the chrome window trim. Towers briefed him.

"Call goes out this morning, 'Shots into house.' Units didn't even bother checking it out. These gangs shoot at each other all night long. Then someone in the neighborhood describes a rocket blast, so finally a unit gets interested. One of the guys who shows up is a Nam vet. He knows what it is right off. Someone shot a rocket through the house, and the target was sleeping on the other side of the wall. Biggest piece the coroner's office found was an arm. Next we get your call from the desert—"

"What did you tell the media?"

"Told them it was a gas explosion. I should tell you that we know who did it. We even got the house staked out. But I can't figure how it ties in with the crazies from down south."

"Neither can I. But we'll find out."

Their driver followed their instructions to another neighborhood. They left a boulevard, went down a side street, turned again. Police barricades blocked the next street. Towers reached from the window of the customized car to show his department identification to the officers manning the roadblock.

"Giving the brass a firsthand view," he told them.

"When do we bust that bimbo in the house?" one officer asked.

"Who knows? We're waiting on permission from the Supreme Court."

Laughing, the officers pulled aside the barricades. Their driver eased ahead. The car rounded the corner and again they slowly cruised. The street appeared normal, but no one sat on their porches, no children played in the yards. Front doors stood open. Inside the houses, Lyons saw the gaudy rectangles of color televisions, blaring their commercials at nobody. In one window, he saw the silhouette of a SWAT rifleman.

"There," Towers pointed to a rundown stucco house with several cars parked in the driveway. They slowed. Lyons gazed at the one-story dwelling. Someone in the living room secretively pulled aside a blanket curtaining the window to watch them pass.

Lyons glanced down each side of the bungalow, saw the rickety fences and overgrown bushes. He caught a glimpse of a slat fence at the back property line.

"The PD got a monitor on the phone?" Lyons asked.

Towers nodded. "Nothing in or out. Maybe they've got a radio."

Lyons leaned forward to the low-rider agent. "Take it around to the other side of the block." Then he keyed his hand-radio. "Politician, I'm in front of the house."

"I'm on the other side. I figure we'll go in over the back fence."

"More or less. There in a flash." Lyons clipped the radio to his belt. He checked the Python he wore in his shoulder holster, touched the two speed-loaders in his left-hand jacket pocket. It was war in the city again, where real life was at its most heavily peopled and most dangerous, where real death came at its most corrosively pointless and, in situations such as those that Able Team had been created to deal with, at its most unavoidable. Lyons had faced this many times and felt the same way many times. He wanted to make a difference, to make life possible for good people. And sometimes he felt he did make a difference, that he had, in Mack Bolan's words, extended the limits of the possible.

He opened his briefcase and took out the modified Colt Government Model and two flash/concussion grenades. Extra magazines of .45 ACP hollowpoints went in his pockets. Towers watched him straighten the grenade cotter pins. Lyons hooked the levers on his belt and pulled his buckle a notch tighter to hold the levers snug.

"Those things'll make trouble for us," Towers told him. Their bizarre-looking low-rider gang car eased through another police barricade.

Towers impersonated a video reporter's solemn monotone, "In yet another cynical attempt to circumvent the constitutional rights of the people of this city, the Los Angeles Police Department ordered a B-52 strike on Boyle Heights."

Lyons laughed, tapped the grenades. "Don't sweat it. These are deluxe models. They got silencers."

CROUCHING AT THE SLAT FENCE, Lyons peeped through. He saw a yard cluttered with car frames and body panels and greasy engine parts. Weeds grew three feet high. Plywood covered the window of the garage that stood at the back of the house. Aluminum foil papered one bedroom window, newspapers another. The window in the back door had been spray-painted red. He heard no sounds from inside the house.

"Can't make it through all that trash," Lyons muttered to the SWAT officer next to him.

"Neither can they," the officer added, pointing to three other SWAT officers who waited in the yard, watching for movement.

At the far end of the slat fence, Blancanales also peered at the building. He looked across to Lyons, shook his head, no. He crawled into the neighbor's yard and peered through the rotted wood of the side fence. He gave Lyons a thumbs-up sign.

Lyons pushed aside vines to look into the other neighbor's yard. A redwood fence overgrown with honeysuckle separated an immaculately landscaped garden from the junkyard next door. Lyons keyed his hand-radio.

"Politician. I can do it. But I need to dodge down one more yard before I go over the back fence. They could spot me here."

"This side, the garage blocks their view. I'll make it to the side of the house and wait for you. Moving."

Blancanales pressed the barrel latch on the front grip of his M-16/M-203. He slid the 40mm barrel forward and chambered a round. He secured the action and set the safety.

"THAT TEAR GAS?" a SWAT officer asked him.

"Multiple projectile," Blancanales told him. "Twenty-seven double-oughts."

"Could hurt someone."

"That's what it's for."

Blancanales tore aside chicken wire and irises, pushed through decayed wood into the adjoining backyard. He walked along the side of the garage. When he came to the corner, he crouched, then chanced a look through the chain link separating the yards.

A bedroom window blocked with aluminum foil overlooked the driveway where he crouched. Farther along the house, he saw a small bathroom window. Blancanales paused to plug the earphone into his radio, then continued on his belly.

Trash cans and geraniums screened him. He crept in the direction of the bedroom window. A three-foot-high chain link fence and four feet of space separated him from the window. He twisted onto his back in the high weeds. He lay there with the M-16/M-203 over his chest, listening.

He heard footsteps crossing the house. They went to the window above Blancanales. He heard the rustle of the foil that papered the window. The footsteps returned to the other side.

Blancanales listened for several minutes. Again, he heard footsteps crossing and recrossing the house. His earphone buzzed. Lyons spoke.

"I'm on the other side, under the kitchen window. I'm going to crawl across the driveway to the kitchen door. What do you hear?"

Whispering into the radio, Blancanales watched the window above him. "I hear two people walking around inside. One walked to the front, the other's—the other one's going to the front too. Now's the time."

"Snake time. Over."

Blancanales keyed the hand-radio again. "Wizard, Mr. Wizard. You there?"

"Monitoring you. What do you need?"

"Just keep the PD back. Don't let them gas the place. We didn't bring gas masks."

"Got you. Doing it."

Footsteps paced the house. They stopped. Then steps crossed the house again. A voice shouted.

Autofire ripped the quiet. Burst after burst punched from within through the walls of the house. A second weapon fired from inside, then footsteps pounded the floor. Slugs smashed the window above, showering Blancanales with glass and tinfoil. The weapons inside the house sprayed the entire area, lines of slugs breaking windows and chipping slabs of stucco off the walls of the neighboring houses.

Blancanales held his assault rifle/grenade launcher by the pistol grip and the magazine, with his left forefinger on the M-203 trigger. He was concerned for Lyons. He tensed to leap for the shattered window.

Suddenly an arm came through the window. The shirt-sleeves had bloodstains past the elbow. Blancanales watched the hand grasp the window frame, then a blond young woman climbed out, pushing through the remaining glass shards. She wriggled upward to reach for the guttering of the roof. Her shoulder supported a slung AK-47 with folding stock.

Don't look down girl, Blancanales thought, looking up at her. *Don't look and you're a prisoner.*

The blonde looked down. She saw Blancanales beneath her. As she struggled to lower the AK and point it at him, Blancanales pulled both triggers.

A simultaneous blast and full-auto burst caught her in the pit of her stomach. The storm of high-velocity 5.56mm slugs and the twenty-seven .30-caliber lead balls tore through her body at an extreme angle, severing her spine where her neck met her shoulders. She died even as the impact tumbled her out of the window.

Blancanales stepped over her body and squatted at the side of the house. Another set of feet pounded across the house to the window. A young man with dark features and curly black hair leaned from it.

"Rosemarie! Where—"

Blancanales thrust the M-16/M-203 up under the guy's chin, the muzzle throwing back his head. Stunned, the guy fell back. But Blancanales's vertical launch of the rifle did not have the force to shock him unconscious. As Blancanales leaped up and scrambled through the window with a powerful push of his arms, the man reached for his AK.

Blancanales advanced fast enough to sight on the reaching arm and fire a burst. The young man

screamed incoherently as he rolled on the floor,
clutching his suddenly boneless arm. Blancanales
stepped over him and began to loop plastic handcuffs
around his ankles and wrists. The man contorted
with agony when Blancanales touched the shattered
arm.

"Ironman!" Blancanales shouted. His radio's earphone buzzed incessantly. He ignored it, shouted.
"Ironman, where are you?"

"I'm okay, I'm all right," Lyons shouted back.

Jerking the Beretta 93-R from his shoulder holster,
Blancanales left his autorifle under piles of newspapers and crept through the house. He kicked doors
open, moving fast but cautiously. He did not stop to
check the closets or bathroom or front bedroom.
Lyons might need help.

Slipping into the kitchen, Blancanales saw a bullet-riddled wall. A breeze swirled through the holes, carrying away the dust of broken gypsum and stucco.
He continued to the back door and stepped out.

Lyons got up off the asphalt driveway, brushing
stucco and wood chips from his coat and hair. Immediately Blancanales saw what had happened.
When the terrorists spotted Lyons, they had simply
fired low through the wall. Lyons had dropped on his
back to sink beneath the house's concrete foundation, which had sheltered him from the wild autobursts. Gouges and holes in the asphalt driveway
indicated about sixty shots.

"You know what it's like to have bullets passing
about one inch past your nose?" Lyons asked him.
"Don't answer. I'll tell you—"

"Joke later. I got two, there might be more."

With their pistols, they searched the house. The wounded man was still screaming in the back bedroom. They ignored him. They checked the front rooms, the closets, finally the bathroom. They found the family.

A teenaged boy, a matronly woman, and a preteen girl lay in the bathtub, their hands tied behind them, their throats slashed. Lyons could only stare at this horror, one of the regular horrors in the barrios of his native city.

"The teenager must be the gang punk," Blancanales guessed. He too knew Los Angeles. "He's the one who supposedly killed the other gang kid with the rocket last night. I guess that's his mother and sister."

"Looks like the crazies considered his action a breach of discipline. Unreliable, die. Witnesses too."

Their hand-radios buzzed again. "Hey! This is the Wizard! You two all right?"

"We got them," Blancanales replied. "One prisoner—"

"The boys in blue are coming in."

Lyons spoke into his hand-radio, his voice neutral, slow. "Keep them out for another few minutes. They don't want to be involved in what's about to happen."

"Will do, over." Gadgets buzzed off.

"Interrogation?" Blancanales asked.

Lyons nodded. They went into the back bedroom and stood over the bleeding terrorist. Lyons saw a sheath knife at the young man's belt. He took it. Blood crusted the handle.

Throwing the prisoner over on his face, Lyons cut the plastic band around his wrists. "Hold him down, Pol."

Blancanales hesitated, looking from the wounded, crying prisoner to the knife in Lyons's hand. The ex-Green Beret looked into his partner's face, saw calm eyes that were beyond hate or compassion.

"No time for drugs or qualified interrogators, Pol. There's more of them out there somewhere. They came to Los Angeles to murder every man, woman and child in the city. And he knows where the gang is."

"Do what we got to do."

Lyons looked down at the prisoner. "Where are the others?"

The terrorist looked up at them, his eyes wide with pain. But he smiled. "I say nothing until you bring lawyer. I know laws of your country. I want lawyer. I no talk until I get rights."

"Where are the others?" Lyons repeated.

The Palestinian pursed his lips to spit at them.

Lyons stepped on the shattered arm.

SUNSET FLASHED from the thousand-faceted glass towers of downtown Los Angeles. In the clear spring evening, Blancanales searched the windows and rooflines of the warehouses and sweatshop tenements surrounding the complex of garages.

From his position seven stories above the street, he spotted concealed FBI and LAPD teams watching the garages. He saw the officers freeze in their places as a terrorist crossed a garage roof. Blancanales stepped back into shadow and keyed his hand-radio.

"One man. I say we do it. I'm ready."

Five floors below him, Lyons lay on top of several filing cabinets, watching the terrorist pace the flat tarred roof. The wide-shouldered Hispanic raised binoculars to scan the windows and fire escapes of the buildings overlooking the garages. The motion raised his shirt to reveal an autopistol in his waistband. Lyons spoke into his hand-radio.

"Want me to hit him?"

"Whenever you're ready. Wizard, you monitoring?"

Gadgets spoke from the back of the FBI taxicab on the street. "You guys do what you want, I'll watch this door."

Sighting through the four-inch-wide space at the top of the windows that backed the filing cabinets, Lyons put a silent burst of .45 ACP hollowpoints into the terrorist's chest and head. Lyons buzzed Blancanales. "All right, Politician."

"I'm ready."

"Then go."

Easing to the edge again, Blancanales peered down to the rooftop. He saw the terrorist sitting on the tar roof, the binoculars beside him. The terrorist stared up at Blancanales. Blancanales whipped his head back, hissed in his radio. "Get with it! He's looking at me, I think he saw me."

"I doubt it. He's dead."

"You already hit him?"

"You said to...."

"Okay, I'm going down." Blancanales clipped his

hand-radio to the belt of his battlesuit. He gave the knot of the rope a last check, then threw the coil over the edge.

It dropped to the roof below. He snapped the hook of his rappelling harness onto the rope and walked backward off the ledge.

Bouncing smoothly down the brick-and-concrete face of the old office building, Blancanales counted the floors. As he passed the fourth row of windows, he kicked hard and let go of the rope. He arced over the tangle of barbed wire and landed on the soft asphalt of the roof. He stepped out of his harness and crept across to the motionless terrorist.

The terrorist stared sightlessly at the darkening sky. A vent pipe behind him kept him upright. Blood drained from wounds to his chest and head.

Blancanales took the pistol from the dead man's belt. He inspected the automatic, a Parkerized Browning High-Power with a defaced serial number. He put the loaded pistol in his thigh pocket. He searched the terrorist for any other weapons, but found only a knife.

He dragged the dead man across the roof to a skylight and wedged the body into a space between the skylight housing and a fan unit. Then Blancanales crossed the roof to the access door. He listened. Far below him, he heard voices and a power drill, but no steps on the stairs.

Lyons rappelled down the building, swinging over the wire. Like Blancanales, he wore a black battlesuit that carried his gear and weapons. Within seconds, he joined Blancanales at the door. They both looked up to see a SWAT officer pull up their rope.

"Well, this is where your interrogation has brought us," murmured Blancanales, looking across the darkening rooftops.

"So here we go...." Lyons slipped his modified Colt from his web-belt holster. Crouching, he eased the door open slightly. He held the silenced Colt Government Model straight up.

A Kalashnikov came at his face. For a long instant, he looked into the muzzle of the automatic rifle, even as he rolled back, bringing the Colt down to point at the chest of a moon-faced Hispanic woman.

"Carlos? ¿Donde...?"

Her eyes glazed too long at the black-clad commando rolling at her feet. Her hand grabbed for the pistol grip of her AK. Lyons silently snapped a hollowpoint into her sternum, shocking her back. She bounced off the frame of the door, staggered forward, her eyes wild, unbelieving. She dropped.

Feet scuffed on the stairs. Lyons grabbed the dead woman and jerked her out of the doorway. Blancanales grabbed an arm to help drag her aside. Lyons closed the door and stood to one side. Feet came to the door.

A young man walked out, an AK slung over his shoulder, looking neither to the right or left. Lyons shot him in the back of his head. The terrorist fell flat. Lyons had done his job again. Who else would do it? Who else *could* do it? His enemies were hardcore, and Lyons responded to that fact in the way he knew best. Justice by fire, as a model not of judgment but of execution. Carl Lyons, like his fellow avengers forged in the caldron of Mack Bolan's war everlasting, was truly a man of the hour.

They waited. The sounds below them continued, the power drill, a hammer on wood, voices. They heard no other feet on the stairs.

Lyons slipped through the door and looked down the stairwell. A flight of steel steps cut through the framework of girders and braces that supported the roof. The stairs went to a platform against the wall, then the stairs continued along the wall to the floor.

When they descended, Lyons and Blancanales would be exposed every step of the way.

Lyons motioned his partner forward, pointed down. Blancanales flattened himself beside Lyons. Creeping down the first several steps, they watched the activity below them.

Men and women worked on a row of twelve commercial vehicles. Some were trucks, others vans. The open trucks carried full flatbeds of fifty-five-gallon drums. Hoses linked the drums in two series, one series red drums, the second blue. The two hoses met at a pump. An electronic supply-shop van contained only two drums and a pump. The flatbed truck immediately below Lyons and Blancanales carried a load of ten drums, five of each color.

Holes had been cut in the sheet-metal roofs of the vans. A nozzle protruded from the roof of one van. The flatbed truck had a nozzle standing six feet above the top of the cab.

They watched the work in progress. Chicano teenagers did the drilling and wiring and assembly of the pump and nozzle units. The terrorists—Europeans, an African, an Arab, Hispanics—directed the work. The leaders, two Europeans and an Arab, stood at a workbench checking details on a map. They called other terrorists to them and issued instructions. The terrorists then relayed the instructions to the workers.

Across the huge garage, a terrorist fitted a young Chicano girl into a plastic suit. She put on a gas mask, then plodded over to the others. She modeled the suit, raising her arms, touching her toes, then climbing into the cab of a truck. She took off the gas mask to let the others try it on.

As the two men of Able Team watched, the leaders rolled up their map. They walked through the maze of trucks and shipping crates, shaking hands with the Chicanos and other terrorists. One of the three, the Arab, stood up on the flatbed truck and began to speak in Spanish.

Lyons turned to Blancanales for a translation. Blancanales hissed a few words at a time.

"A glory for the International Revolution. . . an act of solidarity with the Socialist Peoples of the World. . . cut the throat of Zionism. . . revenge for Vietnam. . . revenge El Salvador. . . smash the Golden Arches. . . ."

"What?"

"My little joke," whispered Blancanales. "It's the standard speech. Seems it's going to happen sometime tonight."

"Why the speech now?"

The Arab concluded his speech to applause and shouted slogans. The two European leaders called to him in Russian. He gave the group a final closed-fist salute, then jumped off the truck and hurried after the other two. They went to a new Mercedes sedan.

Blancanales pushed himself up the stairs, out of view from the floor. He keyed his hand-radio.

"Wizard. We're watching from the roof door. *Todo es bueno*, this far. We have three of them coming out the front door. In a Mercedes. They're the leaders. Ask the liaison to have them followed. They just gave a farewell speech to the local help and the other foreign crazies. The leaders are on their way home."

"What do these three look like?" Gadgets asked. "I'll get the descriptions back to Stony Man immediately."

Getting a hand signal from Lyons, Blancanales paused. Lyons hissed to him, "They're sending out a kid with a walkie-talkie."

Blancanales passed on the warning to Gadgets and the FBI teams, then quickly described the three leaders. He rejoined Lyons.

They watched the leaders. One European and the Arab waited in the luxury car. The other European set his briefcase on the hood and snapped it open. Stacks of U.S. dollars filled the interior of the case. He took out two bundles and put them in his pockets. He closed the briefcase, then got in the car.

The earphones that Lyons and Blancanales wore buzzed. "This is the Wiz. The kid saw something. Give you even odds it's hot time. Over."

Blancanales lifted his hand-radio to his lips to whisper. "Acknowledged. Watching and waiting. Over."

A Chicano tough closed and barred a door behind him. He rushed to the three leaders, leaning into the Mercedes. One of the three leaders called the other terrorists over. All work stopped.

Lyons slipped out his silenced Colt. Blancanales grabbed Lyons's wrist and cautioned him, "We can't have a firefight. Not with all the binary gas down there."

They saw the terrorists and Chicanos run for their Kalashnikov rifles. One terrorist called up to the roof door. Lyons and Blancanales froze. The terrorist called out again in Spanish.

"He wants to know if the ones on the roof have seen any police," Blancanales whispered to Lyons.

When the terrorist received no answers, he rushed up the stairs. Like silent shadows in their combat suits, Lyons and Blancanales crept back up the stairs, then pressed themselves into the blackness of the corners of the access housing. As the terrorist passed between them, they took him, Lyons jamming his Colt to the back of the terrorist's head.

The single .45 hollowpoint ripped away the top of his skull. Blancanales shouldered the corpse through the roof door and dumped it.

The Mercedes' engine revved. Flat on the stairs again, Lyons and Blancanales watched the three terrorist leaders in the German luxury car race from the garage. AK muzzles in the car's windows flashed flame.

Autofire from the police and FBI punched into the car. Slugs whined through the interior of the garage, bouncing off the roof girders, hitting the line of trucks and vans.

The Mercedes screamed backward, tires smoking, into the inner regions of the garage. Its brakes screeched.

Blancanales hissed into his hand-radio. "Stop the shooting! There's at least a thousand gallons of nerve gas in there!"

"Ah...we got a problem, Pol," Gadget's voice announced. "There's been a breakdown in fire discipline."

"Get them to stop!"

Lyons shoved his older partner. "Let's go. Now's our chance."

Below them, the terrorists and Chicanos lined the front of the garage. They sprayed fire in long unaimed bursts, expending magazine after magazine of cartridges.

Lyons went first, cat-footing swiftly down the stairs. He watched the backs of the terrorists. None turned to him. He stopped eight feet from the floor. From his position, he looked over the vans and trucks to the terrorists. He pointed his Colt with both hands, bracing his wrists on the safety railing. He glanced up to Blancanales and gave him a nod.

Blancanales raced down. He passed Lyons to take cover behind a truck. He aimed his Beretta, then gave Lyons a three-finger signal.

Lyons aimed at the back of a terrorist's head. He counted to three. On three, terrorists dropped.

Lyons and Blancanales had snapped shots into the backs of the terrorists' heads, ignoring the Chicano gang punks. Lyons killed three of the nearest terrorists, then aimed a shot at the head of one of the leaders.

The European moved as Lyons squeezed off the shot, the .45 hollowpoint gouging the back of his head. He jerked around, stunned. He saw Lyons and raised his Kalashnikov.

A hollowpoint slammed into the European's chest. He died as he fell. But the other two leaders spotted Lyons and dived for cover. Shouts directed the gang to fire at the commando on the stairs. Lyons snapped the last rounds from the pistol into the scrambling terrorists. He saw two fall as he dived down the stairs, AK slugs punching the concrete wall behind him.

A Chicano with a goatee and tattoed arms rushed across the garage, searching for Lyons. He found Blancanales and took a three-shot burst in the face.

"They're between the trucks!" Blancanales shouted to Lyons. "If you hit the binary gas, everybody dies!"

Lyons jammed a magazine into his Colt. He held the pistol in both hands and crouch-walked between the vehicles. He heard boots running on the concrete. He went flat. He looked under a truck and saw high-heeled boots. He waited until the Chicano stopped, then put a single slug into one of the boots.

The Chicano girl fell to the concrete, clutching the stump of her ankle. She saw Lyons pointing the Colt at her head. She opened her mouth to scream. A hollowpoint punched through her right eye. She died with her mouth open.

On his feet again, Lyons went around the truck and passed between tailgate and the workbenches. In the clutter of tools, he saw a long-handled roofer's hatchet. A loop of leather passed through the end of the handle. Lyons grabbed the hatchet and jammed it under his belt.

Blancanales dodged between trucks and vans. The terrorists now divided their fire between the SWAT teams outside and the two commandos in their midst. High-velocity AK slugs punched through the sheet metal of the vehicles.

Blancanales saw Lyons and sprinted to him. "We have to get out of here! They don't care where they shoot. As long as we're in here, they'll keep shooting. And they'll hit the nerve gas. It'll take out most of downtown L.A."

"Don't sweat it, it's liquid," Lyons told him. "Look at those sprayers. Unless they turn on the sprayers, it'll stay liquid. No gas, no dispersal, no problem."

To prove his point, Lyons pointed to a fifty-five-gallon drum in the back of a van less than three feet from where they crouched. A bullet had drilled through the steel. A pale green liquid trickled to a puddle on the floor of the van.

"But no matter what," Lyons said, "we stop them here."

Jerking the hatchet from his belt, Lyons jumped into the back of the van and hacked the wires from the pump unit. As he returned to the garage floor, he motioned Blancanales to follow him. Lyons peeked out from behind the van, then crept on to the next truck.

One step behind him, Blancanales covered Lyons while he climbed into the back of the truck. A chop of the hatchet severed the power line. Blancanales darted from the truck's tailgate to its cab, to check out the remaining terrorists and Chicanos at the other end of the garage.

AK fire shattered the windshield beside Blancanales. He ducked back. In seconds he stepped up onto the next truck's diesel tank, jumping up from it for a quick look through the windows.

At the end of the line of vehicles, he saw terrorists working on the largest flatbed truck that carried a total of ten drums. Blancanales saw one Chicano with a wrench. Three others struggled to pull on plastic suits and gas masks. The two surviving terrorist leaders—the Arab and the European who carried the briefcase full of cash—directed the desperate efforts. The others held Kalashnikov rifles, watching for a commando or SWAT team attack.

He saw a Chicano swing his AK around. Blancanales dropped as a burst ripped past. He went to Lyons.

"They're making a break for it in the biggest truck."

Lyons took a flash/concussion grenade from his battlesuit. The grenade would produce a brilliant flash and an overwhelming shock of noise, but without shrapnel. Blancanales took a concussion grenade from his rig.

"One behind, one in front," Blancanales said, pointing out the target zones. "Then we rush them."

"Ready to go," Lyons told him. He jerked the cotter pin from the grenade.

They heard the truck's engine start up.

"So are they! On three, one—" Blancanales counted as he went to the cab of the truck to chance a look out. Shots zipped past his head.

He looked back at Lyons, who was at the rear of the truck with his arm back for a throw. "Three!"

The truck lurched into motion as the grenades arced across the garage. The concussion grenades bounced on the concrete and rolled. The Mercedes' engine roared. A terrorist in a plastic suit and gas mask, a wrench in one hand, Kalashnikov rifle in the other, stepped onto the back of the revving truck. Another terrorist in a plastic suit jumped on too, struggling to fit her gas mask over her long hair.

Swinging wide to avoid the slow truck, the Mercedes accelerated for the open door. It passed over Blancanales's grenade.

Two explosions rocked the cavernous garage. The first grenade jarred the Mercedes, but did not stop it. The luxury car continued out the door. The second blast stunned the two protective-clothed terrorists on the back of the truck. They fell among the steel drums of binary agents.

The truck did not stop. Lyons sprinted across the oily concrete, hurdling a corpse. He gained on the truck.

The hatchet dangled by its loop of leather around Lyons's arm. A last lunging stride and he grabbed the stake truck's vertical sidebars, threw a foot to the steel of the flatbed. Lyons hung on as the six-wheel diesel rattled and bounced into the street.

Sprawled on the flatbed, a plastic-clothed terrorist gazed at Lyons. His rubber-gloved hand groped for a Soviet Kalashnikov.

On the industrial street outside, Gadgets crouched behind a bullet-pocked taxicab. He had heard the grenade blasts and seen first the Mercedes, then the flatbed truck hurtle from the auto-shop doors.

Bullets sparked from the pavement as LAPD and FBI riflemen sprayed the vehicles. They had very poor sight of their targets, the dusk a blue half-darkness that dimmed outlines. Above the gray corridor of warehouses and machine shops, the mercury-arc streetlights flickered with low-power greenish light. It would be five minutes before the lights came up to full brilliance.

The Mercedes took several slugs through the windshield. The car failed to hold its tire-screeching hard right turn. The luxury sedan sped out of control at Gadgets. He stepped back as the car missed his taxicab to sideswipe an FBI van. The Mercedes shuddered to a stop in a crunch of metal and sparkling glass.

Gasoline stink choked Gadgets. He saw two FBI agents, in business suits and holding Uzis, run back from the wreck.

"Clear out!" one agent shouted. "There's gas all over the place."

An Arab terrorist staggered from the Mercedes, autopistol in one hand, briefcase in the other. Gadgets raised his M-16/M-203.

The flatbed truck roared past. The Arab terrorist with the briefcase raised his gun hand to try and grab the truck's side rails. Gadget touched the trigger of the M-16. He saw Lyons. He could not risk firing.

Now the Arab terrorist saw Lyons. And Lyons saw the terrorist raising his pistol.

Gadgets watched Lyons produce the hatchet. Lyons's right arm swept out in a hard backhand as the terrorist in the street pointed the autopistol.

A hand and pistol flew into the air, the ax head continuing past the blood-spurting stump to cut into the terrorist's face. Lyons jerked the ax head free, then threw himself back onto the speeding flatbed.

Flames rose in a wave; the gasoline glistening on the streets had ignited. Gadgets sprinted for the maimed terrorist leader and dragged him to safety. An LAPD officer gave the prisoner first aid. Beyond the flames, Gadgets saw the truck speed away. Blancanales ran up to Gadgets.

"That truck's loaded with binary," he said.

The engine of an LAPD black-and-white roared. The uniformed officer behind the wheel threw it in reverse to save it from the fire. Gadgets ran to the officer driving and pointed past the flames.

"That's the nerve gas. We have to stop it."

Blancanales ran to the passenger side of the police car and jumped in. "Go, man. Straight ahead."

"Oh, Jesus and Mary," the officer intoned in sincere prayer.

Gadgets scrambled into the back seat. "If you don't want to risk it, get out."

"Did I say no?" The officer punched the gear lever

into drive and stood on the accelerator. They were slammed back in their seats as the squad car roared through the wall of flame.

In the back of the truck, Lyons kicked at the barrel of the AK automatic rifle. He missed, found himself sprawling between the fifty-five-gallon drums of nerve-gas agent. He was involved in a one-on-one combat. As the truck swayed, then screeched around another corner, Lyons tried to get to his feet. The terrorist in protective plastic clothing swung the rifle. Lyons kicked again.

The rifle flashed. Slugs screamed into the evening sky. Lyons lunged up. He brought the hatchet down on the terrorist's arm. Blood sprayed over the slick white plastic of the guy's protective coveralls.

Lyons threw himself on the terrorist. With one hand he shoved the Kalashnikov rifle aside, with the other he brought the ax head down to bury its steel deep in the terrorist's helmeted forehead. Behind the glass of the eye lenses, the gas mask filled with blood.

Clawing over the dying terrorist, Lyons searched for the other protective-clothed terrorist. He found her unconscious between two barrels. He let the hatchet hang by its strap as he reached for his silenced Colt.

Sirens and flashing red, blue and orange lights gained on the truck. Lyons saw the black-and-white squad car. With backup so close, he now had the luxury of taking prisoners.

He grabbed the woman's autorifle and threw it from the truck, then searched her quickly for other weapons. Plastic handcuffs on her wrists and ankles immobilized her.

Hands held a Kalashnikov from the cab's passenger-side window. Slugs sprayed the pursuing black-and-white one bullet shattering the windshield. The patrol car swerved. Other police squad cars and FBI sedans followed the truck, crowding the avenue behind them.

Crawling behind a drum, Lyons heard wild shots from the passenger window smash a barrel on the flatbed. Greenish fluid sprayed. If a next shot hit the other barrels of nerve-gas agent. . . .

Lyons grabbed the AK from the dead terrorist and jumped up. He slashed the cab with a line of high-velocity slugs. He emptied the magazine.

Out of control, the heavy truck leaped onto the curb. It snapped off a light pole, then another. The impacts knocked Lyons against the drums. The load shifted. Fifty-five-gallon drums banged into one another. Glass exploded.

The squad car smoked to a stop as the truck crashed deep into a furniture showroom. Throwing tables and chairs and couches aside, the truck slammed into the back wall of the huge room. The cab was crushed.

Gadgets and Blancanales ran through the shattered plate-glass windows, their weapons held ready.

"Get back!" Lyons shouted. "Call for decontam!"

"You all right?" Blancanales called out.

"I'm great." Lyons climbed off the truck, the unconscious girl in the plastic coveralls and gas mask over his shoulder. "I even got a prisoner."

They jogged over the sheets of glass. Lyons threw

the handcuffed terrorist onto the sidewalk. "I tell you, guys, these terrorists can't cut it in a straight fight."

Gadgets and Blancanales stared at Lyons. Blood covered him. The hatchet swung from his right elbow, the blade crusted with clotted blood.

Business-suited FBI agents and SWAT officers ran from the arriving cars to peer into the showroom.

They saw Lyons, and they winced. They watched him as they spoke quietly to each other.

Lyons looked around at the agents and officers. "Hey, why are all these people staring at me?"

Gadgets laughed. "Because, man...you are five different kinds of scary, scary dude."

Blancanales turned away. He knew how Carl Lyons felt in this condition, perhaps even better than Lyons knew himself. The warrior has no taste for bloodshed; unlike the jackal, who thinks his power increases when he takes human lives, the warrior feels no power when he ends lives.

Only sadness that it must be so.

29

Virginia

Sunday
1:30 p.m.
(1830 Greenwich mean time)

APRIL ROSE LAY NAKED on the bed. The night breeze from the open window played over her sweat-glistening limbs.

Inhaling deeply, she drew in the cool pine-scented air. She smelled the sweat of the man beside her. His hand rested on her thigh.

Absently her fingers smoothed his dark brow. His eyes were closed. He slept fitfully. But April's eyes were open. She watched his face, savoring the last few minutes with Mack Bolan.

He had arrived at the Farm only hours earlier, from his personal assault on the freighter. It had almost terrified her to see him so distraught, as he leaned over a computer console in Kurtzman's ground-floor office, his shoulders stooped with fatigue, grunting through a question-and-answer routine with The Bear. And Aaron did not like Mack's condition either.

As soon as April entered the room, Kurtzman said to her, "This man needs time out."

Bolan snapped back, "I don't need time out. I need to crash. Two hours."

"Can you? Can you sleep?" she said.

He spoke, but not in answer to her question. He did not look at either of them. His voice had the throatiness that comes from the tight edge of tragedy.

"Too much young blood wasted," he said.

She took his hands in hers. "Come on, Stony Man. Let's see if you can."

He freed his hands to keypunch coordinates into the computer, then called back to Aaron as he left, "The Air Force and Coast Guard are screening all the ship and air routes. They may come up with something on the San Francisco attack any minute. Call me."

April and Bolan walked down the hall to the wide carpeted staircase. Together they climbed to the second floor.

The farmhouse had three above-ground floors. The second held the command staff's quarters. Without speaking, the two veterans of the sacred battle fires moved along a paneled corridor to a steel door.

April took a plastic card from her belt and inserted it into the slot in the doorframe. The door slid open. Mack stepped in first. April followed, and the door closed automatically, locking with a faint click. She rotated a rheostat at a control panel just inside, bringing on a mellow glow from a bedside lamp.

Mack showered. She went to an eighteenth-century Chippendale chair in one corner of the room. Sitting back in its lush upholstery, she slipped off her shoes and waited.

When Mack left the shower, water still dripping from his sinewy frame, he walked to the barred window and operated a complex sequence of electronic locks that lifted the bulletproof glass.

He stood at the open window, hands at his sides, staring into the night.

April came up behind him and raised her hands to his shoulders. "You going to sleep standing up?"

"Done it before."

"Well, not tonight," she whispered. "Sit on the bed."

He sank to the edge of the quilt-covered mattress. He ran his fingers through his hair, rubbed his eyes. Behind him she knelt on the bed to massage his shoulders.

Her slender fingers found the tension in the big man's back. She rolled and pressed the muscles.

"You're all knotted up."

"I'm cringing out, April."

Her hands stopped. She rested her head on his shoulder, her long auburn hair falling forward over his chest. He turned his face to the softness of her throat.

Their lips met. After a moment, she broke away from the long, deep kiss to pull off her sweater in one motion.

He stood and looked down on her. He seemed taller to her, almost forbidding in the faint light. She shuddered under his stare, his eyes for a moment emotionless.

Turning away, he started toward the window, but stopped. He stared into the night, then shook his head suddenly. He came back to her, put his face on her belly. She felt his breath warm on her flesh.

She unsnapped her jeans. Mack's hands took over, finally pulling her Levi's and silk panties off her legs.

At last he lay beside her, holding her long smooth form in his arms. If she were a weaker woman, he might have crushed her. But she enjoyed his strength, matched it.

Their lovemaking became more than the urgent meeting of two bodies, more than a craving for abandonment and release.

They exploded into infinity, April again and again.

Now, she watched him sleep.

Soon he would leave again. How could she slow time?

"Mack...Mack. Look at me."

He opened his eyes. She wished she had not spoken. What she saw frightened her.

She saw love and pain and need. But something other...something awful.

Yet she held his gaze.

All at once, the image of ancient charred forms that were locked together in desire arose from her memory. She had seen them years ago at the Roman ruins of Pompeii; the petrified remains of men and women who—only seconds before being buried beneath the molten lava of an erupting volcano—had sought salvation in sexual love.

Is that what she saw now in those eyes? Was he, she wondered, clinging to her because she represented life to him—and hope—in the face of certain death?

He began to take her again. He thrust into her with

mounting passion and force. His body beat against her, crushing her full breasts against the contours of his chest. Did he seek life and hope in her? Because this could be the last time?

She raised her hands above her head and surrendered herself to him, arching her back. Her hands fell to his shoulders and clawed at them.

Spasming, she wrapped her legs around him, clung to him, held him as his body heaved.

Their storm of desire broke upon them, and their ecstasy came in waves.

Again, he slept. And again she watched his face, wishing that they could be together forever.

The buzz of the speaker-phone shattered he quiet. Before she could move her hand, Mack reached across her to activate the phone.

"Yeah?"

Aaron's voice filled the room. "Sorry to wake you. They sighted the freighter. It entered U.S. waters, on a straight line for San Francisco. It won't respond to Coast Guard challenge. You want to fly to the West Coast?"

"Bomb it."

"What? Who?" Aaron asked, not understanding.

"Anybody who's got bombs. Drop them on it."

SURROUNDED BY PHOTOCOPIES AND MAPS, Kurtzman relayed Mack Bolan's command to California.

Another voice blared from the radio monitor. Kurtzman ignored a "call waiting" light on his telephone to take notes as a data-systems specialist at Eglin Air Force Base reported.

"Got a definite boogie for you. We spotted the flight cutting straight south from Miami. We tried to raise them on the civilian band, let them know they were about to violate Cuban airspace, but nothing. No radio response, no flight plan at the airport. Nothing."

"Did it land in Cuba?"

· "Affirmative. Seems they've put in a new airstrip in the Sabanas—"

"Where?"

"Archipiélago de Sabana-Camagüey. A line of tiny islands along the north coast of Cuba. I don't know if it had anything to do with who you're watching for, but I thought I should get the info to you."

"You thought right."

Clicking off that frequency, Kurtzman listened as Gadgets Schwarz, en route from Los Angeles with Able Team, reported on the interrogation of a prisoner.

"His name's Saeb Shyein. Most definitely Number Ten low-life. FBI's got an Interpol tag on him for atrocities against Christian children during the Lebanese civil war. He's out of that game now. The Ironman pulled a hack job on him."

"What do you mean?" Kurtzman asked. "Is he wounded or what?"

"Like I said, Lyons did a hack job on him. With an ax. Before we let Shyein go into surgery, we debriefed him. He was liaison man between a crazy Japanese Yoshida and a Cuban named Munoz. A Russian named Fedorenko dreamed up Hydra. Then Munoz and Yoshida put it together.

"Fedorenko did the brainwork. Munoz specialized in the equipment and scheduling. Yoshida recruited the crazies. Now dig—what's going on is a mutiny. The Russian just wants to pull this off for the KGB. Same with the Cuban. They worked out this scheme to hold the cities hostage, but they would back off if the President surrendered.

"Not this Yoshida, Aaron. He's been running around the country telling the kill teams to kill the cities even if the President gives in. He intended to kill millions of Americans all along, no matter what the Russian and the Cuban thought.

"Yoshida recruited crazies loyal to him, and he intended to kill Fedorenko and Munoz, then take over Hydra. We know this absolutely, from our interrogation. Fedorenko and Munoz got wise, however. They've stayed out of sight. But Shyein says Yoshida's leaving Miami for Cuba tonight, so if you want to get him, scramble."

"How much information did you get?"

"I got an hour's talk on tape. And there'll be more. There's some interrogators waiting for him to come out of surgery."

"When will you get back?"

"Real quick. How are things on the Farm?"

"Crazy. Be ready to take off as soon as you get here."

"Man, we have broken Hydra. Time to cut some slack—"

"Talk to Mack about Hydra. Like I told you, be ready to go. Over."

Kurtzman grabbed the phone finally. "Stand by,

Grimaldi. It's all coming together. All at once. The Air Force, the interrogations, our people. It's going to happen. Stand by—''

Slamming down the phone, Kurtzman gathered his notes. He read through his scrawls, recopied the details. He checked each point, referred to the maps and high-altitude reconnaissance photos.

The evidence pointed to a small harbor and airport complex in the Sabana islands. The DC-5 of nerve gas that was destroyed in Texas had flown from an airstrip in the Sabana islands. The aircraft from Miami had returned to that same airstrip. The interrogated Cubans and Palestinians all mentioned the base. And now, one of the terrorist captains said the leaders of Hydra would be found on the Sabanas.

But the decision was not Kurtzman's. He did not command the Stony Man forces. The decision was Mack Bolan's.

Phoenix Force was rested by now, but Able Team would be going in tired.

Picking up the phone again, Kurtzman punched the code for April Rose's private quarters.

MACK BROKE THE CIRCUIT. He got up and dressed. April watched his precise, efficient movements.

It's as if he'd been awake all along, she thought as he buckled his belt. In his combat suit, he was a fighting weapon again, no longer her lover. She lowered her head. She could not bear to see him leave her for war.

She listened for the steel door to slide open as he departed.

"April...."

Looking up, she saw him standing over her. He sat on the bed and took her in his arms.

"...I'm not good with words," he started.

"You don't have to be."

He leaned forward and kissed her hair.

"Goodbye," she said, pushing him lightly away from her.

As the steel door slid open, she called out, "Mack?"

"Yeah?" he said, glancing back. He was already gone, his spirit running ahead to the hellgrounds.

She gave him a wry smile, though it cost her. "Stay hard," she said huskily.

THEIR FACES GRAY WITH EXHAUSTION, their bodies bruised and cut and aching from days of nonstop action, the men of Able Team and Phoenix Force waited for Mack Bolan to brief them.

Bolan's eyes seemed to bore through them, as if their souls stood exposed to his examination. But it was he who felt exposed.

For Bolan, these nine men operated beyond the law, guided by their duty and honor to their country and the decent people of the world. They were sanctioned in their fight by the President.

Now he took them beyond that sanction.

This would be a descent into Hell. A strike against the Hydra in its own pit. Who would live?

The leaders of Hydra had risked war to attack the United States. Now Bolan risked war to exterminate the Hydra. Even those of his men who survived the attack—what nation would accept them? Bolan had no illusions about how the international press and the United Nations would react to an attack on Cuba.

There would be no discussion of why, no examination of the evidence against Cuba and the Soviet Union, no consideration of unknown millions of innocent lives saved by these nine men.

They would be international criminals. Men without countries. Doomed to wander the world with false identities. Never to know peace again.

The jackals would never let his men live.

Yet even if it meant the death or lifelong exile of these brave men, Bolan could not avoid this fight. In several days of unrelenting counterstrikes, they had broken Hydra's attack on the United States—in the Atlantic off New York City and Washington, and in Florida, in Texas, in Nicaragua and in Los Angeles.

But the Hydra leadership had eluded the vengeance of his warriors. The body count included terrorists and mad technicians from perhaps every country in the world, but the killer squads had been only pawns—weapons to be used in the attack.

They had not cut off the head of Hydra. And like the monster of mythology, Bolan knew Hydra could grow many more. A thousand killers could again snake through the borders of the United States, more ships with cargoes of poisons could dock in the harbors, more planes armed with devices of mass murder could chance American radar.

But if he struck the head now, at least he bought his country time to prepare for the next attack. He did not doubt that there would be more attacks.

Nothing shook the hold of the KGB on Russia and the other socialist slave states, not famine, not war, not revolution.

While the United States existed, and while the distorted thinking about the United States existed in the minds of the Russians and Eastern Europeans, the KGB would wage unrelenting war. War against faith. War against hope. War against prayers for freedom.

The KGB had killed twenty million Russians to suppress all thought of freedom. Why would they ever hesitate to murder their enemies?

Bolan could not turn from the battle. Even if the pursuit of Hydra to its Cuban lair meant his death, and the death of his men.

Pulling down a map of Cuba, he touched a pointer to the tiny, unnamed island in the Archipiélago de Sabana-Camagüey....

30

Archipiélago de Sabana-Camagüey, Cuba

Monday
5:00 a.m.
(1000 Greenwich mean time)

FOR THE FIRST TIME, they would fight together. All the men of Mack Bolan. The three men of Able Team: Gadgets Schwarz, Rosario Blancanales and Carl Lyons. The five of Phoenix Force: Yakov Katzenelenbogen, Rafael Encizo, Gary Manning, David McCarter and Keio Ohara.

Now they waited a mile from a Cuban beach. The black-painted power cruiser bobbed in the swell, the offshore breeze bringing the scents and stink of tropical night from the island.

The island of Hydra. They stared into the predawn darkness, studying the positions of the lights. From time to time headlights streaked through the palms.

Encizo supervised the inflation of the landing rafts. He checked the internal pressure and the tension of the black neoprene by touch. He positioned and secured the heavy gear.

The others attended to their equipment and weapons. This would be an assault against a hardened base. The terrorist army of Hydra held the advantages of sentries, electronic alarms, prepared defenses. The men of Stony Man knew what they faced. They prepared themselves for a one-day war.

All wore heavy Kevlar and trauma-plate combat armor. Encizo and Blancanales carried M-16/M-203 hybrid assault-rifle/grenade launchers. Bandoleers of magazines for their assault rifles crisscrossed bandoleers of 40mm grenades.

Manning and Gadgets carried lightweight CAR-16 commando rifles. They packed gear for defeating electronic defenses. Gadgets carried a long-distance radio for communication with Jack Grimaldi and Stony Man. Manning carried a device for jamming the terrorist frequencies. Once they attacked, that device would sever the island's communications with Havana and the Soviet army battalions garrisoned there.

To save weight for a load of Viper rockets, which would eliminate concrete obstacles, Ohara also carried a CAR.

McCarter and Lyons manned the heavy weapons. To provide sustained full-automatic fire, both carried M-249 machine guns. Unlike the reengineered M-249 that Lyons had used to annihilate the Hydra ranks in Nicaragua, these weapons had no modifications. The short-barreled folding-stock weapons had been designed to provide deadly fire-support for airborne assaults. McCarter and Lyons each carried a thousand rounds of belted 5.56mm shells.

For pistols, Encizo, Manning, Gadgets and Blancanales had opted for silenced Beretta 93-R autopistols. Though the Italian weapons required subsonic cartridges to fire without a report, the pistols would fire full-power 9mm loads in combat.

Disdaining the 9mm cartridge of the Beretta, Carl Lyons carried a modified Colt Government Model. Reengineered for silence, the bulky, awkward weapon satisfied his demand for a first-shot-every-shot knockdown shock power. He also carried a 4-inch Colt Python with X-head hollowpoints.

Yakov chose a familiar Uzi. For a backup weapon, he carried a snub-nosed Smith & Wesson 9mm revolver. Almost identical to the .38 revolvers carried by police officers in the United States, the Smith & Wesson fired the same 9mm cartridges as his Uzi.

Ohara chose for his backup pistol a Ruger eight-inch-barrel revolver with the same caliber as his commander's AutoMag—.44 caliber.

Carl Lyons, the ex-LAPD detective, surveyed the armament and intoned his familiar sentiment to the others. "Long life through superior firepower."

Unfamiliar with Lyons's cynical humor, Yakov commented quietly, "Considering your occupation, I would not think that concerned you."

"Be cool," Gadgets told Yakov. "The Ironman's jiving. What's with Mack?"

Blancanales went to the door of the cruiser's cabin and glanced inside. He saw Mack Bolan writing by the glow of a tiny blue-tinted penlight.

Bolan folded the pages, placed them in an envelope, and gave the envelope to the 60-year-old Cuban expatriate who owned and captained the black cruiser.

Then he slung an M-16/M-203 over his shoulder and joined his men.

"Ready?"

They all nodded. He repeated his self-imposed directive. "The leaders of Hydra are on the island. We know that much. We don't know where they are. We only know what they look like—from the photos in the files. But we have to get them.

"Photo reconnaissance organized by Kurtzman and Grimaldi from satellite sources shows no villages on the island, only the Hydra base. The prisoners we interrogated say civilians are never allowed to approach or land. Therefore, we have no local people to worry about.

"Every one of the terrorists must die. It's the only way to make sure we take out the leaders. You all understand?"

His men nodded.

"Then let's go."

In silence, they lowered the landing rafts into the ocean. They stowed their gear and eased into their positions.

Taking the first paddle stroke, Bolan led his men toward the dark beach.

Behind them, the power cruiser started its muffled engine and left the warriors alone with their fate.

YOSHIDA PACKED HIS FEW POSSESSIONS: his European-style clothes, his one silk kimono, the old samurai sword set that a Yakuza lord had given him.

A boat waited to take him from the island. But

first, before he departed for Libya to seek sponsorship for a reborn Hydra, he would joke.

He wore a black shirt, black pants, black gum-soled shoes. He wrapped his head and face with a black cloth. In his years as a Yakuza assassin, dressing in the *ninja* suit-of-night shadow had become a ritual for him. Even when circumstances forced him to wear European fashions while he made a kill, he had imagined himself clothed in black.

A silenced MAC-10 submachine gun waited on his bed. He reconsidered his choice of weapons. Now, in the last hour of night, he would demonstrate his strength and cunning, his silence, his skill in horror.

He would kill them. But with an American weapon? A .45-caliber submachine gun?

Images filled his mind. What would create vivid memories? Bullet-punched corpses? The report would simply say they had been killed by gunfire.

No, he would not use the firearm. He wanted to kill in such a way as to shock even those accustomed to and calloused by death. Murder that would scream from newsprint pages. Murder that would lead to a fear of Yoshida that neither time nor distance could diminish.

Unfolding the silk cloth wrapping his sword set, he picked up the shorter of the two swords. In feudal times, samurai always wore two swords, the longer *daimo* blade for fighting in the open, and the *shoto* blade for killing in confined spaces. The *shoto* also served for seppuku, when the samurai ritualistically killed himself.

Yoshida slid the *shoto* blade from its sheath.

Twelve inches of the finest steel alloyed with the holy steel from the nails of the destroyed temple of Nara. A long-dead swordsmith had forged the blade under the light of a rising full moon. Yoshida saw his own face reflected in the shine of the blade.

"With this, I cut my name into their dreams," he said aloud in Japanese.

He packed the MAC-10 in his suitcase, and took the *shoto* into the night.

Standing for minutes without moving, perceiving every sound and movement in the tropical night, he memorized the positions of the compound's sentries.

Several guards paced the walls. Another crouched in a corner, sneaking a smoke. At the far end of the compound, a group of Russian and Cuban intelligence officers argued bitterly about the failure of Hydra.

Let them talk. Soon I will head another Hydra, thought Yoshida. *While they debate and reconsider, while they examine the details of the American victory, while they petition the bureaucrats of the Kremlin to grant permission to make more war, I will make mountains of corpses.*

But first, he thought, *I must make nightmares for the Russians and their Cuban servants.*

Silent as a shadow, Yoshida moved through the night, passing the apartments of the terrorist army's sleeping officers. At the end of the apartment block, a guard paced, with every step his slung rifle tapping against a bandoleer's buckle.

Yoshida stood behind the sentry for minutes as the

young soldier's eyes swept the darkness for intruders.

Two soldiers came from the compound gate. The sentry called out to them in Arabic, asking for a cigarette. As the sentry went to take the cigarette from his comrades, Yoshida crept from the apartments to the wall.

Again he waited. Motionless in a shadow, he listened as soldiers passed, their boots crunching gravel not an arm's length from him. Above him, on top of the wall, other sentries paced.

He heard the sentries on the wall talking. Easing to his full height, Yoshida grabbed the handholds on the concrete wall. Effortlessly and silently, he pulled himself to the guardwalk.

He saw two sentries only ten steps away. He moved like a snake as they talked and laughed. He slipped over the wall and dropped to the soft earth.

A sentry stopped talking. A flashlight's beam swept the cleared perimeter around the compound. But the sentry saw nothing moving in the camp litter and the stubble of weeds. Yoshida waited until the guards above him returned to their banter, then moved on.

Staying against the wall, he continued to the south corner of the compound. Headlights swept the parade grounds between the compound and the private residences of the senior officers. A carload of KGB guards searched the darkness with a spotlight. Yoshida froze until the car rolled past.

Another insult. They quartered Yoshida with the common soldiers while they and their KGB bodyguards enjoyed the luxury of private showers and catered meals. Or perhaps they kept him in the compound from fear.

The thought amused Yoshida.

The thought that they could jail him within the compound. The thought that the sentries would keep him within the walls. The thought that their Russian guards would protect them as they slept. . . .

He heard sentries on the wall above him. He waited until they passed, then snaked across the compound perimeter to the asphalt road. His nightsuit black melding with the black asphalt, he crossed on his belly.

On the other side, the roadside sloped down to a culvert tangled with vines and dead wood. Yoshida heard insects buzzing; he smelled stagnant water and rot.

The culvert paralleled the road. Crawling along the side of the ditch, Yoshida's senses ranged in a hemisphere around him. He perceived every sound, every movement, every faint variation of gray against black.

A rooster crowed from behind the compound's mess hall. Yoshida looked up at the sky and read the time by the position of the stars. Less than an hour remained before the sky grayed with dawn.

But in that time, they would die.

At the far end of the parade ground, he left the culvert and entered the jungle.

Like an island of bourgeois surburbia within the Cuban jungle, the senior officers' small houses clustered in the center of a rolling lawn. Mercury-arc streetlamps lighted the lawn. A chain link fence circled the grassy area and houses. A gated road connected the officers' park to the camp.

KGB bodyguards manned the gate. At the end of the road, other KGB men paced around the small houses.

The lawns required no patrols. Pressure-sensitive sensors ensured no intruder could enter without silent alarms alerting the guards.

But the Soviet designers of the camp, in the tradition of their nation's Asian intrigues, provided for the escape of the leaders. Rising to his full height, Yoshida walked soundlessly through the jungle to the only unguarded, unprotected route to the commanders—their own emergency tunnel.

He had paid gold for the information. Now he used it. Cutting through the palms and tropical brush and vines, he came to a slight rise a hundred yards from the officers' houses.

Tangled vines and years of tropical debris covered the steel-plate hatch. He scraped the matting away with his hands. Though the East German engineer who designed and constructed the tunnel had told him no alarms or booby traps guarded the hatch, he took every precaution. He whisked away the leaves and soil, then felt along the edges.

Rust flaked away. No one had touched the hatch in the two years since its installation. He hooked his fingers under an edge and lifted it away.

He lowered himself into absolute darkness. Cold muck closed over his feet. He found the inner door. Made of sheet metal set in the tunnel's concrete, the door would withstand high-velocity bullets and small explosive charges.

But it also had a lock.

By touch, he inserted a spring steel wire into the keyhole. The German engineer had told him the make of the lock and the approximate date of manufacture. Yoshida needed no key. In less than two minutes, he jerked the steel door open.

The noise of the hinges echoed in the tunnel. Yoshida felt along the frame of the door for an alarm trigger. Again, he found everything as the German had described.

The German had explained to Yoshida the Russian reasoning behind the tunnel's lack of guards and alarms. If the commander posted guards on the tunnel, then the guards knew of the tunnel. The guards could betray or assassinate the commander. Therefore, no guards. If the commander placed alarms on the door, guards would monitor the alarm circuits. Eventually, a rat or rainwater or a short circuit would trigger an alert. Then the guards would know of the tunnel.

With Russia's history of betrayal, intrigue and assassination, only secrecy satisfied the paranoia bred into the Russian architects. After the construction, the Russians assigned the East German engineer to projects in Ethiopia and Yemen. After six months of work in the deserts, the German wanted out. Yoshida's gold bribed border guards, and bought the young engineer a new life in Kenya.

Yoshida followed the tunnel until he came to the second door. His fingers found oil on the hinges.

Again, the spring steel wire opened the lock. He eased the door open, infinitely slowly. More darkness, but now he heard sounds.

He eased through the door and felt around him in the pitch darkness. He found himself in another concrete shaft, with handholds and footholds set in one side.

Above him, he heard faint voices and movement.

He went up the steel rungs and pressed his ear to the underside of the trapdoor. He heard footsteps in another part of the house. Waiting, listening, he heard a conversation, but only one voice.

Somewhere in the house above him, Fedorenko raved to himself. Yoshida slipped out the small *shoto* blade and clenched it between his teeth. He put the top of his head against the trapdoor and gave it a slight push.

No resistance. His head emerged under a rug in the darkness of the Russian commander's bedroom. Soundlessly, Yoshida crept under the rug and into the room.

Curtains muted the blue white light of the security lamps outside. In the bluish glow, Yoshida slipped through the bedroom and stood at the door.

On the other side, Fedorenko paced. He ranted in Russian as if speaking from a podium. Sometimes he was whining and pleading.

Yoshida understood very little Russian. But like all graduates of the Soviet camps, he knew every Communist cliche and slogan. Fedorenko spoke of "inevitable socialist victory," "the relentless progress of history," "the future." Only after he had

listened for a minute did Yoshida realize that Fedorenko was reliving the past.

Munoz the Cuban had once persuaded Fedorenko
to teach Yoshida chess. Fedorenko had explained the
rules and the movements of the pieces. He told
Yoshida he saw the chess game as a metaphor of the
world struggle. For the same reason Fedorenko
studied the victories of great chess masters, he
studied history, "to find pathways to victory," the
Russian explained.

On the other side of the door, Fedorenko relived
that scene.

"History guides us. The lesson of history dictate
my actions. To create the future."

Yoshida had ended the chess lesson by sweeping
the board with a thrash of his hand. Neither the
Cuban nor the Russian ever attempted to force their
philosophies on him again.

Silent, smiling at the thought of the joke he would
play, Yoshida waited. He held one of the Russian's
shirts from the back of a chair; he had it wadded in
his hand.

Fedorenko finally stepped into the bedroom. As he
reached for a pack of cigarettes, Yoshida jammed the
wadded shirt deep into the Russian's mouth and
threw him facedown on the bed.

To reduce his prisoner's struggles as he sat on him,
he twisted the Russian's arms backward until they
broke. Then he tied Fedorenko spread-eagled to the
four corners of the heavy bed.

In his bad Russian, he rebutted Fedorenko's lec-
ture of months before. "Forget the past and future.

History tells us nothing. There is no future.''

Then he played with Fedorenko's body, yet left the quivering, choking mass of raw flesh and agony still living. Whoever found the mutilated, dying Russian would never forget the image. Yoshida started toward the bungalow where Munoz slept.

As he slipped out the Russian's door, he heard a blast of automatic fire.

A VIPER ROCKET punched through a line of parked trucks. Gasoline and oil flashed into flame. The Cuban and Palestinian sentries shot blind into the night with their Kalashnikovs. The burning gasoline had silhouetted the sentries for McCarter....

Lying atop the wall behind the stacked corpses of the sentries, McCarter stroked the trigger of the Fabrique Nationale M-249, sending precise two- and three-round bursts into the compound below him.

Every burst killed. In the confusion of the inferno and shooting and running, the guards died before they spotted the English machine gunner firing from the wall walkway.

Kalashnikovs flashed from the windows of rooms and barracks. Slugs pocked walls, killed running sentries, zipped away into the night. Midway along the compound wall, Encizo crouched in the protection of a sandbagged guard post. With his M-16/M-203's 40mm grenades, he methodically eliminated the officers. The skills of all the years of an adult life came to the fore in Encizo in this latest assault on his native land. A lifetime of trying to live right, by the mind and by the sword, both at once, inextricably, had led to these strange moments beyond all sanction. He put a single grenade through each room's window, alternating fragmentation with white phosphorous.

In the chaos and noise, the flat metallic "whang" of the grenades from Encizo's M-203 went unnoticed by the defenders. They continued firing at shadows.

A group of Palestinians, some in their underwear, one in floral print pajamas, dashed from the barracks and took cover in the darkness between the officers' apartments. As one man surveyed the scene around them, McCarter dropped him with a three-shot burst to the head.

Others saw the flash of the M-249 and sent a storm of AK fire at the Englishman. Slugs tore into the dead men that McCarter used as sandbags. He stayed down as the jackals emptied their Russian autorifles at him.

Encizo put a phosphorous grenade in their midst. Clawing at the specks of metallic fire burning into their bodies, the terrorists thrashed in the dirt. Around them, white phosphorous flamed and smoked. McCarter, going to war with the same high and moral aim that lead to victory in three wars for England this century, gave each terrorist the mercy of a careful burst.

But McCarter and Encizo commanded only one side of the compound in their fields of fire. Officers and soldiers who evacuated the smoke and flames of their quarters found shelter between the barracks and the camp offices. Assembling their men in squads, officers organized a defense.

An officer in midnight-blue silk pajamas buckled a bandoleer of magazines around his chest and took a squad of Al Fatah fighters to the rear of the compound. Dodging from cover to cover, from doorway to doorway, they reached the back of the buildings without a casualty.

All the security lights had gone black. Only the intermittent flares of gasoline flames lit the area. The officer scanned the open ground and the wall for comrades. He saw no one. The attackers had killed every fighter standing guard. He called one of his soldiers forward and directed him to dash across the open ground to the base of the wall.

Only seventeen years old, inexperienced in battle, the soldier hesitated. His officer put a Kalasnikov muzzle against his back and ordered him on.

The boy sprinted, dodging and weaving for his life. No bullets came. Throwing himself against the wall, he panted, fear and exertion drying his throat. The next man ran through the darkness.

One by one, the squad reached the wall, their officer sprinting last. From time to time, flames soared above the barracks, lighting the squad where they crouched against the compound wall. But they stayed low to the dirt. No bullets from the attackers found them.

Their officer ordered them up the wall, directing two men to boost the others to the walkway. As the first soldier stepped onto the braced arms of two others, a couple of small objects fell from the wall.

In a flare of flamelight from the burning trucks,

they all looked down and saw the grenades that killed them.

Gary Manning crept along the wall's walkway, watching for more kills. To quote Mack Bolan, he thought, tonight is the night—every night.

LYONS FOLLOWED THE CAR in the sights of his M-249 machine gun. Flames soared above the compound, the pulsing light illuminating a Russian behind the steering wheel, plus another Soviet in the car holding a radio microphone to his mouth.

Lyons waited until the car screeched to a stop on the parade ground before killing the Russians. He flicked the trigger to shatter the car's windows with a quick burst, then put two more bursts into the interior. He sighted one last time and put three steel-cored high-velocity 5.56mm slugs into the gas tank.

The exploding car lit the parade ground. From Lyons's position on the east, he had a field of fire from the front of the terrorist compound, across the entire parade ground, to the commander's and staff's private houses at the north end of the base.

Watching for targets, he heard the autofire dying away inside the walled compound. It could not be over already. High-altitude reconnaissance had photographed barracks and buildings for a force of perhaps a thousand soldiers.

Even as he wondered, an explosion of autofire tore the night. Screaming, shouting, a mob of terrorists surged from the compound gates. In a coordinated breakout, squads of Palestinians, Cubans and Africans swept the walls with long bursts of Kalashnikov fire, while the others ran for the darkness of the surrounding jungle.

They gained only the escape of death. Lyons swept the parade ground with the M-249, long bursts dropping entire groups of terrorists. With the cool, emotionless, mortal sadness that cannot help but chill even the fires of victory, Carl Lyons was reluctantly but inevitably a man of his hour again. By the light of the burning KGB sedan, he put slugs into running terrorists, into crawling wounded, into silhouettes that motioned other terrorists on.

But Kalashnikovs returned his fire. Prone in the hard dirt of the parade ground, they fired at the muzzle-flash of the machine gun decimating their force.

A Libyan with an RPG cocked his launcher and sent a rocket at the unseen gunner.

The rocket shrieked over Lyons. It exploded in the palms behind him. He keyed his hand-radio, shouted into the mouthpiece.

"Somebody! Kill the one with the rocket launcher!"

Another launch flashed. The warhead fell short and to the side, but the explosion threw the ex-LAPD cop over.

Numb with shock, his left ear screaming, Lyons stared up at the graying sky. Kalashnikov fire zipped over him, slugs ripping through the trees above him. Pain came in a wave. He touched his ringing ear, and his hand came away slick with blood.

He rolled back onto his stomach. He righted his M-249. Yet another rocket flashed from the launcher. Slamming his face into the dirt, Lyons felt the warhead rush past him.

The blast dropped a palm, the tall spindly trunk crashing through branches and vines behind him.

"You gotta die, rocket man!" Lyons screamed out. He sighted on the forms sprawled on the parade ground, swept them again and again with slugs, the bursts kicking up lines of dust, throwing corpses over, killing wounded.

The Libyan rose to one knee and sighted on Lyons once more. Seeing the kneeling silhouette, Lyons jerked the muzzle around and sprayed the guy with a long burst, slugs ripping through the man's chest and gut, doubling him over as he triggered the rocket.

The RPG struck his officer in the legs. The explosion threw the officer's torso twenty yards.

Blood flowed from his head, right arm and side as Carl Lyons held his position, searching the carnage for targets.

AUTOFIRE AND EXPLOSIONS RAGED in the chaos of the attack on the compound. Mack Bolan, Blancanales and Gadgets waited in the jungle around the staff houses. They saw the Soviet bodyguards running from house to house, gathering the officers, herding them and a woman toward the cars.

Bolan waited. Guards ran into the largest house. One staggered out, vomiting. Then the other guard came out, calling to his comrades. One of the officers, a Hispanic in fatigue pants and a pajama top, rushed into the house.

"You see what's going on?" Bolan whispered into his hand-radio.

Blancanales answered. "Something's happened in there—"

"I can't see anything," Gadgets reported. Positioned at the north end of the base complex, the staff houses blocked Gadgets's view of the scene.

The officer came out of the house and motioned to the others. The group rushed in.

No one came out.

After a minute, Gadgets buzzed Bolan. "What the hell's going on?"

"Hold your position. Politician, what do you see?"

"Nothing, Mack. No one outside, no movement at the windows or doors. No one on watch."

"Mack!" Gadgets's voice hissed. "They're out! I hear them thrashing around—"

"They making a break?" From his position, Bolan had no view of what Gadgets saw.

"No, man. Not a break. They are out. I hear them running. They're taking off. They got out somehow—"

Bolan ran through the possibilities in his mind. Only one made sense. "An underground escape, a passage," he said. "Pol, Gadgets—"

"Already moving."

As the sky grayed, the Stony Men pursued the escaping leaders through the jungle.

Sporadic rifle fire came from the barracks. Encizo watched for muzzle-flashes. He sent 40mm grenades through the windows. Below him, dead and dying terrorist soldiers littered the compound. On the other side of the wall, Lyons raked the parade grounds with deadly bursts from his M-249.

Over the sights of his machine gun, McCarter scanned the smoke and flames for terrorists. He heard a firefight break out on the other side of the compound. His hand-radio buzzed.

Manning's voice shouted out, "We got a squad rushing us. Encizo, McCarter, anybody—"

A slug slapped flesh. The radio went silent for a moment, then Yakov's voice came on, "Manning is wounded. We need—"

An RPG blast sprayed fire and stone into the gray sky. McCarter yelled to Encizo, "You just going to bloody *do nothing*?"

McCarter jerked up his M-249 and ran along the top of the wall. Below him, terrorists saw the black clad commando and raised their rifles. Slugs chipped the wall, ripped past him. His leg jerked from a hit. He sprawled on the walkway, but held on to his weapon.

Kalashnikovs sent burst after burst at him. He rolled to the other side of the walkway, pressing himself against the outfacing bricks. The walkway's edge sheltered him, slugs from the gunmen below hitting the wall only inches above his face. Lit by the dawn light and the compound's fire, he had no concealment. If he turned or crawled or stood, he'd be hit again.

"You bloody good-for-nothing Cuban Latin-lover!" McCarter screamed. "Put out some rounds!"

Encizo's hybrid assault rifle/grenade launcher

answered. A 40mm frag killed one terrorist, a burst of 5.56mm slugs ripped through the arm of another. The fire aimed at McCarter slacked off for an instant.

The wounded Englishman heard the sound of cast iron clanking on stone. Two steps from his face, a ComBloc grenade hissed, smoke coming from the fuse. He had no escape but gravity.

Rolling off the wall, still holding his weapon, he dropped eight feet to the pavement, his bleeding leg buckling underneath him. His back slammed against the wall, holding him semi-upright. Above him, the hand grenade exploded.

A Palestinian crouched beside him, a second grenade in his hand. McCarter jammed the muzzle of the machine gun against the man's chest and sprayed a ten-round burst through him. Another terrorist brought up an AKM. McCarter whipped his weapon around, fired point-blank again.

Slugs hit the wall around him. Fire slashed across his ribs. He lurched into a run, his back heavy with plastic magazines of belted 5.56mm rounds, one leg buckling beneath him with every step, knives seeming to stab through his ribs with every breath.

Fighting panic, he did not aim, he did not look for targets, he ran and fired. An Al Fatah killer jumped in front of him, AKM held in his hands like a baseball bat. McCarter fired wild, killing the gunman—but an instant too late, for the Kalashnikov stock smashed his left hand.

McCarter fell over the dead man, rolled, his right hand never releasing the machine gun. Staggering to his feet, he tried to grip with his left hand. His broken thumb and index finger would not close around the machine gun's foregrip.

"ENCIZO!" McCarter bellowed. He held up the front of the heavy weapon with his forearm, his hand dangling numb from his wrist. His eyes searched for shelter as he sprayed slugs at everything that moved.

A slug hit his battle armor, bouncing off the steel trauma plate. Then something hit him from the rear, sending him skidding against the steps of a barracks. He felt a man on him.

His right hand jerked the double-edged blade from his boot top. As he pulled back to stab, Encizo caught his wrist.

"I am here. Give me that machine gun."

Encizo dragged McCarter through a doorway, then threw him down. From the window, Encizo fired into the compound's street, brass casings showering his Phoenix Force partner on the floor. AK slugs smashed through glass and pocked the back wall.

"I tell you, amigo. I think we have problems."

A flash-roar swept past.

"Encizo. McCarter!" Rushing into the room, Keio Ohara threw down a spent Viper launcher, immediately pulled another from his backpack. He glanced outside.

Only gore remained of a group of terrorists.

"What happened to Manning?" McCarter gasped.

"He is wounded," said Keio, blankly sad yet still flame-bright too, in the midst of this crucial wartime that held the balance of democracy's future in its falling numbers.

"Where is he?"

The Canadian staggered in, his right arm hanging limp, blood dripping from his fingers. He slumped against the wall, tried to change the magazine of his CAR one-handed, couldn't. He sat down with the rifle between his knees. Then he pulled out the empty mag, jammed in another, and hit the bolt release to chamber the first round. He looked around at the others.

"Well, do we want to sit here? Or get the job done?" And he stumbled out.

Pulling the pack off McCarter's back, Encizo jerked the near-spent magazine out of the M-249 and fitted on a new one. Then he and Ohara followed Manning.

Alone in the smashed furnishings and broken glass of the small room, McCarter looked at the useless fingers of his left hand then down at his bleeding leg.

"Oh, what the hell...." Staggering to his feet, he pulled out his pistol and headed for the door. "Still got one hand that works."

MOVING SILENTLY THROUGH THE DAWN, Mack Bolan, Blancanales and Gadgets pursued the Hydra officers across the island. The noise of the attack on the base faded behind them. They moved as quickly as they dared, expecting ambush at any moment.

But the Soviets and Cubans did not turn on their attackers. They seemed to want only to escape. They thrashed through the fronds and bushes, left footprints, broken branches, a woman's shoe to mark their path.

Bolan signaled his friends. They crouched in the half-light, their eyes sweeping the jungle around them. Bolan pointed along the path.

"They're going to their boats. We can't chance following them straight to the beach."

"They'll hit us," Gadgets agreed.

A vast roar came from the island's airstrip. Looking up, they saw flamelight glowing on wisps of clouds. Gadgets grinned.

"Someone tried to use a plane."

Blancanales pulled a compass from his thigh pocket, watched the needle find north. He pointed to the southwest. Bolan and Gadgets nodded.

The emerged several hundred yards to the west of the dock. Several moored boats bobbed on the light swell. The Hydra officers, their bodyguards and their girl friends crowded onto a cabin cruiser.

Bolan put binoculars to his eyes. He scanned the group. "Yoshida isn't with them. But...." Bolan passed the binoculars to Blancanales. "Look at the one in the pajama top."

"That's Munoz," Blancanales agreed. "But where's Fedorenko?"

Gadgets took out his hand-radio and keyed the transmit. "Phoenix Force, Lyons, anybody. What goes on?"

Yakov answered. "It is done." Behind his voice, individual shots popped. "Have you finished with the others?"

"They're at the boats, thinking they're going

somewhere. Some of them, anyway,'' Gadgets responded. "Haven't spotted Fedorenko or the Japanese.''

While they spoke, the three men watched the Cubans and Soviets on the dock. The terrorists had finally discovered the sabotaged engines.

"I found the Russian,'' Yakov told Gadgets. "He died very badly.''

Mack Bolan keyed his own radio. "You got Fedorenko?''

"Not me, I could not have done it like that,'' the Israeli answered. "There are limits. One of his own kind did this.''

"Did what?'' Bolan asked.

"I found him in his house. I will not even describe it.''

Then Bolan asked what most concerned him. "And what about our men, Yakov? Who have we lost?''

"God blessed us this morning. We have lost much blood, but no lives.''

"Everyone who can walk and carry a weapon,'' Bolan commanded, "will search for the Japanese.''

AKM fire stopped the talk. Two hundred yards away, unseen gunmen fired from the jungle, slugs shattering the windows of the boats. A woman and two of the Soviet bodyguards fell.

A Russian returned fire. AKM bursts punched death through the gunwale of the power cruiser, sending the Russian staggering backward into the water.

Bolan focused his binoculars. "Munoz is starting the boat!''

Switching on the power cruiser's ignition, the Cuban member of the troika triggered the Stony Men's pre-placed charges.

The explosion destroyed the boats at the dock. Scraps of wood and metal and fiberglass floated from the sky. Palm trees vibrated with shock, the air shimmered.

Two gunmen left the jungle, Kalashnikovs in their hands. Bolan identified them with the binoculars.

"Japanese."

"Yoshida?" Blancanales asked.

"Don't see him," Bolan reported. "But that Palestinian, Shyein, the one you took in Los Angeles, he said Yoshida has two Japanese bodyguards."

Moving silently through the palms, the three Stony warriors watched the two Japanese poke through the flickering flames of the wreckage. They found one of the women still alive and put an AK burst through her face. Then the Japanese returned to the jungle.

Signaling his friends to wait, Bolan set down his M-16/M-203. He pulled Big Thunder, his .44 Auto-Mag. He moved ahead alone, his free hand easing branches and fronds silently aside.

Blancanales and Gadgets watched Bolan disappear into the silent shadows. They listened for the inevitable.

The AutoMag boomed once. For a moment, they heard thrashing. Then the AutoMag thundered again.

The last impact threw a dying Japanese bodyguard through a tangle of branches. Only steps from Blancanales, the man sprawled facedown in the small ferns. The gunman struggled to rise. He threw himself over on his back, spraying the jungle with his AKM.

Blancanales rushed to the dying Japanese and brought down the butt of his M-16/M-203 on the gunman's throat, smashing the larynx. Blancanales cupped his hand over the man's bloody mouth as he choked to death.

Silence returned. Crouching over the dead man, Blancanales scanned the jungle for movement, his hybrid assault rifle/grenade launcher on line, a buckshot load in the 40mm tube. But no other terrorists appeared.

In his peripheral vision, Blancanales sensed a shadow emerging into the red dawn light from the black hole of overgrowth.

Finally weary of all the killing, his hand sticky from the choking of the Japanese bodyguard, Blancanales was relieved to see the black-clad form of his commander padding through the jungle litter toward him.

Mack could have met his match in there. It was good to see him return.

Blancanales casually opened an arm to greet his leader. An *abrazo* was in order on this dawn of destruction. Blancanales was tired.

As he turned to fully face his friend, opening his heart to the nightscorcher who was the one true saint in his life, Blancanales saw his mistake.

Yoshida!

Gadgets screamed. He, too, had confused one black-clad dawnfighter for another. He watched the

Japanese madman slam into Blancanales, slip around the Chicano's rocking form and close his arm around his throat.

Gadgets could not take aim. "Pol!" he yelled uselessly at his stricken friend, his legs locked apart as he moved his weapon's muzzle in search of a safe target.

A twelve-inch blade flashed past Blancanales's face. Yoshida brought the razor edge across the Stony warrior's throat. Twisting against the steel muscles of Yoshida's arm, Blancanales threw his right shoulder forward and up. The *shoto* blade missed his throat, but sliced through the Kevlar battle armor.

As the *shoto* slashed across his chest in a microsecond, it cut deep into his right pectoral and continued to his upper arm. Blancanales felt the blade scrape across the bone. Then he rolled free, and kicked out.

But another black form had already slammed into Yoshida. The two bodies fell on Blancanales. Two writhing beasts of shadow fought on top of him. Blancanales saw Bolan wrestling face-to-face with Yoshida.

They rolled from him in clinging confrontation, rising upright, still locked, as Gadgets rushed to attend to Blancanales's blood-pulsing wound.

The opponents' tendons and neck muscles above their blacksuits stood out from the skin, as each strained to overwhelm the other. Their flesh glistened with chill sweat.

Stony Man's commander glared at the demon mask of Yoshida's insanely nihilistic hatred. It was one man against his absolute opposite. Such a condition cannot exist without the final arbitration of death. In the primal world of physics, death was a wise counselor. So be it.

Bolan gripped Yoshida's wrist in his left hand to push back the *shoto* blade. In his right hand was the AutoMag.

The two unleashed forces that were Bolan and Yoshida struggled without movement, equally matched. Their strength and intensity made them sculptures of violence, extreme to the limit, visibly explosive, but for the moment actually motionless in time.

Bolan snapped his head forward, broke the tension, broke the mood, broke Yoshida's nose with his forehead.

Berserk with pain and rage, his screams spraying blood, the terrorist monster focused his entire psychotic consciousness on plunging the twelve-inch mirror of death into Bolan's throat.

The good mind and the best weapon are one. When the mind is through-and-through right, the weapon is too....

Bolan strained to move the barrel upright, then fired the bucking flesh-shredder that had been The Executioner's companion on his every mile.

The AutoMag blew Yoshida's head away. The heat of the blast seared Bolan's face.

Bolan staggered back. Gadgets caught him as he fell. He let him down on the matted jungle trail. Gasping for breath, Bolan eased the AutoMag's hammer down. Then he wiped Yoshida's blood and brains from his face.

Gadgets returned to Blancanales and tore open more field dressing to put it against Pol's opened-up chest. The wounded fighter pressed it against the bubbling gash while Gadgets put a dressing over the exposed bone of his right arm.

The giant red fireball that rose from the horizon was the sun.

It came like the future itself, a violent thing, full of explosions that sustain and advance life itself.

The red glow of the eastern sky turned to a daylight hue as Mack Bolan stood up and threw his head back in exhaustion, his face staring up at the pale virgin blue.

The dawn of destruction.

He snapped his head forward again. He touched the drying slicks of blood that encrusted the front of his blacksuit. He looked at Gadgets and Blancanales, the two shattered avengers seeming like a still-life of care and attention as the final bandages were tied, and the last empty syringes poked out of the bloodied grass.

"Time for the last act," Bolan said.

THE SHEET OF FLAME SOARED UP to the sky in a crescending roar. It ascended like a terrible curtain that turned the sky from eggshell blue to dirty yellow. The flame, hundreds of yards wide, competed with the sun. It made a warm morning unbearably hot.

The fresh odor of seawater was replaced by the acrid, unmistakable stink that comes from burning the material effects of man.

Mack's order had been to torch the camp. Not a

trace must remain. Now Phoenix Force and Able Team watched from the hillside with their commander, as the terrorist town disappeared in the single sheet of flame.

Their work of righteous arson had taken only an hour to set up, utilizing the gasoline stores of the base itself. Manning and McCarter had arranged the triggering devices in the dry ground and in the straw-roofed, highly inflammable buildings.

Soon the nine men could see each hut burn. Every roof, every wall, every fence, every streetcorner showed the individual flames that had contributed to the opening sheet explosion Fire consumed every detail of a place that had once been very dangerously alive. It was a world in flames.

Mack Bolan knew this to be a sacrificial fire.

It was a sacrifice to save the larger world from the same immolation. Without the blaze that he gazed at below him now, twenty million Americans—more, maybe twice as many, maybe three or four times as many—would never have survived the constant siege that they endured.

Terror had seized the free world in a grip of fear, filling its cities with the paralyzing hopelessness that only hostages can know, scarring the countryside with toxic despoilation that could last for millenia.

This fire cauterized that poisoned reality.

Mack Bolan moved to Yakov Katzenelenbogen's side, away from Phoenix Force and Able Team who stood or sat in a long line in the glow of the fire, their weary faces shining from the crackling light, their weapons held at ease at last.

Bolan knelt on one knee and spoke softly to the seated Yakov. Phoenix Force's senior member worked on a mechanical problem inside his prosthetic arm.

Yakov handed a small screwdriver to Bolan. "I guess it's grit in one of the drives," he said wearily. "Can you see it?"

Bolan peered into an open access plate within the artificial forearm. Yakov rested the arm on Bolan's knee, and Bolan began working to clear the grit from a small nylon cam. The Stony Man commander talked to Yakov in a husky voice.

"Sometimes, my good friend," he said, "when men are thrown together, and every one of them is strong in his own way, it happens that each gets weaker where another is strong, each becomes dependent on his teammates to provide the missing abilities and character traits. But this is not true of Able Team, and it is not true of Phoenix Force. For that I thank you, because I don't have the words to thank all of these men in turn. You must tell that I thank them with my life."

Bolan paused, carefully put a tiny screw under his tongue so as not to lose it while he worked.

Yakov looked at his commander's profile, then at the flames that boiled into black smoke, then over to his partners on the hillside.

"It is we who thank you," he said slowly. "For you know a vital secret. The effectiveness of any army is that a few strategically gifted minds can move many men. You allow us to be as gifted as we are able, and because of that you move the earth."

Mack's eyes were distant, either absorbed in fiddling with Yakov's arm or looking inward at deeper events. "I know only this about leadership," he confessed to the Israeli veteran. "I know that a soldier is critically wounded in his soul when he obeys an order that he does not find just. He will do it, but he will not think it right—he will simply think it is more right than the disintegration of the command system. "Tell me, Yakov. Are my orders just?"

Mack Bolan's blue eyes flickered with reflected flame and shards of blue sky as he looked directly at Yakov, at the man who had lost his only son in a battle that he, the father, had led.

"All over the world," answered the older man, "children are born who will never get to do their best. They will either be killed by cowards who want to hurt their parents, or they will be made into slaves if their parents give in to the terrorists. It is only your orders that will give them their chance. Their only chance."

Bolan finished reassembling the curved metal gates of Yakov's killing arm, and rose to stand upright beneath the drifting black and gray smoke of the fire. "Then may those children grow to be hard," Bolan said, "and may they be ready for competition, and may they win."

He looked down at the man in the red beret. Yakov was staring into the dying fire, his eyes thousands of years—as many miles away.

Bolan strolled over to Blancanales, nodding to each Phoenix Force warrior as he passed, locking eyes with theirs. McCarter and Manning were both confined by their injuries, unable to move much except their faces, but they responded to Mack's look with all the spirit they could muster. McCarter's long hair blew from his face in the hot breeze. Encizo and Keio stood above them as if to protect them from anything that moved.

Blancanales was the most grievously wounded. He lay on his back at the far end of the line of men, his head propped up on a satchel. At his side sat Carl Lyons and Gadgets Schwarz.

Gadgets spoke as Bolan approached. "I've been remembering something, Mack."

"What's that?" Bolan asked genially, standing over Blancanales and looking at him attentively.

"Remember when you called Pol and me at the Able agency, before the terrorist wars began?"

"Yeah, I do."

"All this time we forgot to give you a message. Your call to arms took us just a few seconds to digest. Then we told Pol's sister of our decision. 'We're going to help the man,' we told her. 'You run the detective agency.' And all Toni said was to take care, and to give a message to you."

The narcotic-numbed voice of Blancanales broke in.

"She said, 'Give him my love,'" murmured the Stony warrior. Despite his wound and his dulled wits, Blancanales forced his eyes to convey the message with the brightest clarity.

Mack Bolan ran his hand through his hair. He could not show his face to the graying Chicano hero.

He had two things to say as his gaze rested on the burning base, and on the forbidden waters beyond. He said them to himself.

"We have survived again," he whispered. "By God, there *is* a future."